A MONTH OF DOOMSDAYS

LOOK FOR THESE EXCITING WESTERN SERIES FROM BESTSELLING AUTHORS WILLIAM W. JOHNSTONE AND J.A. JOHNSTONE

The Mountain Man

Luke Jensen: Bounty Hunter

Brannigan's Land

The Jensen Brand

Smoke Jensen: The Beginning

Preacher and MacCallister

Fort Misery

The Fighting O'Neils

Perley Gates

Guns of the Vigilantes

Shotgun Johnny

The Chuckwagon Trail

The Jackals

The Slash and Pecos Westerns

The Texas Moonshiners

Stoneface Finnegan Westerns

Ben Savage: Saloon Ranger

The Buck Trammel Westerns

The Death and Texas Westerns

The Hunter Buchanon Westerns

Will Tanner, Deputy U.S. Marshal

Old Cowboys Never Die

Go West, Young Man

Published by Kensington Publishing Corp.

A MONTH OF DOOMSDAYS

A Brannigan's Land Western

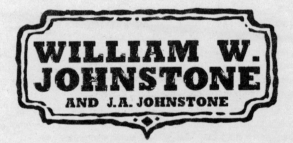

WILLIAM W. JOHNSTONE

AND J.A. JOHNSTONE

PINNACLE BOOKS
Kensington Publishing Corp.
www.kensingtonbooks.com

Chapter 1

"Don't let 'im get away. Cut 'im off!" Tynan Brannigan urged his sure-footed coyote dun to greater speed. The valiant horse did not disappoint him and took off like a Fourth of July rocket. Tynan bent low, played out a loop on his lariat, and let fly.

"You got him, Pa!" Matthew Brannigan threw his arm up high in the air to show his appreciation. It almost got him unseated. His horse veered close to a post oak with a low-hanging branch. The nineteen-year-old ducked at the last instant. Twigs cut at his face and hand but did not slow his exuberant advance.

"Herd him," Ty called. "The ground's turning rocky. I don't want him busting a leg."

Matthew raked his heels against his horse's flanks and cut off the steer as it tried to double back in front of his pa. This tactic was instinctive. The rope would tangle up the dun's legs and give a faint hope of escape, as if the steer had anywhere to go other than the Powderhorn Ranch's wide open grasslands.

Ty let his horse dig in its heels. The rope snapped taut. Together with his son blocking any other possible escape, the steer was caught well and good. The sudden yank on the rope took it off its feet. With a heavy thud, it landed on its side.

"Hogtie him, Pa?"

"No reason to do that. This isn't a rodeo, and that's no calf. You'd get yourself gored if you mess with him."

"He's powerful mad," Matt agreed.

"Give him a second to cool off. He's remembering earlier times when things didn't go well for him. Get him back to the herd. He'll twig to the fact that we're not branding him like was done a couple seasons back." Ty sent a ripple along the rope to loosen the loop. The Circle P brand shone brightly on heaving hindquarters turned up to the afternoon Wyoming sun as if it was made from the purest silver.

Ty tossed his end of the rope to his son.

"Where are you going?" Matthew secured the end of the rope around his saddle horn. He had trained his tobiano mare over the past six weeks. When roundup came in a few months, he'd show off the best cutting horse on the Circle P.

Ty dropped to the ground and stretched his 6-foot-4 rangy frame. A quick sweep took the high-crowned brown Stetson off his head so he could enjoy some of the breeze sneaking down from Baldy Butte. It wasn't that hot a day, but he tired out quicker these days, even if fifty-seven wasn't that old. At least he told himself that was only half a lie. He unfastened his red bandanna from around his neck and mopped a flood off his wrinkled, leathery forehead.

"You doing all right, Pa?"

"Not getting much sleep at night," he said. Ty declined to tell his oldest son any more. His darling wife Beatriz was working him the livelong night after he put in a hard day on the range. The Circle P wouldn't take care of itself, and neither would his wife's desire to have another baby.

Just one more, she said, to keep her from feeling old. At forty, Beatriz wasn't old, not like he felt at this instant, but he hadn't been able to convince her of that. She wasn't one to give in easily—or ever give up. That was something he admired and loved in her.

Usually.

Ty worried that if his wife got her way, he wouldn't see the child grow up. He'd be almost eighty by the time the kid could vote. Working ranchers seldom made it that far, and the way he felt right now, Ty wasn't sure he'd make it to his next birthday. He'd wrenched his shoulder just lassoing the steer all filled with bovine wanderlust.

He watched his son ride away, guiding the wayward critter with assurance and considerable skill. He'd done well bringing up Matt and the rest of the Brannigan clan, even if they did give him headaches at times.

Ty knew he was a lucky cayuse. He had a decent ranch, more than a thousand head of cattle, and the best family any man could ever want. He was proud of each and every one of them.

He caught up his horse's reins and walked to the top of a rise. The exercise got the kinks out of his legs, and even his throbbing shoulder felt a sight better. He looked out over his southern graze with some satisfaction. It was his. It was the Brannigan clan's.

He jerked around as movement on the next ridge over caught his attention. Squinting, he pulled down his hat brim to shield his keen, blue-green eyes. This temporary shade let him more closely see the silhouette of a rider. It wasn't unusual for men to pass through his land. Sometimes they stopped by the Circle P ranch house to pay their respects and other times kept riding. He didn't much care, though Beatriz enjoyed fixing for a new face now and then. It broke up the daily routine and let her hear gossip from around the territory.

Ty was less inclined to like the company. Men on the move were usually running from something and going to any place that didn't know their faces. More than once he had been like that. He'd left towns with no destination in mind simply because the horizon promised new freedoms. The difference between his wanderlust then and most of the men riding Circle P land was that he'd never been escaping arrest.

He shook his head. That footloose, easy philosophy had worn him down over a few years. By the time he'd put down stakes, he had become a deputy marshal and then a full-fledged, badge-toting lawman. For ten years he had gained the reputation of being a town tamer.

Meeting and befriending some of the fastest hands in the West had been pleasant, for the most part. Meeting and gunning down the ones who thought they were the fastest and were intent on proving it eventually brought him to Warknife and Beatriz Salazar, the fiery chile pepper daughter of the town banker. The day he had asked Beatriz to be his wife and she had accepted was the day he turned in his badge. That was twenty-one years ago.

He squinted a little harder and concentrated on the distant rider. Nostalgia was for old men. Ty Brannigan wasn't that old. Not yet, by damn.

As he turned to mount, he stopped and took another, harder look.

"Another rider. Both of them are looking out in yonder direction." He craned his neck around to figure what held those gents' attention. His eyes were not up to the task. The purple, hazy distance was only part of the problem, he realized.

"I need to remember those field glasses," he grumbled. Ty tried to see what they stared at so intently. He squinted hard, closed his eyes, and then popped open his eyelids.

Then he saw it.

"You miserable animal," he muttered. He caught movement in the distant waist-high grass. It might have been the breeze whistling down from higher altitudes, the wind that cooled him still. But he knew it wasn't. He'd been a rancher too long not to recognize the rhythm of a calf breaking off from the herd and hunting for trouble.

Just like the steer Matt returned to the herd far off in the other direction, a calf was heading out to explore when it ought to stay with the herd.

Ty tugged on his horse's reins, swung into the saddle, and headed for the grassy bowl with the wayward calf plowing its way to danger. Halfway there, he looked back at the ridge. The two riders were nowhere to be seen. To vanish that quickly, all they had to do was ride a few yards down the far side of the upland. A stray was none of their business, especially if they only traveled through. He told himself that, but somehow it didn't set quite right and he couldn't tell why.

He reached the bottom of the marshy land and slogged along in the calf's wake. The grass was slowly returning upright to hide the path, but the calf was heading directly for an even lower section of land.

Ty caught his breath when he saw how the ground beneath his horse's hooves changed with every step. The soggy earth was turning into real marsh. There had been heavy rains during the past week. If enough drained to the lowest part of the bowl, the mud might suck the calf in.

He rode on another fifty yards before the piteous shrieks reached him.

The sound made his horse jerk around uneasily. It was too close to the death cries of something in mighty big trouble. He reached for his rope, then cursed. Matt had it, and he hadn't asked for his son to either use his own lariat or hand over the one still dangling from his saddle. Ty urged his horse forward but met with increasing reluctance. The mud sucked up past the fetlocks, making every step difficult and noisy. The horse was smart enough to know what danger it faced.

Ty reluctantly admitted he wasn't as smart as his coyote dun.

Rather than get his horse bogged down, he drew rein and stood in the stirrups. He caught his breath. As he'd feared, the calf had blundered into a bog that slowly sucked it downward. It wasn't quicksand, not exactly, but the more the calf fought, the worse its predicament became. By the time it outright panicked, it would be a goner.

Reaching it on foot was possible. He saw patches of drier land ahead. His horse wasn't going to make it that far, but he could on foot. From there he had a chance to wrestle the calf out of its predicament.

He kicked free and dropped into water over the tops of his boots. He gingerly stepped to the side and found firm ground. From here he hopped from spot to spot, slipping and sliding along the way. His water-filled boots made it feel as if he had hundred-pound weights on each foot.

"I'm on my way. You stop fighting. Stop right now!" His advice to the trapped bovine only caused it to thrash about more.

The calf was already up to its belly in the sucking mud pit. Ty paused a few yards away and considered what his chances were of rescuing the valuable hunk of beef on the hoof. It'd be another year or two before it was ready for market, but it'd fetch top dollar. To be this close to saving it and simply give up would rankle like a burr under his saddle for years.

"Settle down now," he said in as soothing a voice as he could muster. Ty wanted to shout, to rage at the dumb animal for not remaining with the herd in a perfectly fine pasture filled with succulent grass. Nothing he said would change the situation. Only action.

He judged how to approach the calf. It threw its head about and lowed in panic. Ty stepped to the edge of the dry patch closest to the calf. A quick step was all it took for him to realize his mistake. He sank up to his waist in the deep water. Sucking mud pulled at his boots.

Ty frantically grabbed. His arms circled the animal's neck. This kept him from sinking more, but it also caused the calf to strain more to get away. He wasn't sinking any farther but the calf was. And it began taking him down with it.

Instinct caused Ty to swing around, shove out his hips, and arch his back. With his arms circling the calf's head he twisted it around as if he was bulldogging it. Huge muddy bubbles rose from below. He had broken some of the suction drawing the calf under. Continuing to turn, he tried to throw the calf onto its side. That would give both of them a chance to kick free and find more solid ground.

And it did.

With a screech of triumph, the calf jerked free of Ty's grip and landed hard on its side on a dry section. It scrambled and kicked and fought and found its feet on compact soil. Without so much as a backward look at its rescuer, the calf raced off along a firm section, heading for the grass that had lured it into this trap.

Ty let out a whoop of glee. He had saved the blundering animal. Then he realized there was another blundering animal caught in the mud.

Him.

He tried to float, to get parallel with the hidden mire. The mud held him too firmly. Worse, he felt as if it was a huge animal slowly swallowing him down its gullet. The pressure drawing him under was more powerful than anything he'd ever fought—and he was losing inch by inch.

Ty jerked from side to side but failed to break the suction

that had pulled down the calf. As he splashed about, he looked up and saw salvation.

"Hey, help!" His shout echoed through the shallow bowl. "Over here. I'm caught. Pull me out!"

The two riders, likely the ones he had spotted on the ridge above, forked their horses and just stared.

"I'm being drawn under. Get me out!"

The riders never budged. Both men's faces were hidden in shadow cast by the towering cottonwood next to them.

"Throw me a rope. Help!" Ty held down panic as he realized neither man was moving to help. All either had to do was secure one end of a rope to the huge tree and cast the lasso out to him. He was close enough. If they did that, he'd be able to pull himself out.

They didn't even have to exert themselves.

The mud crept up to his thighs. The suction increased. The water sloshed up across his chest and threatened to gag him.

Ty reached under the surface of the filthy water and found his stag-gripped Colt .44. He pulled it free of the water and shook out as much water as he could. Then he took aim. His first shot knocked splinters off the tree trunk to the right of one rider. The man flinched.

The two of them exchanged heated words. Ty shouted for them to help. They turned back and stared at him. Neither moved a muscle to help. This time he didn't aim to get their attention. He aimed to take them out of the saddle.

The hammer fell on a punk round. Water had ruined that cartridge. And the next and the next, which made a dull *pfft!*

The two men wheeled their horses around and trotted off, as if they didn't have a care in the world. Tynan Brannigan watched until their backs vanished. Then he expended the last of his strength trying to pull free.

Water lapped around his mouth, his cheeks, up his nose. He sputtered out his final word: *Beatriz.*

CHAPTER 2

Heaven wasn't anything like Ty had ever imagined. It smelled bad and was dark and burned his eyes and . . . it stunk.

Realizing that made him laugh. Heaven stunk to high Heaven.

As he laughed, he choked and spat out a mouth filled with slime. He fought and heard distant voices. Not choirs of angels. A frightened voice, yet one speaking only to him.

"Come on, Pa. Sit up. Open your eyes."

Hands shook him. Hard. He felt muddy ooze run down his face and drip off his chin. He swiped at it. Somehow his hands still worked. For some reason he had always thought they wouldn't in Heaven. But that was crazy. Everyone in Heaven played a harp. He didn't like harp music, especially not for all eternity.

The persistent voice returned. Something rubbed against his face. He reached up and tried to push it away, but his hands failed. Irritation flared.

"Pa. You're all right." A cloth scrubbed his face and cleared his eyes. He blinked against the sunlight.

"It's Wyoming," he said, the truth beginning to bring him around. He spat again and pushed his Stetson back on his head. Eyes took a few more seconds to focus. "My boots are gone."

"I've got them, Pa. They came off when I was pulling you out of the bog. I swear, they had a hundred pounds of mud in each of them."

He spat a final time and took the boots from his son. For a moment Matthew was reluctant to give them to him, then relented.

"I found your six-shooter, too. You threw it out. Why'd you go and do a thing like that?"

"You didn't hear me firing it?" Ty accepted his Colt and examined it. He had no recollection of heaving it away while he was caught in the mud, but when shooting the two who watched him sink failed, it must have been an instinctual reaction. They'd ridden off without so much as a fare-thee-well, leaving him to die. If he wasn't able to blow them out of the saddle, he'd try to brain them with his flying pistol.

"I might have heard a shot, but sounds in this hollow are weird. The wind blows, and it sounds like someone's moaning. The grass whips around, and there're rocks with crevices that make it hard to hear anything. It's a good thing I did hear that calf."

"It's back in the herd?"

"All safe and sound," Matt assured him. "It came sauntering out all frisky and covered with mud. That's what got me to wondering where you'd gotten off to."

With an arm around his shoulders, his son helped him stand.

"They . . ." Ty started to condemn the two riders, then held his tongue. Burdening his son with what'd happened had consequences. Matt was sure to tell his ma about the rescue. Ty wanted to avoid having to explain to Beatriz how two owlhoots abandoned him the way they had. She got worked up enough. Once angry, his darling wife took a long time to cool off. After all he'd been through, all Ty wanted now was for some peace and quiet.

As if that was even halfway possible with those two devils riding free on Circle P land.

He looked at the mud-caked Colt .44. Peace and quiet would be good so he had a chance to clean and oil his six-shooter. And reload with fresh ammo.

"There's a stream not far from here with clear running water," Matt said. "Ma's gonna ask a lot of questions about how you got so filthy."

"I need to clean up for my own sake. The mud is drying out and it itches. Everywhere." He squirmed about. It took all his willpower not to scratch where it itched the most.

Together they walked out of the boggy area to the edge of the meadow where the Circle P cattle grazed contentedly. They neither knew nor cared that their owner had come within a hair of dying. Now all they noticed was the way he stunk from the filthy mud caking his clothing.

Ty looked for the calf that had caused all the trouble. It blended in among dozens of other calves. The way he felt, if he had picked it out, there would have been one hella-cious dinner of thick steaks for a week on the Brannigan dinner table.

"I'll get those boots clean," Matt said. "I think they'll be all right if I clean them and you get them on while they're still soaked. You don't want them to dry unless your feet're in them. Otherwise, they'd shrink down to a size too dinky for even Caroline to wear," he said, meaning his younger sister. The twelve-year-old had small feet in a family where they were all above average height with equally sized feet.

The stream called to Ty. He stripped off his muddy clothing, leaving on only his balbriggans. He washed his shirt and suspenders the best he could. Wiping mud off his buckskin pants proved easier. The hide chased off dirt and seldom needed cleaning. A quick glance showed him where Matt sat cross-legged under a cottonwood tree, using handfuls of grass to wipe away the mud from his boots.

When he got to town, he'd have the bootmaker give them a fresh cleaning with plenty of polish. Those were expensive boots and worth every cent he had paid. They'd lasted him five seasons already, and two of those years were blizzard winters. Properly cleaned and saddle-soaped, they'd be good enough long enough for him to be buried in.

He intended that time to be a fair amount of time down the road.

Ty splashed around in the water, then found a broad, slick rock and slowly slid along it until he floated face up with the current rushing past. He half closed his eyes and relaxed. Mind drifting along with his body, he remembered the two riders who had left him to die.

He opened his eyes and sat up with a start. Two men stood on the bank, their horses' reins in hand. As the two had done before, they watched him in eerie silence.

Ty's hand went for his six-gun. He splashed water rather than pulling the iron that remained on the stream bank.

"I declare, Kennard, we got ourselves—what do you call them sea critters that sun themselves on a rock?"

"Mermaids," the one called Kennard said. "I read myself a book once all 'bout them, Ron." He grinned, showing two broken teeth and another that had been repaired with gold.

"Naw, that can't be. He ain't no mer*maid*. Are there mermen?"

"Don't see why not. Where'd all the little merbabies come from if there wasn't?" Kennard rested his hand on his holstered six-shooter.

Ty stood slowly. Even dripping wet and almost naked he was an imposing figure. He towered above the two men on the stream bank. More than once when he worked as a lawman, he had stared down a drunk intent on shooting up a saloon. Once he had bluffed the Pecos River Kid into backing down in spite of his six-shooter not being loaded. Town tamer was a moniker he'd come by honestly.

But now he was in his underwear and without a pistol facing down the two men who'd almost certainly left him to die before.

"Have I seen you two before?"

Kennard glanced at his partner, who giggled like a little girl.

"He wants to know if our paths have crossed, Ron. What do you think? Have our paths crossed before this very instant? I ain't got a good recollection of that, myself."

Ron moved to slip his iron from the hard leather holster tied down at his right hip.

"That's a distinct possibility, Kennard." Ron moved as if dipped in molasses as he started to pull his gun. With the pistol only halfway out, he froze.

For good reason.

The heart-stopping sound of a Henry rifle cocking came from behind him.

"So you know him? You know Mister Brannigan?"

Kennard looked over his shoulder. His and Matt's eyes locked, both peering down the long barrel of the Henry repeater. The only difference was that Ty's son was on the end shooting the rifle. His finger curled around the trigger so tight that his knuckle turned white. The eye staring down the length of the rifle aligned the back notch and the bright front bead centered on Kennard's forehead.

"Take him out first, son," Ty said. "You'll have plenty of time to put another round in his partner. His hand's shaking. Isn't it, Ron? Are those nerves you're showing?" Ty knew how to put the fear into an opponent. "That makes you slower. I've seen it a dozen times."

"There's nothing wrong with my reflexes," Matthew said. "And I'm about the best shot within a hundred miles."

"Do you want him to prove it, gentlemen?" Ty saw both gunmen considering their next move.

They decided right.

"We've watered our horses. Let's clear out," Kennard said. "There's no call putting up with unneighborly folks like these two."

"They're called Brannigan, ain't that right?" Ron's hand shook even more. He judged distances and his chance of throwing down, spinning around and shooting Matt before the boy pulled back on the Henry's trigger.

"Enough, Ron." This time Kennard's words carried an edge. He was smarter than his hotheaded partner, not that either of them showed a lick of sense confronting the man they had left to die, even if he was close to naked as a jaybird.

Ron grunted in response. He stepped up. Kennard mounted quickly. Ty was glad to see that his son remained alert the whole time. These sidewinders were dangerous. An instant's distraction would have set them off, hands flashing to their well-used smoke wagons. They trotted away, again not saying a word.

Ty suspected they had ridden together so long that there wasn't much left for them to talk about—other than who to kill next.

"What was that all about?" Matthew asked. "They acted like they knew you and had it in for you."

"I don't know if I've ever seen them before," Ty said, hating himself for the half-lie. If he had to positively identify, to swear on a Bible that this was the pair who had left him to die in the bog, he wouldn't be able to do it. But in his gut, he knew they were the ones.

"You've got a herd of cutthroats gunning for you after all the years you spent as a marshal," his son said. "Maybe they were harkening back to those days when you tossed them in the poky?"

Ty shook all over like a dog, scattered bright water droplets everywhere, and stepped from the stream. The breeze had picked up, chilling him now. Gooseflesh rippled along his arms and torso, but he wasn't sure it came from the wet and wind. Men rode his range, and he needed to protect his family from them.

Watching his own back was part of that from what Ron and Kennard had said.

"The herd's moving out of the pasture and heading south," Matt said. "You want to keep hunting for strays?" He looked up at the sun, now sinking low in the afternoon sky.

"Head on back," Ty decided. He dressed quickly. Strapping his six-shooter around his middle relieved some of the strain he felt. He might be getting up there in years, but his hand was still as sure as his aim, and his reflexes were the match of most of the new crop of gunmen.

Men like Kennard and Ron were better served shooting him from ambush rather than facing him down. What worried him the most was that the kind of varmints they were saw nothing wrong with that. Or leaving a man they didn't even know to get sucked to his death in a slough.

"Here, Pa." Matt held out the Henry. "It was close at hand. I didn't hurt it none."

"Keep it safe for me. I'll stick it back into my saddle scabbard when I get home."

"This is your pride and joy, Pa. Are you sure you trust me with it?"

"If you fire it, don't miss what you're aiming at," he said. He slapped Matt on the shoulder, sank to the ground and pulled on his still damp boots. Ty looked up. "You did a good job cleaning these."

"You've got a few good years left in them."

"A few years and a lot of miles," Ty agreed. "Get on home. And be careful what you tell your ma. I'll be along shortly."

"I should ride with you. You're going after them, aren't you?"

"Do as I tell you. Get on home." Ty waited for his son to step up and ride off. He waved Matt away when the boy looked back.

Walking gingerly in the damp boots, Ty mounted and sat for a moment to get the feel of riding without his Henry repeater pressing into his knee. He drew his six-gun and spun the cylinder. The time taken to dry it reassured him that it wouldn't fail him if he needed to get off a shot or two. While it needed oiling, that could wait. A final check of the cartridges bolstered his confidence in being able to handle any trouble he found.

Or trouble that found him.

He trotted away from the stream, eyes fixed on the ground for the trail left by the two troublemakers. Near the water, hoofprints were obvious. As the pair climbed higher and crossed rocky patches, it took more skill to stay on their trail. A half hour later, Ty topped a rise where he could scan the countryside in three directions. A rocky spine blocked his view toward Baldy Butte.

But the land all around was his. This was Circle P country and the slowly moving, mooing brown and black masses scattered around were his. Ty took his time hunting for the two men. After ten minutes of surveillance he had to admit defeat.

He looked toward Baldy Butte. Kennard and his pal must have made their way into the maze of rocks and canyons surrounding the butte. That proved to him that they weren't pilgrims just passing through. The land there was rugged, and the trails as like as not turned into box canyons. Wherever they rode, it wasn't away from the Powderhorn Ranch.

While reading the future was always a fool's game, Ty felt he hadn't seen the last of the pair.

"Giddyup," Ty said, tapping his heels against the dun's flanks. "Time to go home."

CHAPTER 3

"Whoa, back, don't rear up now. Down, down!" Gregory Brannigan tugged on the halter, but the colt refused to settle down. The fifteen-year-old moved in a circle like he'd seen his older brother do so many times. Keep the horse occupied and spinning. It was stronger than he was, so he needed to tire it out with constant pivots.

He quickly found that what worked for Matthew wasn't working too well for him.

If anything, the frisky colt became more rambunctious. Greg tugged on the headstall and lightly used a long, flexible switch against the horse's front shoulders to divert it. Nothing he did worked, not the way it did when he watched others do it.

Matthew was expert at gentling wild horses. Greg wanted nothing more than to develop that skill, but he could only watch and try to learn that way. His brother never had time to show him, and his pa was always out riding picket, not that he blamed him. The herd had been restive these past few weeks and nobody knew why. It was his pa's job—duty—to look after the cattle.

"Come on, don't do this to me," Greg called in frustration. He snapped the slender switch against an exposed flank and got a reaction he hadn't expected. The colt came to a complete stop.

Pulling on the halter the way he was caused the would-be trainer to fall to his knees. The colt laughed at him. Greg knew a horse laugh when he heard one. And he was on the receiving end of this one.

A whinny replaced the equine merriment, and then it reared, front hooves flashing out. Greg rolled over and under the bottom rail of the pole corral. The horse crashed down inches from him and then backed away. The whinny carried a sense of satisfaction at routing the foolish trainer.

Furious, Greg climbed up to the top rail and threw his leg over. His timing was bad. The colt charged him like a bull, head down as if it'd butt him. It crashed into him and sent him flying. Worse, it knocked down the top rail. From where he landed Greg watched in helpless horror as the colt took two steps back, then galloped forward. It cleared the lowered fence easily, hit the ground running and was out of sight in seconds.

"No, you mangy cayuse! You miserable hunk of horse flesh. Come back here!" He held back certain words he'd heard Matt utter on occasion and his father once in a blue moon when things really went bad and they were out of earshot of his mother.

He looked around to be sure no one had heard him. His two sisters, MacKenna and Caroline, were nowhere to be seen, off doing chores. He saw his mother peering through the kitchen window. She had been preparing something special for their Sunday meal. Greg hoped it needed her constant attention so she wouldn't come out.

She came out.

He used his Stetson to brush away dust. Beatriz Brannigan marched straight for him. He had seen the look on her face too many times when he had done something wrong. About the worst was when he'd burned down the tool shed when he was ten trying to roll and smoke a cigarette. The expression on his ma's face was almost that bad. It took all his gumption to stand his ground and not run and hide.

"What did you do? That colt cost your pa a hundred dollars!"

"It jumped the fence, Ma. I tried to stop it, but—"

"You were trying to break it and left the gate open," she said.

"No, no, it jumped over the corral. See?" He pointed. Anything that diverted his mother's wrath was helpful. She wasn't so easily decoyed away.

"Whatever happened, you let it get out of the corral. I should get a switch and give you a whipping for that."

"No." Greg flushed with anger. His fists hung at his side, and he shook with rage. "That's for babies, for little kids. You'd never say a thing like that to Matt."

"He's a man. You're still a boy," she snapped.

"I'm fifteen!" Greg puffed out his chest and tried to stand a little taller. Even at fifteen, he towered over his diminutive mother. He was four inches shorter than his pa and two shorter than Matt, but he looked down on Beatriz Brannigan. Somehow the height advantage didn't give him the high ground in this argument. He might be bulky, maybe too clumsy and huge, but she was small and fiery.

"That's right. Fifteen," she said. "You're a child yet. Look how you walk around. That's not the way a man walks."

Greg flushed even more. This time embarrassment caused his tongue to get tied up in knots. Both his pa and brother were tall and well-built and walked like cougars on the prowl. They were graceful, their step springy and quiet like they were ready to pounce at any instant. When he walked around, it felt as if he were a bull in a china shop.

"I'm like a bear," he said, more to himself than to his

mother. They were graceful. He was powerful. He reared up just a bit more.

"Whatever you are, you let a valuable horse gallop out of the corral. You go fetch it back. Right now, Gregory Brannigan, this very minute." Her hot, dark eyes bored into him. The set to her mouth and the frown wrinkling her forehead told him how mad she was.

"I was going to," he said lamely. "That old pony's not getting the better of me."

Beatriz Brannigan folded her arms across her chest and said nothing. That was worse than if she had raged and chewed him out, sometimes dipping into Spanish the way she did when she got really angry.

Greg swallowed hard. The way she watched him was even worse than if he'd been told to go find a switch for a whipping.

He tried not to storm off. Trying to march off like a man only caused his clumsiness to trip him up. He stumbled, righted himself, and blushed even more. His mother might have laughed at him. What she did was worse. She made a sound as if she was giving up entirely.

It took him extra time to saddle up a balky horse from the corral and ride out. The last thing he wanted was to hurry tightening the cinch on his horse and have the loose saddle spin around, dumping him to the ground. That had happened to him more than once. Usually able to laugh it off, now it would be like branding himself a failure. Worse, that was something a kid who didn't know what to do when a horse expanded its lungs and then relaxed after the cinch was tightened.

Nobody took him seriously. Being treated like a child rankled with every petty chore he was assigned. Even at the dinner table, he was stuck down with his twelve-year-old sister and not at the other end of the table with the grown-ups.

He wanted to get in on those conversations. They were important and had a lot to do with how the Circle P was run.

He knew enough to contribute. But they didn't listen. Even worse, they discounted anything he did get a chance to say, just as they did Caroline.

She was a child. He was a man.

"Prove it," he said between clenched teeth. The colt was only one way to do it, but right now finding the elusive animal and getting it back into the corral before either his pa or brother returned was all he thought about.

The colt escaping hadn't been his fault. That rail falling down could have happened to anyone. Who knew the horse was such a good jumper when it hadn't been saddle broke yet?

He came to a road cutting through the Circle P property and looked both directions. The double-rutted road was perfect for a young horse to toss its head and then light out at a full gallop. But which way?

Greg was good enough at tracking to find hoofprints in the soft dirt. But was this the colt or another horse? The road was here for a reason. Freight from Laramie came along this stretch on its way to Warknife. A rider alongside a freight wagon could have left those tracks.

He dropped down and knelt. He measured the width of the hoofprint using his hand, then compared it with his own gelding's print. A smug, satisfied smile curled his lips. The horse making these tracks was smaller. He wasn't good enough to measure the stride, but the horse had been racing along.

Greg swung back into the saddle and galloped after the colt. It was young and wouldn't be fully grown for months and months. It tired and slowed, letting him close the distance.

He almost shouted when he saw the colt standing in the road ahead, tossing its head about and stamping with its front hooves. Rather than spook it again, he slowed his pace and approached at a slow walk. The colt spotted him and bolted, cutting away from the road and heading toward a stand of elm trees.

He had ridden this part of the ranch more times than he could remember. The colt had sniffed out water and galloped for it. Following at a more sedate pace, he finally reached the spot where the colt bent low to drink. As he neared, it straightened and took a couple playful steps away from the water.

Greg never hurried now. He reached down and unfastened his lariat. A loop played out, and he held it by the honda.

"Go on, nibble at some of that fine grass. There's none finer in all of Wyoming," he said in a soothing voice. He still didn't swing the lariat around.

The colt bounced around a little, then sampled the blue grama. Greg came closer. Closer. When the colt raised its head, finally realizing the predicament it was now in, it was too late. The lasso spun through the air and dropped neatly around a neck straining to break free.

Greg was good at roping calves. They were sneaky critters. The colt shared many of the darts and dodges, pulls and attempts to loosen the loop around its neck. Greg drew it into a manageable length, then let the horse cavort about all it wanted.

"Gotcha," he said in satisfaction. There wasn't a hand who had ever worked on the Circle P who could have done this better. He took a couple turns around the saddle horn and turned back toward the road. It was time to go home and get the colt back into the corral—after he lifted the top rail back into place.

He was pleased that the colt decided to trot alongside without making another break for freedom. When the horse suddenly stopped, it took Greg by surprise.

"What got into you?" He started to jerk on the rope and get the horse moving again when he saw the reason the colt had shied.

Riding ahead along the road were three men intent on getting somewhere fast. They cut diagonally across the road and headed for the high pasture where half the Circle P beeves grazed. They hadn't spotted him. While riders sometimes came this way, they seldom left the road to head into the Powderhorn's south meadows.

Curious, Greg left the road and trailed the trio down a ravine and up a steep slope. He found the going harder with the colt. It was young and had finally run out of energy. The climb wore it out further. By the time they reached the top of the hill, the colt's flanks were lathered, and it tried to break free again.

"Settle down," he urged. He hunted for the riders but had lost them.

His heart jumped into his throat when he spotted three dark specks moving across the pasture toward the herd—the Circle P herd. Strangers had no business riding among cattle that didn't belong to them.

Greg reached down and touched the shotgun in the saddle sheath. Then he straightened. All he had was his .410 shotgun. It was good for varmints. He'd killed more than one mountain rattler, too. But the varmints he watched intently now were packing. A small-bore shotgun against the firepower those three carried meant only woe if he was stupid enough to challenge them.

He pressed his hand into his hip. He was old enough to carry a pistol like his pa and his brother. There'd be hell to pay if he had a Colt weighing him down because he'd make those three fess up to whatever they were doing.

"What *are* they doing?" he asked himself softly. He pulled

down the brim of his Stetson to shield the setting sun and get a better look.

As far as he could tell, they weren't cutting out any of the cattle. They rode through the herd, occasionally stopping and bending over as if they checked the brands. Greg had never seen any of the three before. The times his pa had taken him to the Wyoming Cattleman's Association meetings, he had met some of the other ranchers and knew even more by sight.

Nary a one of the trio of riders belonged to the local Cattle Gowers group, much less the bigger territorial association. Not that he knew. If only he'd had a chance to sit through an entire meeting instead of being hustled out to run errands for his ma. Matthew had stayed with their pa. Greg had asked what had been said, but his brother had gotten all high and mighty and only said, "Grown-up business" and that he wouldn't understand.

Greg understood all too well.

He touched the slick spot on his right hip again. That was the place where a six-shooter should be secured.

The three riders moved to the far side of the herd, spoke for several minutes, then galloped away in the direction of Baldy Butte.

Greg longed to follow them, but the colt was turning feisty again, having rested up.

"Come on," he told the horse. He tugged on the rope around its neck. "You're going back to the corral." Greg heaved a deep sigh. "After I repair it."

He turned back downslope and returned to the road. The sun was setting fast, and he wanted to be home before dark. Like a good little boy, he should be home to wash up for dinner.

CHAPTER 4

"You're worried, Pa. I can tell. You haven't said a word since you got home." Matthew Brannigan kept currying his horse, but his attention fixed on his father. "It was them two strangers, wasn't it? Have you seen them before?"

"Where'd you put my rifle? I should keep it with my gear for when I need it. I don't want to ride out again and find it's leaning against the barn wall." Tynan Brannigan had been lost in thought not only about how the two strangers, Ron and Kennard, had left him to die but how they were willing to shoot him while he was taking a bath in the stream.

They were low-down cutthroats, of that he was certain. He strained to remember if he had ever seen their ugly faces before. Not even a blurry wanted poster folded a half dozen times came to mind. If he were a gambling man, he'd put down heavy odds they were strangers. So why did they have it in for him?

If Matt hadn't rescued him both times, he would have been buzzard bait. That shocked him more than about anything else had in months and months. He wasn't ready to give up the ghost when the railroad deal was so close to coming true and certainly not—ever!—with most of his family left to raise.

Caroline was only twelve. It'd be another six years before she'd be grown up enough not to worry about her. Only he would. MacKenna was seventeen and he worried about her more than any of the rest. Mack had a way of finding trouble. He smiled grimly at that. She was a lot like him. They never looked for a predicament, but it found them as surely as if they were lodestones and trouble had a compass.

But cashing in his chips now? Not for a while. Not for a long time, he vowed.

"They're sniffing around the herd," Ty said. "I don't like that."

"The cattle have been kinda nervy of late," Matt said. "I've kept an eye peeled for a mountain lion or maybe wolves since the cattle began getting restive a week or two back. So far, I haven't spotted any predator's tracks."

"The snows were wet and heavy all winter long," Ty said. "That should give the little varmints like rabbits and marmots plenty to eat."

"And with a lot of dinners hopping around, the coyotes and wolves don't have any call to come down and pester our cattle," Matt finished. "There might be an old mountain lion, not able to hunt as well anymore. Lose your teeth or strength enough to pounce, a calf starts to look like an easy meal."

"Or the cattle might be nervous because of two-legged wolves." Ty stopped currying his dun and stepped back. The vague uneasiness hardened into certainty. "Saddle up again. I've got a gut feeling that we might find what's upsetting our cattle if we get right on back out there."

"Can I take a Winchester, Pa?" Matt looked at a rack nailed to the barn wall just inside the door.

"Pick one and keep it for your own. You might be needing it sooner than you think."

"Today having your Henry rifle in my hand sure felt good."

"You're man enough to know what it means to pull the trigger if you're aiming at someone." Ty saw the serious look on his son's face. He realized that, as settled as this part of Wyoming was now, that sudden death was always just around the corner. If you pointed a gun at a man, you had to be willing to kill. That was a powerful burden to carry, but he knew his son was up to it.

"Thanks for trusting me, Pa." Matt made a careful selection, loaded the Winchester and hefted it. "I've shot this one before. I like the way it feels."

"It shoots down and to the left. The front sight is skewed," Ty said.

"Not any longer. I sighted it in last month while you were in town to visit Marshal Southern." Matt pursed his lips, thought a moment, then asked, "Are you going to let him know about those two?"

"Chris has plenty on his plate without me adding to it," Ty said. "They haven't done anything to get themselves arrested." He knew it'd be his word against theirs that they'd ridden off and left him to the mercy of the bog. Although he was for certain sure they had watched knowing he would die if they did nothing, he couldn't swear on a Bible in court that they had seen him. Or that they were the ones who'd turned and ridden away.

And for all their talk, they hadn't done anything when they found him bathing.

"What do you think about me wearing a six-gun?"

The question came out of the clear blue. It took Ty a few seconds to sort through what he thought.

"It's about time, but it's a tool, you know what your ma thinks of me wearing my six-shooter." He touched the .44 Colt and remembered it needed a more thorough cleaning and oiling.

"I've got my eye on a Smith & Wesson at Logan's Gun and Ammunition Shop in town."

"We'll talk about it later. Let's ride. And stay alert."

"But don't get jumpy," Matt finished, laughing. "I know, Pa, I know. I've heard you say it often enough."

Ty felt that his son did understand what he meant. Matt had done a powerful lot of growing up in the past year or two. If anything happened to him, he felt his son could keep the ranch running.

"I swear, I'm thinking thoughts I've no reason to think," he said. Ty led his dun from the barn and stepped up. "Let's go check the cows."

A reluctant twilight was surrendering to complete darkness. The moon wasn't going to come up for another hour or two, but the stars already shone brightly. The clouds that had drifted across the sky earlier in the day had all fled to wherever clouds hid. Because of that pristine sky, the stars gave light good enough for riding. Ty trotted out and headed for the south pastures.

Matt rode beside him but wasn't inclined to idle talk. That suited Ty just fine. He turned over everything that had happened during the day and liked it less with every passing minute. His son had asked about reporting the two riders to Chris Southern. The Warknife marshal was an old friend but his wife, Molly, was feeling poorly. Ty wasn't inclined to dump his problems on Southern without more proof. Tending Molly ought to be his primary concern. When she got better, maybe then'd be the right time to mention two varmints willing to let a man they didn't know die.

Proof. Everything he had so far was his word against the two strangers.

"They weren't carrying bedrolls," Matt said suddenly. "Did they leave their gear in a camp? Where is that?"

Ty closed his eyes and tried to calm himself. He was mad now, not at his son for pointing out the way the strangers rode around the Circle P but at himself. He should have been more observant.

"They come and go toward Baldy Butte," he said. "Maybe they've pitched camp there."

"That's rugged country, Pa. Not much water higher up in the hills unless you ride a ways. A man needs good reason to hide out and not camp along a stream."

Questions to be answered. Ty told himself he had missed the details Matthew had spotted because of his ordeal in the bog. But being so tired was a bigger factor. He didn't snap back fully alert and questioning everything the way he used to. Letting things slide by was a good way to die.

His pulse sped up and a thunder in his temples warned him not to get his dander up over this.

"Save it for when I need it," he grumbled.

"Save what, Pa?"

He brushed aside the question. "Do you hear that?" He cocked his head to the side and strained forward in the saddle.

"Something's causing the herd to move," Matt said. "Not wolves. This is unease, not panic. It's good that cattle have so few reactions."

"A stampede's no good under any circumstance," Ty said. Any given wild run meant several cattle died, either from being trampled by the bulk of the herd or by falling into arroyos or stepping into prairie dog holes.

"It sounds like they're quiet again."

Ty and his son struggled up to the meadow from deep in the ravine where they'd been riding. He drew rein and stared over the heads of the cattle. The mass of living, breathing critters looked like an ocean, heaving and rippling with strange tides.

"There, Pa. To the west."

A shadowy rider made his way slowly through the herd. There weren't any Circle P hands working the herd. There wasn't any need until roundup in the autumn when he needed help moving the herd to the railhead—wherever that might be then.

"Stay here and watch over the cattle," he said.

"But, Pa, there might be more of them. There's no call for anyone but a rustler to be poking around in our herd."

"Stay here," he repeated. "Be ready to use that rifle—your rifle," he amended.

Ty edged around the stragglers nervously shifting about. As he passed, they melted back into the herd. He judged where the mysterious rider headed and set his own path directly for the edge of the pasture. The rider began to trot away.

Ty matched the man's pace and narrowed the distance between them. For most of the other's retreat, he was unaware of being chased. Before he reached the spot where a trail disappeared between two tall rocks, the rider spotted Ty. Using his reins as a whip, he lashed his horse to a full gallop.

That retreat was almost his undoing. His horse bounced off one rock and careened into another a few feet to the other side. The rider was thrown around and fought to stay astride his stumbling, protesting horse. Ty never sped up, but he wasn't about to slow down, either. He came within a few yards.

"Hold on," he shouted. "I want a word with you."

The rider recovered enough to guide his horse along the narrow trail. Ty knew this section of his ranch well. The game trail widened a few dozen yards away and opened onto another grassy meadow that went untouched most of the year. Getting the cattle into it required moving them almost a mile to the north before working back through a maze of rocks.

As a result of the lack of grazing by the voracious herd, the grass grew chest-high. That made riding difficult—if you tried it at a gallop.

Ty got through the rocky chute and came out to see his quarry fighting to plow through the tall grass. If he had slowed to a walk, his progress would have been faster. Ty kept his dun moving slowly and again closed the distance between him and the rider.

The man ahead looked around and became frantic. Ty had seen too many men react like this not to know what to expect. He slipped his Henry repeater from its sheath and brought it to his shoulder. From twenty yards ahead, the panicky rider opened up with his pistol.

In the dark and at that distance, even a marksman missed most of the time. Ty heard the hot lead singing past him, but not a single slug came within an arm's length. He snugged his rifle into his shoulder and got off a measured shot. Unlike the man he chased, his aim was on target. He took no satisfaction in seeing the man jerk about and grab for his right arm.

He had been fired on for no reason. The rider got what he deserved.

"Hands up," Ty shouted. "I want to know what you're doing on my land."

Muffled curses danced in the cool night air as the wounded man again tried to gallop through the tall grass. He wasn't big on learning from experience. Ty urged his horse ahead at a walk.

"Stop running," he called. "I don't want to shoot you again."

But he did. Somehow the rider hadn't dropped his six-shooter and got off another round. Or so Ty thought until he realized the shot came from his left. A second prowler riding at the edge of the meadow tried to take him out.

He ducked and kept his horse moving through the grass. More deadly lead came his way. He bent low and urged his horse to get free of the grass. His passage parted the tall, wavy grass and betrayed his every movement. The gathering night was his only protection.

Ty let out a sigh of relief when he reached a stand of trees. The thick undergrowth made plunging on difficult, but now all he did was create a ruckus. He wasn't giving his ambushers a visual target. Deep into the woods, he dropped off and worked his way back to the edge of the sea of grass.

The moon was poking up above the mountains and cast an eerie silver glow to the grass. Only wind stirred the tall stalks. He propped himself against a sturdy tree trunk and waited. So many times he had lectured his children about the need to be patient. Going over those words now kept him from making a foolish move.

He had no idea how many men he faced. Two, at least. But what if there were more? And if they were rustlers, they wouldn't be inclined to leave a witness behind.

"Where is he, Ron?"

Ty recognized the voice instantly. Kennard. He faced the men who had watched him struggle in the bog.

"Be quiet. He'll hear you."

"I think I drilled him. He's dead," Ron insisted.

"Where's the body? No body, no kill. You know what the boss always says."

Ron went to great lengths describing what their boss could do with his advice.

Ty crouched and waited. The two rustlers had him bracketed, one to the south and the other to the north. All he had to do was out-wait them. They'd either light a shuck or get careless and give him a decent target. Either way, patience was always his ally.

Only when it wasn't.

He heard the crunch of a boot coming down on dried leaves behind him and knew there was a third man. Still in a crouch, he spun about. The muzzle flash blinded him, and the searing-hot lead ripping through his shirt drove him back on his heels.

He was hurt and blind and heard the six-shooter cocking again for the killing shot.

CHAPTER 5

"You're not going to tell on me, are you?" Greg Brannigan picked up another stone and tried to skip it along the water's surface. The stock pond was too small for that to be very satisfying. Higher up in the hills he knew a half-dozen lakes where a good flat stone would sail a half-dozen times if he threw it just right.

But not here. He was almost able to heave a rock the entire way to the far side of the pond.

The colt frolicked about as much as it could. He kept it on a short rope. It was frisky and downright sneaky. He had roped it fair and square, even if nobody was around to see it. And that was why he dawdled on his way home.

"Dawdled," he said, turning the word over and then spat it out. "That's what Mack says I do. I'm never fast enough to suit her. 'Why are you dawdling?' she says." He tried to imitate his older sister. His voice cracked, but he got enough of the inflection to give himself a smile. He'd asked what she meant, and she'd told him in a schoolmarmish voice to find out for himself.

Warknife had a tiny library on a shelf in the back room of the general store, but among the few dozen books on its shelves he had found a dictionary.

"I dawdle," he said proudly. "And why not? I go home

and I have to do chores. Kid's chores." He sent another stone skimming across the water. It skipped three times before fetching up on the far bank.

Greg looked up in surprise when an aggrieved moo answered his stone. In the dark he hadn't seen a heifer sampling the water. He hunted for another rock and chucked it at the cow. He missed but came close enough to run it off.

"What am I doing?" He sank to the ground and drew up his knees. Throwing rocks at the cattle was stupid. Worse than stupid, it was childish. If he wanted to show his family he wasn't a kid and deserved to be treated like a grown-up, he had to stop doing impulsive things like that.

He looked from where his horse stood gently cropping grass to the frisky colt. This was the difference between old and young. He admired the colt's energy and even its need to break free and just run. Freedom.

That wasn't the life sought by his horse. The gelding had been broken and dutifully did whatever he wanted. Gallop, canter, walk, it didn't matter. Obey. It was three years older than the colt and had learned its place.

But it was an adult. It was different with people, he decided. The older you got, the more freedom you had. Nobody ordering you around to do this and do that, don't forget your chores, wash behind your ears.

Grumbling, he got to his feet and went to the colt. The horse was skittish but escaping had settled it down. It liked being out where it ran free. While he was a long ways from breaking it to the saddle, he felt he understood the horse better.

"You're going to be a great ride one of these days real soon," he said, patting the horse's neck. The colt shied away and jerked at the rope, but it settled down and came over to nuzzle him.

Greg moved just fast enough to keep it from biting him.

"I wasn't born yesterday," he chided the colt. With heavy steps, he went to his horse and mounted. A couple quick turns secured the colt's rope around the saddle horn. Greg turned toward the road leading home. He had wasted enough time. His untouched chores ahead would take him hours. His ma was sure to insist he finish them before turning in.

Or maybe even before he ate. His belly growled. That was another way the horses were superior. All they had to do was bend over and eat some grass. He snapped the reins and then froze.

Gunshots!

If there had been a single report, he would have ignored it. But the first shot was quickly followed by a half dozen—more!—shots. Torn about what to do, he simply sat astride his horse. His thoughts jumbled up.

Then he started back to the ranch house. Whoever was shooting up the Circle P had to be stopped. Too much gunfire and the cattle would stampede. They didn't have much of anywhere to go, but running around aimlessly burned off weight. The skinnier the cow delivered to a buyer, the longer it had to be kept in a feed lot to fatten up. That meant less money for every cow.

He pulled back on the reins and came to a halt. More gunshots.

A kid ran away and got his pa. Or brother.

"I can find out what's happening and take care of it." He reached down and touched the stock of his .410 shotgun. It wasn't a .44 like his pa carried or anything like his Henry repeater, but it delivered a nasty jolt if he hit somebody in the chest. Shoot for their face and he could blind them or certainly take them out of a gunfight.

The colt tried to jerk free. Greg knew it was foolish to ride into the middle of a gunfight with the skittish colt trailing behind and his other mount unused to him in the saddle. He headed for a stand of trees and secured the colt. Momentarily relieved of that responsibility, he made sure his shotgun was loaded.

He galloped through the woods and cut along a trail leading into rocks along the face of Baldy Butte. This was terrain he had spent most of his summers exploring. There wasn't a trail he didn't know. Weaving in and out, choosing the best route, he rode higher and higher into the hills. The gunfire became sporadic.

"Don't stop. Not yet. I need to see what's going on and help out." Greg wasn't sure who he'd help, but somebody'd need his assistance. Even his pa got into a jam now and then. If he chased off the gunmen with a few choice shotgun blasts, he might rescue his own father.

As he rode, this notion seemed more like he'd been smoking loco weed than anything really possible. Tynan Brannigan didn't need anyone's help when it came to gun handling. Greg almost turned back, but hesitated when the gunfire stopped.

The fight was over.

He didn't know who was exchanging lead, but he was too late to join in.

"Come on. We need to get back to the hideout." The voice was hoarse and deep, booming like a bass drum in the Fourth of July parade.

Greg looked around frantically. His heart hammered so fast he heard the thumping in his ears. He jumped from his horse and led it down the trail to a crevice in the rocks. The horse balked at first, then let him lead it into a sandy spit. He looked around in panic. If they found him, he was trapped. The crevice leading back to the trail was the only possible way to escape.

He grabbed his shotgun and clutched it until his palms turned sweaty and his hands shook from strain. Then he saw it. A dark shape passed down the narrow rock corridor. He lifted his shotgun. If anyone came for him, he'd get a couple good shots off. He swallowed hard when he figured out any bullets they fired at him would bounce off the steep rock walls and then ricochet around the spit.

This cavity in the side of a hill was just about coffin-sized.

Another dark ghost-shape passed the far end of the rock corridor. A third one stopped and blocked his view entirely. Greg held his breath. They had discovered him!

"Quit bleedin' so much, Ron. You're leavin' a trail a blind man can follow."

"I didn't see you mixing it up down there."

"My gun jammed. There wasn't any chance to sneak up and go all bare knuckles on him."

"Kennard, you are yellow all the way through and through," said the third man. Greg watched the man blocking his path out—Kennard?—go for his gun.

"So your hogleg works now? Ain't that convenient."

The three men continued their argument as they moved on. Greg almost collapsed in relief. He had backed himself into a tight spot. Fighting his way out meant weighing a few ounces more, thanks to their lead.

Two of them, at least. If Kennard was telling the truth, his gun had jammed.

He pressed his ear against the rock and heard a click-click slowly fade to nothing. The trio's shod horses were far along the trail leading higher into the mountains.

"'The hideout,' they said." He had no idea where they meant. Exploring Bear Paw Mountain thoroughly required time and effort. It would have taken more time than he had. The rocky canyons and the maze of ridges and valleys was so extensive only the early mountain men knew the extent of the range.

He pulled on the reins and eased his horse back down the rock aisle to the trail. Greg chanced a quick look around. He was alone in the pale light. The rising moon shone down, almost full, and turned the land into an eerie dream of shadows and shining spots where it reflected off fool's gold.

The smart thing to do was retreat to where he'd tied up the colt, then hightail it back home. That was the smart thing, but his curiosity got the better of him.

He walked along carefully heading in the same direction as the three men. They rode and made better time, but he heard them arguing. As long as they kept talking, he wasn't going to stumble across them by accident.

". . . makes sense," the one named Ron said. "Desperado's Den sounds like a place nobody wants to attack."

"Why let him name it anything? All we want is a hideout until . . ." Kennard's voice faded as he rounded a bend in the narrow trail.

". . . two shut up or I'll cut your tongues out," the third man said as they rounded the mountain and came into view. "You're getting on my nerves."

Greg stopped dead in his tracks. The moonlight gave him a perfect look at the men. One of them turned and stared directly at him. He took a step back into shadow, but his horse was too big to join him in the darkness. He started to bring the shotgun to his shoulder. Then the man staring in his direction rode on.

Legs weak in reaction, he leaned back against the rocky face and listened to the sounds of the men fade into the night. In a minute he heard a lovelorn coyote howling in the distance. Only then did he turn his horse around, mount, and ride back down the trail leading to the stand of trees where he'd tethered the colt, unfasten the now-sullen horse, and go back to the ranch house.

He wasn't sure what he'd overheard, but it wasn't about anything legal.

Desperado's Den! Three men talking about a hideout somewhere in the mountains. And there had been a gunfight.

Greg rode faster. He had so much to tell his pa!

CHAPTER 6

"Look out, Ron!" Tynan Brannigan shouted the warning at the top of his lungs.

Confusion to his enemies!

He needed all the time he could steal to get back in the fight. Ty blinked hard. His eyes watered, but the dancing dots that had blinded him faded, and he adjusted to the dark once more. Shapes, even if they were fuzzy and shrouded, darted around that hadn't been there seconds before.

His cry had achieved the intended result. The men attacking him had no reason to believe he knew their names. Using the gunman's name added to the alarm.

Ty rolled to the side and dug in his toes for traction. Straightening his legs scooted him along the forest floor. The detritus cut at his belly, but Ron had missed his chance for a killing shot at his fleeing target. Ty kept moving, rolling, dodging. When he found a fallen log to use as shelter, he dropped behind it and rested his rifle on its decaying top. By now his vision had cleared. The Henry rested in a rotted vee along the top of the log. His shakes slowly vanished as he waited.

Movement. He fired. The cry that resulted was more of surprise than hurt. He swung around and saw another dark form lurching toward him. Three quick rounds drove that owlhoot away. Ty doubted he had winged the man, but driving him off, even for a few seconds, added to the confusion.

To add to the message, he rolled over and fired to his left, then swung back and fired a couple times to his right. He was rewarded with two of them shooting at each other. Let them waste their ammo.

Let them kill each other!

"There's more 'n one of 'em," Ron called. "Let's get out of here."

"One," Kennard insisted. "There's only one."

Ty sighted in on the source of that voice and fired twice. Kennard had been skeptical. Now he voted with his feet to join his partner in running away. Their ambush had changed into a trap they'd triggered. Ty waited. There had been three men attacking him.

When he was at the point of clearing out, he heard slow, methodical footsteps approaching. Ty lifted his Henry and aimed at a spot between two trees looming pitch-black in the night. For a brief instant the moonlight shining between those trees was blotted out. He squeezed back on the trigger. The rifle bucked and gave him a moment of satisfaction.

He hit his target.

The third man sank to his knees. Ty levered in a new round and fired again. He cursed when the hammer fell on an empty chamber. He had fired all sixteen rounds. With a quick move, he dropped his Henry and grabbed at his .44 Colt. Years of practice gave him a smooth draw. He was slowing down from the years, but he still had the moves. Even better, his accuracy was undiminished by his age. All he needed was a decent sight picture to draw a bead.

The six-shooter cleared his holster easily, and his hand was steady as he aimed and fired.

The first shot missed. The next two followed the moving rustler and kicked up dirt all around him. Then the man wiggled out of sight.

Ty stood and stepped over the log. He wanted to capture the rustler and find out more about his partners. Ron and Kennard were gone. The third man knew where they'd run. Find out where they hid out and a heap of answers would drop into his lap.

Who were they and why had they been so callous about letting a man they didn't know die?

Moving quietly, Ty flitted from tree to tree until he saw the spot where the man had stood. Moonlight reflected off a dark black patch staining the leaves. Blood. He had wounded the man, but Ty failed to track his quarry from this spot.

He put cupped hands to his mouth and shouted, "Let me get you to a doctor. You'll bleed to death if you don't give up." Ty listened for any response. The normal forest sounds returned to mock him. He had hit the rustler at least once, probably twice, but none of the rounds had ended the man's life.

If the wounds had been too bad, the gunman ought to be stretched face down in plain sight, moaning for help. Maybe he was dead. Another possibility came to Ty. Serious wounds might have caused the man to pass out. If that had happened, he was bleeding to death at that very instant.

No body. Hunt as he might, Ty failed to find the man. That left one other possibility.

Sweeping the area failed to show how the man had escaped. Ty imagined he heard a horse galloping off in the distance, but he was probably wrong. His ears still rang from the exchanged gunfire.

Back pressed into a tree, he reloaded his six-gun. A

final survey of the area convinced him he was alone. He had survived the ambush. In return he had hit a couple of the men.

"Should have killed them," he said fiercely. Ty retrieved his rifle and hunted until he found his horse. Only when he stepped up into the saddle did he wince. The skin on his ribs stretched and opened the shallow groove one of the ambusher's bullet had left.

He twisted this way and that, raising his arm high to find the limits of movement. His shoulder ached more than the bullet graze hurt. He had wrenched it wiggling along like a snake to take cover. Ty refused to think the joint ached from arthritis. That was for old men.

Shifting about, he turned his horse and retreated through the tall grass. Alert every step along the way, he left this hidden meadow and once more saw the wide-open pastureland where his herd still nervously milled about.

Ty reached for his pistol when a shadowy rider galloped toward him. He relaxed when he saw Matt waving at him.

"What's the hurry?" he asked his son.

"I didn't want to call out to you and spook the cattle," Matt said, out of breath. "There were men riding through the herd. I found evidence of it." From his belt he pulled out a green bandanna. "This was caught on a bush."

"It might have been there for a spell," Ty said.

"I thought about that." Matt held it up. "It was damp with sweat. It's only now drying out."

"There hasn't been rain in the last few days to soak it," Ty said thoughtfully.

"Who could have left it behind?" Matt waved it above his head like a cavalry banner. "I've never seen anyone in these parts with one like it."

"Nobody I know wears a green neckerchief, either," Ty said.

There was a long pause. Both were lost in their own thoughts. Matt broke the silence by clearing his throat. He wiped his mouth and finally worked up courage to ask his question.

"You run them off? The three riders? I heard gunfire and worried."

"It's good you didn't follow. It was mighty confused out there in the dark." Ty sat a little straighter, the wound on his side had gone from burning to throbbing. If he kept his arm pressed close to his left side, the bloody torn shirt wasn't visible. That kept his son from asking questions he didn't have answers for.

"There's something I found you have to see," Matt said. "I can't explain it. Maybe you can."

Ty wanted to get back to the ranch house. Having Beatriz patch him up would require listening to a long lecture on being careful and how he had to let the law handle rustlers. She cared, but he got banged up often enough that her lambasting took on a repetition he wasn't up to hearing right now.

"Please, Pa. This is important."

He nodded and told Matt to lead the way. He trailed his son, thinking hard what to do. Letting his friend, Warknife's Marshal Southern, know was necessary, as much as he wanted to avoid it. Seeing men riding through his herd was one thing. Exchanging lead with them after they rode through his herd was another matter entirely. He had given better than he received, even if the crease reminded him constantly of the need to get patched up.

"This is about where I saw them, Pa. And yonder? That bush is where I found the bandanna."

Ty looked around and saw nothing out of the ordinary.

The cattle moved about sluggishly, not sure what to do. Keeping his horse quieted kept the herd from running. A stampede always ruined several head, not to mention being deadly dangerous to anyone caught in front of the rampaging herd.

"Come on over here, Pa. Take a gander at the brand."

He circled the steer and bent over to get a clear look at the brand on its haunch. Moonlight caught the burn mark. He pulled himself back up and studied the cow.

"It's not ours. We've got a stray from someone else's herd. It happens."

"I don't recognize the brand, either, Pa. Nor that one. Or the one over there." Matt pointed out several cattle.

"All of them?"

"I tried to count. The best I can tell, our herd's more than a hundred head to the good. All with the wrong brands."

"Not good if those aren't ours. Can the brand be from the Lazy 8? That's Caleb Young's spread quite a ways north of here."

"The name's not familiar," Matt said.

"It's been a spell since I talked with him. He wasn't at the Cattle Growers meeting when we voted on funding the railroad spur."

"The brand doesn't look a thing like a Lazy 8," Matt said. "I can't make heads or tails of it. But I can count. We're at least a hundred cows over what we had even a week ago."

"Having that many new head isn't an accident." Ty pressed his hand into his side. The bullet wound leaked blood again and turned him a little woozy.

"Are you all right, Pa? You're wobbling in the saddle."

"Those weren't rustlers looking to steal our beeves," Ty said, hardly hearing his son over the roar in his ears. "They're hiding cattle already rustled among ours."

He didn't put into words the rest of what had to be the rustlers' scheme. Combine the herds, then steal them all.

It was definitely time to see what Marshal Southern had to say.

But first he let Matt lead him from the pasture so they could head home. Somehow, finding the right trail back to the house was a mite hard for him to do.

CHAPTER 7

Greg Brannigan led the colt into the corral. In spite of his work with the spirited animal, he made a mistake taking the rope from around its neck. The frisky colt turned and studied the section of corral where the top rail had yet to be replaced.

"No, you don't," Greg cried. He jumped and threw both arms around the colt's neck as it lurched forward, ready to jump out of the corral to freedom again.

His extra weight caused the horse to stumble and fall to its knees. Learning from his earlier blunder, he grabbed the horse's halter and secured it to a post. Only then did he get the chance to replace the upper corral rail that had been knocked down. This time he made sure it was secured and wouldn't fall off if anyone—or any horse—smashed into it.

After he finished his bit of carpentry, Greg glared at the pony and said, "This isn't over. You and me, we've got to work out our differences. Meaning, you're going to be saddle broke or I'll know the reason."

"He doesn't understand you."

Greg backed from the horse and climbed to the top of the corral, legs dangling over. The rail was rock steady under his weight now.

"Oh, he understands, Caroline," he said to his younger

sister. "We've tried each other's patience already. He's not going to win. We're both stubborn, but I'm more stubborn than he is."

"Let Matt train him. He's got skills you don't."

"I'll do it." Greg gritted his teeth. Nobody, even his twelve-year-old sister thought he was any good.

"Says you. Oh, good, there's Papa and Matt." Caroline ran out, waving to them. The ranch dog, Rollie, barked and jumped about at their return.

Greg took a moment to free the colt from its halter and let it dash around the corral. He'd get back later, after he told his pa what he'd seen up on the mountain trail.

"Mama is fit to be tied," Caroline said to her father. "You're late for dinner. Both of you." She turned and fixed her accusing stare on Greg. "*All* of you."

"The herd's been restless," Ty said. He picked up the girl around the waist and spun her about and immediately regretted it as a sharp twinge poked into his side. It wouldn't do to worry the girl, so he forced a smile. "Not as restless as you, it seems."

"You tore your shirt," Caroline said. She had as sharp an eye as her mother for such things. "Can I sew it up for you? What happened? Is that blood soaking into the shirt? I'll have to ask Mama how to get it out since it dries into the cloth real fast."

"Caught it on a twig going after a stray," Ty said. He glared at Matt to keep him quiet. Greg saw the silent exchange and knew there was more to the story than riding too close to a tree branch. The blood splotch made him uneasy because it explained a lot of the ruckus during his way back with the colt.

"I heard gunfire," Greg said. "I was out by the southern stock pond and—"

"What were you doing out there?" His father's stern

question irritated him. He had important news to pass along and this sidetracked him.

"I was chasing the colt. It got out and—"

"Tynan Brannigan, you'd better have a good reason for being late to dinner. I should throw it out and let the pigs have it. It'd serve you right to go hungry."

"Yeah, Pa, it was real good tonight. Dumplings and—" Caroline fell silent when she saw her comments weren't helping any.

Ty went to his wife, took her in his arms and kissed her to cut off the string of Spanish telling him how hard she'd worked and he'd run off and . . .

Ty broke off the kiss. Beatriz started to relaunch her diatribe. He kissed her again. This time when he pulled away, she looked up at him. She was tall for a woman, but his six-foot-four height towered over most everyone. She stood on tiptoe and kissed him.

Greg was impatient to tell about the men he'd seen and how he'd almost been caught by the trio up near Baldy Butte.

"I wish you would not get yourself into gunfights," she said. She sniffed. "The stink of gunpowder is fresh. And something more? Have you been walking in a swamp?"

"I'll tell you all about it." Ty turned and put his arm around Matt's shoulder, drawing him close. "And how my son pulled me out. He really saved my bacon today."

"I saw riders," Greg piped up. He spoke to the backs of his family. They all went to the house and paid him no attention at all. He might as well have been telling the colt to obey his every command.

He threw his hands up in resignation and trailed them in. His ma fussed about making sure everyone had a plate heaping with her dumplings. Somehow when she made this recipe she added a mound of chiles and turned something bland into a spicy treat.

Although he usually wolfed down dumplings, Greg wasn't in any mood for the sharp bite of the food. His tongue burned from the need to let the others know what he'd seen out on the trail. As they talked, though, he sank down and realized they had found more exciting, more important, things than just watching three riders heading for higher ground.

"So you think these men are turnabout rustlers?" MacKenna cleared the plates away as they talked around the table. "Instead of stealing cattle, they leave them?"

"Reckon that's so. I don't recognize the brand, but someone's missing quite a few head of cattle," Ty said.

"And sooner or later they'll come in and try to steal *all* the cattle," Matt rushed on. "The rustlers, I mean. What are we going to do?"

"We need to find the extra cows' owner," Ty said.

"Pa," Greg spoke up. "I saw them!"

"I know, son," Ty said. "Matt and I saw the extra head, too."

"I mean—"

"Go help your ma and sisters clean up. It's your turn to do the dishes." Ty turned back to his older son. They swapped stories of all that had happened once they spotted the three rustlers moving through the herd.

Greg wanted to blurt out "Desperado's Den" and that he'd gotten a good look at the third gunman, but he saw they weren't interested. He had done more than either of them, and they ignored him. Like always.

He began clearing the plates from the table and went into the kitchen. His mother and two sisters huddled together. Whatever they gossiped about, it had nothing to do with

him or what he'd seen. They weren't even talking about
how Pa had been in a gunfight and been wounded.

Then he realized they had believed it when his pa had
said he'd scratched himself riding through a forest. Low-
hanging tree limbs and dried twigs were always an annoyance. Some of them cut like a knife.

"He was shot," Greg said in a level voice. "Him and the
rustlers traded lead. I heard the gunshots."

"Have you finished your chores out in the barn?" his
mother asked. She hadn't heard a word he said. Like always.

"I'll get right to it, Ma," he said. Greg left, slamming the
kitchen door behind him. Somebody shouted at him. One of
his sisters. Probably Mack. She thought she had the right to
boss him around like she was his ma. Just because she was
a couple years older.

Greg trudged to the barn and threw himself onto a
haystack. He lay in the dark, his mind racing about in tight
circles, getting nowhere. Fingers laced behind his head, he
stared up to the loft. Something moved about there. A
mouse, maybe. Then he saw one of the barn cats leaning
over the edge, glowing green eyes staring at him.

"What do you want? To boss me around, too?" He spat.
The cat returned the gesture, hissing at him before it disappeared, returning to its nocturnal hunt.

Greg's mind raced. There had to be something that
brought him to the family's attention. He deserved a bigger
role than cleaning the dishes off the dinner table or even
mucking the stalls. Those were jobs that had to be done, but
his pa didn't do any of them. Matthew occasionally cleaned
up the barn and corral, but he spent more time breaking
horses and riding herd. He did grown-up things, not kid
brother jobs.

He'd show them. He'd show all of them, but he didn't
know how. His pa always preached patience. If he waited

for the right time, he'd prove himself. They'd have to stop treating him like a child. Or worse, ignoring him entirely the way they had tonight when he had important facts to report.

Greg heaved to his feet and got down to his chores. He liked working with the horses, but what went in the front end came out the back and required someone to shovel it out.

He was that someone. For the time being.

CHAPTER 8

"Quit bleeding so much," Race Cooper said. "You're leaving a trail for the wolves. I don't want them sniffing around camp."

"That's easier said than done. That cowpuncher shot me three times," Ron Marcus said. He bent forward over his horse's neck and clung to the pommel to keep from tumbling off.

"We shoulda left him," Kennard said.

"If you'd been the one shot, should I have left you behind?" Race Cooper snapped.

"He'd have left me, if it'd been up to him." Kennard clutched his arm. "And I got hit, too. That rancher was a real whirlwind. I've never seen anyone handle a gun like him."

"He got lucky," Ron Marcus said. "That was the same one who got himself stuck in the bog. There wasn't no way he coulda escaped that quicksand, not the way it was sucking him down."

"Somebody helped him out. There was another rider, a kid, with him riding night herd."

Race Cooper stepped down and stretched tired muscles. The trail to this pocket hidden away in the Wind Mountains was treacherous and required more vigilance than he cared to give after shooting it out with the rancher. He rubbed his thigh. The rancher had gotten lucky with two of his shots, and Race had gotten luckier that they barely scratched him. One graze burned like hellfire, but the other was all scabbed over already. He took a few steps and flexed his injured leg. The stiffness and pain faded as he walked.

He looked around and smiled grimly. Desperado's Den one of them had called it. Probably Ron Marcus. That man daydreamed too much. But the name fit. A dozen men lounged around the rocky bowl with a small stream gurgling along at the base of the slope. There wasn't one of the outlaws that didn't carry a hefty reward on his head, just not around here. Cutthroats, the lot of them. It had taken him almost six months to recruit them from Nebraska and Montana, and now he was waiting for the final one to arrive.

And that made him antsy. He had accumulated a pile of rewards on his own head through the years. He had a small sheaf of the wanted posters stuffed in his saddlebags. Some people kept diaries. Cooper saved the posters to remind him of where he'd been and what crimes he'd committed. A few were trumped up. Most weren't.

He was willing to fess up to any and all of the crimes. It puffed up his ego to be wanted in so many places.

"There's no call to play around, Race," Kennard said. "Why risk them finding the beeves we already rustled? Let's swoop on down and take the whole damned herd. We got enough men to move a thousand head."

"We're waiting for Dexter. He's got the schedule we need."

"To rob the damned bank?" Kennard growled deep in his throat. He wasn't sold on that robbery. "When we've got a thousand head of cattle waiting for us to run north? You said that Montana rancher was willing to pay top dollar for cattle, no questions asked."

"His herd got wiped out by Texas fever," Ron Marcus

pipped up. He tried to tie his spare bandanna around his arm to keep it from bleeding. No one offered to help him. He had lost his bright green one somewhere along the trail. "That's what you said, Race. Ain't that right?"

"It's right." Cooper wasn't in the mood to argue. If the rancher they'd traded lead with got wind of the extra head in his herd, he'd go to the sheriff. Chances were slim they'd find where the cattle had been stolen very fast, but if they had long enough, they'd find that eastern Wyoming ranch eventually. When they did, the six killings required to get the stolen herd on the trail would be revealed.

No rancher liked a rustler. And nobody at all liked a killer. If they got caught for the theft from the Broken W Ranch, not a single neck in his gang would go unstretched.

"There's nothing this Dexter fellow can tell us that's worth wastin' our time settin' around and lollygaggin'," Marcus said.

"It don't happen often, but this time Ron's right. You know the Montana rancher's name. That's enough to find his spread. Let's take the cattle and move out real soon." Kennard pressed his bandanna into a shallow wound that hardly bled. He made a big deal of it after seeing how badly his partner had been shot up.

"Dexter has another job to share. One that'll take all of us, and one that'll pay us all twice what we'd get for a month of moving a herd that big."

"You want to change horses in midstream, is that it?" Kennard wasn't pleased. Ron Marcus wasn't, either. Worse, their petulance was drawing some of the other owlhoots to listen. More than one of the gang nodded slowly in agreement. At least none of them joined in the argument.

Cooper was the boss. He had to keep them under his thumb or lose any chance at both the robbery and the rustled cattle being moved north.

"I've told you. This will be worth our time. But Dexter's the only one with the timetable."

"What timetable's that?" Kennard demanded.

"Look, I told him I'd keep it under my hat, but if you've got to know, there's a powerful big gold shipment being sent to that little town of Cutbank. Dexter can not only tell us when it'll arrive but how it's being guarded."

"Guarded?" Marcus looked around to see if anyone else understood that meant there'd be added danger.

"It's an Army shipment." Cooper looked around the circle of men hanging on his every word now. None of them knew he was winging it. Dexter had told him there'd be a pile of money in the bank but hadn't divulged any of the details. Without embellishing what he did know, though, Cooper saw he'd lose his gang, thanks to Kennard and Marcus. "If it's half as good as Dexter says, every man's share will be two thousand dollars."

"You're saying it could be two thousand?" Ron Marcus licked his lips, then bent to use his teeth to pull a knot tight on the bandanna tourniquet on his arm. He spat out some cloth and blood and repeated, "Two thousand?"

"And the cattle, too? You said that'd be five hundred for each of us," Kennard said.

This caused a buzz around the camp.

"What if this Dexter fellow doesn't show up?"

Cooper wasn't sure who asked. It didn't matter. He read the question on every face so intently watching him. This wasn't the time to chicken out. He plowed ahead with his speechifying.

"If he never shows up or does make it here and says something's wrong—no gold, it's shipped somewhere else, too many troopers guarding it—we get the herd moving and we're not out anything but a few days."

"It's dull layin' around camp," someone said. "If we had a woman or two, that'd be better."

"And whiskey," chimed in another.

The desire for liquor and whores was agreed on by everyone. Cooper let them talk for a minute or two. They'd come to the conclusion those things would be theirs if they successfully robbed a bank and drove a herd of rustled cattle to an unethical rancher's spread.

Before Cooper suggested how rich they'd all be, one of the thorns in his side had to shoot off his mouth.

"The longer we wait to start the trail drive, the more time that rancher has to figure out something's wrong. I've heard the Warknife marshal is a rough character," Ron Marcus said.

"Southern," Kennard muttered, nodding in agreement with his partner. "I tangled with him before over in Cheyenne. I got away by the skin of my teeth."

"He knows you by sight?" Cooper felt a knot form in his belly. Part of his plan required that the law, if they got on their trail very soon, not have any idea who they were chasing.

"Enough to put my picture on a poster," Kennard said. "It wasn't a very good picture." He laughed.

Race Cooper was becoming less confident in either Marcus or Kennard. He'd had to pull their fat out of the fire when they tangled with the cowpuncher. The pair of them should have gotten rid of him without any fuss. Instead, he'd shot them up and left them bloodied.

He touched his own minor wound. Those two were bringing down a curse on him and the rustling. If Dexter was right about the bank robbery, Cooper wasn't going to let the two owlhoots hoodoo everything.

"Who is this Dexter, anyway, and why do you trust him to know about the bank?" Ron Marcus rubbed his arm and then pulled his shirt away from his body where it had matted to skin. He had been shot twice in the arm and once in the side. That wound wasn't serious. The bullet had gone clean through and left holes front and back. Like many bullet wounds, the holes closed up on themselves and he hardly bled.

"I served with his brother over at Fort Sill."

"You were in the Army? You never said." Kennard's accent spoke to which side he'd favored in the War Between the States, if he had served at all.

Cooper had hardly been in the ranks for a month when he deserted. The Army wasn't for him, but he had made some friends. Sergeant Dexter had been one because Cooper early on figured how to supply the quartermaster with profitable items—like illicit cases of whiskey. Dexter had been one of those soldiers willing and able to cut corners. He and Race Cooper had been birds of a feather.

Race had to smile remembering how true that was. They both flew the coop at the same time to keep from being court-martialed. He had lost track of the sergeant, but when Dexter had approached him a couple months back, riding with another, he recognized the man's brother in a flash. They might have been twins, other than his brother being several inches shorter and stockier. The sandy hair, the nose like a potato and ears that flapped in the wind—the Dexter family had produced singularly ugly males. The sergeant had mentioned a couple sisters, and Cooper knew he'd have nightmares if he ever chanced on any of them.

When the two got to arguing over the brother's wife and family, he had let them be. He wanted no part of it and had ridden away. After that he hadn't seen the brother, Thomas, again, and Frank Dexter had been bubbling over with promise about the bank robbery.

"I ran into Dexter in Cutbank. It took a few drinks to loosen him up, and then he spilled everything about the gold." Cooper swallowed hard. "It'll be worth it, even if we abandon the cattle."

"I know cattle," complained one man. "I ain't never robbed a bank." This sentiment went around the camp. Cooper tried to keep track of those who shared that sentiment and those who obeyed the Siren's lure of gold. The numbers were about even. He could have the cowboys get the cattle moving while the rest tore open the bank vault.

If nothing else, the stolen cattle served as a diversion. Any posse on their trail for the bank robbery was easily decoyed by the rustlers. But Dexter had assured him he had a plan where no one would know the gold was missing for at least three days. Even loaded down with that much gold coin, Race knew he could put a lot of miles between him and a posse in three days.

But how much did he trust his fellow deserter? Dexter had always been the best spinner of tall tales around the campfire.

"Who's tending the remuda?" he asked suddenly. "We'll need every horse we've got."

Those horses were vital not only for the rustling but for the bank robbery. A rider with two or even three spare horses could put more than a hundred miles between him and a man wearing a badge in a couple days of hard riding.

"It's Ron's turn," someone called. "I took his watch a couple nights ago."

"I'm wounded," Marcus whined. "I need to rest up and save my strength for the trail drive." He paused, then said, "Or the bank robbery."

An argument started over his condition and standing watch. Cooper was getting sick of listening to the men. All they did was bicker. If he didn't need them all, he'd start eliminating them one by one and force the survivors to dig the graves. But recruiting in this part of Wyoming was hard. The towns were few and far apart, and most of the layabouts normally knocking back whiskey shots in saloons worked on the ranches. Without them to recruit, he had to hire on men who wanted to be outlaws or who were on the run already.

It was so hard finding the right cutthroats these days.

He made sure someone watched over their spare horses, saw that a couple sentries were posted high up on the sheer rock walls and then spread his bedroll out near a low fire. If today was any indication of what was to come, he had a rough road to travel.

And where the hell was Frank Dexter?

CHAPTER 9

"This is serious, Ty," Beatriz Brannigan said, her words on fire. "You almost got yourself killed." She pursed her lips and scowled at him. "Again."

"The brush with the rustlers wasn't all that much," he said.

"Brush? You call this a brush!" She poked him in the ribs. He expected it and tried not to wince.

"It's hardly a scratch. I've done worse to myself putting up barbed wire."

"This is open range. When did you ever string barbed wire? I've heard you cursing that Joe Glidden for inventing that devil's rope. You're trying to distract me."

"Really, my darling, getting caught in that bog was worse. If Matt hadn't pulled me out, I'd have been a goner."

"He's getting to be quite a man," she said, distracted from her anger. "I've seen how he looks at that little slip of a thing working as a schoolmarm."

"Miss Tanner?" Ty shook his head. He had been too busy to even notice her. All he remembered of her was that she wore her mousy brown hair pulled back in a severe bun. She was tall. That he recollected, that along with her brown eyes, and moved with a precise way. He imagined her in a classroom writing on a blackboard with a long piece of chalk. Each word would be exactly the same height and nothing would be misspelled. Ever. She spoke in clipped tones, as if getting ready to lecture anyone daring to talk to her. She had been hired a few months ago when the old schoolmarm married away. "She just graduated from some finishing school in Boston."

"Philadelphia," Beatriz corrected.

"She's too old for him."

"He's nineteen. She's not more than twenty-two."

"See?" Ty said. "She's over the hill. A spinster. Way too old for our son."

"Like you're too old for me." Beatriz poked him again, then wrapped her arms around him and snuggled closer on the sofa.

"Your pa thinks so."

"So does *mi madrecita*," Beatriz said. "You took me away, swept me off my feet when I was only eighteen. They wanted me to marry a businessman."

"Or another banker like your father. Instead they got a broke-down old gun slick who never stayed in one town for more than a few years."

"That's because you ran the outlaws from those towns. When your job was done, you moved on. They call you 'Town Tamer' for a reason."

"Nobody calls me that," he said.

"I do," she said softly. "Except in bed. You're a wild man then. Never then do I want to tame you."

He kissed her, then said, "Let's find out how much wild is left in this old man after the day I've had." They stood. Ty hesitated. Greg had come in from finishing his chores and stood in the doorway, looking like he was going to explode if he didn't get something said.

"Pa, I need to talk. About what I saw this evening, just about when you were shooting it out with those rustlers."

"In the morning, son. I'm real tired." Ty jerked when his wife squeezed him around the middle. She wasn't one to hesitate when the mood moved her. And right now, he felt the heat from her and shared it.

They left Greg standing in the middle of the big room and went upstairs.

Greg clamped his teeth together and fought not to grind them. That didn't get him anywhere. His parents treated him like a child to be dismissed when they wanted. They'd never turn their backs like they'd just done on either Matt or Mack.

He turned around a couple times in indecision. There had to be something he could do to show them he mattered around here. With a determination he hadn't felt in a long time, he left the house and went to the barn. His gelding opened one big brown eye as if accusing him of some terrible deed.

"Yeah, it's gonna be terrible," he assured the horse as he tossed the saddle blanket over the horse's back and went to fetch his tack. "We're gonna ride all night, if we have to. Those rustlers aren't escaping us this time."

He hesitated when he slung his saddle up. His shotgun still rode in the saddle scabbard. If he crossed paths with the outlaws again, he'd need more firepower than the puny .410 offered. It was good for varmints, but not the big two-legged kind. His pa kept a few rifles in a case on the barn wall, just in case. It saved hiking back down to the ranch house should anyone need a long gun. Only a week back a fox had tried sneaking into the chicken coop. His pa had calmly removed one rifle, slipped a single cartridge in and shot the fox as it came out, feathers and blood all over its snout.

He looked up above the barn door. A fluffy fox tail dangled there.

"One shot," he said softly. "He knew it'd only take a single shot."

Greg considered the two rifles still in the case on the far wall. The slot where a third usually rested was missing. If it had been stolen, there'd be hell to pay. Only no one had crept in to take only a rifle.

"Matt," he said, fuming. "He took it and kept it."

This almost made him grab one for his own, but his pa was strict about who could take a rifle and who couldn't. Greg patted his shotgun. It'd be good enough. He led his horse from the barn and swung into the saddle. He rode past the corral where the colt leaned against the rails, eyes closed. It slept and dreamed of boundless freedom again. What else would such a frisky animal want?

Greg wanted the same thing.

He rode toward the southern pasture. The herd had slowly migrated to the west. Seeing this made him suck in his breath and hold it. Baldy Butte lay in that direction, and the trail winding up into the mountains where the rustlers had ridden ended not far from the edge of the pasture.

Sure the rustlers would be back to take their extra cattle, he skirted the edge of the herd. A few cows turned sleepy eyes in his direction as he bothered them. He gave the bull a wider berth. The bull protected his herd from all comers and considered any rider at night to be a threat.

Greg found a spot among a sparse stand of pines, with a post oak or two elbowing their way in. He dismounted, tethered his horse and set up his watch. He gripped his shotgun as he stared out into the darkness. The cattle moved about sluggishly, and an occasional one lowed, complaining about some bovine annoyance. But the night was still, and Greg failed to spot any of the rustlers, either coming to take the stolen beeves—and likely others with the Brannigans' Circle P brand—or add new stock.

He dozed off now and then, only to snap awake. When faint pink on the horizon promised a new day, he climbed to his feet and stretched cramped muscles. He had done his job but had nothing to show for it. If he galloped all the way, he'd be back at the ranch house before anyone else arose.

He'd return for another day of being treated like a kid and not the man who had guarded the herd from real rustlers.

CHAPTER 10

"You're not doing a very good job," Caroline Brannigan said. Her tiny fists rested on her hips, and she looked the world like their mother. Her eyes flashed and the set to her jaw showed the same strength and determination for chores to be done right. "See? You're leaving dust everywhere."

Greg glared at her. He tossed the broom to her. She tried to catch it but missed. It clattered to the front porch floor.

"You want it done. You do it," he said.

"Mama told you to do it. I've got windows to clean."

"You're just standing there."

"I want to be sure you're doing a good job. And you're not. If you don't do better, I'll tell Mama!"

Greg started to retort, then remembered he was bickering with his twelve-year-old sister. He said nothing as he picked up the broom and shook it. A small dust cloud drifted down just off the porch. With a swing he could chase his annoying sister off the porch and work in peace. Before he had a chance, his pa came out.

"You're looking better, Pa," Greg said. "You were all bunged up yesterday."

"A good night's . . . sleep will do that," Ty Brannigan said. Greg thought there was more meaning in his pa's words but wasn't sure what they were.

"You have anything for me to do today?" He held up the broom to silently make his point. Was there a chore to do that wasn't menial and befitting a small kid.

"Ride with me into town. I need to tell Marshal Southern about the extra cattle in the herd. He might have heard something about rustlers and be able to identify the brand."

"Sure thing, Pa!" He dropped the broom and vaulted the porch railing. Greg hit the ground hard and took off at a run for the barn. Staying up most of the night keeping watch for those very same rustlers had left him tired. The fatigue disappeared in a flash. He'd get to tell the marshal about what he'd seen, the three riders and how they headed up into the mountains.

And where. He knew the path to their hideout. Desperado's Den. The name said it all. The outlaws had let him find out where they hid and never knew it.

He saddled and was ready to ride by the time his father got to the barn.

"You're eager to get to town," Ty said. "Any reason?"

"I've got things to tell the marshal. About the rustlers. I've been thinking about them a lot and—"

"Wait a second," Ty said. He stepped out of the barn and yelled, "Matthew! Get to breaking that colt. Then see to the mare I've penned out back. She looks like she's starting to bloat. If it looks real serious and you need help, go tell the vet."

"That'll cost a lot, Pa."

"Take the money from the strongbox in my desk."

Greg listened to the byplay. His pa trusted Matt with the family money and to deal with a valuable mare, if it was beginning to bloat. Worse, he told the older boy to finish breaking the colt Greg had worked with the day before.

He wanted to show he was able to do a good job, and

now his brother was going to get the pat on the back for it. It wasn't fair.

"Come on, Greg," Ty said.

He only nodded. No matter what he did or said, nobody paid any attention. Nobody except Caroline who only wanted to torment him. If he tried to get even with her, he'd be in a world of trouble for picking on his little sister. And doing nothing let her win. That encouraged her to keep bedeviling him. He was caught in a no-win situation.

His pa wasn't much of a talker, but it seemed that he yammered on about this and that all the way into Warknife. This suited him fine. If nobody in the Brannigan family wanted to know what he knew, Marshal Southern was sure to listen. More than a family friend, the marshal was a top-notch lawman. He'd know how important everything Greg had to say was.

There might even be a reward in it, he thought. After all, he had seen one of the rustlers plainly and could identify him again. A moment's thrill made his heart race. Looking through the wanted posters could be dull, but he'd never done it before with a particular outlaw in mind.

They rode to the jailhouse. It was a low structure, one story and made of sawn planks that had been whitewashed. Three barred windows along the side wall provided fresh air for the prisoners. Otherwise, there weren't any openings other than the door opening out onto Main Street.

The front door was open to provide ventilation inside. Greg got a quick look and saw Chris Southern behind his desk, poring over a stack of wanted posters. He hopped down and started to go inside. Those posters had to have a picture of the man he'd spotted on his way to . . . Desperado's Den.

"Let me have a word with the marshal," Ty said. "You go on over to the barbershop. Mister Dempsey can cut some of that shaggy hair off. There might actually be ears under that mop of yours."

A quarter flashed over and over as Ty flipped it to his son. "Give Merlin his dime for the cut and tip him a nickel."

"What do I do with the remaining ten cents?"

"See what Angus O'Reilly's got in the way of hard candy. That much ought to get you a pocketful."

Greg looked at the two bits and started to run off. The sooner he got his hair cut the quicker he could see if Mister O'Reilly had any butterscotch. That was his favorite. Then he closed his hand around the coin and realized the truth of the matter.

He was being chased away so the grown-ups could talk without being bothered by a kid hanging around.

"I need to tell the marshal about—" Greg was cut off when Marshal Southern called out to Ty to come on in and have a seat.

"Run along, Greg. I'll find you, either at the barbershop or the drugstore."

Greg stared at his pa's broad back. Ty grabbed a chair and pulled it around to the side of the marshal's desk so they could put their heads together and talk in confidential whispers. There must be a prisoner or two in the back they wanted to keep their talk from.

Greg felt like a prisoner only without the iron bars all around. What held him wasn't even visible.

He walked down the middle of Warknife's main street, flipping the quarter as he went. He watched the merchants and workers and wondered which of them would give him a job if he left home. He was plenty old enough. He knew men who had gone on the trail at his age. Younger! If he found a job that paid enough he could get a room over at Mrs. Jensen's boardinghouse. That was a decent enough place, or so his ma said.

He shook his head. Decisions to be made had to come from what he wanted balanced against what he needed. His parents treated him like a little kid. If he made choices on his own, he'd show them.

And those rustlers. Before he rode home, he had to tell Marshal Southern about them. It'd be easier when his pa wasn't taking up all the lawman's attention.

He came to a stop in the street in front of the barbershop. The red-and-white striped pole appeared to turn but it was only a painted post. The movement was a trick of the light, but one that he enjoyed. Inside Merlin Dempsey stropped a razor to give a shave to someone in the chair. Greg tried to identify the man on the receiving end of that razor, but he was covered in a white sheet and had his face wrapped in a steamy hot towel to soften up the prickly beard.

Greg ran his hand over his own chin. There were a few bristles sprouting, but getting Mister Dempsey to razor them off was a waste of money. He took off his hat and ran his hands through long, dark hair. It had been a spell since he'd hacked off an inch or two. Trying to do it himself had left ragged ends. Mister Dempsey'd take care of that ragamuffin look.

He tucked the quarter into his jeans watch pocket and went in. He caught his toe on the doorsill and stumbled. Merlin Dempsey jerked around, startled, pulling the razor away from his customer's throat.

"Careful, boy," he said. "You don't want me to nick Walt, would you?"

"Sorry, Mister Nobles," Greg said. The man in the chair was part owner of the town lumberyard. He was as opposite in appearance from the barber as he could be. Tall and thin, his boots stuck out over the footrest on the barber chair.

Merlin Dempsey was hardly five feet tall, maybe more. Nobles had a full head of hair and a thick beard. The barber must have gone into this business so he'd see a decent head of hair. His bald pate had been polished until it shined like a crystal doorknob. A thin ring of sandy hair, as fine as carded cotton, curled around his skull. He wore wire-rimmed glasses perched on a long, thin nose.

Walt Nobles' dark eyes snapped this way and that, never missing a detail. If he'd needed eyeglasses, fixing them onto his potato-big nose would have been easy. Greg thought he'd never seen a man with nostrils as big and hairy as Walt Nobles'. He started to tell the barber not to miss slicing back that jungle growth but kept his peace. For some reason Nobles had never much liked him, and he had to admit the feeling was mutual. He suspected the real animosity ran between the lumberyard owner and his pa, but no one ever talked about it.

"You're in need of my skills, son," Dempsey said. "It'll be ten minutes or so before I get Walt here all spruced up." Dempsey returned to working on removal of the stubbled beard. "You thinkin' on goin' to the church social this week, Walt?"

The man in the chair mumbled something, not daring to speak with a freshly sharpened straight razor moving along his throat.

"You'll look good enough to ask that purty schoolmarm. No woman can refuse a man with a clean-shaven chin and a perfect haircut done by yours truly. No, sir, Walt. The ladies will flock around."

Greg guessed that Merlin Dempsey wasn't inclined to think of the lumberyard owner charitably, either. The way he poked and prodded bordered on the cruel. There wasn't any way Nobles could respond, in spite of getting a little squirmy.

"Get yourself a magazine to read while you're waitin'," Dempsey said, pointing with the razor blade. "Not the ones up high on the shelf. You're too young for them. Yeah, those. I just got a couple new dime novels in. Don't go tellin' your pa I let you look at those. They're pretty racy. Now, let me get back to my precision barbering."

Walt Nobles got out a muffled comment that the barber ignored.

Greg reached up and took down three of the dime novels. The covers all appealed to him, but one title jumped out. *The Sunset Kid's Deadly Showdown*. The cover had two cowboys facing each other. The gun slick facing the gaudy dressed Sunset Kid had his iron almost all the way out of his holster, but Greg knew the Kid would pull through. He settled down in a straight-backed wood chair and leafed through the brittle yellow pages.

Then he thumbed to the first page and began reading. It took Mister Dempsey calling his name a second time before he came out of the spell cast by the lurid novel.

"You raced right through that one," the barber said. "You're within a couple dozen pages of the end."

Greg didn't trust himself to relate the plot. The Sunset Kid was everything he wanted to be. If only he had the chance.

"Don't wiggle, and I'll get done before you know it." Merlin Dempsey finished Greg's haircut and pulled the sheet away, sending inch-long shorn locks flying. "There you go, young man."

Greg fished out the quarter and passed it over.

"Keep it all," he said.

"That's more than generous. Are you sure?"

He clutched the almost completed dime novel like a rope tossed to a drowning man.

"If I can keep this to finish."

"Tell you what, son. You bring it back when you're done. No charge for running a lending library." He handed Greg fifteen cents change and got back a nickel as a tip. He laid the coin on the back of his hand and walked it from one finger to the next like some tinhorn gambler. "You deserve a little sideshow for such a handsome tip. Now run along. That's Bernard Weaver coming in. He always wants to look his finest."

"Best saloon in town, my pa says," Greg said.

"Reckon it is, yup, it certainly is." Dempsey turned from Greg to greet his highfalutin customer.

Greg slipped out, the dime novel tucked under his arm.

He marched back to the marshal's office, full of determination to be as honest and forthright as the Sunset Kid. Marshal Southern once more sat alone at his desk, working through piles of wanted posters.

"Marshal, I got something to tell you. About the extra cattle."

"Your pa told me everything, Greg." Southern waved. "Ty, your boy's here."

"There you are. Let's get on back to the ranch," Ty said, coming from the back of the jail.

"But, Pa, I have to tell Marshal Southern about—"

"It'll be sundown by the time we get back. Your ma will chew us out if we miss dinner again. Once in a while is all right if there's important work to do, but two nights running is pushing our luck."

"Marshal, I saw—"

"Greg. Come along. Now." Ty Brannigan's tone brooked no disobedience. It was sharp and told that his time with the marshal hadn't been productive.

He followed his father and mounted. He made sure the dime novel was securely tucked away in his saddlebags. It wouldn't do to lose it, not when he wanted to find how the Sunset Kid got out of that ambush the cattle thieves sprung on him.

As he rode, Greg imagined himself in that predicament. How the Sunset Kid would escape he didn't know, but he'd find out. It had to be some clever trick he'd never think up himself—and one that he could use against the rustlers threatening the Circle P herd.

CHAPTER 11

"Hey, boss, somebody's comin'." Ron Marcus hobbled over to the fire where Race Cooper boiled a fresh pot of coffee. "He's lost, from the way he's lookin' around."

Race Cooper dashed his coffee into the fire and watched the curls of steam rise. Tossing his tin cup onto his bedroll, he made sure his Colt rode easy in its intricate holster. The leather had been tooled by a Mexican who was shot down less than a week after finishing. That was a shame. Cooper would have paid him to similarly decorate the saddle sheath where he carried his Winchester. All good work, but the leather smith had never learned not to spark a woman claimed by a fast hand.

"Which way's he approaching?"

"From the north. He had to ride a powerful long way to find that trail, or he took the wrong fork east of here. I get mixed up there's so many ways to the camp."

Cooper left Marcus babbling to himself. The man was a liability, but he needed all the guns he could recruit. The bank robbery needed at least six men, but rustling cattle took all dozen he had in camp. It was greed on his part wanting both the gold locked up in the Cutbank vault and the stolen cattle. But why not? His thievery had been far more successful than profitable. Two train robberies on the way to Wyoming had put less than a hundred dollars in each of his gang's wallets. If he didn't deliver a big payoff there wouldn't be a single one of these cutthroats following him in a month.

In a week.

He trooped up a steep slope into the rocks where a sentry with a pair of field glasses watched the northern approach. The canyon's high walls made attack from that direction impossible, at least by a cavalry troop. The only possible assault had to be done by a handful of lawmen sneaking in. They might follow a stream coming from higher elevations, but he had chosen well when he pitched camp here. It wasn't invincible, but any attack was more likely to fail. The distant clop-clop of a horse's hooves provided warning long before any rider came into view.

"What do you see?" He took the field glasses from Kennard's hands. The man started to yank them back, then fell into a sullen silence. Such behavior was all he expected from him and his partner Marcus. They'd joined solely to rustle cattle and didn't understand the lure of a mountain of gold sitting in a bank vault.

Cooper was surrounded by men with little ambition and feeble imaginations.

"Never mind," Cooper said. He adjusted the lenses and saw the rider working his way along a narrow, rocky trail. It was Dexter.

The two of them had gotten drunk together, reminiscing about the old days. Neither had mentioned their time in the Army, as if that laid a curse on their heads. Being caught, they'd be hanged before sundown the next day. But both had ridden the long coulee long enough to brag on other robberies, even a shooting or two, and enjoy the bragging.

Eventually Dexter had spilled everything he knew about the gold shipment because it gave him a leg up on his old crony. Cooper had listened with intense interest. A dozen surrounding ranchers pumped in the specie to pay for a railroad spur to be built from the main line a hundred miles south. The Wyoming and Colorado Railroad, Dexter had said, wasn't interested in servicing the towns because of the lack of population, but the ranchers worked it out that they'd save money over a few seasons shipping their herds to the main line rather than driving them to a distant railhead.

Speed of transport, not needing to fatten the cattle as much when they arrived at market, requiring fewer cowpunchers, it all made sense to the ranchers. And it made sense to Cooper. The only problem was that Dexter had to find out the whole story. He'd played it cagy and refused to say who gave him the details.

Without a good tally of how much gold and when it was to be put into the vault, any robbery was likely to match Cooper's earlier pathetic attempts at being a crook. Hit the bank too soon and he'd end up with hundreds of dollars and not tens of thousands.

"Come on, you mangy dog," he muttered as he watched Dexter follow the meandering stream toward camp.

Sunlight must have reflected off the field glasses. Dexter drew rein and sat staring straight at Cooper. It became a standoff. Who'd give in first?

Race Cooper lost this battle of wills. He tossed the field glasses to Kennard and slipped and slid down the steep rock face to the trail. A quick hitch to his fancy gun belt satisfied him he was ready for anything Dexter threw his way.

They were linked forever because of their desertion from the Army post, but Cooper knew better than to trust Dexter. For two cents he'd turn Dexter in to the Army if enough money rode on it. He expected no less from Frank Dexter.

He stopped twenty yards from the still mounted man. No

matter what Dexter had discovered, he needed a gang to
pull off the robbery. This wasn't anything one or two men
handled on their own. The gold had to be loaded in wagons.
That'd take a pair of men an hour. A dozen robbers made
short work of it. And if a cavalry detachment guarded the
hoard, a small army had to oppose them to make a getaway
succeed.

It'd be a bloody fight. And worth it.

"You want to shout at each other?" Frank Dexter made
no move to ride closer.

Cooper saw the battle of wills brewing between them.
Dexter tried to get the upper hand. Give an order and have
it obeyed established who was in charge. Cooper wasn't
going to let Dexter take over either the planning for the
robbery or his gang. Those cutthroats weren't reliable or
even the best at what they did, but he had recruited them.
Letting anyone else muscle in when he was in charge got
Cooper's dander up.

"You have the details? I need to put a plan together."

"Come on over here," Dexter shouted.

"Let's go to camp. You can tell the rest of my men about
the bank. They've been waiting to hear." Cooper tilted his
head down a side trail that led to camp but made no move
to precede Dexter. He wanted the rider to go ahead of
him. He saw no reason for Dexter to double-cross him,
but following Dexter kept a bullet from finding its way into
his back.

"I ain't got it."

Cooper widened his stance and rested his hand on the
outside of the tooled holster. At this range he'd likely miss
with the first few rounds, but if he fanned off all six bullets
one had to hit this treacherous snake. The gunfire would
bring the rest of his men running. He knew Kennard
watched but had no confidence that he'd use his rifle on

Dexter. It had surprised him that Kennard had bothered to let him know someone had come up this trail.

"Then what good are you to me?"

Dexter heaved a deep sigh and snapped his horse's reins. He walked forward slowly. His occasional glance into the rocks where Kennard waited told Cooper he dealt with someone alert and not foolish enough to ride into a trap. If Kennard had been even a little more alert, Dexter would have galloped away, fearing he had come into a trap.

The rider stopped a few yards away and swung down. When he hit the ground, a small cloud of trail dust billowed about him. Dexter had been on the trail for a long time.

"I'll tell you what good I am. It's my brother who has everything we need to know. Thomas is reliable."

That last sentiment put Cooper on guard. The man's brother said one thing and thought another. The way he said it, the tone, the set to his mouth—Dexter and his brother weren't on good terms. They might look like twins, but putting a bullet or two in his sibling's gut would count as a red letter day.

"You're supposed to know it all. We can't stick around here much longer." Cooper already considered abandoning the bank robbery and moving the cattle right away. Two crimes at the same time might not have been his best idea, but he cursed such bad luck. Stealing cattle was profitable enough, but taking a small mountain of gold from a bank? If Thomas was right, that was a robbery of a very crooked lifetime.

Race Cooper seemed doomed to *almost* make the big score. Piles of gold coins slipped through his fingers like sand. This time was different. This time *had* to be different.

"We've got this one," Frank Dexter assured him. "I've scouted out that bank. When the gold's stored inside, it'll be as easy as pie 'withdrawing' it." Dexter laughed in a way that set Race Cooper's teeth on edge.

He didn't have to read the man's thoughts to know Dexter intended to double-cross him. Cooper wished he had more reliable men than Kennard and Marcus at his back.

"We need to know if robbing the bank will be easier than tackling a guarded wagon train on its way south."

"The railroad won't send their bulls to protect the money. It won't belong to the railroad until all the contracts are signed. There'll be at least a squad of cavalry guarding it once it leaves the bank."

"It might be better to hit the bank before all the gold's brought in. They won't expect that," Cooper said, more to himself than to Dexter. Even as he spoke, he saw the problem. Robbing individual ranchers as they brought their gold to the bank meant he'd miss the entire amount loaded into the vault before the Army picked it up.

Bits and pieces, not the entire mountain of gold. This was his problem before. Taking a few dollars and losing out on the bigger payment to the railroad marked his history as a thief. Petty payoffs and never the one that gave him bragging rights the rest of his life.

He wanted notoriety. He wanted lawmen to shiver in fear at his name. The name Race Cooper had to be on everyone's lips for him to consider this robbery a success.

"This is the kind of reconnaissance Thomas will give us."

"When?" Cooper turned his attention back to what mattered. First the details, then the renown.

Dexter shook his head and looked annoyed.

"In time. He knows that."

Cooper again considered what to do. Take the cattle and make a few dollars. Or wait days or even longer for Thomas Dexter to spill the details about the Cutbank gold.

Greed won out over common sense.

"Two days," he told Dexter. "I either find out what we need to rob the bank or we're out of here. In two days."

"Yeah, I heard about you being seen by that rancher prowling around his herd. Has he figured out there are too many newcomers butting heads with his cows?"

"Two days," Cooper said coldly. The hair on the back of his neck rippled as he whirled around and stalked back to camp.

Camp? Desperado's Den Marcus and Kennard called it. For Race Cooper it was turning into Desperation Den.

CHAPTER 12

Frank Dexter looked around and didn't like riding into the steep walled canyon. There weren't many branches that didn't look like box canyons, forcing him to ride straight or make the decision to retreat. He kept riding although it felt as if he rode to his death.

He didn't trust Race Cooper as far as he could throw him. The man was a small-time crook who thought he had big plans. Dexter admitted knocking over the Cutbank bank was rolling the dice on a big pot. Such a pile of gold seldom showed up in Wyoming anymore. The real wealth was in cattle and crops, not in mining.

He snorted at that. There was one big mining industry in the territory. Coal for the railroads. He tried to imagine how low a crook had to be to steal a carload of coal.

But the cattle and railroads gave the chance to live in luxury. The ranchers had plenty of gold to pay the railroad to bring in a spur line. This saved them payroll for a couple dozen cowboys and a lengthy trail drive come autumn. If the railroad owners were to be believed, the railroad promised to lay the hundred miles of track in a month. That'd let the ranchers ship their cattle to market right away. That gave the ranchers an incentive to hand over the money as quick as they raised it.

He'd heard a rumor that the ranchers offered a huge bonus to the railroad if the spur line was completed before snows came.

Dexter looked at the canyon rim and imagined them cloaked in heavy snow. The heat trapped in the narrow canyon right now made it seem as if winter would never come. This branch of the hills was part of the Wind River Mountains. Aptly named, he thought. A year back he had ridden this range and felt the wind and snow pelting him in the face. He had barely escaped with his life after being caught in a sudden early blizzard.

Wind blowing through the narrowed mouth of the canyon whipped his bandanna back and forced him to grab to keep his flat-brimmed black felt hat on his head. Dexter pushed it back just a little to sop up the sweat off his wrinkled forehead. His hairline had not retreated, it had abandoned the field entirely. Once it had been sandy and now only existed in a few strands flopping wetly across his skull. If he had any sense, he'd shave his entire head, all the way down to his bushy eyebrows. That'd give him a look to intimidate the most crotchety drunk.

He spat as that idea crossed his mind. Race Cooper hadn't been cowed. If anything, Cooper came close to ordering his sentry to shoot him out of the saddle. He needed a more menacing look. If it wasn't so hot, he'd consider dressing all in black.

Before he realized it, he left the constricted walls of stone. Dexter looked around. He cursed not only Cooper but also his own brother. Thomas had the information and couldn't care less that a fortune danced in front of him. The man had gone off the rails a year or two earlier, and it was all his wife's fault. If she hadn't disappeared one night, without even hinting to Thomas she was leaving, he would still be a reasonable, if sometimes cantankerous, man.

Frank Dexter turned due north to once more wait at the rendezvous where his brother had promised to meet him— three days ago.

The road was empty, and the weather good. Dexter made good time to the stagecoach way station where he'd checked three days earlier for Thomas. The station master had been a tetchy old geezer whose idea of being accommodating was waving around a long-barreled shotgun and promising to gun down anyone he disliked. From what Dexter could tell, that was pretty near everyone who walked and breathed.

He had lounged under a large shade tree for the livelong day, waiting for Thomas and watching the station master insult stage passengers. One had come close to putting the cranky man in his place, then saw that the station master had been out in the sun too long and had cooked his brains.

That was about what Dexter thought, too. The loneliness and the sun were a deadly combination. He wondered if that was what had turned Thomas' wife so touched in the head. She and their brats had been alone out on the Kansas prairie for more than a year while Thomas was in Minnesota trying to find a decent job.

Frank Dexter thought his brother should have ridden with him. The pickings hadn't been great but he'd ended up with more than a few feathers from a stolen chicken. After Evangeline had lit out and Thomas came home to an empty sod-roofed house, convincing him to try his hand at some banditry had been easier.

If only he wasn't still hunting for his wayward wife. That distracted him at a time when Frank needed his brother's full attention most.

He stayed a fair distance from the way station. Tangling with the station master again wasn't in the cards, though he supposed he had to talk with him to find if Thomas had been by in the past three days. Dexter worried he had missed his brother because he had to assure Race Cooper that he— and Thomas—were still part of the bank robbery.

Dexter daydreamed about what he'd do with his share of the gold. Before the robbery, he'd make sure he had three or four horses scattered across Wyoming. Ride one until it dropped, switch to a fresh horse and repeat until he was miles beyond any possible posse. What Cooper did to escape was his own business.

He'd take part in the robbery, giving Thomas all the time he needed to buy and stake out the horses for their escape.

That's how he'd do it if Thomas could be trusted.

Dexter perked up when he heard a rider coming. Cautious, he slipped behind a tree and waited, hand on his iron. The rider came closer, then dismounted by the way station's front door. He chanced a quick look, then blurted, "Thomas! Come on over here."

His brother spun, hand going to his six-shooter. Dexter tried to piece together what happened then but everything came apart all at once. A shot sounded. Thomas jerked around and fired into the station's dark interior. He staggered forward and disappeared.

Dexter saw the bright white-orange lightning of repeated rounds being fired. Half of them blasted from his brother's gun. Whoever else was in the tumbledown shack supplied the rest of the noise.

"Thomas! Thomas!" Dexter slid his pistol from the hard leather holster, unsure what to do. Barging in after his brother wasn't a good idea since he had no idea who was inside the way station. One? A dozen?

The gunfire ceased. The sudden silence clamped down hard, as if someone boxed his ears. In a crouch to present as small a target as possible, he dodged back and forth, dropped to his knees in the mud beside the watering trough, then took careful aim at the door where Thomas had entered.

He edged along behind the wooden trough, then rolled through the dirt and pressed into the splintery wood wall beside the door. Dexter fought to keep his heart from exploding in his chest. His breath came fast and short until he became dizzy. He closed his eyes, opened them, and whirled around. He leveled his gun at . . . nothing.

The darkened room was empty. A kerosene lamp on a long table had been broken. The acrid scent of kerosene made his nostrils flare. And like smelling salts, it cleared his head of the fog of fear.

"Thomas?"

The silence reminded him of a grave site. He flopped onto his belly and crawled toward the table. Shoving a chair ahead gave him some cover. More than this, he wanted the movement to draw fire.

Nothing. No one moved.

He curled up under the table and pivoted around. His heart galloped away again when he saw a pair of boots poking out from behind a stack of crates at the side of the room. He recognized those boots immediately. Thomas had taken them off a deputy sheriff he'd gunned down over in Nebraska. Not only were they fancy boots, they'd fit him perfectly.

Thomas had taken that as a sign the deputy was destined to die so he could pass along the boots to someone who'd appreciate them. Dexter gave his brother that much. He had spent more time polishing them than he had earning an honest living.

A quick peek from under the table let him see that the back door was ajar. The inch or two between the door and the doorjamb showed the clear blue Wyoming sky. Whoever had gunned down Thomas had hightailed it without hesitation. A quick look around behind the station made him wonder if his brother had been cut down by a ghost. Nothing moved. He kept his six-shooter pointed outside for another few seconds, then crept back into the way station.

He felt exposed. Anyone with a rifle hiding behind one of the nearby cottonwoods had a perfect shot. Ending up dead like his brother was in his future, but not today.

"Thomas?" He called out louder, sure they were alone. Dexter crawled on hands and knees to where the boots stuck out.

They weren't alone. *He* was alone. His brother had taken three bullets in the head.

Dexter rolled him over onto his back. He was glad those dead eyes were closed. It always spooked him when a man died staring at nothing. If Thomas had cashed out that way, he'd have been staring at the fiery gates of hell.

"May you not have seen it coming," Dexter said in a low voice. He and Thomas had never gotten along. Hardly ever had they seen eye to eye, but he was blood kin. That counted for something.

Dexter scooted around and tugged hard to get the boots off. He pulled off his own and then tried on Thomas'. They fit better than his own, though they were far from being a perfect fit like his brother had always bragged. Dexter shifted his feet around, wiggled his toes and settled the heels. The boots were too large, but not that much. What they lacked in fit, they made up for in style. The curlicue patterns tooled into the sides were flashier than the ones on his own battered boots.

Satisfied with his new acquisition, he turned to searching his brother's body. A wallet stuffed into a coat pocket spilled out a half-dozen sheets of paper onto the floor. Not taking the time to look at them, Dexter returned them to the wallet and counted the money. Thomas had eight dollars in greenbacks. In a vest pocket he found another dollar's worth of change. All of it went into his own pockets.

He tugged at the gold watch chain, then dropped it. When Thomas had crashed to the floor, his body had broken the watch. It might run a little or even be worth selling for the gilt case, but Dexter had no desire to take it as a souvenir. If it had belonged to their pa or another relative, it'd have been worth taking. All either of them had ever gotten from their pa was a hard time driven by drunken rage. Frank wasn't even sure what fate their pa had met, but he hoped it was long and painful to repay all the hours of endless punishment he had dished out to his boys.

A search through the rest of his brother's pockets revealed nothing worth mentioning.

Dexter grunted as he unbuckled the gun belt and yanked it free. The six-gun was worth three or four dollars, and the cartridges tucked into loops on the belt would prove useful.

Thomas Dexter's body stripped of everything of value, Frank made his way to the rear door. Indistinct prints in the dirt just outside showed where Thomas' killer had lit a shuck and disappeared.

Six-shooter in hand, Dexter followed the trail to a tree near a well. A bucket had been filled and left for a horse.

"Your killer, brother mine, your killer took care of his horse. At least he's a decent enough fellow."

Dexter stared into the distance for a moment, then walked back to where his horse cropped a tuft of grass under a tree. He swung up into the saddle and trotted to the well, then got on the trail. He had all he needed from his brother. Thomas had been a prickly fellow, not inclined to being polite to anyone, much less his younger brother. Dexter considered that he had the papers Thomas used to take notes about the Cutbank heist. There was no need to chase down his killer.

But he did anyway. Blood debt demanded it. Returning to Cooper's camp put him in an awkward position. He'd ride with a gang of strangers. He knew too little about Race Cooper to trust him. And from Cooper's attitude they had something more in the works than stealing a pile of gold. What that was baffled him. Running his brother's killer to ground gave him time to think.

How valuable was the information Thomas had collected?

Dexter was a fair tracker, but his brother's killer made no effort to hide his trail. He seemed to head directly for a distant slash in the mountains, thinking it was a pass through the range. Dexter knew enough of the terrain to appreciate how the obvious turned into a lie. That sharp notch in the mountains might lead to safety for the killer. It had as much chance of being the mouth of a box canyon.

The trail into the winding canyon split into a fork, one side curving around in a way that'd bring a rider out farther south but heading back in the direction of the way station. Dexter considered the matter, then took the trail. The rider he followed thought to double back and had found a hidden way to do it.

He picked up the pace. In the twilight he caught sight of the distant rider. The man who'd shot down Thomas wore a long dark duster and had a hat pulled down low on his forehead. He wore not one but two kerchiefs, one red and the other a blue-and-white check pattern. They were pulled up to protect his face from the dust stirring in the late afternoon wind.

Dexter came out of the U-shaped canyon, hot on the trail. Somehow the rider he pursued caught on that he was being tracked. One instant the dark-cloaked figure was ahead. Then he vanished.

This put Dexter on edge. He slid his six-shooter from its holster and rode slower now. The towering trees and dark patches along the trail made perfect spots for an ambush. He jerked around at movement and fired.

"Damn," he said. His aim was perfect. The target was wrong. He'd shot a rabbit flushed from cover.

Dexter had given himself away and now any chance at running his brother's killer to ground was gone. He hopped down and retrieved the rabbit. If he wasn't able to bring a tad of justice to a cold-blooded killer, he'd fill his belly with freshly cooked rabbit. It took a few minutes to find a small stream gurgling along nearby and pitch camp. More than once he jumped at an unusual noise in the distance, but Dexter finally convinced himself he was alone.

He had chased off Thomas' killer. After poking the fire to get decent heat, he stretched out for the night. His eyelids turned heavy. The final thing he saw before sleep possessed him were the new boots. It hadn't been a wasted day. Not at all.

CHAPTER 13

"When's Marshal Southern coming out?" Greg Brannigan shuffled his feet and tried to look at his pa, but he was too nervous. He kept looking at his boots rather than his father. "The rustlers are going to clear out any time now."

"Chris—Marshal Southern—has personal problems. His wife Molly's not feeling too well. He can't up and leave her until she's better."

"But the rustlers!" Greg was outraged.

"The cattle they stole are still mixed in with our herd," Ty said. "Do you think they'd leave without trying to cut them out?"

"Or taking a bunch of Circle P cattle, too," Greg said.

"You're right about that, son. Matt can ride out to the southern pasture now and again to watch for that. So far, he hasn't found any trace of them returning since he and I ran them off." Ty shook his head, bemused. "It may be up to us to find where those beeves were stolen and return them."

"You think the rustlers have left?"

"Don't sound so disappointed. Whenever you tangle with cutthroats, you're likely to catch an ounce of lead or two. Avoid that, son, and don't go looking for trouble."

Greg saw that his pa wasn't wincing and trying not to show it anymore. The bullet crease on his side was about healed up. How he tangled with such desperate men and made light of it was a puzzlement. It had to be something he'd learned during his years as a town tamer lawdog.

"The Sunset Kid would go right after them," Greg said before he realized it.

"Who?"

"Nobody," he said lamely.

Ty studied his son closely. Uncertainty about what he'd just said convinced Ty that Greg was building fantasies. What was real mattered because that got people killed.

"Get to your chores. It's mid-morning, and the day's about over." Ty slapped Greg on the shoulder and headed into the house.

"Chores," Greg said sourly. Matt had taken over breaking the colt. But cleaning out the corral? That was Greg's chore. And the barn. And feeding the chickens. He was supposed to repair the roof on the chicken roost. Part of it had come loose during the windstorm the night before.

All they wanted him to do around the ranch were trivial chores. Kid's chores. Caroline ought to be feeding the poultry. She was younger and nowhere near grown up. She actually liked poking around in the chicken coop hunting for eggs. Caroline cackled and cheeped every time she found an egg and put it into a basket.

She could pretend to be a chicken and nobody mentioned it. He mentioned what the Sunset Kid would do and his pa looked at him as if he'd been out in the sun too long.

He headed for the barn. Before going in he looked around to be sure no one watched him. Feeling like he was doing something he shouldn't, he took the dime novel from his saddlebags. Greg sat on a bale of hay and leafed through the tattered pages until he came to where he had stopped reading. The Sunset Kid was in dire straits, and Greg had no idea how he was going to get out of his predicament. But he would. The Kid was in charge of his own life. Nobody told him what to do.

"The marshal's not coming out any time soon," Greg said softly. Determination gave him the steel spine needed to do what the Sunset Kid would. He tucked the pulp novel into his waistband, grabbed his shotgun, and then saddled up.

He led the gelding from the barn. It took some willpower not to look back toward the ranch house. His pa, or more likely his ma, might see him and wave him back. With rustlers running rampant on the Circle P, he had to protect the herd.

"Maybe I can find Desperado's Den," he said. The name rolled off his tongue. He knew what the outlaws called their hideout. Marshal Southern didn't. Neither did his pa nor Matt. They refused to listen to what he knew about the owlhoots. It was up to him to bring them to justice.

Just like the Sunset Kid.

He rode fast out to where the herd had been a couple days earlier. They had slowly moved on, hunting for fresher grass. Greg stared across the meadow toward the trees where he had gone after the rustlers before. Hidden away at the foot of the hills was a path leading higher into the mountains, past Baldy Butte, losing itself in the Bear Paws.

A choice between following the Circle P cattle or following the trail deeper into the hills faced him. The cattle weren't in much danger of being driven off, he decided. Cautiously riding into the trees, he sought the head of the trail he had followed days earlier.

He found it.

"What now?" He wanted to get on that path and climb higher into the hills, but being so far from home turned him even more cautious. The Sunset Kid was brave. He wasn't reckless. "Wait. That's what I'll do. Those rustlers have to come down eventually if they want to drive off their cattle."

He hunted for a place to hide his horse and then sit and watch the trail. If they came charging down from Desperado's Den, he'd be ready for them. Greg rested his .410 against a tree and moved around so high grass hid him from sight but let him have a good view.

After a few minutes of sitting and staring intently at the empty trail, he grew restless. Watching a bug crawl along the ground and clamber up onto his boot took a minute or two. And then the bug flew off. Bored, he pulled out the epic story of the Sunset Kid. In a few minutes, he was caught up in the story.

He lived every word of the story. It took him a few seconds to realize he wasn't reading about a horse galloping along. He heard it. Greg jerked around from where he spied on the trail and saw a rider come around a bend in the trail. Reaching out, he grabbed his shotgun but didn't level it. He recognized the rider as one of the rustlers. The one called Ron. He had been shot up when Greg saw him before.

As Ron rode, he made faces, as if jabs of pain bothered him. But he wasn't so badly shot up that he'd surrender quickly if Greg trained his shotgun on him. He stood and started to block the end of the trail. The outlaw might not notice that he swung a .410 shotgun around. That'd make it easier to get the rustler to surrender.

Then any chance to capture himself a rustler disappeared. A second rider came trotting along the trail. This might have been one of the others with Ron when he'd spotted them before.

A third rider joined the first two. They were far enough away that he wasn't able to make out their words, but their argument grew hotter by the minute. One waved his arms around like a runaway windmill, thrashing around and pointing both back up the trail and out toward the herd.

Another sat as still as a statue, but his partner reached down and slid his rifle up and down in its saddle sheath.

Greg gasped when Ron yanked out his six-shooter and fired at one of the others. The argument grew louder. And deadlier.

The man Ron had shot at jumped to the ground and slipped the leather thong off his Colt's hammer. He squared off and yelled at Ron.

"You're a complete fool, Kennard," Ron declared. He waved his own pistol around.

"Get down off that horse and let's settle this."

"I'll do that very thing. You've insulted me for the last time!"

Greg tried to follow what the two angry men did. Both rammed their smoke wagons back into their holsters. Stomping around, they stopped ten feet apart. They faced each other, hands on their holsters, waiting for the other to draw.

"You two cut that out," snapped the third rider. He still fiddled with his sheathed rifle. "Neither of you have any call to throw down like you're fixing to do. Save that for when it counts."

"Yeah," Ron said. "It'd be a waste of bullets to shoot him." He backed away and turned his back on Kennard. Ron crossed his arms and sulked.

"Get your hand off your iron. I'm not telling you twice." The rider slid out his rifle and aimed it at Kennard.

"Aw, Race, we don't mean nothin' by it. We're just havin' ourselves a little fun," Kennard said. "That's the way we are. It keeps us from gettin' bored."

"You're both such bad shots, you're likely to put a bullet through your own foot." The rider spat. Greg took him to be the leader, if anyone had a chance of telling either Ron or Kennard what to do was possible.

"I've never done that," Ron said. He pointed wordlessly at his boots to show they didn't have bullet holes in the toes. He shifted toward the mounted Race. "I'm a sight faster than Kennard. And I'd wager I'm faster than you, too."

A deathly silence fell. Greg knew that Kennard had called out the man who was likely his boss. In an outlaw gang, this was a challenge that meant one of them had to die. The winner became the undisputed leader.

He had read all about it. Greg tucked the story of the Sunset Kid back into his waistband. With hands turning sweaty and his muscles shaking from strain, he held the shotgun. If any of the trio came in his direction, he'd have to open fire. Which one would the Sunset Kid shoot first?

"Ron," said Race in a cold voice. "Set up a dozen targets. Stack them along that fallen log."

"A dozen?"

"Rocks, pine cones, whatever you can find. Line 'em up." Race resheathed his rifle, then opened the gate on his Colt. He spun the cylinder to check its load. Satisfied, he thrust the six-shooter back into his holster.

Ron kept looking over his shoulder at his leader as he found rocks the size of his fist, lengths of wood, and a couple pine cones as Race had demanded. One by one, he balanced them on the log, then backed away.

"What are you gonna do?" he asked.

"Watch and learn," Kennard said, sneering. He made no effort to make a fast draw. He pulled out his six-gun, cocked it, and took aim. One by one, he sent the targets flying until he got to the last one. He missed.

For a moment, he simply stared. Then he shook his six-shooter as if it was somehow to blame.

"It moved on me," he complained. "It musta been the wind or something that deflected the bullet and ruined my aim."

In reply he got a nasty laugh from both Ron and Race.

"Your turn," Kennard finally said. "You're not gonna do one whit better."

Race filled his fist with his Colt. He fanned off six shots, sending six targets flying. With a quick move, he spun his gun around his finger using the trigger guard and smoothly dropped the Colt back into his holster.

"That's how it's done, old buddy." Ron slapped Kennard on the shoulder. He was greeted with a snarl. Ron stepped back and said, "Your gun's empty. You want to call me out? Not even you's that dumb."

Ron staggered away when Kennard swung his empty six-shooter and landed the barrel alongside his partner's head. Ron went for his gun. Greg caught his breath. He was going to see a man cut down before his very eyes.

"Stop that," Race said, grabbing Ron's wrist and forcing him to point his six-gun at the ground. "You, too."

"Are you gonna make me?" Kennard began reloading, then looked up.

Race trained his gun on the man's gut.

"I've reloaded. This squabble's got out of hand. You bury the hatchet now or I'll bury you. Both of you."

From the way Race spoke, Greg believed him. So did the feuding men.

"What's that?" Race spun and stared straight at Greg.

Somehow, he had given himself away. A million choices ran through his head. If he fired, he might wound one of the rustlers. A leg shot kept them from chasing him. But the other two? All three were dangerous gunmen. Their bickering had almost turned deadly. Killing anyone spying on them would come easy.

"Riders," Kennard said. "Let's clear out."

"For once, he's got a good idea," Race said. He shoved Ron in the direction of their horses. With a last glance into the bushes hiding Greg, Race turned and jumped onto his horse.

The three rustlers hit the trail and vanished in seconds. Greg stayed frozen until his muscles gave out and quakes shook him. He sagged down, dropping to one knee. When the realization of how close he had come to getting ventilated passed, he stood. His cramped legs failed to hold him. He braced himself against a tree, then stepped out.

"Greg!"

Hearing his name almost caused him to collapse. He swung his shotgun around, then heaved a sigh and lowered the muzzle.

"Pa, am I glad to see you. What're you doing out here? You said you were going to wait for Marshal Southern to come out."

"Chris is right behind me. I heard gunshots. Pistols, not a shotgun." He stared hard at the .410 in Greg's shaking hands. "What happened?"

"I came out to check the herd," he gushed. "Rustlers. They were here. Three of them. I spied on them while they were having a shooting match." He pointed to the log where a single target remained erect.

"I don't understand why you're even out here," Ty said.

"Marshal Southern wasn't coming. I wanted to—"

"Chris!" Ty called. "Over here. It's all right."

The Warknife marshal worked his way through the trees and drew rein beside Ty.

"He wasn't the one doing any shooting. Who was?" the marshal asked gruffly.

"They went up the trail," Greg said, excited. "Three of them. I saw them before and—"

"Get on back to the house, son," Ty ordered. "We'll run them down."

"Wait, Pa. I can identify them. I heard them talking about

their hideout. They call it—" Greg spoke to empty air. Both his pa and Marshal Southern hit the trail leading up toward Baldy Butte. Somewhere beyond the sullen mound of brown stone lay the outlaws' camp.

"—Desperado's Den," Greg said. Anger filled him. He had scouted out the rustlers. He had learned so much about them, and neither his pa nor the lawman listened.

"This'd never happen to the Sunset Kid," he said bitterly. Greg lifted his shotgun and aimed it at the solitary remaining target Kennard had missed. He fired.

He missed.

CHAPTER 14

"What was your boy doing out here?" Chris Southern asked.

Ty Brannigan guided his horse over a pile of rocks in the middle of the narrow trail. When he reached the far side, he hunted for hoofprints. Finding them was easy. Without jumping down and examining the trail more carefully, he made out at least two sets of tracks. The way the ground was chopped up hinted at more riders.

Three. Like Greg had said.

"He thought he was helping. I tried to tell him how dangerous it was tangling with rustlers. If they're willing to steal few hundred head of cattle, they're the kind of men who'd shoot down anyone trying to stop them."

"Hanging is too good for them. They're like horse thieves. Or murderers." Southern pulled the brim of his Stetson down to shield his eyes to get a better look at the trail ahead. "I don't see any riders."

"This path winds around a considerable amount," Ty said. "They can be around a bend and we'd never see them." He considered stopping for a few minutes. What he said was true. If he and Southern stayed in one place, the rustlers might show themselves as they negotiated the switchback trail farther uphill.

"Where do you think they're headed?"

"The trail goes into the Bear Paws. There's a hundred places for someone on the run to hide out. We're lucky that it hasn't rained in a couple days. The ground's soft but without rain, the hoofprints aren't washed away."

"It's still dirty out here," the marshal said. He brushed a handful of dirt off his duster. "I should have sent Conrad out and stayed in town."

"You're out here where you belong, Chris. That brain of yours is concocting a dozen different ways to catch the varmints. That pistol report we heard means something's going on that we need to investigate." Ty gave up waiting for any riders ahead of them to show themselves. This part of the trail wound around the hill. If they moved slow enough, anyone ahead of them on the trail might take another half hour to appear.

"I've got a question for you. Why hide when they have cattle to steal? It makes sense they'd mix their stolen head with yours for a day or two, if they had to wait."

"Wait for what?" Ty asked.

"As much as I hate to say it, some of the local ranchers'd be willing to buy stolen cattle at the right price. I won't name names but you know who I mean."

"Bartell, for one," Ty said.

"Not naming his name, mind you, but he's one." Southern pointed out a fresh pile of road apples. They were steamy hot and had only just started drawing flies. The horse responsible had passed by within the past half hour.

"Most all of us are pressed for cash right now," Ty said. "More than usual. Jack Lowry dickered with the Wyoming and Colorado to run a spur line from their southern line up to Cutbank."

"I heard something about it, but I thought the deal fell apart. Didn't the railroad want too much money?"

"Close to twenty thousand dollars," Ty said, "but with enough of us anteing up we can get ourselves a dedicated line to ship cattle real easy."

"Is everyone in this deal for the same buy-in? That don't seem fair to the smaller ranchers."

"Lowry's got it all worked out. A credit is given for every head shipped. The smaller ranches won't have to pay anything for the first year. The Circle P came out in the middle. I'll have to pay a couple dollars a head after putting in about all my spare cash, but the quicker sale makes it worthwhile."

"What's your father-in-law have to say about that?"

Ty heaved a sigh. Beatriz's father, Diego Salazar, was owner of the Warknife bank. Never had Ty seen a man more cautious with a dollar, whether it was his own or his depositors'. He and Beatriz had discussed the possibility of her pa making a loan to the Circle P to keep from drying up all the ranch's available cash. A week of back-and-forth argument had brought them to the same decision.

Her pa would oppose the deal on a dozen different points. Not the least of which was the railroad spur running to Cutbank and not into Warknife. The chance he'd approve a loan, even collateral using a successful ranch like the Circle P—and his own daughter—ran close to zero.

Ty wasn't sure her father had ever forgiven her for marrying a drifter. It didn't matter that Ty had run the Circle P for more than twenty years, Diego Salazar still considered him to be a newcomer. The worst crime Ty had committed, though, was marrying Beatriz. Salazar had intended for her to marry a successful businessman, not a cowboy.

Keeping the banker in the dark wasn't that hard since Jack Lowry and the rest of the ranchers in the Cattle Growers Association worked to keep the deal a secret. Ty wasn't sure how well that worked since too many of the ranchers liked to brag on their wealth, their ranch, their power in the community, but so far there hadn't been any gossip.

At least there hadn't been any he'd heard. Or Beatriz. And even better, his daughter MacKenna hadn't heard so much as a whisper around Warknife about the proposed spur line into the neighboring town. If Mack hadn't heard it, it wasn't out there.

"Still don't understand why the rustlers haven't moved their cows by now," Southern said. "It's been a week or so, if you're right about when the strays showed up."

"Strays," scoffed Ty. "That's one name for stolen steaks on the hoof." He stood in the stirrups and caught his breath. "There they are. Three of them, like Greg said."

"They've spotted us," Southern said. "What'll we do? They must be a half mile ahead of us along this here twisty trail."

"Why not make them come to us?" Ty slid his Henry from the saddle scabbard and jacked in a round. He sighted along the barrel and took a couple calming breaths.

"You can't hit them at this distance. Even if you did, how's that gonna make them come back?"

"If they can't go forward, they have to return this way if they want off the trail." Ty squeezed down on the trigger. It bucked into his shoulder. He began firing with a methodical rhythm until the air around him filled with gunsmoke. After the sixteenth round, he lowered the rifle.

"That barrel's got to be red hot," Southern said. "And you weren't coming anywhere near them . . ." His voice dropped to a whisper when the ground began to shake.

Ty began feeding cartridges back into the Henry's magazine. He'd need the rifle again real soon and not to create a rockslide. His horse began crow hopping as the ground continued to shake.

"You started a gol'danged avalanche," Southern said in

awe. "Look at that. The whole side of the hill's coming down on them."

"It'll block the trail in front of them. There wasn't an overhang above them so I had to shoot at one ahead along the path."

"That worked just fine, old friend," Southern said. "You always were a sneaky one." Southern laughed. "And about the best shot I ever did see." He pulled his six-shooter and cocked it.

"It'll take them a few minutes to backtrack," Ty said. "We might want to take cover behind the rocks higher on the slope."

They left their horses downhill where random flying lead wouldn't accidentally hit them. The boulders Ty had scouted were perfect for what was to come. He covered the trail from higher on the hill, and Southern was closer and able to prevent any rider from rushing past and escaping.

"Here they come," Ty said, using his vantage to spot the lead rider. "And he's coming hard." He swung up his rifle and took a shot to get the range.

The bullet careened off a rock and sailed farther than Ty expected. Even better than giving him the range, the bullet ricocheted past the rider. Ty wounded the rustler more by accident than intent. The man jerked away and grabbed for his face. His six-shooter went flying. In the sun it became a blue-steel cartwheel spinning from his hand and landing on the steep incline to the side of the trail.

Ty kept firing. Southern added a few rounds to the attack. The rustler's horse dug in its heels and kicked up a dust cloud that hid anyone behind.

"You can't get past us," Southern yelled. "Give up. Lay down your guns and walk out with your hands up."

"Who are you? Road agents?" The question was meant to buy time.

"I'm Marshal Southern out of Warknife. Anything you do from now on will be resisting arrest."

"A town marshal? You ain't got any authority out here."

"I'm also a deputy sheriff, and that gives me all the authority I need since you're still in the county."

"Let's see a badge."

Both Ty and Southern laughed out loud at that. They faced crooks without much imagination. Even the dumbest lawman wasn't going to march out to flash his badge.

"You're penned up. The rock fall blocked your escape going up the mountain. And there's no way you're getting past us," Ty shouted.

A curtain of lead came his direction as an answer. It was all he expected.

"We've got you dead to rights for rustling. That's not too bad," Southern said. "If you keep this up, it'll get worse. Resisting arrest is piled on top of the rustling. And you're about to commit the worst crime possible."

"What's that?"

"Pissing me off," Southern answered.

"You don't want us to stand trial, even if we'd done something wrong. You've got a bee in your bonnet about us, for some reason, and you got plenty of rope to put around our necks." Another couple rounds whined from the direction of the voice.

Ty settled down and drew a bead. When a man wearing two neckerchiefs showed himself, Ty fired. His target stood up, stretched out and then fell forward. He kicked a couple times and slid over the side of the trail, out of sight.

"Two of you varmints left," Southern warned. "Don't make us put you in the ground, too."

A half dozen shots replied to his words. The marshal hunkered down and let the rustlers waste their ammo. Ty watched for another rustler to incautiously expose himself.

The two remaining gunmen had learned the lesson after seeing their partner tumble over the side. At this point in the trail, it was a hundred feet down a rough, steep incline to where the trail curled around below.

"We can wait you out." Southern chanced a quick peek around the rock and ducked back immediately. His hat flew off his head. A bullet ripped through the crown. "Now you're makin' me mad. That was a new hat."

"We'll bury you in it, Marshal." The taunt went unremarked. Chris Southern reloaded and signaled Ty.

Ty exploded from behind the protecting boulder and ran full out toward the spot where the first outlaw had taken a tumble off the trail. The two rustlers jumped up to take shots at him. Southern's marksmanship wasn't dulled by dust or distance. Both gunmen turned and fired at him, giving Ty his chance.

He slid behind a rock just above the two. From this spot, he cut off any chance they had of retreating down the path. Unable to go ahead without catching lead from Southern's deadly six-shooter, they turned around and bumped into each other. Ty let fly with several rounds that herded them in the marshal's direction.

"Drop those irons," he called. "This is the only chance you're getting."

The two looked confused, then realized their predicament. As if controlled by the same puppet strings, they dropped their guns and raised their hands in unison.

"I've got 'em covered, Chris. If they move a muscle, we can bury them where they fall."

"Don't kill us," whined one of them. "I'm all shot up. I'm not a problem."

"Shut up, Ron." His partner lowered his hand and tried to punch him. Ty sent a round singing inches from his head. The outlaw jerked his hand back into the air.

Ty made his way down the slope to stand behind the pair as Southern advanced.

"Did we shoot them up that much?" The marshal pointed to the wounds causing both men to bleed onto the dry trail.

"You hit me a couple times," whined the one named Ron.

"Don't give 'em no satisfaction," the other said. "Suck it up and quit your grousing."

"I'll do any damned thing I like, Kennard. You're not the boss." As the words came from Ron's mouth, both men turned and looked over the edge of the trail.

Ty edged around, keeping his Henry pointed in their direction. The steep slope was impossible to climb. Anyone hitting it from this point had to roll downhill until fetching up in the roadway below.

"I don't see him. I'm sure I hit him at least once," Ty said. "What was his name?"

"That was none other than—" Kennard grunted when his partner elbowed him in the ribs.

"Don't say anything, you fool. Let them do all the work. They're the law and don't deserve our cooperation." Ron squinted as he looked over Ty. "You're the Circle P rancher, ain't you? You're not a lawdog."

"He used to be," Southern said. "He was about the best there was. Now, with you two, I tagged along just to keep from getting bored. He's able to bring both of you—all three of you—to justice."

"Chris," Ty chided. "You make it sound like I'm running for your job. I had it and don't want it back."

"Good. These old bones need a steady paycheck. Fighting you for the job's a sure loser. I ain't up to speechifying, kissing hands and shaking babies."

"It's the other way around," Ty said. He had to laugh. His friend knew and was joshing him.

"It's a wonder I got elected then. Those babies are always squalling and sticky."

Ty studied the rocky slope again, sure that the falling body had left some trace. Either one of those flashy bandannas or a hat or piece of clothing should have been ripped off in the headlong descent. He didn't see anything. Spotting blood from this distance wasn't too likely, but if the body had crashed into a big enough rock, it'd have stuck there.

Nothing.

"What do we call them?" Southern asked.

"We call them prisoners. Let's get them back to War-knife."

"I've got a couple empty cells just waiting for gents inclined to rustle cattle. And both of their ugly faces must show up on a wanted poster from somewhere else."

"You can't collect any reward," blurted Ron. "You're a lawman."

"I'm not," Ty said. "The way I look at it, you owe me for all the time I've wasted chasing you down."

"We're innocent. No matter what you're charging us with, we didn't do it," Kennard said.

Ty and the marshal worked hard not to bend over belly laughing at that. They retrieved the outlaws' horses, tied the men in place and then started back for town.

The only time they stopped was directly under the precipice where the third rustler had taken his nosedive. It worried Ty that he didn't find a body. There wasn't even a dried puddle of blood to show where he'd landed. Then he forgot all about it as he brought up the rear, his Henry laid across his saddle in case either of the prisoners tried to make a break for it.

It had been a good day for him and Chris Southern. The rustlers in their custody proved that.

CHAPTER 15

Greg Brannigan fumed and kicked at a rock. He sent it flying but almost lost his balance. He was big and bulky and a little clumsy, but anger made him unsteady on his feet.

"I'm not going home. Not now," he said. "Those rustlers are on the trail, and Pa and Marshal Southern won't catch them. They have too big a head start."

His horse turned a big brown eye in his direction. It slowly chewed a mouthful of blue grama, swallowed, and bent low for another mouthful. Greg felt irrational anger at the horse for not being concerned, but he settled down. The unflappable gelding neither knew nor cared about the rustlers or how his family treated his rider.

Greg walked the horse away from the trail head and cut through the woods, coming out in the meadow with chest-high grass. He knew the quick way back to the main herd lay directly to the east, but to the north? He and Matthew had come here hunting too many times for him not to know that there was a gap in the hills. A ride of a few miles would take him around to the stage road.

He stepped up and headed north. Making it back for supper seemed unlikely if he rode much farther, but what did any of the family care? They treated him like a little kid.

He might not even be missed unless they had some menial chore for him to do.

Putting his heels to the horse's flanks let him pick up speed. He emerged from the grassy area and passed through another forested area. The gap in the hills gave him quick access due north. If the rustlers found a branch on the trail they rode, they'd come out on that road.

He looked up into the purpled peaks of the Bear Paw Mountains. The outlaws had a way to find their hideout. Stay on the path past Baldy Butte or did they cut off and head north?

With luck there might be another way into the hills where they hid out. No self-respecting owlhoot camped with only one way in or out. Desperado's Den must be reachable in a lot of different ways. He intended to scout along the stage road to see if the rustlers sneaked in this way. Any traveler would think nothing of seeing a few men riding together. The old stage road curled around and went to Warknife.

Greg wasn't sure how much traffic came along this way anymore, but even a gang of riders wouldn't cause much concern. This made it perfect for reaching the outlaws' hideout.

Desperado's Den.

The longer he rode the more sense it made. They hadn't driven the stolen cattle down that narrow path they took to and from the Circle P graze. The very gap he had used to leave the ranch had to be the quickest way of bringing the stolen beeves into his pa's herd. Greg hunted for evidence that a hundred head had come this way, but there'd been rains on and off during the past week or two. Not knowing how long the cattle had been hidden among the Circle P–branded cows made it impossible to guess about the condition of the ground.

It took two hours, but he finally reached the far side of the gap and began the descent to the road. Curling up from Laramie, the stage road made its way around before going straight into Warknife. In another hour he crossed the road.

He hunted for any travelers. Asking if they had seen Ron or Kennard or Race came to mind. After watching them in their shooting match, he knew their appearances perfectly. Greg shivered as he thought of how they acted. And how Race had stared right at him without knowing he peered back through the bushes.

Race had dead eyes. He'd heard his pa talk about gunmen with that look. Life meant nothing to men with . . . dead eyes.

If there had been anyone on the road, they'd remember seeing Race or the others, shot up as they were. Both Kennard and Ron argued endlessly and complained about their wounds. From the bloodstains on their clothing, they had been through a battle matching anything fought against the Arapaho or Cheyenne. Even a casual traveler had to notice.

Greg rode faster and looked and listened hard for the sound of wagons or horses. Nothing. He was starting to get tuckered out when he saw a sign telling that the way station was only a mile ahead. This kept him going. He could rest at the way station, get some food and drink his fill of water. His horse was sore in need of some water, too.

He slowed when he spotted the shack with the crudely lettered sign declaring this to be the stagecoach stop. Out back an empty corral warned that the station was abandoned. Any stage rattling in wouldn't have a fresh team to hitch up.

"Hello, anybody home?"

He rode closer, itching to pull out his shotgun. Rather than look like he was a threat, Greg tried to sound all peaceable.

He called again. Still no answer. The eerie silence stabbed at him like a knife. There was a feel of recent occupation. But not now. Deep in his gut he knew something was wrong here. Terribly wrong.

The shotgun came free as he dropped to the ground. He gripped it tightly. Just before going inside he broke open the gun and made sure he had a shell in the chamber.

"I'm Greg Brannigan. I don't mean anybody any harm. Hello?"

He stepped in and looked around the large room. If a cyclone had whipped through, the room couldn't have been in greater disarray. Stepping cautiously he went to the long table dominating the room. He imagined stagecoach passengers seated along each side, chowing down on their way into Warknife and beyond.

The uneasy feeling gave him the shivers. Moving slowly, he turned. Bare feet stuck out from behind a crate pushed against the wall.

Greg stepped closer and prodded the feet with the shotgun. No movement. Grabbing a corner of the crate, he yanked it free. The movement sent a cloud of flies buzzing away angrily. He swatted at them to clear a space so he could check the body. There wasn't any doubt the man was dead. And whoever had killed him had stolen about everything of value.

Greg frowned when he saw the pair of boots neatly placed beside the body.

"Why'd you take off your boots? Or did whoever gunned you down do that?" Try as he might, nothing logical suggested itself as a reason for the boots being beside the picked clean body.

His gut twisted around at the sight and smell inside, Greg went out back. The fresh air worked miracles on him to settle his rumbling belly. He had seen dead men before. Not many, not often, but not a one of them had looked like that. Walking away from the way station toward the well, he noticed the footprints in the dust.

More than one person had come this way, not too long ago. How many he couldn't say. His skills at tracking weren't that good, and the boot prints were indistinct. He dropped the bucket down the well. It splashed. At least the well wasn't dry. He used the crank to pull the half-filled bucket back up.

Splashing water on his face and taking a couple good swallows of water perked him up.

"What do I do now?" he asked aloud. "What'd the Sunset Kid do?"

Greg wasn't fond of the answer. A similar situation had faced the Kid while he was on the trail of real desperados. It would be easy to just ride on and ignore the body. But the Sunset Kid would never do that.

Greg Brannigan wouldn't do that, either.

It took the better part of an hour to dig a grave near the empty corral and drag the body over using a sheet of canvas he'd found in the barn. Greg shoveled back the dirt and finally tamped down the mound.

"I'd say a few words like the padre does every Sunday, but I don't know your name." He satisfied ritual by reciting the Lord's Prayer and wishing the dead man Godspeed. Somehow, Greg doubted the man was bound for heaven, but he didn't know for sure.

Not sure why he did it, he took the man's boots and

slung them in a gunnysack over his horse's rump. The only thing he could do now for the dead man was report his death to Marshal Southern. The boots might mean something or nothing at all.

Warknife was another couple hours away, if he hurried along. After the day he'd had, Greg wanted nothing more than to let the marshal know what he'd seen and done. If the marshal was even back from chasing down rustlers Greg had flushed. And if Marshal Southern could force himself to listen instead of brushing him off like his family did.

A combination of anger and despair filled Greg by the time he rode down Wyoming Street in Warknife.

CHAPTER 16

"This might be the ugly one," Chris Southern said, holding up a wanted poster and comparing it with Ron Marcus. His prisoner hung on the cell bars and made a face.

"That's not much of a description for either of them," Ty Brannigan said. "It fits them both to a tee."

"There's a hundred-dollar reward on this one's head," the marshal said. He leaned back in his chair and hiked his feet to his desk, careful not to let his spurs scratch the wood. "Yes, sir, if there's money on one of them, there's got to be something for the other."

"They're partners," Ty agreed.

"You ain't got nuthin' on us. Either of us," Kennard said.

"Rustling is a mighty big offense. I don't need this to bring you to trial." Southern tapped the wanted poster.

"Do you think these two are smart enough to think up the idea of hiding the rustled cattle among the Circle P head?"

"Well, no, Mister Brannigan, I don't."

"Who are you calling stupid?" Marcus rattled the bars. "We're plenty smart enough to do it."

Ty and Southern exchanged amused looks. It'd take a minute for their prisoners to understand. Ron Marcus figured it out first.

"Are you saying we might waltz on out of here if somebody else thought this up?"

"We're smart enough, Ron. What are you sayin'?" Kennard growled like a feral animal.

"Help your partner out, Ron," Ty said. "Explain it to him."

"If we're the only ones doing the rustling, they'll hang us."

"And that's the end of it, as far as the law is concerned." Southern laced his fingers behind his head and watched the two closely. "It'd be a shame if whoever's responsible walks away scot-free."

"These two'll take the fall, if you know what I mean. We have them dead to rights. If you know what I mean." Ty wanted both men to think what having a noose around their necks meant.

"I know what you're saying. They don't." Southern dropped his boots to the floor and swung away from the pair. Ron Marcus kept rattling the bars.

"What if we tell you?" he asked.

"Shut up, Ron. They'll never let us go. Can't you see that?" Kennard swatted at his partner in the next cell. He missed by inches.

Ty had the impression of two hungry rats willing to savage each other. It was hard to believe they were partners for long, yet he had seen others acting like this. Something about the mutual abuse told them they were not being ignored.

"He's right," Southern admitted. "As much as I'd like to make a clean sweep of you owlhoots, it's good enough that I have you locked up."

"I've got to get back to the ranch," Ty said. "It's been a pleasure riding with you again, Marshal."

"Anytime, Ty. Why don't you and Beatriz think on coming by for dinner sometime soon? The missus would love the company."

"Let's do it after these two do a midair two-step. That'll give me time to cut out the stolen cattle and take a decent inventory."

"That's a good idea. If the Cattle Growers Association recognizes the brand, we can invite the rancher over to see the execution. Why, he might even be skilled as a carpenter and help build the gallows."

Ty and Southern shook hands. Ty went to the door, moving deliberately. He knew what would happen any instant. He wasn't disappointed.

"Wait! Wait!" Ron Marcus rattled the bars even harder. "What if we told you about a bank robbery?"

"Race'll kill you for spillin' your guts," Kennard said.

"Race doesn't give two hoots about me. You, either. He'll come to our hanging and cheer on the executioner. That's how he is."

"Well," Kennard said, indecisive. "He might try to save us. You heard him say he needed us for the robbery."

"Save us?" Ron spat on the cell floor to show his disdain for that notion. "When hell freezes over."

"What's this about you boys and Race robbing a bank?" Chris Southern asked. He sounded as if he wasn't much interested. After all, he had them for cattle rustling. Any further crime was only icing on the cake.

Ty paused at the door, then closed it and went to perch on the corner of the marshal's desk. The two cutthroats finally said something that caught his attention.

"If we tell you, will you let us go?" Marcus and Kennard looked at each other. Ty saw that they came to a silent agreement to save their own necks. It probably wasn't the first time this had happened. They fought like two badgers stuffed into a gunnysack, but they were partners.

Southern picked up the wanted poster and carefully tore it in half, then dropped the pieces into the corner of the room. He said nothing. Ty waited to hear what the prisoners had to say.

"Will you believe we don't know nuthin' about the

rustled cattle?" Kennard took over the talking. This convinced Ty that the two outlaws had been in a similar spot before. This division of labor worked for them.

"That depends. Who's Race?" asked the marshal.

"Race Cooper. He's always thinkin' and plannin', always has an iron in the fire," Kennard said.

"Especially if it's a running iron," Ty said.

"He stole all those cattle and had to hide them for a few days since they were so scrawny and weak. He was going to take the lot of 'em and a bunch more after they got their strength back."

Ty looked at Ron Marcus. This seemed to be true. Neither man pulled off guileless, but what Kennard said had the ring of truth to it.

"Why've the cattle been on my graze for the past week? Maybe more? The longer the stolen beeves were with mine, the more likely I was to notice."

"A better deal came up," Kennard said.

Both said at the same time, "A bank robbery."

"Let me get this straight. Race Cooper is leaving behind cattle he's already stolen to rob a bank? The one here in Warknife?" Ty looked at his friend to see if Southern believed that for an instant.

"Señor Salazar would tell me if there was anything but rat droppings in his vault worth stealing," Southern said. "He never keeps too much in the vault. There's no call for it this time of year."

Ty wondered if his father-in-law would share with him if a considerable amount of money was already deposited— or coming into town to be stashed in the vault. Where it'd come from was a poser, unless Diego was foreclosing on a ranch, or another owner was buying adjacent land. In either case, Ty was certain rumors would have reached him.

If nothing else, Beatriz would be buzzing about how her *padrecito* has proven himself to be an astute banker. Again.

"You boys aren't talking about the Warknife Ranchers and Merchants Bank, are you?" Ty saw the prisoners' bemused expressions.

He felt as if he had stepped off a cliff and fell endlessly.

"Cutbank," Ty said in a hoarse whisper.

"That's where," Kennard said. "That's where the bank is. Race never told us the bank's name."

"He never told us anything about the robbery, only that there was going to be more gold than any of us could carry. Race made it out to be a robbery everyone would be talking about for years to come."

"That's the kind of thieving I want to do," Ron said.

"We tell you what we know and you let us ride off, no posse or anything following us. Is that a deal?" Kennard looked anxiously from Southern to Ty and back.

"No," the marshal said.

"Yes," Ty cut in. When his friend started to protest, he motioned for him to go outside.

The late afternoon wind was picking up and drove away the day's heat. Ty took a deep breath and faced the marshal. He held up his hand, palm out.

"Wait, Chris, let me have my say."

"You can't make a deal with them! They're double-dealing, backstabbing, low-down, no-account—"

"Chris, please. You know about the deal Jack Lowry's made with the railroad."

"You mentioned it out on the trail. I don't know the details."

"The money will be stashed in the Cutbank vault. At least twenty thousand worth of greenbacks will be shipped after the ranchers all ante up their share."

"How's the money being sent?"

Ty shook his head.

"All the details are up to Lowry. Him and the banker. I haven't heard of anyone paying off his share in gold. I don't know where those two cutthroats got the idea there'd be that much gold."

"It might be this Race Cooper's way of keeping his boys in line. Stealing greenbacks is profitable, but what self-respecting road agent wouldn't prefer to get paid off in gold?" Southern rubbed his chin as he considered all the possibilities.

"It'll likely be soon that all the money's deposited in the Cutbank safe," Ty said. "My share's already there."

"Why are you the one telling me and not Lowry? Or Marshal Buckman?" Southern scowled. "Secrets are never kept long. Not around here."

"You know Paul. He wouldn't tell his own ma the sun was coming up in the morning. I can't blame them on this, though. The fewer people who know the details, the safer moving the money will be."

"Except those two yahoos know about it." Southern stabbed a finger back in the direction of his two prisoners.

"Them and this Race Cooper. Have you ever heard of him?"

Southern shook his head.

"He's a new one, but then if he's riding through our part of Wyoming to rustle cattle that makes him a drifter and not likely to be staring at me from a pile of wanted posters."

"Somebody working for the Cutbank bank or Paul Buckman must see this as a way of making a heap of money fast. He must know Cooper or someone in his gang. That'd explain how all the details leaked out."

"I'll send a telegram to Buckman," Southern said. "He won't pay attention to it, though."

"He's a know-it-all," Ty agreed. "But I've got a dog in

this fight. All my spare money's been sent along to Lowry last week. I can't afford to lose close to fifteen hundred dollars, not with the market like it is this year. That'd wipe out all my profit for the livelong year if Cooper makes off with it."

"I understand, Ty. Look, we're friends. About the best I have in Warknife, but I'm not letting those two go free."

"They'd ride straight to Cooper," Ty said. He considered possible ways of snaring all the outlaws. "We can follow them and round up everyone in the gang."

"That sounds good, especially since we don't even know the names of the rest of Cooper's gang. But tracking Kennard and Marcus without them spotting us isn't possible. You know the trails in the mountains. They're narrow and treacherous, and we'd need a dozen men in a posse. Maybe more since it sounds as if Cooper's got at least that many guns itching to rob the bank."

"There's no way to sneak up on a hideout with that many men," Ty said. "Why don't we get what we can out of them, tell them we have to hold them until Cooper and the rest are in custody, then we can let them go free?"

"Pretend we're protecting them from their partners?" Southern sounded doubtful. Ty felt the same, but it was a better plan than letting the two ride away scot-free.

"Maybe it's good enough knowing the gang intends to rob the bank," Southern said. "We can set a trap."

"Cooper has to come to the money," Ty agreed. "If we let it leak the money's moving out earlier than Lowry wants, the gang has to move in fast or miss their chance."

"It'd be easier if we knew who was feeding all the details to Cooper," Southern said. "I'll see if I can't worm that out of those two."

"They probably don't know," Ty said, "but it's worth a try."

He shook hands with his friend, then said, "You can send a 'gram to Buckman, but he's too uppity to pay attention. I'll send one right now to Lowry. He's got the most to lose."

"He's putting up the most money?"

"Without the money there won't be a spur line laid up to Cutbank. I've heard tell that his herd's big but not in the best shape for a trail drive. He might be hit twice if Cooper's successful."

Ty stood for a moment, thinking there should be more to do or say. The marshal disappeared into the jailhouse and started dickering with his two prisoners. Until something more came to light, Ty was going to be uneasy. He hurried down the street to the telegraph office when he saw his son riding toward him.

"Greg! Good that I found you. We're heading back home as soon as I send a telegram."

"Pa, wait. I have something to tell you." His son dropped to the ground and fell into step. "Out at the way station."

"Along the road coming in from the north? What about it?"

"I found a dead man there. He'd been all shot up. It wasn't the station master. This was somebody else."

"How'd he die?"

"He caught a lot of lead. I . . . I buried him and I've got his boots. That's the strange part. He was all dead and his boots were beside his body, as if he'd taken them off."

"Boots, yeah," Ty said. "You did the right thing burying him. Bringing him to town would stir up everybody."

"I should tell Marshal Southern about this. He was killed. Somebody'd pumped at least three slugs into him. I don't know if he was even packing an iron. I didn't see one. And there wasn't any belongings I found. He—"

"Greg, I wish this wasn't true but too many men meet their Maker in terrible ways out on the road. Did you recognize him?"

"No, but—"

"I've got to get this telegram off in a hurry."

"Should I tell Marshal Southern?"

"There's not a lot he can do. Right now he's got his hands full of rustlers and . . . other problems."

"You're telling me to ignore a man that got himself killed and robbed? I checked. His pockets were all empty."

"Was there a watch in his vest pocket?"

"What? I . . . yeah, there was. What's that got to do with him being shot?"

"A robber'll take the watch first. Chances are good the man was broke."

"But he was *shot*!"

"If he got into a gunfight, his opponent's not going to stick around."

"We don't know it was self-defense. Whoever shot him might have murdered him!"

"Without witnesses, there's nothing anybody can do about that, son. We're heading back to the ranch after I send the telegram. Don't stray too far." Ty left his son in the middle of the street, silent, sullen. He'd have a talk with Greg later, after the bank robbers were safely locked up.

And he had to cut out the stolen cattle and find their owner. That was easier, so he could do it later. After Race Cooper was brought to heel. After . . .

CHAPTER 17

"Don't bother me," Matthew Brannigan said, irritated at the interruption. He tugged on the colt's lead and used a long, thin pole to tap its front legs to keep it from rearing. "I've about got this one broke. It'll take a few more weeks to saddle break him because I don't want to rush him along. He's going to be a fine saddle horse."

"Why are you taking so much time with him?" Greg hung on the corral and watched with some envy. He had been doing just fine with the colt. He wasn't as skilled as his brother, and he lacked his older brother's experience. A touch of envy crept in as he watched how expertly his older brother worked the feisty colt.

"Don't tell her, but I want to give him to Caroline for her birthday." Matt kept the horse dancing and prancing in a circle, wearing down the animal's wildness bit by bit.

"My birthday's before hers. Why can't I have him?"

"You've got a horse. Besides, you can train your own." Matt moved about and spoke softly to the colt.

Greg muttered, "I was training him, but you took him away."

"Gregory, have you cleaned the chicken coop and brought in the eggs? Do it before I die of old age." Beatriz

Brannigan held open the kitchen door and waved to get his attention. There wasn't any need for that. Her whiplike voice carried.

Not only did it carry, it cut into him like a real whip.

"Yes, Ma," he called. He stepped back from the corral, casting a final longing look at the colt. It was going to make a dandy gift for his younger sister. If he couldn't have the horse for his own, he was glad she'd be able to ride the colt. But still . . .

He spent the next half hour cleaning out the hen house, then collected the eggs. He only had to use a chicken stick he carried to whack the rooster a couple times. The rooster objected to him carrying away his progeny but all Greg thought about was a couple of fried eggs.

"You're going to end up as dumplings one day," he warned. The rooster fanned out his thick red comb and tried to peck him again. Greg swung and missed with his stick. The rooster was too quick for him. It scratched at the ground, bobbed its head up and down, and prepared for another attack. This time Greg was ready. He tried to whack the bird a good one but missed by inches.

It was just as well. He wasn't in the mood to clean up a pile of feathers if he had whacked the fowl a good one.

Trudging into the kitchen, he put the egg basket on the table. His sister MacKenna worked to chop onions and vegetables for the evening meal. She turned to him, her usually lustrous hazel eyes red and watering.

"The onions are really powerful," she said, sniffing.

"Do you want me to do that for you?" he asked.

"You'd only mess it up. Besides, Mama told me to do it."

Greg sank into a chair and glumly stared off into space. Mack noticed. She laid aside the eye-tearing onions and sat across from him.

"You're moping around the past couple days. What's wrong?"

"I found out something important and Pa won't listen to me." Greg took a deep breath. That wasn't exactly true. Ty Brannigan had heard him out and then dismissed his concerns. A man had died. An unknown man. Greg felt he ought to find out what had happened. It was what the Sunset Kid would do.

"Someone out at the way station?" Mack used a corner of her apron to dab at the tears welling in her eyes. Then she sniffed, considered using the apron for her nose and decided against it. It wasn't ladylike.

"I should have gone to the stage office in town to report it," Greg said.

"Was the dead man the station agent?"

Greg shook his head. He had seen the station master a few times and hadn't liked him much. The feeling had been mutual. But the man he'd found on the floor with his boots neatly placed beside him was a stranger. What had happened to the station master was a complete mystery. Considering how ornery he was, he might have just gathered the stage company's horses and ridden off with them, thinking they were his due for being alone so much.

"He died with his boots off. Maybe that's what he wanted."

Mack looked quizzically at him. He explained about the boots.

"So you took them? Why?"

Greg shrugged. He wasn't sure why.

"You should scout the area and see what you can find. If the station master's back, you'll know everyone who ought to be notified has been."

"If the place is still abandoned? What do I do then?"

"You were right wanting to tell Marshal Southern. Pa

can be so pigheaded at times he might as well be riding a different range from everyone else." Mack wiped her eyes once more, then took off her apron. "Let's ride out there and see if it's occupied."

For a moment Greg wasn't sure he heard his sister right. Then he brightened.

"You believe me?"

"Of course, I do. You're not inclined to lie. Exaggerate, maybe, and certainly see something and come to the wrong conclusion. You've got the makings of a fine spinner of tall tales. Riders will appreciate that on a trail drive."

"You believe me," he said again, amazed.

"Of course I believe you, Greg." She leaned across the table and put her hand on his.

He lit up like the summer sun coming from behind a cloud.

"Let's go!"

"I need to change. Meet you at the barn."

Greg raced outside and ran until he panted harshly. Matt still worked with the colt and never paid him any heed. Working fast, he saddled his old horse and Mack's, too. He was anxious to get on the trail. He hesitated when he touched the shotgun in his saddle sheath.

"Take it," Mack said, coming into the barn. She went to the rack on the wall and pulled down a Winchester. She stuffed a handful of cartridges into her pocket, then mounted. Her rifle slid easily into the sheath. With an impatient gesture, she beckoned Greg to follow.

He didn't have to be goaded into it. At last someone treated him like he knew what was going on.

They found the trail and cut across the south pasture to reach the stage road. Greg had spent hours before to get to the way station. Knowing his destination let him use shortcuts he'd pioneered over years of just riding around, exploring.

Scouting, he thought. Like the Sunset Kid.

He called out to his sister. "I saw the rustlers. The ones Pa and Marshal Southern locked up."

"Did you poke them with a stick?" Mack laughed at this. "You don't do a very good job using that chicken stick. That old rooster gets the better of you every time."

"I don't mean after they got put into jail. Before. There was a third one. He might have been the ambushing snake that shot Pa."

"Are you saying there's still a rustler out there?"

"They're hiding in a place they call Desperado's Den. I overheard them talking when they rode past me on the trail."

"How many rustlers are there?"

Greg shook his head. He didn't know. But that third rustler? He had to be out there somewhere. Maybe he was the one who gunned down the man in the way station.

"There weren't too many in that gunfight," he said out loud.

"At the way station?" MacKenna held out her arm to stop him. The station's main building poked out at the bend in the road. "It's still mighty quiet up ahead."

Greg slid his shotgun from its scabbard and rode ahead. He quaked inside but didn't let his sister see how scared he was. The killer might have come back. Or the station master had returned and was willing to shoot anyone who wasn't in a stage.

"Greg, don't—"

He ignored her and rode to the side of the station. Over the whistle of wind through cracks in the wall came a rustling sound like a giant rat snuffling around inside. Greg swung down and edged toward a window. He chanced a peek inside.

"There's a horse out back," Mack said, riding up.

The dark figure rummaging through the station's cabinets froze. Greg held back his irritation that Mack alerted the looter. He broke the window with the muzzle of his shotgun and thrust it through.

"Don't move! I'll shoot. I swear I'll shoot!"

A tiny, frightened squeak echoed. Then the pillager dropped a gunnysack and sprinted for the back door. Greg had a fraction of a second to decide. Shoot or let the looter escape.

He called to Mack to get to the horse and prevent any escape. By the time he rounded the building, she had not only grabbed the horse's reins but had pinned a young girl against the wall. Mack's horse kept sidestepping, using its bulk to repeatedly knock the would-be fugitive back in place.

"Whoa, don't fight. We're not going to hurt you." Greg came up. The girl's wide, frightened eyes fixed on his shotgun.

He lowered it and held out his hand like he was gentling the colt.

"He's right. That's my brother. You don't have anything to be scared of. Not from us, at least." Mack stepped down and handed the captured horse's reins to the girl. "You can go, if you want," she said.

"Or we can help you," Greg piped up.

"Hungry. I'm real hungry. I know it's wrong to steal, but we're starving."

"We?" Mack asked the question in a low voice. "You're not alone?"

The girl shook her head, then said, "Me and my two little sisters."

"Where're your parents?" Greg took a step back at the reaction. The sudden animal fury on her face frightened him.

"I'm MacKenna. You can call me Mack. Everyone does. That's my brother Greg. The two of you are about the same age. How old are you?"

"Fifteen," the girl said.

"See?" Mack grinned ear to ear. "Exactly the same as Greg." She motioned for him to come closer.

"Pleased to meet you. I'm Greg Brannigan. My family owns the Circle P about ten miles from here." He held out his hand to shake. Just when he considered pulling it back out of embarrassment, the girl put her filthy hand in his. Her nails were broken and caked with dirt. A dozen small cuts, most recent, were beginning to show signs of infection.

He refrained from wiping his hand on his jeans when she drew back.

"Where are your sisters?" Mack asked. "We can do what we can to help them, too."

The girl's eyes darted along the road toward Warknife, then returned to the ground.

"My name's Anna."

"Pleased to meet you, Anna," Mack said.

For a long minute they stood and stared at one another. Greg finally broke the uneasy silence.

"Did you find anything inside? To eat?"

Anna smiled weakly and said, "Some. I dropped it when you tried to shoot me."

"I didn't—never mind," Greg said. "I'm sorry about that. I thought you were the man who had—"

"Greg," Mack cut in. She glared reprovingly at him. "She might like you to help gather food and a blanket or two. Do your sisters need blankets?"

Anna nodded.

He started to complain about how Mack kept him from talking about the man killed here. He had done exactly what the marshal or his pa or any grown-up would have done and wanted to brag on it. Just a little. Then he realized Mack was right. Anna didn't need to hear about men filled with lead in a shootout. Whatever she had been through was all she needed to cope with.

And she had younger sisters to look after, too.

Greg burned with curiosity about Anna's parents, but he had seen how she reacted when they were mentioned. He began dropping air-tights of peaches and beans into the gunnysack Anna had dropped. He glanced over his shoulder. Mack and Anna talked outside, the girl slowly coming out of her fright and answering questions.

He wished he had the gift of gab his sister did. At times she'd talk the ear off a cornstalk, but she learned about everything worth knowing by just listening.

"Got it," he said, holding out the heavy sack. "Let's take it to your sisters."

Again Anna recoiled, then settled down. She took a quick step forward and grabbed the sack. She held it close but made no effort to mount.

"We can help, Anna," Mack said. "If you let us."

"Yeah, let us help," Greg said.

Anna bounced up and down like a rabbit ready to run from a wolf. Then she nodded and handed the sack back to Greg. With surprising agility, she vaulted into the saddle and reached down. Greg handed the gunnysack back to her. Once more she clutched it tightly to her. Then she got her horse moving.

"Let's go," Mack said.

"After her?"

"If you want to help her, that's the only way." MacKenna stepped up and trotted after Anna.

Greg felt good about the way the rescue had gone. He hurried to his horse, mounted, and galloped after Mack and Anna, giving a wild yell like the Sunset Kid.

CHAPTER 18

Race Cooper stretched out on the rock like a lizard, closed his eyes and let the warm Wyoming sun soothe his aches and pains. Nothing went according to his plan. Not only did he take a tumble down a steep slope, barely grabbing onto a bush before he rolled another hundred feet but Marcus and Kennard were both arrested and locked up in the Warknife jail.

He had been lucky to avoid the marshal and that rancher. Scrambling along the slope in spite of cuts and bruises had saved him. By the time he found a ledge wide enough to sit on where he regained his strength, his men were being herded away by the lawdogs. Worse than losing the two loudmouths, the marshal had taken his horse.

Walking all the way back to the hideout gave him blisters and feet that hurt like the very devil. Answering the questions of the men still in the shallow bowl hidden by the tall peaks had hurt even more. With as much tact as possible, he had kept from blaming Marcus and Kennard, but his gang had absorbed his words. The faces of three men changed as he talked, warning him they were going to slip away at the first chance. They wanted no part of a gang where the leader let the law arrest his partners.

Cooper turned his head to the side and spat, then returned

to let the sun soak into his weathered, scratched-up face. Others in the gang grumbled about leaving the cattle in the Circle P herd. That was a bird in the hand for them. The two in the bush offered by stealing the ranchers' money from Cutbank was nothing but a fantasy.

One had said he'd rather have a two-bit, broken-down whore right now than wait a day to fork over a dollar for the pretty-as-a-picture madam running the brothel. His intentions were obvious, and caused Cooper to seethe.

Even dangling the promise of a couple thousand dollars in gold each from the bank robbery against a couple hundred dollars selling the rustled cattle didn't move his men. Cooper recognized the signs.

He was losing control of the gang. He was going to begin losing his men as they drifted away. He'd be lucky if they didn't shoot him in the back before they left in the middle of the night.

"Damn you, Marcus. Double damn you, Kennard."

When he finished conjuring up appropriate punishments for those two, he moved on to Dexter. He hardly knew the man and yet depended on him to give enough warning about the loot being stashed in the Cutbank bank. Everything Dexter reported to him was important.

When was the money going to be deposited? What guards were placed at the bank? When they moved the money south, how was the shipment protected? A company of cavalry troopers made stealing the money impossible once they started on the trail south. They'd have to hit the bank and blow the vault. But if only a handful of deputies rode south guarding the gold, that was the best plan.

Which was it? An entire cavalry company or a handful of deputies? Without knowing such details, he'd never be able to make a plan to steal the bank vault's contents.

"Triple damn you, Dexter."

"Do tell?"

Cooper sat up and reached for his six-shooter. Ten feet away at the base of the rock where he sunned himself, Dexter watched. The feral glint in the man's eyes almost caused Cooper to finish the draw and fire. It'd go a ways toward venting all the frustration he felt at how everything fell apart around him.

"Shoot me and you'll never find out all the details of that money in the Cutbank safe."

"You took your sweet time getting back." Race Cooper slid down to stand beside Dexter. "So? When do we hit the bank? Or do we wait for them to load it all into a strongbox and take it to the railroad?"

"What'd you think? That I double-crossed you?"

"You need my gang. Wherever they have the money will require ten or more guns to pry it all loose."

"There's plenty of time before we need to go after that pot of gold," Dexter said.

Cooper tensed. Something in the way Dexter spoke rankled. Dexter knew something he wasn't sharing.

"I'm the boss around here," Cooper said. "Tell me everything, and I make the decisions."

"And I said there's plenty of time before we need to ride." Dexter stepped back and rested his hand on his six-shooter.

Cooper saw how he was being called out. With his hold over everyone in the gang weakening, he dared not let Dexter get the upper hand. If he did, he might as well mount up and hightail it for the horizon.

If he did that, he'd leave with empty pockets. No gold from the Cutbank vault, no cattle he'd worked so hard to rustle. Cooper wasn't up for enduring such humiliation after all his hard work.

"You don't know, do you?" It looked as if the time to move the rustled cattle was at hand.

"Yeah, I have all the details. Maps and places all laid out." Dexter patted his coat pocket. "Before then, I need to borrow a couple of the men for a little job of my own."

"No."

Dexter's face hardened. His thumb flicked back and took the rawhide keeper loop off his Colt's hammer.

"Someone gunned down my brother. Let two or three of the boys ride with me and settle scores. It won't take long."

A million things ran through Cooper's head. From the way Dexter talked, he had the facts about the ranchers' money and wasn't sharing. Worse, he made an obvious play to take over not only the robbery but Cooper's gang.

In spite of Dexter ready to throw down on him, Cooper took three steps forward. His fist was coming around in a haymaker as he took the second step. He planted his feet with the third and landed the hard punch on the side of the upstart's head.

Dexter stumbled and went to one knee, stunned. Cooper moved in fast. He kicked out and caught Dexter's right wrist. This sent the man's gun flying. By the time Cooper recovered his balance and prepared a second punch that would end the fight, his opponent was scuttling away.

Cooper's blow missed an exposed chin by an inch. He stumbled, off balance. When he recovered, so had Dexter.

They faced each other. Both breathed heavily. Cooper considered whipping out his iron and ending the fight here and now. But what if Dexter wasn't carrying the information with him as he had suggested with that tap to his coat pocket? If he hid the information on his way back to the gang hideout, there was no way to ever find it. The mountains were rugged and vast.

All thought of cutting his foe down disappeared. Dexter

feinted, then drove a hard left jab into Cooper's ribs. The jolt shook him all over, like lightning hitting a tree. He dropped his elbows and took another punch, this time a right. He staggered away.

A flurry of blows came at him. Dexter punched for his face, then his gut, and landed a couple hard blows to his ribs. As Cooper turned to avoid another, he caught a hard fist to his kidney. He sagged. All he could do was keep his arms lifted to ward off a new series of blows.

But Dexter wore himself out with such furious punching. His guard dropped, and he opened up his midriff. Cooper's first reply was weak but enough to make Dexter stumble back. Then it was over. Cooper drove three hard punches into the man's solar plexus. He folded like a bad poker hand with the final blow.

Towering over him, Cooper pushed back his hat and grabbed a handful of thinning sandy hair. Gripping it, he turned Dexter's face up so he saw the cocked fist ready to drive down and rearrange his nose.

"Don't cross me again," Cooper gasped out. He reared back as if to deliver a devastating blow. Instead he released his grip on Dexter's hair. The man recoiled and fell to the ground.

His eyes were wild and dangerous. Shooting him was the smart thing to do. But he'd claimed he had everything Cooper needed to rob the Cutbank bank.

"When do we hit the bank?" Cooper stood with his hands balled into bony fists. He shook all over. During the fight, he had opened a few of the cuts from falling down the side of a mountain avoiding the lawmen. New cuts leaked his lifeblood, but he ignored it all. One thing alone burned in his head. "When?"

"Not yet," Dexter said crab-walking away. He got to his feet and reached for the pistol that had been kicked from his grasp. He looked hard at Cooper, then picked it up and slid it into his holster.

If it came down to gunplay, Cooper wondered how it would go. His hands felt like rotted stumps. Hardly any sensation in them. His skinned knuckles leaked blood, and his entire body shook like aspen leaves in the autumn wind.

"I'll see if any of the men will come with me. You don't have to ask," Dexter said. He backed away, then turned and disappeared among the rocks.

Cooper knew that if he had a lick of sense he'd stop Dexter right now. That'd mean giving up any chance of robbing the bank, but keeping his gang intact and loyal meant more.

"Twenty thousand dollars," he muttered. Trading that for leading desperados who barely respected him seemed like an increasingly bad trade. With money like that, he could recruit a new gang somewhere else. He'd heard Indian Territory was wild and wooly, even if Hanging Judge Isaac Parker had legions of lawmen prowling around.

Race Cooper hitched up his drawers and followed Dexter to camp. If he wanted to keep his men loyal he had to show them nobody else was good enough to lead them.

CHAPTER 19

"How much farther?" Greg asked.

Anna looked at him out of the corner of her eye. She didn't give an answer, but from the way she leaned forward a bit more than usual, Greg wondered if their ride was nearing an end. The girl had plenty to be afraid of, he thought, but with him along things would be better. With him and Mack.

He watched his older sister confidently riding ahead of them. She was alert but never seemed to be anxious about riding into trouble. Considering what she had been through the past few months, she had learned from her troubles how to cope. For all Greg knew, Anna's problems were even worse than what his sister had faced, with her beau being chased down for murdering his pa and then losing him because he had to marry after getting another girl in trouble.

Greg wanted to ask MacKenna what she thought about that, but he knew better. If she wanted to confide in him, she would. More likely she'd cried her heart out to their ma. Greg sucked in his breath. Or to their pa. Tynan Brannigan was a man of few words and great deeds. Whatever advice he had given her would be exactly what she needed.

For a moment Greg compared his pa with the Sunset Kid. Both were courageous, and in similar ways. The elder

Brannigan had tamed towns and faced outlaws and raised four children on a ranch that'd break a lesser man. He stayed and fought. But there was a big difference between Tynan Brannigan and the hero of the dime novel.

The Sunset Kid rode on to find new troubles to solve.

"A penny for your thoughts."

"What? Oh, nothing," Greg said, blushing. He hadn't realized Anna studied him so intently.

"We're almost there," the girl said. "I think we are."

"You don't know?"

"I told my sisters to run if anybody found them. None of us know the countryside. Where they'd run is . . ." Anna shrugged her thin shoulders showing she had no idea where her sisters were.

"That's all right," Greg said quickly. "I know every inch of the land around here. My pa's ranch—the Circle P—is on the far side of those hills. There are a half dozen passes through. And this side? The road goes smack dab into Warknife."

"Momma said that's where we were going. Once she was sure it was safe."

"Why don't you come on out to the Circle P? After we find your sisters?" Greg tried not to sound too anxious. Having them come to the ranch was the smartest thing he could think of. Ma would take care of them, and Mack would help. Caroline would only get in the way, but maybe Anna's sisters were young enough to tolerate a noisy twelve-year-old.

Maybe Caroline and the young girls would become friends. He cast a sidelong look at Anna and blushed. He wanted to know Anna better but wasn't sure how to go about it. She had no reason to trust anyone, so he needed to win her confidence. The best way to do that wasn't to tell her he was a responsible gent.

Actions spoke louder than words. Whatever he did had to benefit her without being self-serving. Greg tried to remember a homily Father Simon had delivered a month or two back. It had been hot and Greg was tired and had drifted off more than once, but the words exhorted everyone in the congregation to look after their brothers and sisters. At the time, Greg thought that meant family.

He realized now that Father Simon also had meant neighbors and friends . . . and newcomers.

"No." Anna spat out the word as if it burned her tongue.

"If you're afraid you ma might not find you if you went there, we can hunt around. If we don't find her, we can let people know where you are and—"

"No!"

Anna's reply was so vehement that Mack turned to look. Her accusing stare fixed on Greg. He had no idea what he'd said to get such an adamant response.

"Don't worry yourself over it, Anna dear," Mack said. "We'll work it out so you're comfortable."

"What's wrong with coming to the ranch?" Greg asked. "You'd be safe there. And Ma's cooking is about the best anywhere. Unless your ma's cooking is better, that is." He began floundering for words.

"There's a bend in the road ahead," Mack said. "See that stand of trees? It's on the bank of the creek. If your sisters camped anywhere, that'd be a good place."

"They'd want to wait for Ma," Anna said. "Or me. Ruth'd want to water her horse. She thinks the world of that nag."

"Ruth?" Mack prodded. "That's a pretty name. How old is she?"

"Eight. Jasmine is a couple years older. We think she's ten or eleven."

"Why don't you know?" Greg blurted. Mack tried to

shush him, but he ignored her. "If she's your sister, wouldn't you know?"

"Tracks," Anna said, pointing. "More 'n one horse. This must be where they're hiding."

"Let's go," Greg urged. When Anna came to a complete stop and said nothing, he wheeled around and faced her. "What's wrong?"

"They'll be scared if they see you. I'll tell them there's nothing to be frightened about. Because of you."

"Go on," Mack said gently. "We'll wait out here beside the road. As long as it takes."

Anna trotted off the road, heading down a winding trail that led to the creek. Trees hid her within a few yards.

"What if she runs off?" Greg asked.

"Then she runs off. She's not our prisoner, Greg. We don't know what she's been through, other than her mother's scouting for someplace safe to hide."

"Yeah, safe," he said. "I saw how she acted when I mentioned her pa. That's got to mean something, Mack. It does."

"It means the reason they're on the run might just be her pa. Let's step down and get in the shade. We might be here for a while, and it's still hot out in the sun." She swiped sweat on her forehead. "I'll be glad when it cools off, even if it means the snows will be up over our heads before we know it."

"Anna and her sisters need to find a place to stay before the first snow."

"A couple months later and it'd be downright dangerous for them," Mack said. "Not that it's safe now, for different reasons."

"At least we know her sisters' names. But that's strange how she doesn't know how old Jasmine is. That's a pretty name, but not knowing how old your younger sister is?"

Greg snorted. "Can you imagine Caroline letting us forget her birthday?"

"Anna's family's not like ours," Mack said. She settled down, back pressed against a tree. Her horse was broken to ground reins and wandered about, nibbling at sparse patches of grass. This near the trail other horses had grazed away most of the taller grass.

Greg was too het up to sit. He paced around. Once he pulled out his copy of the dime novel about the Sunset Kid and stared at it. There must be a page or two somewhere telling how the Kid would handle a situation like this. But there wasn't. He had read through the book until the pages began to crack from being turned repeatedly.

"You're wearing a hole in the ground," Mack said, smiling.

"What if she runs off?"

"Anna? Her sisters? We've seen her safely this far. Has she ever said what she's running from?"

"It's obvious, isn't it? She's running from her pa. What else would make her act like that?"

Mack nodded as she chewed on this. She finally said, "That's a good observation, Greg. Her ma is the one running, and she took her girls with her. They're too young to be dodging the law, so it has to be their mother's choice to leave wherever they called home."

Greg laughed at that. The girls being wanted by the law? With wanted posters? Anna was only his age. Then he sobered. He was all grown-up but nobody admitted it. That meant Anna was a grown-up, too, even if she looked years younger. She had missed quite a few meals from the way she was all skinny and her eyes were sunken into dark pits and her skin stretched tight on her cheekbones. He had seen an Arapaho brave who'd broken both legs and had been stranded for a week up in the Winds who looked like that.

He spun at the sound of someone moving toward him. Anna peeked out from behind a cottonwood. She smiled shyly.

"The girls say it's all right if you come on down to the creek."

Greg and Mack led their horses into the wooded area and then onto the bank of the shallow, fast-running creek. For a couple seconds he thought the girls had run off. Then they came from the underbrush. The bigger one he took to be Jasmine, had a dull look about her. The youngest, Ruth, clutched a rag doll that was more tattered than she was.

"They'll help us find Ma," Anna said.

"Why?" Jasmine made no bones about her skepticism.

"We help out people who need it," Mack said. "That's what we do in these parts. Where are you from? Is it different there?"

The three girls huddled close and turned away.

"I didn't mean to pry," Mack said hastily. "Where'd your mother go?"

"Town," Ruth said, peeking out from around Anna.

"Do you mean Warknife? That's a few miles down the road. Has a stage passed by? She might have caught a ride."

The silence greeting his question made Greg uncomfortable. Getting the three girls to safety was taking more of a toll on him than he expected. Rescues in the dime novel were so easy and always done by the end of the chapter.

He realized the chapters for these three were going to be long and not likely to end happily. He doubted any parent abandoned her children without a good reason.

"We can ride with you into town and ask around," he said. "It's not that big a place. Not like Cheyenne or Laramie. If your ma's there, we'll find her in lickety-split time."

"Greg's right about that. And if she's not there yet, we

can find you a place to stay. It gets chilly out in the open this time of year."

Greg saw what MacKenna was getting at. The three had nothing more than their saddle blankets. Whatever bedrolls a traveler usually carried were missing. Nowhere in their gear did he see coats thick enough to hold back the nighttime cold.

"You only have two horses?" He looked around.

"You won't turn us over to the law?" Anna's question ate at him.

"Are you on the run?"

"We don't like the law," piped up Ruth. "Papa says they're out to do us a bad turn." She ducked back behind her two sisters as if expecting some terrible retribution for what she'd said.

"Marshal Southern's not like that," Greg said. He started to explain how the marshal and his pa were best friends, but his sister put her finger to her lips to shush him. Whatever he said only made matters worse. The trio might not be criminals on the run from the law, but their father had instilled a suspicion in them that wasn't going away any time soon.

"We can get to town before sundown," Mack said. "You two ride together? Up you go." She boosted Jasmine into the saddle.

"Me, too, me, too. Do that to me!" Ruth squealed in glee as Mack hoisted her up behind her sister.

Greg watched Anna's reaction. She tensed when Mack touched either girl, but then she relaxed once she stepped up and sat her own horse.

"Back to the road and thataway!" Mack said cheerfully. She mounted and trotted after the other two horses.

Greg brought up the rear. He watched their back trail and

kept an eye peeled for any sign of the girls' mother. The ride into Warknife was uneventful. He wasn't sure if that pleased him or not since he never got the chance to show anything more than his ability to guard the rear of the small procession.

CHAPTER 20

"I don't like leaving Conrad in charge," Chris Southern said. He snapped the reins and got his horse moving a tad faster. "He's wet behind the ears."

"There won't be any trouble," Ty Brannigan said. "He's a strapping fellow. He's as tall as I am and outweighs me twenty pounds. Not a whole lot of that's fat, either."

Southern made a rude noise.

"All the muscle's between his ears. He's not lazy, though. I'll give him that. But still . . ."

"He needs experience. What is he? Nineteen?"

"About that. If you'd let me deputize Matt, I wouldn't think twice about riding out of town with those two outlaws locked up. But Conrad?" He shook his head.

"My son's got better sense than to let you pin a badge on his chest. He's heard my stories. He knows what it takes to be a marshal, even in a quiet town like Warknife."

"You just want to hog him because he's so good at breaking horses. I saw that colt he's working now. That's a mighty fine-looking animal."

"That's true, and he enjoys working with horses, but if he even hinted that he wanted to be a deputy, Beatriz would snatch him bald-headed. She still hasn't gotten over me being a marshal for so long, and I turned in my badge the day before we got hitched."

"I can always deputize Matt as a secret lawdog. He wouldn't have to tell her. He could sneak around and arrest people on the sly."

Ty snorted at such a notion, then pushed it out of his mind. The two talked of this and that until they reached the outskirts of Cutbank. Seeing the sign marking the edge of town, Ty felt his gut tighten. Peaceful was the only way he could describe everything around him as he rode down the main street. Merchants went about their business, wives bought supplies, men hefted fifty-pound sacks of feed or seed into wagons. Cutbank was prosperous, and Marshal Buckman did a good-enough job of keeping the peace.

"Why didn't he answer my telegram?" Ty wondered aloud.

"Because he's a stuck-up fool who thinks he knows best."

"You don't like him, do you?" Ty laughed. He knew his friend wasn't on the best terms with Marshal Paul Buckman. They had locked horns on more than one arrest. Jurisdiction meant everything to Buckman and almost nothing to Chris Southern, as long as the crooks were brought to justice.

Not once had he heard of Southern claiming a reward. And not once had he heard of Buckman not claiming one, in spite of being on the town's payroll. There wasn't a town ordinance in Cutbank preventing him from collecting the money on outlaws' heads, but Ty considered it wrong. The marshal's salary should be all he worked for, unless he collected extra money serving process and other legal services dictated by the mayor or a judge.

Otherwise, the temptation to throw anyone and everyone in jail for the reward overwhelmed some lawmen.

But he could overlook that, just a little, even if Southern couldn't. He suspected the rivalry between the two lawdogs went deeper, but he never asked. If his friend wanted to share the details, he'd listen. Otherwise, prying into personal matters was downright rude.

"There's the bank," Southern said. "There aren't extra guards posted outside."

"Snipers on the rooftops across the street and on the second-story balcony of the hotel are the best places," Ty said. "Give me odds on whether there are extra guards inside?"

"Why bother until that mountain of money's locked in the vault? If old man Hutchinson is like all the other bankers I've ever known, he's a tightwad. He won't bring in hired guns until the money's here."

"I don't know when that's supposed to be," Ty said. "That makes it even harder to set a trap."

"If those two mangy coyotes weren't lying."

"That's a possibility, but what would they gain by making you mad?"

"Not a thing. If they lied to make me come all this way for nothing, I'd be inclined to use a short rope to hang them both. Let 'em choke on their own lies that way."

"There's Buckman. It looks like he's got his dander up already," Ty said.

"That's because he's spotted me."

Southern nodded in the other marshal's direction and got a string of invective in reply.

"You just turn that maverick you're forking around and ride on back to Warknife. There's no call for you to be here, Southern."

"Pleased to see you, too, Marshal Buckman," Southern said.

"I don't care if you're a deputy sheriff, this ain't your

jurisdiction." The man puffed himself up and glared. His piglike eyes narrowed even more. "You're here after some outlaw with a big reward on his head and you never told me."

"Paul, you know it's not like that." Ty cleared his throat. "You know it's not true because I sent you a telegram explaining our concerns." He almost added "my concerns" but held back. The Cutbank marshal was still steaming at having another lawman in his town.

"You're all upset because Jack Lowry talked you into putting up so much money, aren't you, Brannigan? That ain't my problem. You don't have to come babysit your poke."

"I haven't deposited it yet," Ty said. "Isn't Hutchinson keeping you up to date on how much is in the bank?"

"I'm in the dark all the time," Buckman snapped. "Lowry told me about the stash after him and you and the other ranchers held a meeting to which I was not invited. And that banker's not been any better telling me about the contents of his safe. How am I supposed to properly protect him if he don't tell me? I ask you that. How am I supposed to guard him?"

Ty stepped down and stretched his aching muscles. Riding all day was a young man's job. His old bones jangled, and his muscles tensed up. There wasn't much of him that didn't hurt from the hard ride. He needed a hot bath to soothe away the twinges. Either that or Beatriz rubbing him down with horse liniment. He was never sure if that cured what ailed him because of the liniment or her strong hands.

Right now, since his wife was back on the Circle P, he'd settle for the hot bath.

What he didn't want to deal with at all was Buckman's belligerence. The marshal stepped up and almost bumped bellies. He craned his neck to glare up at Ty. Buckman stood a full foot shorter but weighed as much. Mostly bald, he had a ring of long, stringy black hair dangling out from under his tall-crowned Stetson. Short, pudgy fingers poked at Ty's chest, each thrust emphasizing a point.

"You," he said, "have no business in Cutbank." Buckman tried to step even closer, but Ty stopped him by simply placing the flat of his hand over the top of the marshal's hand when he tried to poke him again.

Pulling the fleshy hand into his chest so it lay flat, Ty leaned forward. Buckman yelped. His wrist was bent backward, and he couldn't pull free.

"I sent a telegram warning that the bank was going to be robbed. What have you done to stop the outlaws intending to blow the vault open and make off with its contents?"

Buckman gurgled in pain. Ty stood a little straighter and released the pressure bending the other man's wrist backward. The marshal pushed hard and pulled free, stumbling. He crashed into Chris Southern, who held him upright. The small man must have felt he was riding in a canyon with tall walls. Only this time, those walls were a towering Chris Southern and Ty Brannigan.

"The money's not there. Lowry's still got it. I asked the banker man."

"We're going to spread a rumor around town that every last dime is stored now," Southern said. "This'll draw the robbers so we can nab them. How many deputies do you have?"

"Two. That's all."

"The three of us, two deputies, do you think five guns will be enough?" Ty looked around town. Commerce went on as if they didn't exist. There was no reason for any of the merchants to lock up and hide. Not yet. He'd have to give them one. Having innocent citizens caught in a crossfire with determined bank robbers had to be avoided.

"Your deputies with rifles on roofs across from the bank can cover the street. Are they good shots?"

"I don't know. There's never been any call for them to use their rifles. Or their six-shooters. I run a peaceable town, Brannigan." Buckman grumbled some. "At least it was until you two blew in."

"Should we tell Lowry what we're planning to do?" Southern asked, speaking over the Cutbank marshal's head.

"No," Ty said, giving it a moment's thought. "He'd leak out that the money's not there, just to reassure the other ranchers."

"And Lowry likes to be in charge," Southern said.

"You two, what are you up to?"

"Marshal Buckman," Ty said tiredly. "We've told you. Spread word around town all the ranchers' money is deposited in the bank and that it moves out at opening tomorrow morning."

"Would it be better if we let it known the money was being shipped before the bank opened? That way there's not any customer to get in the cross fire." Southern always considered the citizens first, even in another town.

"That can keep innocent customers from getting shot," Ty agreed.

Buckman sputtered and started to make another point by using his finger to stab out into Ty's chest. He drew back, remembering how he had been twisted up when he tried that before.

"This is all on your head. Both of you."

"Start the gossip," Southern said. "We're going to talk to Hutchinson now. We can set up the ambush inside the bank lobby."

Paul Buckman went off, sputtering. He started past a saloon, then veered as if a powerful magnet pulled him through the swinging doors.

Ty laughed.

"Everyone in town will know about the money within the hour."

"And Buckman doesn't even have to miss a round," Southern said.

They trooped over to the bank. The tall oak doors were secured. Ty rapped hard on the door until a muffled voice told them the bank was closed.

"It's Marshal Southern," Ty answered. "And me. Ty Brannigan. Open up. It's about the money Jack Lowry's collecting."

The door opened a fraction. Light glinted off a six-gun held in the banker's trembling hand. Hutchinson stuck his head out and looked around nervously. He stepped back and opened the door wide enough for them to slip inside. The banker Hutchinson slammed the door immediately. He fumbled a little, sliding a locking bar into place. From the look of the wood, it hadn't been used in a while.

Life in Cutbank was too peaceable for the banker to secure the door with anything more than the heavy key lock.

"I'm glad to see someone's taking it seriously guarding my money. The ranchers' money," he corrected.

Ty pushed the long-barreled six-shooter away. The banker waved it around carelessly.

"Let me lay out for you what we intend," Southern said. He took Hutchinson by the elbow and led him back to his desk beside a knee-high railing. Immediately behind the president's desk the giant spherical-shaped safe looked like some remnant from a giant's cannonade. The circular door was secured and a timing mechanism clacked loudly. Only when the clock reached eight A.M. would it be possible to open the safe without blowing it to hell and gone.

As his friend engaged the banker, Ty prowled around the

lobby. Two places looked like decent spots for a guard to hide. Both platforms were fixed up high, near the ceiling and both had iron sheets to protect the guard. Slits ran down the middle of each iron plate to allow rifles or shotguns to be thrust through. From what Ty estimated, both of those aeries were properly positioned to control the entire lobby.

"What will the robbers do to the tellers," Hutchinson asked, "when they find there's no money in the safe? Or not what they expect. I have barely a thousand dollars in there right now."

"Are you afraid they'll shoot you out of disappointment?" Southern laughed harshly.

"No, not at all. That's my job taking risks for the bank's employees and customers. But these are desperate men. Vicious killers. If they don't get what they expect from the safe, what's to keep them from opening up on everyone in sight?"

"Not a thing, Mister Hutchinson," Ty said. "Nothing except for Marshal Southern and me being in those sniper's nests. When the robbers come in, we'll have them covered."

"But I'm exposed. By the safe. Nothing but my desk between me and the robbers."

"That cherrywood desk is sturdy enough to stop about any bullet that comes your way. Be sure to dive and take cover."

"Are you going to spend the night?"

"There's no reason for that, Mister Hutchinson. Unless Jack Lowry's already deposited the money."

"No, no, he hasn't," the banker answered.

If Ty had to bet, he wouldn't lose money claiming the safe held a considerable amount of greenbacks and gold coins more than Hutchinson claimed. He looked at his friend. Chris Southern thought the same.

"I've got my Henry outside," Ty said.

"And Old Suzy's ready for action," Southern declared. His ten-gauge shotgun was a formidable weapon. In a closed-in lobby, he'd reduce a dozen men to bloody ribbons if he discharged both barrels.

"You'll stay inside. Overnight?"

"We'll see you an hour before you usually open. That'll alert the bank robbers we're ready to move that mountain of money to the railroad office down south."

"Good, good." Hutchinson looked around as if expecting the gathering shadows to come alive and pounce on him. He tucked his pistol into his waistband and went to the door.

A quick peek out, then he slipped through like a cat sliding around a table leg.

Ty looked at Southern as the metallic click of the front door lock sounded. They were locked in.

"Let's get comfortable," Ty said. "It's going to be a long night."

"A long night," Chris Southern said, "with dawn coming mighty early."

Chapter 21

Frank Dexter kept watching his back trail. He expected that Race Cooper put at least a couple men to follow him. His jaw hurt, and his head felt like it was ready to split open. If he'd reached his six-gun none of this beating would amount to a hill of beans. With his skinned knuckles wrapped around the reins, he kept moving, finding high points to look back, places to let his anxiety grow.

Was anyone on his tail so good he failed to spot them? Or were they even there? He cursed Cooper. The man was sneaky. Not sending some of the gang to come after him served an even better tactic. How did he ever see someone who wasn't there? It made him jumpy. And Cooper kept his gang intact. Dexter had seen the distrust among the rustlers. If Cooper had dispatched one or two to come after him, they might hit the trail and keep on riding.

Dexter had always told his brother how dumb he was for not thinking things through. Thomas managed to act first and regret his actions later. That got him into a world of trouble, but it had also brought him things to envy.

Thomas had an open, sort of stupid look to him that made people ignore him. Frank had no doubt this was how his brother had come by the information about the ranchers' money and all the details. Those had to be known to only a couple men, and yet Thomas had learned the plan and was smart enough to enlist help stealing it.

Dexter touched his coat pocket. He had always joshed his brother on how he failed to think ahead. The crinkle of paper under his fingers told him that trait ran deep in the Dexter family. There had been plenty of time to hide the sheets of paper with the details of the bank and money shipment, but he had barged on into Cooper's camp carrying them.

Relying on Race Cooper to be this stupid in the future was a good way to end up dead.

"He looked like he'd been whupped good and proper before I started to whale away on him," he said softly. "That musta addled his brain."

The longer he rode the better he felt. Whatever hell Cooper had gone through before their fight, anyone seeing him afterward would think it was Frank Dexter's doing. He took his jaw between thumb and forefinger to wiggle it back and forth. In a day or two he'd be able to eat without it hurting too bad to even swallow. Until then he'd do what Cooper had denied him the manpower to do: find Thomas's runaway wife.

Dexter circled and came around one last time to be sure no one followed him. Here and there he had done his best to confuse his hoofprints. Rocky patches in these mountains gave plenty of chances to cross stone fields where even an Arapaho couldn't track.

The trail spat him out on the edge of the graze where Cooper had hidden the stolen cattle among the Circle P head. This buoyed his spirits a tad more. Cooper was a small-time crook with no imagination. When he had come along with the promise of robbing a bank and making off with twenty thousand dollars, he had perked up like a prairie dog from its burrow.

No matter that he had maybe a thousand dollars in stolen cattle waiting to be moved. Cooper dropped the sure thing for a chance at robbing the bank. Dexter wasn't sure if he would have done the same thing, had their positions been reversed. A surefire payoff? Twenty times that for a robbery depending on men he hardly knew.

Bird in the hand, two in the bush.

"If Cooper knew Thomas, he'd never have set his gang to the robbery." Dexter himself hardly believed his brother until he had taken the papers from his dead body.

As he rode, he looked down at the stirrups and the fancy-toed boots poking out. His brother had been a wastrel and a little on the dim side, but he had good taste in boots. Dexter wiggled his toes. They even fit pretty good, and his brother wasn't going to need them where he had gone.

"Hotfooting it through hell," he said, laughing out loud. That was all Thomas had earned in a life mostly misspent.

He stopped to let his horse drink from the meandering brook. As the horse slurped up the sweet water, Dexter walked around. He had no idea where to go to find Evangeline Dexter. She had abandoned Thomas in Kansas and taken her three brats on the road. All he knew of her background was that she'd worked as a whore on a riverboat running along the Missouri River.

Thomas and the mousy soiled dove had married and stayed away from him for ten years. He had come across them by accident. Thomas had agreed to join him in a little bit of stagecoach robbery. When they'd returned to Kansas, Evangeline had hightailed it.

No matter how he tried to convince his brother to let her go, Thomas had insisted she was his woman and had gone after her. Part of that hunt had been useful. Thomas had found out about the ranchers piling their money up, but it had also brought him a chestful of lead.

Dexter wanted to square things with Evangeline. She had to be the one who ambushed Thomas and left him to draw flies.

He mounted and began the long ride to the way station. That was the only place he had a ghost of a chance of finding Evangeline.

It stood abandoned and lonely along the road. Dexter rode to the way station and dismounted.

"Hello, anybody here?"

His only reply was wind whistling past exposed timbers in the station's decaying roof. The stage still ran past here, he knew, by the look of the road. Deep ruts showed a heavy coach had come this way in the past few days. But the stationmaster was nowhere to be seen.

Dexter quickly decided that somebody had been here. His brother's body was gone.

"They even took my boots," he said, grinning crookedly. Once more he admired the fancy boots for which Thomas had given his life to pass along to his brother. He rubbed the top of one against the back of the opposite leg, then repeated until the boots gleamed like new. If nothing else, he'd gotten decent boots out of coming to Wyoming.

Dexter explored and found the fresh grave. He kicked at the stones laid across the dirt in the shape of a cross. Thomas wasn't well served by such a gesture. Let the worms eat him without worry about the cross over their heads.

He began a hunt for tracks and found sets of hoofprints. The riders had to be the ones who buried Thomas. Evangeline wasn't riding with anyone.

"Or maybe it was her entire clan," he wondered aloud. Three distinct sets made sense. Evangeline and two more horses for her three kids.

Dexter walked along the tracks until they reached the road running toward Warknife. His head still hurt, and whenever he shook it, something rattled around inside. Cooper had done a good job pummeling him. But Dexter wasn't completely addled. Evangeline had avoided towns smaller than Warknife on her way here.

She wouldn't seek out a town with people who'd gossip or lawmen who'd ask questions. Her intent had been to ride as far and fast as she could to keep Thomas from finding her.

He backtracked and looked for other tracks. A fainter set cut away from the road and went toward a butte a few miles off to the southwest. Dexter tried to picture a map and the route Evangeline had taken from Kansas. Mostly heading south, angling away to the west made sense. It let her avoid the ranchers and Warknife and Cutbank.

"Salt Lake City? Is that what's in her crazy head? To go to a big city and lose herself there?" That ran counter to what she'd been doing so far. The chance that she'd considered it to throw off pursuit wasn't to be discarded. She was downright sneaky.

He walked another quarter mile and found more distinct impressions where a mud puddle had dried. Then a rocky stretch made tracking impossible. He dropped to his knees and hunted for a half hour. He found a few bright cuts made by a steel horseshoe across barren rock, but he had to admit this was guesswork. Dexter got to his feet and looked toward the butte.

"There. She headed there."

The tiny cooking fire was banked to keep anyone from seeing it. Dexter happened to see the curl of smoke because he hunted for it. Otherwise, he'd have ridden right on by.

A game trail curled up into the rocks and showed some promise to reach the fire.

He dismounted and tethered his horse. In the twilight, the horse was almost invisible. He wanted to be entirely invisible as he trudged up the trail. Dexter pressed close to the rocks and kept a sharp eye out in case Evangeline waited for anyone coming up the trail.

Her horse was tethered near a small stand of trees. It dozed, snorting and swaying in its sleep. Careful not to disturb the horse and warn the woman, he moved silently to a spot behind a large-boled spruce tree that let him study the campsite.

The fire was partly hidden by a rock cliff face. Stacks of stone all around the fire pit hid the flame even more. The fire had burned long enough to leave soot marks on the rock above. He took a deep whiff. Roasting meat mingled with wood smoke. Still unmoving, he sought the woman. This had to be Evangeline Dexter. Who else would go to such extremes to hide their camp?

He almost cried out when a dark form moved to the fire and took the roasting meat—a rabbit?—from a spit. In the dancing light he saw the sharp planes and Roman nose and washed-out blond hair he remembered from back in Kansas.

Dexter let her begin eating. She nibbled at the meat and occasionally licked grease from her fingers. If she was armed, he didn't see it. With her hands occupied with dinner, reaching for a gun, no matter where she kept it, presented a problem for her. Greasy fingers made gun handling even more difficult.

He slid his six-gun out and cocked it.

The metallic click rang out like thunder. She dropped the meat and grabbed for something hidden by a rock.

"I'll shoot you down if you move a muscle. Don't try to

raise that gun." He took aim. At this range he wouldn't miss, and she realized it.

"You," she said, spitting out the word like a curse.

"I told Thomas I'd help find you."

"Where is he?"

The question took Dexter by surprise. Then he thought she only meant to confuse the issue by playing dumb. She knew where he was. If she hadn't buried him, she had filled him full of lead and left his body out for anybody to stumble across.

That was cold.

Pretending she had no idea her husband was dead by her hand was even worse. Dexter tolerated most things in a woman, but lying about gunning down his brother went miles beyond his sufferance.

"Where you left him," he said with emotion burning his words.

"Back in Cutbank? Good. I figured I was headed away from him."

"At the way station, not Cutbank." Dexter stepped closer and circled. A small-caliber pistol balanced on a rock beside her. He gestured for her to toss it away.

"You don't owe him anything, Frank. Let me go. I promise neither of you will ever see me again."

"Where are your brats?"

She tensed.

"I left them behind. They slowed me down."

"You're scouting ahead. You intend to retrieve them when you get somewhere you think's safe."

"Please, Frank. He beat me. Thomas was terrible to the children, too." She swallowed hard. "Real terrible. What he done to Anna was . . ." She choked up. A bright tear glistened on her cheek. Firelight caught it and turned it into pure gold.

"Nothing you didn't deserve, any of you."

"I'd kill him if I had the chance." Evangeline swiped at the tear. "I'd kill you if I had the chance. You're just like him."

He stepped closer. Her reaction when she saw the boots puzzled him.

"What's wrong, Evie? You didn't think I would take my legacy from him?" He lifted one foot so the firelight caught the intricate tooling. The toe gleamed like a tiny sun.

"Those are his boots," she said. "I'd recognize them anywhere. He . . . he used to kick me while he wore them, then make me shine them. Getting blood off leather's real hard, especially when it's your own."

"You did a good job. They're all clean and bright."

"How'd you get them?" Her voice hardened. "He'd never give them up. He loved those boots more 'n anything else in the world."

"You know how I got them. He had no reason to wear them anymore."

"You killed him? You killed your own brother for his boots?"

"What're you saying, woman? You're the one who gunned him down. *You*!" His anger flared and he pointed his six-shooter at her. His hand shook with emotion.

"I wanted to, but I didn't. Where'd it happen?"

"Don't matter," he said. "You're a widow woman now."

She sat straighter. Her pale blond hair was pulled back in a bun. She had lost weight but was still an attractive woman. Her cheekbones thrust out prominently due to lack of food. Her pale blue eyes peered at him from sunken pits. If he didn't know better, he'd think she had used mascara to darken the lids. More likely, that was trail dust.

Her thin dress clung to her body and showed her curves.

Her neckline had been ripped and hung down low, showing off her small bosoms. The flash of bare flesh in the flickering firelight made his heart race just a little.

"Stand up," he ordered.

She did so without a word. Evangeline looked beaten.

"Lift that skirt enough so I can see a bit of ankle. There, yeah, that's good. You've got nice legs. Real nice. I like a woman with good legs." He stepped closer. He reached out with his left hand and stroked her cheek while keeping her covered with the pistol in his right.

She flinched away. He slapped her. The sound of his callused hand hitting her cheek rang out like a gunshot.

"Don't be like that. I inherited my brother's boots. No reason I can't inherit his woman, too."

He grabbed at the neckline and yanked the dress hard. He ripped away cloth until it hung in tatters around her waist. She wore a thin camisole that hid nothing. It clung to her thin body and accentuated the curves. Dexter grinned wolfishly. He liked what he saw.

"Yeah, you and me," he said. "There's no reason we can't spend some time together. Thanks to Thomas, I will be coming into a heap of gold soon. You'd like to spend some of it, wouldn't you? I don't see any call to get married, but who knows? If I cotton to the sample, I might want to get it exclusive. Just like Thomas."

"He sold me to his friends," she said in a flat, emotionless voice. "He liked to watch when they—when they did things." She wrapped her arms around her body and shivered. Evangeline closed her eyes as memories flooded back and turned her even paler.

"That's a lie. He'd never share a sweet young thing like you." Dexter started to rip away the camisole when Evangeline spun sideways and grabbed a stick in the fire.

She stabbed at him with the firebrand. Dexter yelped as the hot tip prodded into his chest. He recoiled in pain, caught his heel and fell hard.

Evangeline grabbed for her gun in the dirt a few feet away. She held it in both hands, cocked it and fired.

Dexter fired first. Her bullet missed him and dug a tiny hole in the dirt beside his head. His lead tore through her heart. She was dead before she collapsed to the ground.

He sat up and stared at her body. It lay in shadow now and hardly seemed human.

"Were you lying with your last breath?" he asked the empty night. "And if you weren't, who killed Thomas?"

He sat up, searched her meager belongings and found nothing worth taking. Dexter left her where she lay, saddled her horse, and led it through the stand of trees. At least his hunt didn't leave him entirely empty-handed.

CHAPTER 22

"Are you asleep?" Ty Brannigan asked softly.

"Of course not. And I knew you wasn't sleeping either. There wasn't any snoring. You sound like a crosscut saw going through hardwood." Marshal Southern imitated the noise he claimed was Ty's normal snoring as he slept.

"Do not," Ty said. He got to his feet and walked around the bank lobby. He pulled out his pocket watch and peered at the face.

"It's four A.M.," Southern said. "I already looked."

"Something's not right," Ty said. "It's eating at me, and I can't figure out what it is."

"Does it have to do with being locked up in a bank about to be robbed? Robbed, that is, if our carefully planted rumors reach the right ears?"

"It's too easy," Ty said. He peered out a barred window into the street. Cutbank was as silent as a graveyard. If Marshal Buckman's deputies were in place on the roofs across the street, he missed them.

He heaved a deep sigh. There wasn't any reason for them to be visible. If they knew their job, they'd stay hidden until the outlaws rode in and dismounted to rob the bank. That was the plan, but he wished he had some hint they were in place, though. The best chance they had of capturing the bank robbers lay in catching them in a crossfire.

From other robberies he had thwarted, the gang wouldn't ride into Cutbank with fewer than a half dozen men. If they thought they had to blow open the safe, a couple more men experienced in hard rock mining and use of dynamite would ride along. More than once he had seen robbers use too much explosive and destroy everything in the safe.

Him and Chris Southern inside the bank, the deputies with rifles on the far side of the street. It was going to be enough to arrest the gang. It had to be, yet an uneasy feeling wormed its way through his gut.

Something was wrong.

"You think we should crawl up into those hunting blinds?" Southern pointed at the armored perches at either corner of the lobby, way up high.

"We'd need ladders to climb up there. These creaky old joints aren't agile enough so I can jump up from the top of the teller's cage."

"I wondered about that. Does Hutchinson ever position snipers there? Ever?"

"Are you saying the perches are for show?"

"That makes more sense to me. Let folks—possible bank robbers—think somebody's in there. That'd act as a discouragement."

"Do you think Hutchinson is sneaky enough to do that?" Ty had to smile at the notion. Just asking the question answered it.

"He's a banker. Of course he's underhanded enough. Have you ever come across a banker who wasn't a scoundrel and a cheat, deep down inside?"

Ty cleared his throat and looked hard at his friend.

"Sorry. For a second there, I forgot your father-in-law's a banker," said Southern.

"Diego's a sharp character, but I've never known him to cheat anyone. Or even outright lie." Ty chewed on his lower lip. Diego Salazar stretched the truth until it bounced around like rubber, but, for a banker, he was honest enough.

For a banker.

Southern joined his friend in going to the windows and looking out. He echoed Ty's sentiment about seeing Buckman's deputies.

"We could go check," Ty said.

"How do we get out? We're locked inside. I don't have a key and neither do you."

"That wasn't very smart letting him box us in." Ty examined the window. The bars kept him in as well as keeping out unwanted visitors.

"It's been my experience that any cell is easier to get through in one direction. In a jail, it's hard to get out, but breaking in? Simple as pie." Southern laid his hand on the heavy wood double doors secured with a complex lock. "Likewise, it should be easier to get out of a bank built to keep people from breaking in."

He pulled out his knife and stuck it between the doors. With a little bouncing and rattling, the lock snicked open.

"It's good that you decided to be a lawman and not a crook," Ty said. "That's as slick a way to open a locked door as I've ever seen."

"Feeling locked-up eats away at me," Southern said. "It's a good thing I'm wearing the badge and not running from it."

He tugged on the doors and they opened. "You want to scout those deputies or should I?"

"You go. You're the one with the badge."

"But you're the one who sounds like an Army sergeant. You snap out commands and people who don't know you jump to."

This surprised him. Ty wondered how others saw him. That wasn't the way he saw himself. If anything, he felt as if folks walked over him. At least his family did because he always gave in to them. Whatever Beatriz wanted, she got. And his children? The girls wheedled him. With the boys he had a more commanding presence. They did as he told them without any backtalk. Or without much argument.

"A sergeant, eh?" Ty considered that.

"I'll be back in a few minutes. As you pointed out, these old bones have a mite of trouble climbing the way they used to." The lawman crossed the street to the darkened store.

Ty watched his friend fade into shadows, only to appear outlined against the night sky a few minutes later. Southern walked the length of the roof, then stopped. He put his hands on his hips in a signal of disdain. Ty didn't have to be over there to know what Southern had found.

Or hadn't found.

The deputies weren't at their posts.

Ty waited for his friend to come back down. Southern cursed under his breath the whole way.

"What are we going to do?" Southern asked. "How many owlhoots do you reckon will take our bait? Ten? Twenty?"

"Not that many," Ty said. "They will have a half dozen. And a couple to cart off the money."

"Eight? We can't tangle with that many and expect to arrest very many."

"We won't have to," Ty said. "If we take out enough of them that'll warn them off."

"I want them in jail alongside those two we already caught. Chasing off most of the gang's not good enough."

"It'll make them think twice about going after the actual shipment," Ty said. "That's good enough."

"We can get a posse and chase them down to wherever their hideout is."

"Marcus was vague about where this Race Cooper is hiding."

"Desperado's Den, he called it." Southern spat. "We're up against a gang of greenhorns."

"That makes them all the more dangerous," Ty said. "The other one, Kennard, was willing to fess up to being a rustler. They turn on each other because they don't have confidence in Cooper."

"So they're giving up stealing cattle and going to bank robbery." Southern spat again. "I prefer chasing down rustlers."

"You would. It gets you out of town and onto the range. Let's get back inside and rethink what we're doing."

"Why go inside? If the robbers hit before the bank opens, why don't we try to trap them inside? You're about the best shot with that Henry I've ever seen. And Old Suzy here'll be plenty happy to bottle them up. A blast or two of ten-gauge puts the fear into most everyone, greenhorn or grizzled veteran bank robber."

"You're right. Without the deputies, we have to think of a better plan." Ty saw the first fingers of dawn working to claw away the night. "And from the sound of hooves coming fast, you'd better think real fast."

"How's this for a plan? Don't get yourself boxed in," the marshal said. He broke open the shotgun and made sure two shells rested in the chambers. "Here they come."

Ty hefted his rifle and ran for cover across the street, sitting on the boardwalk and using a chair to hide himself. Southern dropped down behind a water trough near the bank. Ty worried about his friend being so close to where the robbers had to dismount.

Then his full attention focused on the men wearing

bandannas pulled up over their noses. Four of them. This wasn't anywhere near the number he expected, but Race Cooper must think striking this early wouldn't be hard. The fewer the robbers, the bigger the share for each.

Two of the masked men dismounted and went to the bank's tall doors. One pushed it open and chanced a quick look inside.

"It's a trap!" The robber swung around, his six-shooter hunting for a target.

Ty had to act. If Southern ordered the robbers to give up, they'd open fire. He was almost in the middle of the nervous, crow-hopping horses.

"You're surrounded. Give up!" Ty fired his rifle in the air. Then he lowered it and sought human targets.

The four outlaws all began firing. A few rounds came in Ty's direction and tore through the store wall behind him. A plate-glass window shattered. Nasty shards cascaded down around him, forcing him down. From the scatter of lead, they didn't have any idea where he hid. The four bandits fired wildly, hoping to hit something on their way out of town.

He heard Southern ordering the robbers to throw down their guns. Then his ten-gauge shotgun roared. All the robbers answered with a curtain of lead from their handguns. The air filled with choking smoke and dust kicked up by the frightened horses.

Ty stepped forward to get away of the broken glass. He drew a bead but didn't fire. The rising cloud hid both the outlaws and Chris Southern. Firing blindly was as likely to hit his friend as the robbers.

Old Suzy blared a couple more times. From the sound following the report, the marshal fired in the direction of the bank. Ty didn't want to know what damage was done to the building. At that range Southern had likely blown fist-sized holes in the walls.

Moving fast, Ty slid along the street to find a spot where the smoke cloud parted. He got off a couple shots and missed with them. Before the cloud finally settled, he saw the four riders bent low over their horses' necks, whipping their mounts and galloping away.

"Did you hit them?" he called to Southern.

"Missed the whole danged lot. Get our horses. I'll see if anybody's stirring around town who's willing to join a posse."

"Buckman. His deputies. Start with them," Ty advised. He circled the bank to where they'd tethered their horses. A running vault took him into the saddle. Bending low, he snared the reins to Southern's horse. He tugged insistently and got the animal moving.

He zigzagged through Cutbank's streets and got to the marshal's office to hear his friend haranguing Paul Buckman. The Cutbank marshal had pulled on his britches. His suspenders hung down along his legs, and he hadn't strapped on his iron. The union suit covering the man's torso was dirty and filled with holes, letting his chest hair poke out in thick tufts. Southern had awakened him from a deep sleep from the look of Buckman's bloodshot eyes.

"It was a dumb idea," Buckman said. "I wasn't going to tucker out my deputies by having them hide all night long waiting for something that wasn't going to happen."

"We drove off four robbers," said Southern. "Mount up. Get as many men as you can for a posse and follow us."

"There were only four?" Buckman rubbed his chin whiskers. "You shouldn't need a whole army clambering after them. Get after them yourselves. This is your party."

Southern remarked caustically on Buckman's ancestors.

Tiring of new insults, the Warknife marshal spun around and stepped up into the saddle.

"That way," Ty said. He already heeled his horse to a gallop. Southern wasn't far behind.

After a few minutes, Ty slowed. The new sun burned hot on his back. A long shadow cast forward along the trail hid much of the outlaws' tracks. He looked around and finally pulled up to a halt.

"What's wrong?" Southern asked.

"I don't know. This isn't right."

"You want to wait for Buckman to roust his deputies and get a posse out here?"

"If he bothers to pull on his boots, it'd be a surprise," Ty said. "He'll be along eventually, but not soon enough to do us any good."

"Ambush?"

"That might be their plan," Ty said. "That wasn't much of a robbery attempt. Four men? No scouts. Even a complete fool wouldn't ride up like that."

"Race Cooper might be new to robbing banks, but there's nothing to say he's a fool."

"Not like the pair in the Warknife jail," Ty said.

They stared at one another for a moment. Both came to the same conclusion.

"This was intended to lure us away from the jailhouse. Your deputy's big, but he's new to the job."

"Big, burly, and a trifle slow, if you catch my meaning," Southern said.

"He's a few cents shy of a dime," Ty said, distracted.

Ty looked farther along the road.

"What do you make of that, Chris? There was a flash from those bushes alongside the road."

"Ambush," Southern said. "If I keep saying it, I'll be right eventually."

"How do we handle this? Those gents won't wait for the posse to come trotting up. They'll be gone long before Buckman leaves town."

"I've got plenty of room in the jail for more prisoners. There're four of them varmints on the loose."

"I'll ride along, slowlike, while you circle. By the time you get behind them, I'll be in position to catch them in a crossfire. They won't expect that."

"A good plan, Ty. Only I'm the one wearing the badge. I'll be the bait. Just don't go after them unless that Henry repeater of yours has all sixteen rounds in the magazine."

Much louder, Ty said, "I'm going back to town. You can keep on their trail if you want. I'll lay you odds they're in the next county by now."

"I'm too consarned stubborn to give up, but you get on back to Cutbank. Let me do the lawdogging."

They exchanged broad winks.

Ty wheeled about and trotted away. When he hit a bend in the road, he veered away and galloped hard to make the big circle that'd bring him behind the sniper waiting along the road. Hidden by trees, he had to rely on his friend to ride along at just the right gait. If he got there too soon, he'd be cut down. Too late and they'd have a devil of a time flushing the ambushers.

Ty was glad he and Southern had ridden together so many times it was like they shared the same brain. Counting slowly, he estimated where the marshal was along the road. He cut straight for the double-rutted dirt path when two men rose from hiding ahead of him. Both snugged rifles to their shoulders, ready to gun down Southern.

Shooting from horseback was tricky at the best of times. Ty knew he had to make the first shot count. As well trained as his horse was, it'd flinch and shy away when he opened fire. He picked the outlaw closest to the road. His finger came back smoothly, and the Henry barked.

A puff of smoke came from the muzzle, and the outlaw let out a death cry as he fell face forward. His partner hadn't expected attack from the rear. He swung around, frantically searching for their attacker. Ty got off another shot. This one missed, but from the way the owlhoot danced around, the slug had passed between his legs, close enough to the family jewels to cause him to yelp and jump about.

Ty swung back and fired across his body. He missed again, but the robber had enough. With a huge thrashing and crashing, he tore through the undergrowth. A few more rounds from the Henry kept the cutthroat running for his life. Not a single round touched him, though.

His part of the fight done, Ty pressed forward toward the road. A pitched battle filled the air with gunsmoke and deafening noise. Most of that earsplitting sound came from Old Suzy barking repeatedly.

He burst out onto the road and took in the details in a flash. Southern had dismounted and knelt behind a low rock. His ten-gauge rested atop the rock to steady it as he fired methodically into a cluster of boulders twenty yards away. Ty saw two men pop up every time the marshal reloaded. He steadied his horse and aimed for the spot where one foolishly staked out territory. A better tactic would have been to fire, duck, and move.

A head rose. Ty fired. The man's hat went sailing.

He cursed when the head ducked back. He had shot through the crown but had missed the head inside the hat. A second chance afforded itself as the man realized he had to clear out. Ty fired as fast as he could lever in a new round and pull the trigger.

Southern was busy, too. His shotgun barked out enough pellets to blast a barn wall to splinters.

"They're hightailing it," the marshal shouted. He waited to see if he lured out any of the robbers. They were all melting back into the maze of rocks above the road.

"How many were there?"

"I counted four of them. But you were shooting," Southern said.

"Drilled one but another escaped."

They looked at each other.

Ty spoke what was on both their minds.

"They never intended to rob anything. They wanted to lure us out here and kill us. If six of them were waiting, and only four shot up the bank, two were already in place."

Ty dismounted and hiked back to the outlaw he'd shot in the back. Using the toe of his boot, he rolled the man over. Southern looked over his shoulder.

"You recognize him? I don't," Ty said.

"His ugly face don't show up on any of my wanted posters. I spend a fair amount of time memorizing them. He's a new one to me."

"His horse ought to be around here somewhere. We can lash him down over the saddle and take him back."

"No reason," Southern said. "Bury him where he fell. It's more than he deserves."

Ty considered the possibility that Paul Buckman wanted this cutthroat for some infraction in Cutbank. He finally agreed with his friend. Bury him where he died.

After piling stones on the shallow grave to keep the coyotes away, at least for a little while, they mounted and rode slowly back toward Cutbank. Before they got to town, Ty said, "You know that uneasy feeling we were missing something about this whole sorry robbery? I'm getting that feeling twice as hard now."

"Let's go straight back to Warknife," Southern said.

"I've got the same feeling that we'll find the jailhouse empty as a whore's promise."

They bypassed Cutbank and got on the road, keeping as fast a pace as they could without having their horses falter. With every passing mile the feeling in Ty's gut that they had been gulled grew.

CHAPTER 23

"I've lived here all my life," Greg Brannigan said, riding a little closer to Anna. She muttered enough to show she listened to him but offered nothing about her own background. "I've got two sisters. I suppose you're lucky you do, too. And I've got an older brother who hogs everything. Oh, Matthew's all right, I suppose, but he thinks he's so much better 'n me just because he's older."

He looked at the girl sidelong. She rode staring straight ahead as if she was a stone statue. No hint of emotion crossed her face, even when a bug flew up and landed on her forehead. She let it crawl about for a few seconds and never moved to brush it off. It got tired of exploring the dusty, dirty expanse of her eyebrows and flew off.

Greg swiped at his eyebrows in reaction.

"Is it hard, having Jasmine and Ruth depend on you?"

Anna nodded slowly and finally spoke in her little girl voice. "They help, but they're kids."

"I know what you mean. My sister Caroline is a real pest."

"They're too weak to scrounge for victuals. I have to do it all for them since Ma left." She clutched at the gunnysack with the food taken from the way station. A quick, fearful look in Greg's direction made him think she worried about him stealing what she'd found in the way station.

"I wish I'd packed up enough to help out," Greg said. "Me and Mack weren't going to be gone long. But when we get to town, you'll have all the food you want. You and your sisters. Just wait and see."

Anna said nothing. They rode in uneasy silence. Greg felt the need to say something, anything, to fill the emptiness. But he saw that the silence went all the way down into Anna's soul. He wanted to ask what she'd been through but knew she wouldn't answer.

Worse, she'd clam up and never say another word. Being on the run like she was had to be awful. Having her mother disappear was even worse. Fifteen years old and the weight of taking care of her family fell on her thin shoulders.

"Why'd she leave you?" he blurted. Greg bit his tongue to keep from making matters worse.

"Ma? She wanted to lure him away from us, I reckon. She never told me. Maybe she told Jasmine. Her and Jasmine would sit and talk for hours. They ignored me."

"You mean she decoyed your pa away? I understand that," Greg said, hurrying to change the subject. "My folks and Matt and Mack all put their heads together and stop talking when I come in. They ignore me."

"Your sister, too?"

"I—" The question caused Greg to consider this. "Yeah, Caroline, too. That's because they don't think I'm grown up enough. But you and your ma. Why did she talk with your sisters but not you?"

"Greg!" Mack called to him again. "We're going to take the cutoff into town. That'll save us a half hour's ride."

"That's a good idea," he said. "We'll come out by the church. Father Simon has a spare bed or two at the back of the church where he can put them all up." Greg started to expand on this to let Anna see who was in charge, but MacKenna put her arm high in the air and pointed to the shortcut trail. She let out a loud "yee haw" like she was leading a cavalry charge. She raced off hooting and hollering like a crazy woman.

The two girls on the horse beside her giggled and galloped off after her, delighted to be playing a game. Anna smiled, just a little. It was the first real emotion Greg had seen her display since they had hit the trail. Having his sister steal his thunder was annoying, but if it brightened Anna's disposition, he was willing to endure it. He kicked at his horse's flanks and charged after the others.

"After them! They're getting away!"

Greg let Anna draw even and then shoot past so he brought up the rear. The steep trail crested above Warknife and then meandered down the far side of the hill where the church steeple stood tall and proud like a beacon. By the time Greg drew rein, his sister and Anna's sisters had already dismounted.

Anna remained in the saddle, unsure.

"The father's a nice guy," Greg said. "You'll like him. Father Simon Drysdale. He's new to town, too. Well, new meaning he's only been in Warknife for a few months. Everyone's taken to him, though."

Mack walked over and looked up at Anna. In a conspiratorial whisper she said, "He's really handsome, too." She looked over her shoulder as Father Simon came from the side door. "See?"

Mack reached up and helped Anna jump to the ground. Greg hurried after them as the priest greeted Mack.

"What have we here? Pilgrims on the road to Bethlehem?"

"Girls in need of some charity, Father," Mack said.

"Yeah," Greg cut in. "Their ma's out there looking for a safe place. If you take them in, at least for a night or two, she's sure to find them here."

"This is a sanctuary," Father Simon said, holding out his arms. Jasmine and Ruth stepped closer, taking to the man.

As Greg suspected, Anna was harder to win over. She held back and looked skeptical that anyone offered charity so easily.

"It's all right. He'll see that you get something to eat and have a place to sleep," Greg said. "A safe place."

Anna nodded, then smiled her weak smile.

"He is good-looking, like your sister said."

"I suppose so, if you like that type. But he *is* a priest."

Anna went inside when Mack waved for her to follow her sisters. Almost immediately Mack returned and stood beside her brother.

"They're in good hands now. Mrs. Ralston's inside cleaning up. From the smell, she's baking bread."

"She does that good," Greg said. His enthusiasm had cooled for bringing Anna and her sisters here.

"I envy her," Mack said, a dreamy look on her face.

"Why? She's married to that old wastrel Blaine Ralston. If he's not drunk, he's gambling away their money."

"She gets to work with the father." She heaved a deep sigh and came out of her reverie. "We'd better get home. Ma's worried about us. Practice our story. She'll act mad but really won't be when she finds we helped out three orphans."

"Their ma's out there. They aren't orphans."

Mack looked at him with a touch of pity in her hazel eyes. Tears welled up but weren't shed. She hugged him and then quickly released him.

"You're always so optimistic, Greg. Now, let's get on home."

"Go on ahead. I'll tell Marshal Southern what's happened." Greg pointed toward the church.

"Good idea. He'll want to know. I should stay here until you tell him and get back."

"I'll catch up. You know how Ma is."

MacKenna hugged him again and said, "You've done some good things today, brother dear."

She started to kiss him on the cheek, then backed away as he resisted, grabbed her horse's reins and stepped up.

"Don't be long." With that Mack trotted off.

Greg wondered if he should tell Anna goodbye. It seemed like the polite thing to do. He reluctantly mounted and walked toward the marshal's office rather than disturb her. Father Simon could get Anna and her sisters settled. Later on would be a better time to pay his respects.

Right now the lawman would know what to do about finding Anna's mother. And Greg would finally have a chance to tell everything he knew about the body he'd found at the way station. He glanced back. The gunnysack with the dead man's boots still bobbed gently with every stride his horse took. Those weren't much but a sharp man like Marshal Southern could figure out who'd died.

After all, the Sunset Kid could perform miracles like that. If a fictional character in a dime novel was smart enough, a lawman with the marshal's experience would be, too.

As he approached the marshal's office, he heard a commotion. Wondering what caused the ruckus, Greg tapped his horse's flanks and trotted closer. He pulled back hard on the reins as two men wearing bandannas over their faces rushed out. Both waved their six-shooters around.

"Your horses. Get on and let's ride," one of them barked.

Greg caught his breath. Two men followed. They struggled to strap on their gun belts as they ran, but neither wore a mask.

The four galloped from town. In seconds only a lingering dust cloud showed they'd even been in Warknife. Greg dismounted and walked on eggshells to the still-open jailhouse door.

"Hello? Anyone in here?"

A moan answered him. He backed out and took the shotgun from its saddle sheath. He bolted back into the jailhouse. Anyone left inside was on the right side of the law. A quick glance around led him to the closest cell. A burly man stretched out on the floor. Blood leaked from a cut on his forehead where he'd been slugged. From the length of the wound, one of the cutthroats had raked his pistol across his head. The gushing wound had been opened by the front gunsight slicing through flesh.

"Deputy?" Greg hesitantly stepped forward. He'd never seen the man before but he wore a badge pinned on his shirt.

"Help. Jail break. They slugged me."

Greg hesitated to open the locked cell door. Marshal Southern only had a couple deputies, but they never lasted long. Deputy marshal wasn't a high-paying job, and even in a peaceable town like Warknife breaking up fights and the occasional gunplay was dangerous.

The deputy sat up and pressed a meaty hand into his forehead. The wound continued to bleed around his sausage-sized fingers.

"You need a doctor," Greg said.

"I need outta here. Keys." The deputy gestured vaguely with his bloody hand.

"I'll fetch Doc Hickenlooper." Greg got to the door and looked back. "Where's Marshal Southern?"

"Him and a rancher fellow lit out for Cutbank. He left me in charge and they slugged me and locked me up in the cell. Ohhhh." The deputy put his head in his hands and dripped more blood onto the floor.

Greg tore out, jumped onto his horse and rushed to the doctor's surgery. He had to rouse Clarence Hickenlooper. After pounding on the surgery door for what seemed a lifetime, the doctor opened and peered out.

"It'd better be the biggest emergency this town's ever seen for you to get me out of bed right now. It was one terrible long night I spent with a patient."

Greg blurted out everything. Hickenlooper came awake as the story unfolded.

"This deputy fellow in the jail. Is he named Conrad?" The doctor pulled up his suspenders, then snapped them.

"I didn't ask. So much blood. He was leaking all over the place."

"Head wounds bleed like a son of a gun. Let me get my boots on and find my medical bag." Doc Hickenlooper pushed the door to. Greg heard him rummaging about inside and then say to someone, "Sorry, my dear. Duty calls. Maybe we can continue this tonight?"

The muffled reply followed the doctor out. He tucked in his shirttail and swung his medical bag around as he hurried along.

Greg hung back and let the doctor enter the jailhouse, in case the man in the cell wasn't Deputy Conrad. He relaxed when the doctor laughed and used the keys to open the cell door.

"You got yourself bunged up good this time, Conrad.

Not as bad as when you let that mule step on your foot a couple weeks ago."

"Aw, Doc, my head hurts something awful."

"I've got no idea why. It's as empty as a henhouse after the fox's been inside. This will hurt."

Conrad yelped. Greg peeked inside. Doc Hickenlooper poured something from a dark brown bottle onto the wound that caused white froth to bubble the entire length of the cut. Deputy Conrad moaned constantly. The doctor pressed his thumb against one side of the cut.

"No need to put in stitches. You've got a hard enough head that I'd break my needle if I tried." He mopped away the bloody foam and taped a clean white bandage on.

"I've got to go, sir," Greg called. "Is there anything I can do?"

"Don't interrupt me when—" The doctor cut off his complaint. "No, son, clear out. The deputy and me've got this under control."

As Greg turned the deputy bemoaned his fate when he had to tell Marshal Southern what had happened. A smile crept onto Greg's face at the thought. His pa had a way of chewing out anyone who made such a monumental mistake. He suspected Marshal Southern was even more vocal, dealing with drunks and hard cases all the time the way he did.

Wanting to catch up with Mack, he galloped a ways until he was on the road leading toward the Powderhorn. At any bend he expected to spot his sister, but she had ridden faster and he had taken longer following than anticipated. Greg grinned at the prospect of telling the family of his adventures in town.

He'd seen the men breaking out of jail and had freed the deputy after the outlaws locked him up. And then there was Doc Hickenlooper and his friend. Greg wasn't sure who he should mention that to. His pa wouldn't like it. He and the doctor were friends. It certainly wasn't a fit topic talking about the doctor's lady friend with his ma or even MacKenna.

"Matt. He'll enjoy it and maybe even know who the doctor's seeing. Yeah, he—"

Greg pulled back on the reins and stared. He swallowed hard. Four men walked around partially hidden by a stand of pines. They came together and talked. He jumped at a gunshot.

The four edged away. Two mounted and raced off. The two remaining argued and then both mounted a single horse. Slower, they trailed the other two.

The chance of finding another group of four riders on this road—the road likely taken by the escaping prisoners and their rescuers—was pretty low. If Greg had a lick of sense, he'd go back to Warknife and tell the deputy. Conrad seemed to be the only lawman in town. He had a good reason to come back and capture the escapees.

Greg rode to the copse and wove his way through the trees to a large dark form stretched on the forest floor. He didn't bother dismounting. The horse had broken its leg, and its rider had shot it in the head to put it out of its misery.

He looked over his shoulder, in the direction of the road. Back to Warknife? On to the Circle P?

Greg snapped the reins and trotted after the fleeing outlaws. He knew he was no Sunset Kid. Capturing any of the men wasn't likely, not with them all armed killers and him carrying only a .410 shotgun. But he could find where they went.

He could find Desperado's Den.

CHAPTER 24

"How close? How close can I get before they see me?" Greg Brannigan chewed his lip as he worried over the best way to track the four outlaws. The last thing he wanted to do was tangle with them. With cutthroats like these, breaking prisoners out of the jail and pistol-whipping a deputy, he didn't dare take risks.

He wasn't the Sunset Kid.

That notion caused him a moment's despair. He wanted to be. If he built a reputation like the Sunset Kid, everyone would look up to him. His ma and pa wouldn't treat him like a kid. Greg sucked in a deep breath. Especially his pa.

He crested a rise and realized he silhouetted himself against the clear blue Wyoming sky. Urging his horse on he followed the trail a few feet more and still had the view of the terrain ahead without exposing himself. All the outlaws had to do was look at their back trail and spot him if he'd stayed on the top of the rise.

"They won't get you," he said, patting his horse on the neck. Sitting upright, he studied the trail for as far as the eye could see.

Empty.

Greg waited a minute. Another. Still no sign of the four escaping outlaws.

He knew the land well enough, though he seldom came this way. Their hideout had to be hidden away in the canyons ahead, even if he didn't see them right now. Turns and twists in the mountain trail hid them. It had to be that. Losing them on the narrow path was out of the question.

Another couple minutes watching frustrated him. He still failed to spot the men. Greg rode down the slope and tried to pick up their hoofprints. The rocky trail prevented such an easy solution to his problem. Here and there he saw broken twigs on bushes growing out across the trail, but the bushes were low, and none of the signs told him they were recent. A large cat or a wolf was as likely to leave the spoor.

A half hour of slow, cautious riding brought him to a crossing trail he didn't remember. Again sign of recent passage was lacking.

"Which way?" He dismounted and walked a few yards along the right fork, then returned and studied the left. Greg dropped to one knee and ran his finger over a rock. It had been dislodged and had fallen back into place. The dirt around the rock's edge had crumbled.

He stood and stared ahead. This trail led over the mountains, through a pass that eventually fed into the stage road.

"Would they head that way? Not to catch a stage but to escape? They're hightailing it," he decided. "They're giving up on rustling and getting away from Warknife."

This conclusion left him feeling defeated. He had wanted to give the marshal enough detailed facts about the owlhoot hideout as possible. If the four men rode off, intent on escape, there wasn't any way to shine in the eyes of the men he most wanted to impress.

"A little farther," he said to his gelding. A snort and shake of the head told him what his mount thought of the scheme.

He stepped up into the saddle and continued along the

trail. A few minutes later, he turned cautious. Two hoofprints showed in softer dirt—but they went in the wrong direction. If they had been made recently he would have met the rider head-on.

"They have to leave their hideout as well as go to it," he said softly. The hard ground prevented him from finding the tracks left as the four went to their camp. The prints he found were old enough to have been left as they went into Warknife to spring the other two in the gang.

But this was all guesswork. He had nothing solid to tell the marshal.

Just a little farther. That'd show where the riders had gone. He vowed to give up his hunt if he failed to find any trace of their passage. The prior day had told him he needed more skill in tracking. His pa was good. So was the marshal. But they had their hands full with outlaws and rustlers and who knew what else.

When he had time, finding the Cheyenne camp deep in the Wind Range would give him a chance to barter with some of the younger braves. In exchange for a cow, they'd show him how to track better.

"An entire cow?" Greg shook his head. His pa would never agree to that. He touched the dime novel tucked into his waistband. "They might like reading about the Sunset Kid." Even as the words slipped out, he knew none of the braves cared anything about a fictional frontiersman. Indian life was real and constant. There wasn't any room for made-up stories.

Dejected, he vowed to find other ways to hone his tracking skills.

He crossed a narrow meadow, keeping to the game trail. Crushed grass and a pile of road apples showed recent travel, but it was all coming toward him. Nowhere did he see a trace of three horses heading in the direction he took.

Past the meadow and into a sparsely wooded area eventually brought him to a forest of rocks. The game trail broke apart, but he kept to the broader one. He turned increasingly uneasy when he had the feeling that someone watched him.

He jumped a foot when a coyote bolted from between two large rocks and dashed away. Greg looked above as a shadow crossed his path.

"Buzzards," he said softly. "Something's died." His mouth turned dry when he began to wonder if that wasn't "someone."

Wending his way through the rocks where the coyote had hidden, he came to a wider trail that led to a small camp. A fire had been built against a rock face. Belongings were scattered around where animals had fought over a blanket and the contents of saddlebags.

He swallowed hard when he saw the woman's body half dragged from the camp. The tracks in the dirt showed the coyote had tried to take her away from the buzzards' insatiable appetite for dead flesh.

Greg dismounted and pinned his horse's reins to the ground with a large rock. The stomach-turning stench of decayed flesh made him sick. It spooked his horse even more. He sidled up, pressed against a rock until he got a look at the body. The woman's soft parts had been eaten and bugs worked all over her.

The sinking feeling in his gut came from realizing this had to be Anna's mother. How many other women riding alone were there? What fate had befallen her wasn't obvious. Not wanting to touch her but knowing he had to, Greg turned her over. From the small hole and bloodstain on her dress, she had been shot once through the heart.

He edged away and picked up the blanket chewed over by the coyotes. A quick snap sent a cloud of dust into the air. He continued to beat it against a rock until it was a little cleaner. With as much care as possible, Greg draped the blanket around the body and started rolling it until he had a cocoon.

Gripping the ends he pulled her free and to a spot near where she'd built her campfire. Sadly, he shook his head. Whoever had found her had been attracted by the fire.

Whoever had killed her left the trail Greg had followed back to this spot. He shivered. Luck had been with him avoiding such a meeting.

A quick look around told him the woman's horse was gone, either run off or stolen by her killer. This forced him to come to a decision he didn't like one bit. His horse was even less thrilled as he wrestled the body up and draped it over the haunches. With a few turns of his lariat he tied the body in place.

He carefully mounted, avoiding contact with the corpse. Taking everything into account, he made his way down the hillside and reached the stage road. Burying the woman was the smart thing to do, but Anna and her sisters deserved to know if their mother was dead. Identifying the body would be hard, but her clothing might be enough.

Whether it was the girls' ma or someone else, he didn't envy them seeing the body.

It was a long trip into Warknife, made even longer when he had to spend the night on the trail. Too often, he awoke to stare at the dark shape of Anna's ma, imagining her stirring, trying to tell him who had killed her so brutally. By the time he reached Warknife the next day, he was jumping at every sound and worrying about Anna's reaction.

CHAPTER 25

Doctor Hickenlooper couldn't do anything for the woman, not that Greg expected it after spending a night on the trail with the corpse. Still, some unrealistic hope had made him wonder what might be done. He'd never been around anyone who'd died for so long.

"Nothing short of resurrection brings her back," the doctor said. "On my best day, fixing what ailed her is more'n I could handle. A bullet through the heart?" Hickenlooper shook his head sadly.

Greg looked behind him and wrinkled his nose. The smell had gotten worse as the sun beat down during the last half hour ride into Warknife. In the doctor's office, it became overpowering. Besides, he had disturbed the doctor before when he fetched him to fix Deputy Conrad's cut forehead and wasn't likely to be held in high esteem because of that.

Greg left the surgery, wrestled the body over his horse, looked around and finally turned down a side street. He took a couple shortcuts between buildings until he came to a solitary building on the far side of town.

Clarence O'Dell's Funeral Parlor and Rest Home, the sign said. Greg wasn't sure exactly why but his pa never spoke of the undertaker in polite terms. Some of the words he used were those Greg'd get his mouth washed out with soap if he tried to say. Others were foreign, mostly Spanish with some Arapaho, but he caught the meanings as uncomplimentary.

Kicking his leg up high he dismounted and dropped to the ground. Two quick turns of the reins secured his horse. He went inside. He'd been here more than once. People died. That was how it was, but he'd never brought a body in before and wasn't sure what to do.

"What's your pleasure, young man?"

He turned to see the mortician part long black velvet curtains. It looked as if he flowed out of those hangings, dressed all in black the way he was. Clarence O'Dell matched Greg in height but weighed forty pounds less. His bony hands folded across his belly as if holding in his guts. Colorless eyes fixed on him and made him uneasy.

"Sir, I've got a body outside. Some woman. I'm not sure who it is but it might be the mother of some girls staying with Father Simon over at St. Nicholas."

"You found the body?" The words rapped out sharp and brittle. Greg felt as if he might cut himself on the edges. All he did was nod.

The undertaker went to the door and looked out. He spun around and stabbed a bony finger in Greg's direction, as if accusing him of some terrible crime.

"Money. Did she have money on her person?"

Greg shook his head.

"A charity case, then. Potter's field." O'Dell sounded as if he wanted to spit. "Haven't had a paying funeral in weeks. The city's always late paying for the burials in the potter's field. Never make a dime off them, anyway."

"I don't know about any of that, sir. The mayor's the one to ask, I reckon."

"The mayor, the mayor. That wastrel. Now when he drinks himself into an early grave, that'll be a proper funeral. He can pay for it, and if he doesn't the city will show proper monetary gratitude for getting rid of him."

"He wouldn't pay for his own funeral, would he? He'd be dead."

"You're the Brannigan boy, aren't you? Will your father pony up money for her funeral?"

"I . . . he doesn't know I brought her to you."

"You didn't kill her, did you?"

Greg bristled at that. He only wanted to do what was right. Being accused of such a crime offended him.

"I did not, sir. I'm on my way to the marshal to report this. He'll want to see the body. And keep it for those girls I told you about to see if it's their ma." He swallowed hard. Putting Anna through looking at the decomposing body wasn't much of a kindness.

"Pennybacker!" The undertaker roared out the name again. A small, mousy man scuttled from behind the same curtains where O'Dell had come. "Get a gurney. There's a stiff outside slung over a horse."

"That one's goin' to the potter's field?" Pennybacker asked. He flinched when O'Dell yelled at him again. "On to it right now, Mister O'Dell. Right now, sir." The undertaker's assistant vanished into the rear of the funeral parlor.

O'Dell followed him, leaving Greg alone. He shuffled his feet a couple times, then went back outside. Pennybacker had come around the side of the building with a flat board mounted on wheels. Greg started to offer his help getting the woman's body onto the gurney, but O'Dell's assistant, for all his stature, was more than up to the challenge. A knife flashed. The securing ropes parted and the body began to slide off.

Pennybacker bent low and caught the corpse across his shoulders. With a quick twist, he dumped it onto the gurney. In seconds, he pushed it around the side of the funeral parlor and disappeared. Greg heaved a sigh of relief. He hadn't realized the load that body put on his shoulders.

He mounted and galloped off, glad to be away from this unpleasant chore.

His heart jumped when he saw his pa's coyote dun tethered beside the jailhouse. Telling Marshal Southern everything that'd happened would be harder, maybe, but it saved him effort in the long run if his pa heard it at the same time.

Nervous at having to report the death, he went inside. Marshal Southern sat behind his desk. Ty Brannigan faced him across the nicked, battered surface. Deputy Conrad leaned against the wall by the gun rack, a confused look on his face.

"Marshal," Greg greeted. "Howdy, Pa. I got something to report."

Southern looked at him, then over his shoulder at his deputy.

"I've heard. Doc Hickenlooper gave me quite an earful about my deputy's dereliction of duty. Thanks, Greg, for seeing he got all patched up after the escape."

"This is about something else."

"The girls Mack and you brought in? We've heard. She did a good job with them, seeing them to the padre's care," Ty said.

"No, not that. Well, it's part of them being left on the road. See, I found—"

"Later, Greg. The marshal and I have some serious matters to discuss."

"But—"

His father's sharp look silenced him. He started to go stand next to Conrad, but the man's expression warned him to move to the other corner of the office. The deputy must have found himself in a huge pot of boiling oil for letting the two rustlers get away.

"We were decoyed, Ty. Pure and simple, they duped us into thinking they were robbing the bank when they wanted us out of Warknife to spring those two varmints."

"I don't know how they did it," Ty said. "If Kennard and Marcus hadn't told us about the bank robbery, we would never have gone to Cutbank."

"They never talked to anyone after I locked them up, did they, Conrad?" Southern never turned to his deputy for the answer, which was a surly grunt. "I didn't think so."

"One of the gang must be in town and watching," Ty said.

"There aren't any newcomers I know of," the marshal said. "Except for those girls Mack escorted in, and that was after we were lured up to Cutbank."

"They don't have anything to do with rustlers," Greg piped up. "They're on the run from—"

"It's a poser," Ty said, ignoring his son. "We'll have to figure out how big a threat there is to the money."

"I'd say we let Buckman worry on that a while," Southern said. "We saw how seriously he took this robbery attempt."

"The next one will be for real. We have to be ready for it. I'm not going to get robbed because he's falling down on the job. My reputation is at stake! And so is my money!"

"Well, Ty, we won't be welcomed with open arms. Banker Hutchinson might want to see us and a few deputies, but Buckman will do whatever he can to make us look bad."

"Again," Ty said in resignation. He heaved to his feet. Reaching across the desk he shook the marshal's hand.

"There's an answer somewhere," Southern said. "We need to keep thinkin' on the matter a bit harder."

Ty nodded curtly, put his arm around Greg's shoulders and steered him from the office.

"It's time to get on home. Your ma is going to have a litter of kittens that we've been gone so long without letting her know."

"Pa, I—" Greg bit off his words. His father was deep in thought, worried about rustlers and something about a bank robbery in Cutbank, and spies in Warknife. He wasn't ready to listen to his son's grand adventures. But then he never was.

CHAPTER 26

"So what did you say then?" Caroline Brannigan scooted her chair closer to the table, propped her elbows on it, and put her chin in cupped hands. She listened intently to her sister's every word.

"It was hard figuring out what to say," Mack said. "Even harder was trying not to say anything that would spook them. They were like timid little rabbits."

"They have such beautiful names," Caroline said. "Anna and Ruth. I really like Jasmine. Maybe I'll change my name to Jasmine."

"You'll do no such thing, young lady," their mother said sternly, coming from the kitchen. "Get your elbows off the table. People will think you were raised in a barn." Beatriz Brannigan sniffed loudly. "Jasmine. What kind of name is that?"

"She's certainly not named after a saint," Mack said. "You can't believe the mouth she has on her, and in front of her little sister."

"Ruth's probably the same when you're not around," Beatriz said. "You're a good influence. And if I ever hear you saying anything like that . . ."

"You won't, Mama," MacKenna assured her.

Greg listened with half an ear. Whenever he spoke, the

topic always changed to how his sister had herded the youngsters into Warknife and the padre's care. He wasn't sure they had even understood how he'd buried the man gunned down in the way station or taken the woman's body into town.

"Ma, how can you figure out someone's name who's dead?"

Beatriz frowned as she turned toward him. He read disapproval, but he pushed ahead.

"I mean other than asking relatives or friends. What if the body's all rotted and falling apart?"

"That's not a fit topic for the breakfast table, Gregory. If you're finished, clean off the plates. Is it your turn to wash them?"

"It's Caroline's," he said. "Why doesn't Mack have to do the dishes anymore?"

"She's got other duties around here, that's why. Now get on with it. Clean the table and then get to your chores. You've not been doing them recently."

Greg did as he was told, then slipped out before Caroline found some excuse to make him do the dishes. His other chores were all simple and tedious. Tending the animals was fine. The chicken coop was always tedious and smelly, but if he kept the rooster from pecking at his legs, the job wasn't hard. He enjoyed working in the barn, even if he had to muck the stalls, but he wanted his brother to let him help with the colt. Matt spent hours a day training the frisky colt. Every time Greg asked to help, he was brushed off.

Just like the rest of the family brushed him off. It was as if he existed only to clean the chicken coop, gather eggs, and tend the barn. And dishes. Endless cleaning of dishes from breakfast, lunch, and supper.

He started for the large building, then slowed. His pa and Matt walked around the barn, pointing to spots high up that needed repair. Winds took their toll on all buildings, and the summer had seen violent thunderstorms that often lasted for days. It was a miracle that those gusty winds hadn't taken shingles off both the barn and house.

His pa might repair the roofs, but if he wanted to patch the broken planks, Greg'd be the one tapped to paint the entire barn. His arm ached just thinking about it. It was a huge barn.

Moving like a ghost, he slipped into the barn and saddled his horse. Leading it from the barn when his pa and brother were on the far side, he swung into the saddle and galloped off in a cloud of dust. He thought he heard Matt calling his name, but he ignored his brother. All that Matt could possibly want was to pass along the responsibility of one of his chores so he had more time with the colt.

When Greg rounded the bend in the road leading to Warknife, he slowed and thought about what to do. If he goofed off the rest of the day, he'd catch hell from everyone. Even Caroline would join in telling him what a wastrel he was and that he'd never amount to anything being lazy.

He sucked in his breath. He might even get a switching for playing hooky from a full day's work. Too much of the past couple days had been spent on the trail, hunting outlaws, finding dead bodies. And no one cared.

The purple-hazed mountains hid the owlhoots' hideout.

"Desperado's Den," he said. The name rolled off his tongue. It carried some mystical meaning. In the dime novel, the outlaws had a fancy stone building they used as their headquarters. The Sunset Kid snuck in and rescued the shopkeeper's kidnapped daughter and escaped. After a gunfight or two that proved his courage.

Greg had his shotgun. It was a puny weapon compared to any sidearm slung at men's hips. Better used to shoot birds than cutthroats, the gun needed serious improvement.

A ten-gauge like Marshal Southern carried put the fear into any coward's heart.

He smiled grimly. It put the fear into him. That was a powerful, deadly weapon in the lawman's hands. Even the Henry rifle his pa carried was adequate to use in a gunfight, though his Colt .44 was a real man's gun. It filled his steady hand and showed that he meant business when he drew it.

Any outlaw worth his salt would laugh at Greg if he leveled his .410 and gave the order to grab some sky.

He reached behind and touched the dime novel crammed into his waistband. Reading the last chapter or two of the book appealed to him, but it felt like betrayal. He was supposed to do chores. Running off and spending the day riding with the Sunset Kid was . . . wrong.

A smile crept onto his lips. He knew how to do something useful and read more in the book that had captured his imagination so completely. With a tap on the sides, he brought his gelding to a trot. Warknife wasn't that far off.

Before he knew it, the hustle of the town disturbed his daydreams of being like the Kid, going where he pleased and doing whatever struck his fancy. He took a winding route down alleys and across shortcuts that brought him to the church. Its steeple had held a bell once. A storm brought it crashing down. The padre had sent for new iron fittings to hold it, but the wood holding the crossbeam needed to be replaced, too. One thing led to another, and it was close to three months since the bell fell.

Dismounting at the side door, he hesitated going in. There was no telling what he disturbed. Then his dilemma was settled for him.

"Hello, Gregory," Anna greeted him. She stood in shadow just inside the door. He wasn't able to see her clearly—and yet he pictured her perfectly. She looked down shyly and held her hands behind her. Maybe she shuffled one foot around nervously.

She was as uneasy as he was.

"How're you doing, Anna?"

He stepped closer. For a moment he thought he saw an angel. Light behind the girl lit her hair and turned it into a fiery ring around her head. Shadows played over her face and gave her the look of something wild and free, not shy and held back by the need to find her parents.

"Did you want to see Father Simon? He's gone out to, I don't know, see someone," she finished lamely.

Greg guessed Anna and church services were strangers. He started to ask if she had gone to identify the body he'd brought to Mister O'Dell, then chickened out. She was in a good mood and actually smiled. Kinda. It seemed wrong to break whatever good feelings she enjoyed right now. She had been through so much. Let her enjoy being . . . normal.

"No, not him. It's you," he said, suddenly the shy one.

"What do you mean?" Anna stepped into the daylight. Any hint of angelic lighting vanished. She was once more the plain waif he'd found out on the trail, but she'd had a bath and her dingy clothing was clean now. Her hair had been combed back and all the rat's nest knots worked out. Anna wasn't beautiful or even pretty. But Greg didn't much care about that.

"Want to take a walk? Can you, I mean? I don't want to—"

"All right. Is there somewhere special you want to go?"

His mind raced. Then the idea blossomed.

"There's a stream not far from here. It's quiet and, well, not many folks will be poking around this time of day." He saw her hesitation. "If you want, ask your sisters along." He suddenly realized how inappropriate his request was. It was almost as if he was sparking her. Being alone would cause tongues to wag if anyone in town saw them. And someone would. He knew his neighbors too well not to think eyes would follow them and cause gossip to erupt.

"They're busy, I think. If it's all right, we could go. Me and you."

Greg smiled ear to ear. Let the gossip begin! It'd give the busybodies something to do, and he truly wanted to spend the time with Anna.

They walked slowly, occasionally arms brushing. Greg wasn't sure what they said until they got to the stream. The quiet rush of water calmed the race of his heart. Anna relaxed, too.

"There's a grassy spot. We should have brought a blanket," Greg said.

She shrugged. Her dress was spotted and thin. Getting grass stains on it wouldn't be noticed.

They sank down and watched the water tumble over the rocks. Greg's mind was blank. No words came until, "Would you like to borrow my book?" He pulled out the epic tale of the Sunset Kid that had so excited him. If he found it thrilling, it might be equally fun for Anna.

"I . . . No thanks." She turned from him and looked uneasy.

From her reaction he suddenly realized that she wasn't able to read. Greg covered their mutual embarrassment by saying, "Why don't I read some of it for you?"

"I'd like that," she said. She drew her knees up and hugged them close. She rested her cheek on her knees so she could watch him.

He pulled out the battered copy and leafed through to the spot where he had stopped. A quick summary of what had happened so far prepared her for what he knew was a good section.

Greg cleared his throat and began reading. He was hesitant at first and then fell into the story. The Sunset Kid was trapped by the villain, but he had a way out.

"He's the fastest gun in the West," Greg explained. He went back to reading, "'. . . and the Kid whipped out his six-shooter and blazed away. He never missed. Every slug hit right where it should. Blackie groaned, clutched his chest and keeled over. "You got me, Kid," he said with his final breath.'"

Greg jerked away from his recitation when Anna gasped. She leaped to her feet and let out a cry of pure anguish. Never had Greg seen such abject fear on anyone's face. Hand over her mouth, she ran away. For a moment, he wondered if she was acting out the characters. The disappearing thud of her feet told him she wasn't playacting. She was hightailing it away from the stream. From him. He heard her sobbing.

"Anna, wait. Don't go. What is it?" He took a few steps after her and then stopped. There wasn't anything to say if he overtook her. She was frightened by the words in a crummy dime novel.

He flung it away and stormed off. Greg got a dozen paces before he slowed and finally turned back to the stream. The book had fallen into a bush. Some of the pages were torn. Carefully pulling it away from the impaling twigs, he smoothed out the lurid cover and tucked it back under his waistband in the middle of his back.

He should have stayed home and done his chores. Whatever had frightened Anna was beyond him soothing her right now.

Dejected, he returned to the church and mounted. There wasn't any reason to go inside to speak with her. He turned his horse toward the Circle P and galloped away. The sooner he got to familiar territory the better.

CHAPTER 27

"That one. I want that one," Kennard said. He climbed up on the corral railing and leaned in. The colt reared and lashed out with its front hooves.

"Get down, you fool," Race Cooper whispered. He grabbed a handful of Kennard's shirt and pulled him to the ground. He wanted to shake some sense into Kennard, but that'd take more time and effort than he wanted to expend. Right now he wanted to steal a horse and get away before the rancher caught them.

If beating sense into Kennard's thick skull wasn't possible, Race Cooper wanted to try persuasion.

"That one's not broken yet."

"It's a good-looking horse." Kennard wasn't backing down. If anything, denying him the horse made him more obstinate.

"Race is right. Look at it. The horse is too small yet to support you," Ron Marcus said. "Lose fifty pounds and maybe then it would make a good mount for you."

"Quiet, both of you," Cooper snapped. "If you wake them up in the house, we'll have a fight on our hands. That's not gone too good for us."

"I want to steal all his horses." Kennard snarled like a

feral animal. "His name's Brannigan, and he's responsible for catching us before. Make him suffer."

Cooper pushed the men toward the corral behind the barn where a dozen Circle P horses were penned. He was tired of dealing with these two, but he needed them. Three more of the gang had left camp and never returned. While the Warknife marshal was always on the prowl, he hadn't left town after suffering that fiasco in Cutbank. That told him he lost riders with his gang because they no longer trusted him to bring them good jobs. They certainly had nothing to fear from the marshal, not hidden up in the mountains far from Warknife.

Cooper wondered if it had been worth the effort to lure Brannigan and Southern away from the jailhouse so Kennard and Marcus could be sprung.

"We'll need more horses than just one for me," Kennard said. "We can do it like the Hole in the Wall gang. Leave horses all along our escape route. After we rob them ranchers of their money, we can get on and ride and ride and ride, if we have plenty of spare mounts."

"One horse," insisted Cooper. "They might not miss it or think it got out and is on the loose hunting for a maverick herd."

"We ain't seen any mavericks," Kennard said. "The ranchers in these parts catch 'em and break 'em. Look at that one."

"The dun?" asked Marcus. "It's a good-looking horse. You taking it?"

"He's taking the gelding. That one," Cooper said. "It's not flashy and won't be missed."

"How do you know it's not one of them Brannigans' personal horses? They'd notice it missing straightaway," Kennard said.

"So taking the colt wouldn't warn them?"

"You said they'd think it escaped. The colt's more likely to jump the corral fence than any of them." Kennard walked the perimeter, studying the horses.

Cooper rested his hand on his six-shooter. Then he reached out and shoved Marcus.

"Go lasso the gelding. Be quick about it. The longer we stand around yapping, the more likely we are to get caught."

"You afeared of Brannigan?" Kennard thrust out his jaw. "I ain't. If that rock fall hadn't bottled us up along the trail, he'd never have caught us. Him and that tin star lawdog from town."

Cooper still stung from the cuts he'd taken falling down the side of the steep hill. He had escaped and these two had been too stupid to get away. And they had been too cowardly to go out in a blaze of glory, shooting it out with Brannigan and Southern. That rankled now because he had to nursemaid them.

Kennard's horse had broken its leg after the jail escape. Shooting it had left the gang one short on mounts. The Circle P was the closest source of replacement horses. As he looked at the remuda, he seriously thought Kennard and Marcus might be onto something. Steal all the horses. They would come in handy after the bank robbery—if Dexter ever told him what he needed to know to do decent planning.

The half-hearted bank robbery attempt had been a diversion and nothing more. Still, he had learned valuable details about the roads to the bank—and from. The quick look he'd taken into the bank showed the spherical safe. If they had to blow that, even the indolent Cutbank marshal would have time to gather a posse. They had to hit when the safe wasn't locked, steal all twenty thousand and be gone. Fast.

For that to happen, all his men needed to be astride a strong horse.

Cooper looked at Kennard with some scorn. He wondered if the man had even reloaded the round he'd used to put down his broken-legged horse.

"Got it," Marcus said. He balanced on the corral rail and tugged on the lariat. He cast and roped the gelding on the first try.

"Lead it out of the corral," Cooper said. "Don't let any of the other horses get out."

"They're mighty skittish," Kennard said. "Can't stand the smell of freedom, maybe. Come on, you cayuses, run for the hills. Go on!"

Cooper swung his six-gun and connected the barrel in the side of Kennard's head. He yelped and clutched his temple.

"What'd you do that for?"

"Don't let them out. I told you."

"You're mighty quick with pistol whipping folks, ain't you?" Kennard said. "I saw what you did to that deputy."

"You wanted to shoot him down," Cooper said. "There wasn't any call to do that. A dead lawman would have angered the whole town, and they'd still have a posse out hunting for us."

"He's right, Kennard," Marcus said, leading the gelding out. "The deputy's feelings got hurt. He wasn't too bright so they won't think much of how we got out. Lay him out in a coffin, though, and he'd become a hero."

"A martyr," grunted Cooper. "Go into the barn and get yourself enough tack to stay on the horse's back."

"I ain't ridin' bareback," Kennard said, still rubbing his temple. He glared at Cooper but obeyed.

"Don't think too much about what my partner says,"

Marcus whispered to Cooper. He tried not to spook the horse. "He'll be there to help out when we rob that bank."

"I know he's just a mite touchy," Cooper said. He rested his hand on his six-shooter again. The way everything came down against him, he was ready to lash out. Pummeling Dexter had given him a moment's satisfaction. Shooting Kennard between the eyes might give a more lasting gratification.

He looked over his shoulder as Kennard returned, a saddle hoisted up onto his shoulder. Without a word, he saddled the gelding and stepped up. The horse was well trained and didn't try bucking off its new rider.

Cooper cringed when Kennard let out a rebel yell and galloped off.

No light came on in the ranch house. It was a still night, but the corral was some distance from the house. Luck rode with him enough that night to keep from a shootout with Brannigan and his boys. Before the bank robbery, he wanted to keep a low profile. Afterward, let the whole damned territory come after him. He'd be rich and far, far away.

He silently mounted and galloped after Kennard. Marcus brought up the rear. It only took a few minutes for them to overtake Kennard. He had gotten lost and wasn't able to find the trail head leading back to their hideout.

Cooper said nothing as he studied the stars to get his bearings. A few wispy clouds obscured the Big Dipper, but finding the North Star was easy enough as wind blew the clouds away. He trotted past Kennard on his way up the new trail they'd found leading to their hideout. The old one was still blocked by the rock fall. Nothing less than a few sticks of dynamite would open that route again. But this way was as convenient.

He heard the cattle moving about in the distance. He caught his breath. How many rustled head mingled with the

Circle P beeves? A hundred? More? He had left them among the properly branded cows when the lure of the Cutbank robbery had been dumped in his lap.

Trading a few dollars for thousands still made sense to him, even if it split his gang down the middle.

He led the way up the winding trail into the mountains. Kennard and Marcus trailed him, arguing the entire way. When they had first joined up, he thought they hated each other's guts. Now he realized they hated the idea of not arguing over the most trivial things. He shook it off. They would only be riding with him for a few more days.

If Dexter didn't fail him. And if he did, he'd round up the cattle and be on his way. Getting in touch with the rancher willing to pay him ten dollars a head would be easy enough—if the blackguard had any money left after chipping in to pay for the railroad spur.

Too many problems and not enough solutions. Cooper had to focus his attention on one thing at a time or everything would fall apart.

"Finally," Kennard called. "Back to camp. Think there's any coffee left?" He trotted past Cooper toward the nearest campfire. Marcus followed.

Cooper veered away and headed for the back of the camp where he had pitched a lean-to. This was as close to a headquarters as he wanted. He sucked in his breath when he saw a horse staked nearby.

He slid the leather thong off the hammer holding his Colt in its holster while he rode. Kennard had his horse in preparation for the bank robbery. And now Dexter had returned. Once and for all the matter of times and guards would be settled.

Cooper remained in the saddle as he looked down on Dexter. The man hunkered down beside the low-banked fire. He poked it with a stick to coax the embers back into small flames to heat the coffeepot.

"There's not much left. I got the first cup," Dexter said. "If you want any, you'll have to fix it yourself. Might be just as well. That's terrible coffee."

"This is my campsite," Cooper said. "That's my coffee."

Dexter stood and looked around the camp. He laughed harshly.

"You barely have enough men left to pull off the robbery. Maybe I should rustle up my own gang." He laughed even harder. "That's what I need to do. *Rustle* up some help."

"Do you have the information or not?"

"Are you fixing on shooting me if I don't?"

"Will it come to that?" Cooper twisted slightly to free up his six-shooter as Dexter reached for his six-gun.

"Don't go for that iron. You are one nervy gent." Dexter reached into his coat pocket rather than pushing the coat-tail away from his holster. Showing infinite care, he drew out three sheets of paper.

"Is that everything I need?"

Dexter shook his head. He spread the sheets out and held them up.

"A detail or two is missing. That's my insurance against you throwing down on me and finishing off the robbery without me."

Cooper dropped to the ground and walked over. The fire lay between them. The aroma of burning pine mingled with harsh coffee. He reached out. Dexter hesitated for a moment, then passed over the papers.

Cooper didn't bother looking at them. He pointed to a rock.

"Set yourself down. We've got a few matters to discuss."

"That sounds serious," Dexter said. "Am I going to like it?"

"We can both come out of this richer, if we cooperate."

"You want us to throw in together? To be partners?"

"Equal partners," Cooper said. "You've got everything we need to know about the bank and when the money will be moved. I saw the safe. If we have to blow it, getting away will be chancy."

"Unless you have a miner used to blasting, you can blow the money to hell and gone," Dexter said. "I've asked around. There aren't any miners, current or former, in this camp."

"Recruiting one now is out of the question." Cooper poked at the coffeepot. From the slosh there was enough left for one good cup.

"We'll need six men, minimum. Eight or ten are better," Dexter said.

"You heard what happened out on the trail? I got away, but Kennard and Marcus ran afoul of the Warknife lawman."

"I've been wondering about that," Dexter said. "You sprung them real slick. Decoying the rancher and the marshal to Cutbank was smart."

"I got a chance to look over the bank," Cooper said.

"That's not what was on my mind. How'd the marshal know about the bank robbery?" Dexter watched Cooper. The gang leader's face slowly showed a trace of anger. The truth of it all dawned on Dexter. He grinned ear to ear. "Kennard and Marcus spilled their guts about the Cutbank robbery, didn't they?"

"I knew they would the instant they were taken into custody. Southern and Brannigan wouldn't have been at the bank if one of their prisoners hadn't told them everything about the plan. Nobody else knew of the robbery."

"They thought to set a trap for you, but you used them leaving the jail unguarded to spring your two loco weeds."

"Two loco weeds who warned the law about the robbery." Cooper grit his teeth together. "I knew they would when they got caught." He fixed Dexter with a steely stare.

"It'd be a real shame if they got shot during the actual robbery."

"That'd be real fitting, wouldn't it? But it comes with a price."

"What price, Dexter? You'll get more from the loot."

"I got family around here somewhere. Help me find my nieces. Three girls."

"In exchange for losing Kennard and Marcus?" Cooper saw all sorts of possibilities.

Dexter spit on his palm and held it out over the fire. Cooper duplicated the action and shook.

"There's enough coffee left for each of us to get half a cup," he said.

"Seem fair. For partners."

Race Cooper knew their partnership lasted about as long as it took to drink the bitter coffee. But that was all right. He'd end up rich and a hundred miles out of Wyoming Territory.

CHAPTER 28

"He's playing his cards close to the vest," Chris Southern said. "I flat out asked when the money was going to be stashed in the bank and he refused to tell me."

"I can't fault Hutchinson for that, but I asked Jack Lowry. He wouldn't tell me, either," Ty Brannigan said. "I let him know I didn't appreciate that. It's my money he's going to be using to pay off the railroad."

"Some of it's your money," Southern corrected. He lounged back in his chair and stared at the corner of his desk. He itched to lift his boots up, lean back and take a nap. The only thing stopping him was his deputy sweeping up the jail.

Conrad hummed to himself as he worked.

Ty saw this annoyed Southern as much as it did him.

"Let's take a quick patrol around town," Ty suggested. "Deputy Conrad can hold down the fort while we're gone."

Conrad looked up with dull eyes and muttered something about Ty not being a lawman. Ty almost told him he didn't think Conrad was much of one, either, but sowing discord among men supposedly on their side of the law wasn't a good idea.

Southern got to his feet, hitched up his gun belt and said

to his deputy, "If you take a nap in one of the cells, don't lock yourself in."

He herded Ty from the jail into the bright morning sun. Warknife was peaceable enough with the citizens going about their business. It was hard to believe rustling and robbery and all manner of killing had swept through the land around town. This was the Warknife Ty knew and called home, not the one filled with gunfights and jailbreaks.

"Lowry should stash all that money here and not in Cutbank," Southern said. "Buckman's as likely to let them robbers tote the money away as he is to catch them."

"I admit Diego Salazar is a better banker. Even if he is my father-in-law," Ty said. "But Lowry has his reasons for dealing out of Cutbank. After all, that's where the railroad depot will be."

"Just as well," said Southern. "Having a locomotive spewing out soot and making noise'd ruin Warknife. Let Buckman get the blame for things going wrong."

"He's an honest enough marshal," Ty said. "He's just . . . lacking in certain skills." He looked over his shoulder in the direction of the jailhouse. Conrad had closed the door to keep his nap from being disturbed by anyone passing by in the street. "I've sent a telegram to the railroad home office asking when they needed the money. That'd give me an idea when Lowry would muster his guards."

"Didn't get an answer, did you, Ty?" Southern grinned crookedly. "I tried the same trick. They ignored me, too, me the Warknife marshal and deputy sheriff of these fine lands all the way to Baldy Butte."

"It's good for them to be cautious, but I've got the feeling the robbers know exactly what Lowry is planning," Ty said.

"I tried to find out who knew those details," Southern said. "The Cattle Growers Association doesn't. Or nobody'll fess up to knowing."

"If we think this through logically there ought to be an answer buried somewhere. To get enough firepower, he'll have to go to the Army," Ty said.

They looked at each other. The same thought bubbled up.

"The post commander's told his second in command, who told his sergeant," Ty said.

"Who got drunk at the sutler's and told anyone who'd buy him a drink every mother-loving detail."

"Chris, we need to convince Lowry to let us escort the money."

"Or change the details around. We can get the robbers to come galloping up again and fall into a real trap."

"Not even if you deputized every man in all of Warknife and surrounded Cutbank with our posse would that work. We can't go to the well too often."

"I'm not gonna be out a dime, Ty. Your money's fixing to be snuck away. Or outright stolen. But having such a big robbery done almost under my nose is worse than having a canker sore where I set myself down. Every move reminds me of my predicament."

They walked in silence for a block. Ty finally put together pieces of an idea to share with his friend.

"Let's see about the cattle mixed in with my herd. I haven't checked them in a while."

"You want to get your boy to come with us?"

"Matt's got his hands full training a colt. He's doing a fine job of it."

"I'm going to need a new mount soon enough. Mine's getting a little long of tooth."

"Like its rider," Ty joshed. "You'd better not let Blue hear you talk about getting a replacement. I'm not sure he's ready to be put out to pasture."

"Out to pasture," mused Southern. "That sounds like a decent future. But me, I'd rather be put out to stud."

"You're spouting off all kinds of nonsense today," Ty said. "Blue will buck you off. And Molly? Your wife's likely to bury you where not even the coyotes'd dig up your bony carcass if she caught you cheating on her."

"That'll never happen. She's feeling poorly, and there's no call to make her exert herself burying my bony old corpse. I think too much of her."

The two men got their horses headed in the direction of the Circle P southern pasture, enjoying back-and-forth banter to take their minds off more serious matters. As they came to the edge of the grassy expanse, Ty said, "It's getting strange out here of late. Greg claimed one of our horses was missing. Some gear is gone from the barn, too."

"Just one horse?" Southern hiked his leg up and curled it around the pommel, leaning forward. His popping joints caused Ty to look in his direction.

"You're scaring the herd. Keep that up and they'll stampede."

"You do have the strangest problems," Southern said. "Too many cows and not enough horses. Did you ever identify the brand on your adopted strays?"

"Never did. I should ask Lowry. He can post a notice with the Cattle Growers Association. Truth is, it's slipped my mind with all the riding around trying to capture bank robbers and men escaping from your jail."

"Want to capture some rustlers?"

"I reckon so. What did you have in mind?" Ty jerked around when the marshal pointed to the far side of the grazing herd.

"Those aren't your cowhands, are they?"

Ty slid his Henry from its sheath and checked the magazine. It was fully loaded.

"I'll take that as a 'no,'" Southern said. He checked his smoke wagon, then pulled out Old Suzy. The ten-gauge shotgun had reach, but they were still too far for it to be of much use.

Without a word, they rode toward the herd, slowly to avoid drawing attention. The rustlers worked through the herd, cutting out a hundred head. Ty wasn't close enough to see the brands, but a few were the Broken W. The rest were his. Circle P cattle. The outlaws finally came to take what they thought had been so well hidden.

Fattening the rustled cattle on his graze was one thing. Stealing his prize cows was something else.

He and the marshal made their way through the cattle. Some reluctantly moved out of their way. Others stood their ground, defying him to make them move. Ty had spent long years on the range and knew which to prod aside and which to avoid. Some were downright ornery. Others only wanted to be left alone to eat the juicy tufts of grass and soak up the sun.

He and Southern had ridden together long enough to work as a team without exchanging orders. Ty lifted his rifle and took a bead. He counted to three, then fired. His rifle bullet sang through the air toward a rustler the same instant the marshal's shotgun belched out its heavy load of double-ought buckshot.

Ty's target slumped forward and seemed to melt. He ran down the side of his horse and thudded to the ground. Southern's victim seemed to erupt. He threw his hands high in the air, stood in the stirrups, and then was lifted away to fall in a bloody shower.

For a moment the world froze like a painting. Ty and Southern took aim again. Cows looked up. Rustlers hunted for the source of the death coming their way. Then it all changed in an instant.

The cattle stampeded. The rustlers, caught among the cattle, fought to stay astride their horses. If they landed on the ground, thundering hooves would pound them to grisly pulp.

Ty and Southern fired again. This time their shots missed, but the reports added to the confusion.

"Hands in the air. You're under arrest!" Southern's gravelly voice carried over the thudding of so many cattle's hooves.

Ty didn't expect the rustlers to give up easily. And they didn't. He got off four more shots, winging one and scattering the others. Southern chose not to shoot again. He charged forward toward the rustler who gave the orders. Capture the boss and the others would be thrown into confusion.

More confusion, Ty thought. If the rustlers thought for a second, they'd see that they outnumbered the law by three to one.

Ty and Southern fought to keep their horses under control. Cattle smacked into them and sent them reeling. Ty called out an instinctive warning when one rustler tumbled from horseback. The downed man's cries were short-lived. A heifer stepped on him, let out an aggrieved moo and ran off.

"They're getting away!" Southern reloaded Old Suzy and got off two more shots. All he did was encourage the rustlers to ride faster.

Ty had better luck. He knocked another rider out of the saddle.

"One got away," Ty said.

"Two. One cut away from his partners and is riding alongside the stampede."

"Let 'im go."

"That's you, Ty, that's purely you. Always going for the big payoff."

They bent forward and brought their horses to a full

gallop. Wind whipped past Ty's weathered cheeks. He felt more alive than he had in weeks. Finally he saw an end to his troubles—some of his troubles.

His dun veered sharply and splashed through a stream as he pursued what looked to be two rustlers. Muddled trails hinted at other rustlers that hadn't been in the gunfight. Not knowing the actual number made chasing any of them downright dangerous. Not seeing Southern warned him he had to deal with this pack of wolves all by himself. That didn't slow him. He struggled up the far bank and reached a rise.

All of the outlaws rode hell-bent away, caught up in rolling land that made it hard to figure how many he chased as they hit a rise and then dipped down on the far side of a hill. He brought his rifle to his shoulder and took as careful aim as possible on his heaving, shaky horse. The Henry barked. The trailing rustler grabbed his shoulder. He tried to stay in the saddle. Before Ty got off another shot, his target fell heavily.

The others never looked back or gave a second's thought to saving their partner. They kept riding. Overtaking them was out of the question. His dun was tired from so much flat-out running. Ty walked his horse forward, keeping his rifle trained in the direction of the rustler sprawled on the ground.

His caution proved necessary. When he came within ten yards, the outlaw reared up and began fanning his six-shooter. At that range and fanning the gun hitting anything was a matter of luck.

He had run out of luck. Ty hadn't. The Henry barked again. The fallen man sagged onto his side. He had been playing possum before. Ty doubted he was this time.

"Toss your gun away," he called, coming within a few feet now. He trained his rifle on the prone man.

The outlaw tried to crawl away but lacked the strength. Ty fired. The bullet grazed the man's wrist. Even with his six-gun inches away, there wasn't any way he'd point it at Ty.

Ty dismounted and approached slowly. The man lay belly down and kicking feebly. One arm was pinned under him. More than one outlaw carried a hideout gun. Ty was ready to end the man's life if he rolled over with a derringer clutched in his good hand.

The tiny trapped animal sounds convinced Ty all the fight had gone out of the rustler. He knelt beside him and rolled him onto his back. All the blood had drained from the man's face, but his eyes carried nothing but pure hatred.

"You want to die here or stand trial? There's a chance a judge won't sentence you to hang."

Blood dribbled down the man's chin. He gurgled out, "I give up."

Ty wasn't sure if he was happy about it. Then he reflected on the matter. Satisfying his own sense of justice wasn't in the cards. Let a jury and judge decide.

The sound of an approaching horse caused him to swing around, rifle ready. He relaxed. Chris Southern trotted up.

"You got yours all hogtied yet?"

"He gave up. What happened to yours?" Ty asked.

Southern patted the empty spot on his saddle where a lariat usually hung.

"He's all trussed up. Unless he uproots a big oak tree, he's not going anywhere."

"Catch this one's horse. He's in no condition to walk back to your jail."

"Reckon not. You shot him up good," the marshal said. "This time let's see if I can't do a better job of keeping a pair of prisoners locked up." With that he trotted off to fetch the outlaw's wayward horse.

Ty looked at his prisoner. It hadn't started as a good day, but it ended that way. He could hardly wait to get home and tell the family. Beatriz would protest that he'd risked his life, but she'd be proud of him. She might not put that pride into words, but actions spoke louder with her.

That was fine with Ty. It was the Brannigan way.

CHAPTER 29

Race Cooper pored over the papers Dexter had given him. Everything was spelled out. Lowry had altered the original plan of collecting and depositing the money. Each rancher delivering his share made holding up Lowry before he got to the bank impossible. The money would be deposited in the bank from a dozen different sources. Any one of those streams of rancher money wasn't worth bothering with. Hold up one or two and the rest would be skittish and possibly back out of the deal entirely. The pile once they'd all been dumped into the Cutbank bank was the only prize worth the risk.

One detail annoyed him. There weren't any gold deposits. The ranchers all contributed greenbacks. He knew having so much scrip drawn on local banks was a problem. Gold coin could be spent about anywhere in the US of A. But having the entire deposit in paper money carried one benefit.

He wouldn't need a wagon to cart off the heavy gold coins. Cooper heaved a deep sigh of resignation. He had dreamed of running his hands over gold bars. Now he had to console himself with saddlebags full of bills.

In a way that was a distraction. Selling the robbery to his gang when they expected gold might be hard. The ones that remained were greedy enough to agree to any robbery where they each made off with a thousand dollars.

Or more.

Cooper read through the notes and let a plan form to take new facts into account. Most interesting to him were the details of the cavalry company sent to guard the money as it was taken from the bank to the railroad office down south. Twenty or more soldiers were tasked with protecting the shipment. Attacking once the Army patrol assembled outside the bank was impossible. He'd need ten times the gang he had, and even then success was not guaranteed.

The longer the soldiers held off the robbers, the more likely that reinforcements came rushing to their aid.

"No way can I fight every bluecoat in the territory," he decided.

A dozen crazy plans fluttered past, teasing him with possibilities and being dashed by a simple question: what can go wrong? In every scheme something simple prevented him from waltzing away with the money.

"Simple. Keep it simple," he said aloud. He stretched out on his bedroll and stared up at the gathering clouds. Heavy dark underbellies promised rain later in the day. Cooper tried making patterns out of the clouds but saw nothing. Nothing. Nothing.

His anger mounted.

The sound of horses coming up the trail leading to the Circle P pastures brought him around. He got to his feet and watched the two men as they looked around the camp in panic. When he called to them, they hung their heads and looked as if they had ridden a thousand miles without a single stop.

Something bad had happened. Cooper looked up to a sentry posted high in the rocks, expecting to see the warning flashed down that a posse thundered up on them. The sentry waved an all clear. Whatever had gone wrong had saved the camp from attack.

"Where have you been?" he called. Seeing neither man intended to answer, Cooper hitched up his gun belt and walked across the campsite to stand between them.

When he did, they averted their eyes. He rested his hand on his Colt.

"Where have you been?"

"We took a ride, Race." The man on his left sounded like a little boy lying about stealing the family egg money.

He turned to the other.

"Yeah, that's it. Just out ridin' 'round, not doin' nuthin'."

Cooper reached up and grabbed a handful of denim shirt and pulled hard. The man crashed to the ground. Before his partner had a chance to light a shuck, Cooper jumped and got a double handful of this one's vest. His weight coming back down plucked the rider from the saddle and sent him flying. When the rider crashed into a cooking fire, he upset the iron tripod and spilled coffee from the dangling pot. He yelped and rolled away, swatting at flames trying to set fire to his vest.

"Where'd you go? I gave orders that nobody was to stray far from camp."

When neither man spoke up, he drew his six-gun and pointed it at the one closest to him on the ground.

"Three," he said loudly. Others in camp came around to see what the fuss was all about. "Two." He cocked the pistol. "One."

"Wait, Race, please, don't shoot. We didn't mean to try to rustle them cows. It was all Clay's idea."

"Where's Clay?" Cooper forced himself not to pull the trigger. From the way these two had returned, he already knew the answer. When he got the answer he wasn't the least bit surprised.

"He's dead. Or caught. No, I'm sure. He's plumb dead."

"Don't you go pointin' that gun at my partner," the other rustler said. He finished brushing embers off his clothing and came over.

Cooper saw movement from the corner of his eye. With a wide, smooth, powerful swing he brought his Colt around to crash into the side of the man's head. His eyes rolled up and he fell forward, stiff as a board. He was knocked out before he hit the ground.

"Tell me everything. Clay decided to go take the cattle we hid in the Circle P herd, right?"

The man's head bobbed up and down. He kept looking at his motionless partner stretched out on the ground.

"You decided to take more than the cows marked with that Broken W brand. You cut out Circle P beeves."

The man's head threatened to come loose from all the nodding.

"What went wrong?"

It took two tries before the story finally spilled out. Everything Cooper worried about had gone wrong. The stolen cattle were his backup if he had to abandon plans for the Cutbank robbery. Now even a few hundred dollars off those cows was denied him.

"Are you sure the Warknife marshal was with the rancher?"

"The two of them ambushed us. Shot us out of the saddle 'fore we knowed what was happening. Stampeded the herd and Elfego, Elfego he got all trampled to death. Clay got shot in the back."

"Did they capture anyone?" Cooper read the answer. He came as close to giving up and riding away as he'd ever been. He wasn't always right, he wasn't always too bright, but he never gave up.

He came within a hair's breadth of giving up now.

"Yeah, two guys. I don't know their names. They were pals with Clay."

The man stared at him, fear growing as he read death in Cooper's expression. Before he pulled the trigger, the steady clop of a horse caught his attention. Cooper looked up to see Dexter motioning to him. He lowered the hammer on his pistol and stalked off without another word. A collective sigh of relief went up not only from the man on the ground but everyone else gathered to watch.

"I got something to pass along," Dexter said. He dismounted and looked around the camp. A crooked smile twisted his lips. "You've been busy with discipline problems, haven't you?"

"They tried to steal the cattle hidden in the Circle P herd," Cooper said.

"That was a damn fool thing to do. Why get everyone stirred up, but it does explain what I heard. I ran into a rancher on his way to a meeting in Cutbank tonight. The Cattle Growers Association is about ready to put out the call for the money."

"After Clay Quinn got himself killed and two of his men arrested, the meeting will call for added vigilance watching their herds."

"Added vigilance, yeah," Dexter said. "The Cutbank marshal's not worth a bucket of warm spit, but the one in Warknife is trying to patrol the entire county."

"Spread himself thin," Cooper said to himself.

"I was thinking this is a golden opportunity tonight. If we snuck into the meeting, there's no telling what we'd overhear."

"The ranchers know everyone else," Cooper pointed out.

"There's always a steady tide of cowpunchers moving through. Some of them don't know their own crew. What's said in public's nothing compared to whispered conversations. We get an earful of those and you can come up with a decent plan for the robbery." Dexter fixed him with a sharp stare.

Cooper bristled. It shouldn't be that apparent he hadn't figured out how best to rob the bank yet. With even fewer men in the gang, his options were shrinking. Taking on the Army troopers had never been a good idea. With Clay and his crew all shot up or arrested, they weren't even able to tangle with a squad, much less a company.

Not stealing gold looked better and better with his diminished gang. Greenbacks could be stuffed into a few gunnysacks without need of pack animals to cart it all off.

He looked around. The two who'd tried to take the rustled cattle huddled together, licking their wounds. If he had swung a tad harder, he would have crushed one skull. Not gunning down his partner felt like a missed opportunity now.

"I haven't forgotten," Dexter said softly. He looked to the tiny fire where Kennard and Marcus huddled, whispering furiously. "They might make good decoys instead of shooting them." He held up his hand to keep Cooper's protest at bay. "Not that I won't waste a couple rounds on their worthless carcasses, if you still want me to."

"This is going to work out fine. Has anyone in Cutbank seen you? The marshal? The banker?"

"Nope. I've been real careful about that. No idea what Thomas did, and we look a lot alike. But with the excitement of the deal finally commencing, nobody'll pay me a bit of attention."

"Let's go sneak in and find what secrets the Cattle Growers Association has to reveal." For the first time in days, Race Cooper felt a surge of confidence.

"I was right. There's so many crowding into the town hall nobody'll spot us, even if they'd caught sight of us earlier." Dexter pushed his hat back on his forehead and began moving around the perimeter to get to a spot near the head table.

"Wait. Them. They're here. The Warknife marshal and Brannigan."

"Have they ever seen you? This is the first time I've been close to them. The fact is, I'm thinking of asking after my three girls. They might know." Dexter sounded eager to bring unwanted attention to them. Cooper restrained himself from pistol whipping the man for such stupidity.

Cooper grabbed Dexter's arm and held him back.

"Don't get cocky. They've killed and jailed half my gang."

"Not the good half," Dexter said, laughing.

A tall, thin man stood and rapped the butt of his six-shooter on the table. He had to do it a second time to get the ranchers to quiet down.

"Y'all know me. Jack Lowry. You've entrusted me to head up the Cattle Growers Association this year and do what's necessary."

"Get on with it, Jack. We've got ranches to run."

"Before the big business, Ty Brannigan's going to say a few words."

The tall, lanky rancher rose and waited for the murmurs to die down.

"That there's the man you got away from? You're either a slippery little weasel or the luckiest varmint in all of Wyoming," Dexter said.

Cooper considered the ruckus he'd cause if he slugged Dexter. He turned away and faced Brannigan squarely. The rancher stood behind the table with less than ten feet separating them. Brannigan was too intent on saying his piece to notice. Cooper stepped behind a portly rancher to hide himself. Brannigan might not know whom he looked at but the man's sharp eyes could pick out a stranger. That might be good enough for him to spring into action.

Worse, the Warknife marshal lounged against the far wall. He balanced his long-barreled ten-gauge beside him where it'd come into his grip as fast as lightning. Cooper doubted the marshal cared much if he took out a few ranchers if he killed himself a rustler.

"Don't see the Cutbank lawman anywhere," Dexter whispered. Cooper waved him to silence. Brannigan cleared his throat and his baritone voice boomed out, filling the courthouse.

"My sons and I found stolen cattle grazing with my herd. The cattle were scrawny. I think they were rustled but too weak to go much farther so the rustlers left them, thinking we'd never spot a few extra head as they fattened up."

"I ain't had any of mine stole," piped up the man directly in front of Cooper.

"Neither Marshal Southern nor I recognize the brand. But we'll find where they came from eventually. What I wanted to warn you about was how the rustlers swooped down and tried to take not only the ones they'd left but a couple hundred head of Circle P stock. Marshal Southern and I stopped them. Killed a couple and put two into the Warknife jail."

"Where's Marshal Buckman? He has to protect us!"

"Not likely to happen," said another. "He's hardly stirred from Cutbank since he was hired. Truth is, he told me guarding my herd was my business."

"We need a vigilance committee!" That cry went up and circled the room before dying down when Brannigan used his Colt .44 as a gavel to bring some order to the rowdy gathering.

"I just wanted to let you know. What we do to stop further

thieving can be talked over later. Right now, what Mister Lowry has to say is more important."

A few grumbled that nothing was more important than protecting their livestock, but they quieted when Lowry again took the floor.

"We're getting real close to collecting the money to send to the railroad headquarters. I can't give you any details to protect the money, but rest assured I've got plenty of firepower to make sure the money gets to the right people."

"Soon?" someone hollered.

Cooper saw from the corner of his eye that Dexter was pushing his luck calling out the question.

"Real soon," Lowry said evasively. "We got other details to hash out. Where's the terminal going to be in Cutbank? Outside of town or down the block from the courthouse?"

"Have the station depot put in near the Lulu Belle Saloon," a man in the back suggested. "There ain't much else to do but drink ourselves cross-eyed once we load our cattle onto a train car."

Arguments about the location flowed about like the ripples in a big lake. Cooper stepped back, then made his way to where Dexter leaned against a supporting wood column.

"Let's clear out." Cooper felt a curious blend of fear and exhilaration. There wasn't much chance Brannigan or Southern recognized him, but he had heard all he needed to know. The ranchers were riled up about rustlers. That took away any hint that they would ride herd on the money.

"Two days, just like my spy said." He saw that the men were growing skeptical and needed something more certain or they'd all desert.

"What do you mean?"

"They're bringing in money from all over in two days.

The soldiers will arrive a little after dawn, be given the money, and escort it to its rightful owners at the Wyoming and Colorado headquarters."

"How much rank does your spy have?"

Dexter frowned. Reluctantly he said, "It's the company sergeant."

"Better and better. Come on. I'll tell you what I need from him. This is going to be one quick and easy robbery. Mark my words, easy as pie."

"If it's not, we'll all get strung up," Dexter said.

Race Cooper felt the last of his uncertainty evaporate. Only exhilaration remained. They wouldn't get strung up by a vigilance committee formed by the ranchers. But more than one of his gang would find out that going against his orders was downright dumb.

CHAPTER 30

Greg Brannigan moved like a ghost. He picked up each foot and placed it carefully to keep from stepping on the squeaky floorboards. The second floor of the ranch house needed considerable work, but his pa always put it off. That made sneaking out dangerous.

"He likes going to town and hanging out with the marshal," he said to himself. Greg paused outside his sisters' bedroom. The door was ajar. Soft snoring greeted him.

That was MacKenna. She denied she snored, but he knew better from prowling around after the rest of the family had gone to bed. Tiny sniffles helped him find the dark lump in the other bed. His younger sister Caroline had bad dreams most nights, but never anything reaching the intensity of a nightmare.

Walking faster now, he came to the head of the stairs. Matt's room controlled access like some guardhouse on an Army post. Greg chanced a quick look in. His brother was a light sleeper, but tonight he had slumped over his desk. Whatever book he'd been reading lay open just above his head. The candle had burned down to a nub and snuffed itself out.

Greg gingerly took the steps down one at a time. To trip now meant rousing everyone. More than once he had seen his pa come boiling out of the big bedroom with his Colt gripped for action. It took a loud noise to accomplish that, but he'd seen it happen.

Tynan Brannigan protected his house and his family completely, around the clock and every day of the week.

At the bottom of the stairs, Greg moved faster. He went through the kitchen and sat on the back stoop. His boots slid on easily. From here he ran across the yard to the barn. The closer he got, the more cautious he became.

Someone had stolen one of the horses. He was sure of that, although nobody paid him much heed. To avoid what his pa would say about him not being responsible and tending the horses properly, Matt said the horse had jumped the corral fence and was roaming free, hunting for a herd of mavericks. He had felt guilty about the lie, especially when his pa had agreed that one missing horse didn't mean much.

But what horse stole a saddle and all the rest of the tack?

"Dollars to dimes, that horse is in Desperado's Den now," he said. "Them rustlers stole the horse right out from under our noses."

Why they hadn't taken all the horses in the corral bothered him. But those outlaws were cagy. Take one and they got the response the other Brannigan men showed. They hadn't counted on him, Gregory Brannigan, figuring out their dastardly theft.

He took down a coal oil lamp and lit it, then trimmed the wick enough so only a faint glow showed. Greg put the lamp on a barrel and flopped into the hay beside it. The copy of the dime novel had seen better days. Pages were cracked from being read and reread several times and more than one fell out. Those he stuck back in, but the glue holding them was long gone. He wasn't going to miss a single detail of the thrilling story although he was on his fourth reading. Each time he had stopped short of the final chapter. Savoring that ultimate experience wasn't to be rushed.

He opened the epic story of the Sunset Kid and felt a little let down. Only one more chapter. When he finished it—tonight!—his good friend, his partner, the Sunset Kid would be at the end of his trail.

Greg read each page twice before going on to the next. When the last page emblazoned with THE END faced him, he heaved a deep sigh. Faced with the conclusion of the Kid righting all the wrongs and then moving on with his faithful horse under him, Greg flipped through the brittle pages to the cover. He ran his fingers over it, then opened the book and stared at the first page again.

Realizing he had memorized the entire book, he closed it and tucked it back under his waistband. He should return it to Mister Dempsey. There wasn't any reason to offer it to Anna. He had seen how she reacted when he had read a particularly good scene to her.

"She can't read," he said softly. His mind raced. Maybe he could teach her. Without a pa or ma, she was the head of the family. Every family should be able to read. That's what his ma claimed.

He looked at the faded cover. She had been right about that. Reading had let him ride along with the Sunset Kid.

But Anna? Where would reading get her? He sagged down into the pile of hay. There wasn't a lot of reason for her to learn. Better she find a job somewhere around Warknife.

He came to his feet when the horses in the corral began kicking up a fuss. He looked at the rifles racked on the wall, then grabbed a Winchester. If a horse thief returned for another night's plundering, he had to be ready. The rifle felt heavy and awkward in his grip, though he had fired it many times. But it wasn't his .410, which was back in the house.

Greg slipped out the side door and climbed onto a water barrel to get a better look at the horses. They were all spooked now. He waited, hunting for any sign of movement.

When he saw it, his heart sank. He had wanted the predator to be a human thief, not a prowling coyote. He cocked the rifle. The dark shape froze at the sound, then turned glowing yellow-green eyes toward him. They stared at each other. Neither blinked. Greg took aim but didn't fire. The report would bring everyone in the house running to see what was wrong.

Coyotes and even wolves out roaming by themselves weren't such a big concern. There wasn't a horse in the pen that couldn't fight off the scrawny predator.

The eyes never blinked. Then they vanished. The dark shape turned and ran off into the night. Greg lowered the rifle, feeling as if he had done something good for a change. His pa wouldn't let him go hunt rustlers. Marshal Southern had been with him, but he'd heard them arguing over whether to take Matt.

"Matt," he grumbled. "He's good enough to ride with them. I'm not."

He lowered the Winchester's hammer and jumped down from the barrel. A quick scout of the area showed the horses had settled down, and the coyote was long gone. Greg returned the rifle to the rack, then reluctantly returned to his bed.

Sleep eluded him. He kept asking himself if the Sunset Kid would put up with being ignored the way he was. Finally deciding that he had to find a way to prove his worth, he closed his eyes and dreamed of open ranges and running rustlers to ground.

CHAPTER 31

"You ain't gettin' me to wear that." Kennard stepped back and put his hand on his six-shooter.

Race Cooper looked up. His anger flared. For two cents he'd plug Kennard now. Or signal Dexter to do it. Dexter sat nearby running his fingers over the wool jacket of a Federal soldier's outfit. The brass buttons were tarnished and the hint of gold braid was filthy and looked like black seaweed dangling down. A closer inspection showed tiny moth holes in the wool and more than one that had been inexpertly patched.

Whatever officer who had worn it before had shown no pride at all being in the Army. Cooper squinted. There were even darker patches on the sleeves hinting that the former owner had been stripped of rank. Cooper wanted to tell Kennard the jacket's history matched his own sorry life of being a loser. Instead of arguing, he chose to clear his throat and adapt a command voice.

"Wear it."

"No." Kennard was adamant.

"All right. You don't have to, but you have to ride with us and pretend you're a Union soldier. Only not wearing a uniform. That's part of the plan."

"Ain't pretendin' to be a Federal."

"Keep him at the end of the column," Dexter suggested. "We've only got three uniforms."

Cooper held up his own jacket. It was a tad small across the shoulders and around the waist but it had a captain's bars on the shoulder epaulets and the hat fit. Dexter held up a jacket sporting faded sergeant's stripes. The third uniform—the only other one they had—was a private's. He had checked to see if any of the men remaining in his gang could wear it.

Kennard was the best fit, and he refused. Cooper looked at the man's partner. Marcus came close but the sleeves were too short by a couple inches. Such a misfit always drew unwanted attention. If whoever noticed laughed, that was almost as bad as if they detected the fraud and started slinging lead.

Being noticed was not part of the plan.

"You don't want a share in that twenty thousand?" Dexter slid into his jacket and tugged at the spots where it proved too tight. A seam popped. If the threads gave way, the right arm would fall off entirely.

"Get more uniforms," Ron Marcus suggested. "Ones that fit."

"These are the best we can do. The quartermaster was lucky to steal these. There'll be hell to pay when the captain's uniform is reported missing from the wash." Dexter turned this way and that, as if asking for someone to compliment him on his new look.

Cooper considered telling him to shave. His ragged beard was not very military, even for a frontier post sergeant. As part of his own disguise, Cooper had shaved as clean as he could, even to the point of taking off his mustache.

"You all know what to do?" He eyed Kennard, waiting for him to protest.

"We all ride double file, like them cavalry patrols do. Only we don't have to wear the uniforms," Marcus said petulantly.

"You will line up on Dexter, and I will ride at the head of the column with Marcus beside me, as if he is my striker."

"How much are you gonna pay me for my services, Mister Lieutenant sir?" Marcus sneered.

"You get a cut of twenty thousand dollars," Cooper said, irritated. "And these are captain's bars." He hadn't expected so much opposition to wearing the Federal uniforms to disguise the robbery for what it was.

"Sorry, *sir*," Marcus said. "Is everything else going the way you want, *sir*?"

"Yes, we know the money's in the bank." He glanced at Dexter, who nodded. How Dexter had come by so much information was a mystery, but Cooper knew it had something to do with the man's brother and his connections. That was all he wanted to know.

"This better be good," Kennard said. "Wantin' me to wear *that* uniform and gettin' up so much before dawn."

"It'll be worth it, partner," Ron Marcus said. "Think of that gold. Imagine runnin' your fingers across the smooth, hard gold coins and knowin' they're all yours."

Cooper sucked in his breath. He hadn't told them yet they were stealing greenbacks, not gold. Before he figured out what to say that wouldn't cause a fuss, Dexter spoke up.

"What if there's twice as much money in that there safe? Only it's not gold but greenbacks? Would that bother you much?"

"No gold?" Kennard turned dark and angry. His partner put a hand on his arm to calm him.

"Twice as much?" Marcus said.

"For everyone," Dexter assured him.

Cooper almost laughed. Neither Kennard nor Marcus

saw the way Dexter ran his fingers over the butt of his six-gun. He might as well promise them a ton of money each. They weren't going to live long enough to spend a single nickel.

"No gold?" Kennard repeated. "What else ain't you tellin' us, Cooper?"

"If we don't get on the trail right now, we won't see anything but a future of poverty and regret. Let's ride," Cooper said. "You all know what you're supposed to do."

"If we get split up, where're we supposed to rendezvous?" Kennard's belligerence irritated Cooper even more.

"Back at the camp, that's where. You've been told a dozen times. What's so hard for you to get through your thick skull?"

"I got the feelin' when we show up back here at Desperado's Den that we'll be mighty lonely."

"Go rustle some cattle, then," Cooper snapped. "That worked real good for Clay and his partners. Or fall in line and ride into Cutbank, acting like a soldier out of uniform." He glared at the man. Cooper wondered if Kennard was simply suspicious or if he had gotten wind of what Dexter was going to do after they'd ridden far enough from the bank.

It didn't matter. As long as Kennard played his part, he could be as wary as he wanted—of his leader. Cooper could face him, hands open and empty. Dexter was the one going to pull the trigger.

He'd never see that coming. Cooper smiled, just a little. Then things turned complicated.

He stepped up and settled into the saddle. If they left the horses a ways from the bank, the president or his tellers would never notice they weren't riding with McClellan saddles like a real horse soldier. So much of the plan depended on the banker being nervous and unobservant.

And the rest depended on how fast the robbers rode out of Cutbank.

They made their way the last few miles to the outskirts of Cutbank. He stared at the still-sleeping town and asked Dexter, "Any word from the sergeant about delaying the real company?"

"He said someone had left the corral gate open and the horses all scattered to the four winds. It won't take long to catch them and get on the trail, but he's sure that'll mean at least a half-hour delay."

"Imagine that, a soldier being so careless."

"Imagine that, a sergeant pocketing a hundred dollars for nothing more than forgetting to slip the latch around the corral gate," Dexter said.

"You get a hundred extra out of the loot to make up for that expense," Cooper said.

"I get five hundred extra. The uniforms cost an arm and a leg."

Cooper looked at the man riding beside him decked out in the sergeant's uniform. He knew Dexter cheated him. It didn't matter. They were close to waltzing away with a heap of money. That was a dance he'd enjoy for a good, long time.

"The sun's just poking up over the horizon," Cooper said. "To me, to get rich." Just as if he was a commanding officer, he lifted his hand and then dropped it in the direction of the city. He felt like a commander at that instant, and knew the rest of the robbery would go like a military campaign.

His military campaign.

They galloped into town. Cooper kept looking over his shoulder to be sure the rest of the gang didn't break formation. Anyone seeing them had to believe they were a cavalry unit with only a handful in uniform.

And Cooper also wanted to make sure Dexter didn't shoot him in the back. At this stage, he wasn't sure if the banker would fork over the money to a sergeant or not if their officer wasn't present. Dexter—and Marcus—were ruthless enough to force the banker to open the safe.

He led the gang through Cutbank streets he had scouted earlier. The bank loomed in front of him. A quick breath to settle his nerves and he hit the ground running. Dexter and Marcus followed closely. He straightened his ill-fitting uniform and rapped smartly on the bank door.

"Captain Jones," he bellowed. "Hurry it up. We've got to hit the trail."

The double doors opened an inch. A large eye peered out. He saw the glint of a six-gun in the man's hand.

"You're not the officer who's supposed to take the money." The banker's voice quavered.

"He's got Montezuma's Revenge. I'm his aide-de-camp."

"Jones, you say?"

"Captain Jones. Are you going to open up or do I go back to my post and let you take the money to the railroad yourself?"

"No, don't go. Don't do that!" The door opened farther. The banker's shocked expression told Cooper all he needed to know. His plan worked. Having so much money for so little time in his safe put a tremendous strain on the man. From his pinched face and pale complexion, he might have a brain stroke at any instant.

Cooper crowded past, Dexter and Marcus quickly joining him in the lobby.

"Where's the money?"

"It's still in the safe, Captain. You . . . you're here early. The time lock has to open before I can dial in the combination."

Cooper took a hard look at the safe.

"Open it, sir," he said, trying not to get too anxious.

"It . . . it's a Sargent and Greenleaf Model 2. It's my pride and joy. There's no way I can until the clock allows it."

"How long?" Cooper saw both Dexter and Marcus reaching for their holstered six-guns.

"Well, as I said, you're here early." The banker took his pocket watch out and popped open the lid. He held it up to catch a ray of sunlight slanting in through a high window. "It's any time now. The mechanism is quite accurate, though it seems to be late today."

He shook his pocket watch and turned the stem a couple times to wind it.

Cooper wasn't going to let this obstacle stand in his way. Not after all the work and danger he'd experienced. He didn't have dynamite to blow open the safe. Taking the bank president hostage was his only chance if the cavalry showed up. And they would. It didn't take that long to wrangle their horses, no matter how effective the post sergeant had been shooing them from their corral.

"It's a good thing we got seven men backing us up," Dexter said.

Cooper knew he had the same idea. The only trouble was keeping the men outside from running if they spotted a real bluecoat trotting toward the bank. He hadn't ridden with many of the gang before. The ones who had faced the law all buckled. That made him look hard at Ron Marcus. He and Kennard had spilled their guts about the robbery to avoid standing trial, as if Marshal Southern would have let them go, no matter what they confessed to.

They were untrustworthy cowards and yammered about anything that came into their heads.

"Enough of this," Cooper said, turning. He reached for his gun as a loud click sounded.

"There! That's the time lock releasing the mechanism. My pocket watch is running a trifle slow." The banker bustled over to the spherical safe, used a key and then dialed in a combination.

The circular safe door swung wide.

Cooper stared at the pile of money. The *piles* of money. It hadn't occurred to him that a bank had plenty of cash on hand to run its ordinary business. The twenty thousand of the ranchers' money was only the start.

"The bundle in the center," the banker said. He dropped to his knees and leaned in to pull out what the Army was supposed to guard.

Cooper swung his pistol in a short, vicious arc that ended at the back of the man's head.

"Drag him out," he ordered. He didn't care who obeyed as long as the bank president no longer plugged up the safe door.

Marcus grabbed the banker's ankles and pulled him out, bouncing him along the floor face down. He started to shoot him. Dexter stopped him.

"The money. There's no need to wake up the whole danged town."

Cooper worked like a gopher shoveling out stacks of greenbacks. Behind him Dexter and Marcus stuffed the money into sacks they'd brought in tucked under their belts.

"Both my bags are full," Marcus complained.

"Mine, too," Dexter said. He backed off, staring at Marcus.

"That's six bags of money." To Dexter, Cooper asked, "Can you carry three?"

"I reckon so."

"What? Why'd he?—"

Dexter fired once. His bullet caught Marcus just under the chin as he looked up, and the bullet angled up into his skull. He fell like a soldier at attention, stiff all the way to the floor. The garrison cap he wore quickly soaked through with his blood.

"Let's go. The banker shot him."

"So why didn't we shoot the banker?" Dexter asked. Then he saw the reason.

Cooper fired and hit him in the chest. Dexter staggered back and got out the door, clutching two bags of money.

Kennard rushed in demanding to know what went wrong. Cooper took careful aim and ended him. So much for the other tongue-flapping varmint who had almost cost them the chance to empty the safe.

"Here," Cooper said, heaving two bags of money to the men anxiously waiting. They all had their guns drawn. "Time to hightail it."

He struggled with four bags, slinging two over his horse's haunches and stuffing the other two into his saddle-bags. As he went to mount hands yanked at him, pulling him back. He lost his balance and fell.

Dexter towered over him. His fists were drenched in his own blood. The expression on his face was one of pure hatred.

"You double-crossed me," he snarled. He reared back to drive a hard punch into the supine Race Cooper but stumbled when his victim kicked out hard and crushed a kneecap.

"They're coming. The whole danged town's coming!"

Cooper wasn't sure who shouted the warning, but the rest of his gang turned tail and ran with two bags of money. He fumbled for his own six-shooter but discovered he had lost it.

Dexter moaned and clutched his knee. The blood oozing from his chest soaked the blue wool cavalry trooper's coat.

Cooper shoved him hard. Dexter grabbed wildly and

pulled the two money bags tied to the horse with him. A quick decision put Cooper into the saddle and galloping off. If he'd fought over those other two bags, Dexter would have delayed him long enough for the horde of Cutbank citizens to catch him.

He put his head down and rode. He had two gunnysacks stuffed to the point of straining the seams. That was enough. He wasn't greedy enough to risk losing everything—his life included. But he wished he had aimed better when he shot Dexter.

Race Cooper had to be content with pulling off one hell of a robbery and getting away with it.

CHAPTER 32

"I'll be at the marshal's office," Ty Brannigan told his son. "Can you find something to keep you busy?"

"I reckon I can find something to do," Greg said, trying not to sound too excited.

"You might ask Walt Nobels if there's any day work you can do for him. You might earn two bits." There was always menial labor at the lumberyard. Sweep up sawdust. Move cut planks in the warehouse. Count nails and put them into paper bags so the clerk didn't have to waste time sorting them when a customer asked. There were a lot of small jobs. For a kid.

"That's a good idea, Pa." Greg already looked toward the far end of town. The church steeple poked just above the roof of the town newspaper where lights blazed inside and a steady stream of people came and went. Most of the crowd was Greg's age. The *Warknife Caller* was already being distributed. He saw two youngsters, both a couple years his junior, lugging stacks of the freshly printed paper around to the merchants. If he really wanted a temporary job, asking the editor, Lemuel Wilkins, was better than breaking his back lugging sawn boards around the lumber-yard for Mister Nobels.

Nobels had it in for his pa and any Brannigan, for that

matter. If he got a temporary job, it'd likely be a nasty one. Then Nobels would complain that he hadn't done it well, no matter how diligent he'd been.

Asking for a few hours' work in the newspaper office was a better choice. Greg wasn't sure but he thought he would be the only one working for the editor who could read and write. There had been a reporter who spent more time drinking in the Tophat Saloon or pretending to interview the girls at the Crystal Palace Theater. He had disappeared within a couple weeks. The only other employee Wilkins had ever kept around for longer was a man barely five feet tall but with shoulders as broad as an axe handle. Something about his colorless eyes had always given Greg the willies.

Rumor had it that the short man had left town suddenly after serious allegations about him surfaced. Greg never heard what that might have been, but it had something to do with Josiah Hancock's twin daughters.

Greg knew he could get a couple hours' work out of Wilkins, if he wheedled a mite.

Only earning a few cents while his pa engaged in endless flapdoodle with his friend wasn't near as exciting as talking with Anna.

Ty Brannigan walked off, leaving his son in the middle of the street. Greg wasted no time running past the *Warknife Caller* where Mister Wilkins worked to print more copies on the flatbed press. From the way he cussed, he'd hire Greg in a flash to help out. It was messy, backbreaking work, running that printing press.

But the church beckoned. Anna beckoned.

He slowed when he saw her two sisters outside the church, tending a small garden plot the padre had put in. What he didn't eat, he sold after Sunday mass to pay for small repairs and to help out those needing his charity.

"Gregory!" Jasmine waved when she saw him. Ruth said something behind her hand. The older girl snickered.

He tried to saunter up, all dignified and adult.

"Girls," he said. "Where's—"

He never got the name out. Both of them shouted, "Anna!" at the same instant. Before Greg had a chance to caution them about yelling, Ruth said, "Your boyfriend's here! Don't you go keepin' him waitin'!"

"I'm not her boyfriend," Greg said in horror. Then he thought a moment and amended, "Maybe I am. Is that so bad?"

Jasmine and Ruth chattered away, but Greg ignored them. Anna came from inside the church, walking with slow, hesitant steps. She still looked like a poor ragamuffin. Her sisters no longer had their original emaciated look after several days of decent food and a safe place to sleep. Anna was drawn and pale. Her eyes were dark in sunken pits as if she hadn't slept in a month of Sundays.

He wondered if being in a town wore on her. She had resisted coming to Warknife, not that it was that big a town. It certainly wasn't as big as Laramie or Cheyenne. They had a thousand people in them. Maybe more.

He couldn't help himself. An ear-to-ear grin spread on his face. He was glad to see her, even if her own enthusiasm left something to be desired.

"Hello, Gregory," she said in a thready voice. "You've come back."

"I wanted to see how you were doing. You and your sisters." He chanced a quick look at them. They both snickered at the idea of their sister having a beau.

He paused for a moment. A beau. Was that the way to describe what he felt? What she did? Greg decided half that was true. He wanted to do for her, but she remained remote.

She was as wild as a meadowlark and twice as flighty. If he said "boo," she'd jump up and fly away.

"I never expected to see you again."

"Why not?" He frowned. He'd never given her that idea. Never had a single word hinting at that crossed his lips. He remembered too well how MacKenna had reacted when her beau had left her and married another girl he had gotten in the family way. Mack never spoke of it anymore, but he knew the emotional bruise was still deep inside and caused her to be touchy at the oddest times.

"I . . . I identified her. Mama. At that awful man's funeral parlor."

"Mister O'Dell?"

"He demanded money to bury her. The only way I recognized her was by her clothes. He wouldn't even give me her ring. It was all she owned."

"You want it to remember her?" Greg's indignation rose. "I'll have a talk with him. He's not the nicest man in Warknife."

"No, wait, Gregory. You don't have to. Father Simon argued with him. But in a nice, gentle way."

"The padre's like that," Greg said uneasily. He had wanted to be of help. Father Simon had beaten him to it.

"She'll still be buried in the potter's field because none of us have any money, but the reverend talked O'Dell into giving her an old pine box."

Greg wished he had money enough to bury Anna's mother properly, but he had less than a dollar to his name. Asking his pa was not likely to get him far and asking his ma would bring down the wrath of the heavens on his head. She'd hate the idea of him getting involved with the remnants of a family like this.

Of getting entangled with Anna.

"How much does O'Dell want to do it right?"

Anna shook her head and shrugged her thin shoulders. If possible, she looked even more forlorn.

"Lots, I bet. I'll see what I can do."

"Father Simon said he'd ask for charity after the sermon on Sunday."

Greg closed his eyes and remembered what Anna's mother had looked like after being in the open for so long. He had never seen that many dead bodies. He wasn't sure he'd ever see worse even if he lived to be a hundred.

"Don't fret, Gregory," Anna said. She laid her hand on his shoulder. "It'll work out all right." Something in her tone caused him to look harder at her. "Everything will be fine when I find our pa. He killed her. I know he did."

"Your father killed your mother and left her for the buzzards?" Shock robbed him of more words.

"He did. Who else would do such a terrible thing? He's a terrible man. He deserves whatever he gets. But he's out there free as the wind."

A dozen things fluttered through his head. Before he realized he was speaking, he said, "I'll bring him in, dead or alive. I give you my promise."

"You don't have to say that, Gregory. You're not a lawman or a gunfighter or . . . anything."

Her words stung him.

"I said I'd bring him in for murdering your ma. I will. I keep my word."

The Sunset Kid always kept any obligation he undertook. If her pa was out there, anywhere, he'd track him down and . . . and . . .

What?

At that instant Greg Brannigan felt righteous anger and strength enough to pull the trigger on another human being. For Anna, he'd do it.

He ran his suddenly sweaty palm up and down along his

right hip where a six-gun ought to hang. He'd have to get one. His pa had a gun case back at the ranch with plenty of irons stored in it, along with the boxes of ammunition.

"I'll track him down if I have to go to the ends of the earth." He pressed his fingers into her bony hand still on his shoulder. On a sudden impulse, he bent over and kissed her. He'd intended to kiss her on the lips. He missed and instead touched lips to her cheek.

Embarrassed, he pulled back. Anna's sisters were giggling. Greg felt a hot flush rising to his cheeks.

"I'll get him or know the reason."

He ran away, heading toward Marshal Southern's office. The only place he knew where a sighting of Anna's father might be reported was behind that half-open door. Greg started through but was almost bowled over when the marshal's other two deputies, Bob Early and Glenn Beach, rushed out as fast as he had been going in. Neither of them paid him the smallest notice.

From inside the office came loud voices. His pa and Chris Southern carried on about something.

"You keep things all peaceable in Warknife, Conrad. I don't know how long we'll be gone."

The giant lumbering deputy replied, but the words were too muffled for Greg to make them out. All he knew was something big had happened.

His heart jumped into his throat. Anna's father had been found! That had to be it.

"Pa, wait," he said as Ty Brannigan came out of the jailhouse. "What's going on? Is it the man who—"

"They robbed the bank in Cutbank. They left the president, Hutchinson, with a busted skull and shot each other."

"Double-crossing each other's what they done," Southern said. He pulled the door shut after him. "Let's get on the trail."

"Your deputies? They'll form a posse?"

"As many as they can round up," Southern said. "They'll track us if we get on the trail first. If not, we'll meet up in Cutbank."

"What's Marshal Buckman have to say about a Warknife posse?" Greg asked.

"He won't have a thing to say. The robbers made fools of me," Ty said. "I don't take kindly to that."

"You and me both," the marshal declared forcefully. "If I have to turn in my badge and spend my next two birthdays on the high coulee trail, I swear I will find them." He glanced over his shoulder at his lockup. "There'll be plenty of cells waiting for the whole gang." Southern ground his teeth together. "For the ones who make it back alive, at least."

"Let me ride along, Pa. Please." Greg ran alongside his father toward the stables.

"These are dangerous men, cutthroats, cunning outlaws. We've tangled with them before."

"We've shot it out with them," Southern corrected. "Your father's right. It's too dangerous for a youngster." He slapped Greg on the back in way of consolation, then ducked into the livery.

In minutes the marshal and Greg's father galloped out, heading toward Cutbank.

Greg called after them, but the thunder of hooves drowned out his protests at being left behind. Like a little kid.

He went into the stable and saddled his horse. There were other criminals out there who had to be brought to justice. Let the posse and his pa go after bank robbers. That was only about stolen money. He'd find Anna's pa—the man who had savagely murdered her mother. Bringing him to justice, to hang for everyone to see, would be better than catching any old bank robber.

All Greg had to do was figure out where Anna's pa might have hidden himself.

"What would the Sunset Kid do?" he asked softly. He wasn't sure but knew what Gregory Brannigan would do. He'd keep his word.

CHAPTER 33

"What'll it be? East or west?" Marshal Southern looked from side to side at the junction in the road.

"Straight ahead leads us to Cutbank," Ty Brannigan said. "Any action there is over, except for stacking up the dead bodies." He chewed on his lower lip a moment, then pointed west. "To the mountains. They'd stand out too much if they hit the plains."

"Like that?" Southern pointed to a cloud of dust rising due east.

"The rider's in too much of a hurry and isn't coming from Cutbank," Ty observed. He fished out field glasses and fiddled with them a moment to get a good focus. His eyes were filled with trail dust and, he hated to admit it, the dust of years. Vision failed him at odd times because he was getting old.

He knew that and took it into account. All he need do was spot the bank robbers before they saw him. His hand was still steady and his aim had never been better.

"He's got wind of us. Can you make out any details?"

"Corporal from the look of the stripes on his arm." Ty tucked the field glasses back into his saddlebags. He itched to be on the trail, but the soldier was in such a powerful hurry, he had an important message to pass along.

More than that, the Warknife posse hadn't caught up with them yet.

Ty had no problem going after the robbers with Southern. Or all by his lonesome, if it came to that. But having a dozen armed men anxious to enforce the law against such cutthroats made him ride a mite easier. It'd make the story-telling better, too, when he related it all to Beatriz. There wasn't much way she could chew him out for being a loose cannon if he rode with his best friend and a gaggle of determined, law-abiding men.

Even if they'd been recruited from the saloons and promised a shot of whiskey along with a dollar or two, she'd appreciate he wasn't standing alone, beating his chest and demanding for the bad hombres to either surrender or shoot him.

As the soldier approached, he took off his garrison cap and waved it about, as if they hadn't seen him a mile back.

"You, you two are the Warknife lawmen?" The corporal was sweating hard and his uniform clung to his thin body enough to show he was a skeleton astride a horse.

Southern introduced them, then added, "We've got a posse on the way out of town."

"That's good. Major Wallenstein's ordered the entire post out on patrol. Every last pony soldier, yes sir. He's fuming mad about this."

"Why was he late getting to Cutbank?" Ty thought he knew but wanted to hear it officially.

"He was there on the dot. The clock was striking eight when he dismounted, but the robbery had been done by then. They got there 'fore him and his detachment."

"What'd he do?" Southern asked.

"He lit out after the biggest bunch of them as they ran. They scattered all over the landscape, they did, but he'd run two of them to ground."

"They went east?"

"He thinks they all did, that being the quickest way to get out of Wyoming." The corporal mopped his forehead. "I ain't heard if he recovered any of the money." The soldier grinned as if in approval. "They surely did make off with a pile of money. The bank president—"

"Hutchinson," Southern supplied.

"Yeah, him. He said they carried off six bags of money. And those bags were crammed full. You got to hand it to them robbers. They got brass balls to sneak in minutes 'fore the major showed up and steal the money like they did. They snatched it from right under his nose, and a big nose it is, too." The soldier grinned broadly. He knew he was siding with the outlaws, but his distaste for his commanding officer came through loud and clear.

"Has any of the money been recovered?" Ty shifted anxiously.

"My friend here's got a stack of greenbacks taken from the bank," Southern said to temper the soldier's enthusiasm for such criminal daring.

"Sorry, sir," the corporal said. "The major, he didn't mention getting any back. Not yet. Just that he'd caught two of the robbers and was sending the entire command out to find the rest."

"To the east?"

The corporal nodded in agreement.

Ty turned toward the Bear Paw Mountains. They were majestic this morning, crowned with thick white clouds that blocked the sun and sent daggers of shadow down the rocky sides. A purpled haze turned them into something from another world.

If he'd robbed Hutchinson's bank, heading out onto the plains was the last place he'd ride unless he had a remuda of horses so he could switch from one tired horse to a fresh one and ride the livelong day. It was too easy to be seen, even with gently rolling hills obscuring the view. Worse was being spotted by anyone else out on the plains for more legitimate reasons. A robber might as well leave a trail of bright red confetti.

"We're headed into the mountains," Ty told the corporal. "Pass that along to the major, will you?"

"Yes, sir, that I will. I'm going into town to send some telegrams. There won't be a widening in the road between here and St. Louis that won't be on the lookout for the robbers." The corporal took a deep breath. "The major's *real* mad about this."

"He's got some turncoats in his command," Southern said. "Somebody passed along all the details of moving that money."

"He never liked our quartermaster," the corporal shared. "Even if he didn't have a danged thing to do with this, he's standing for a court-martial. Good luck to you in your hunt, Marshal." He gave Ty one last look.

"When you get to Warknife and finish sending all your telegrams, head on over to the Longhorn Saloon," Southern shouted after the departing soldier. "Tell him the first drink's on me."

The corporal kept his head down but acknowledged with a raised arm.

"The first drink?" Ty scoffed. "That boy's going to tell Willewaug you said to give him all he could pour down his gullet."

"Normal's not stupid enough to fall for that line. He's been tending bar too long to believe anything a horse soldier tells him when it comes to free drinks."

"If he runs into the posse, he'll send them our way," Ty said. He heeled his horse into a trot. Time slipped away. The longer the robbers were on the trail, the better their chances of escaping. All Ty thought of as he rode was losing the money he'd entrusted to Hutchinson. Losing fifteen hundred dollars was a blow to the family finances. The Brannigans wouldn't be bankrupt and the Circle P wouldn't have to sell off land to make ends meet, but the winter would be mighty sparse when it came to any luxury.

He rubbed his belly. More than luxuries might be a thing of the past. That much money was most of the Circle P operating cash. He recoiled at the idea of having to go to Beatriz's pa and asking for a loan. Still, if he failed to get the money back, he'd have to. The railroad would never build the spur, he'd have to hire an entire crew to drive his cattle a hundred miles south, and then there were extra expenses like fattening the cattle after they'd walked it off.

The railroad saved him money and got his beeves off to market faster, which meant he'd be paid sooner.

"It was a good deal," Southern said, reading his mind.

"I know it. That railroad spur will make trail drives a distant memory. But getting the tracks laid is the first problem. It won't be done if they don't get money."

"It'll be profitable for the line. The railroad might advance you the money as a loan."

Ty looked hard at his friend.

"You're not giving up on catching these crooks, are you? It'd be a pity if I had to ride on alone."

"There's a chance they will get away. There always is, Ty. You know that. The robbery was carefully planned and everything worked in the thieves' favor. All it'll take is another day's good luck and . . ." Chris Southern let his words trail off.

Ty understood. But in his gut he wondered if the robbery had been as slick and easy as it seemed. Catching Kennard and Marcus had alerted them to a robbery no one outside the gang had known about. Being on guard meant they should have done better protecting the money when it was actually deposited. Lowry thought keeping everything secret was the way to protect the pile of greenbacks.

Letting everyone and their second cousin know was a better tactic. If everyone jumped about on pins and needles, getting close to the money with intent to steal would have been a damned sight harder.

"Greg had mentioned a hideout in the mountains," he said. "I don't know if it was something his wild imagination conjured up or if he knew."

"The boy listens. You never catch him beatin' his gums for no good reason," Southern said. "Where do we go to find where the gang'd hole up?"

"If they are," Ty said. "Better for them to ride and keep riding."

"They might want to wait for the posses to get tired and all go home," Southern said. "If they're secure in their hide-out, they might take a breather."

"Desperado's Den," Ty said, chuckling. "That's what Greg called it, I think. I wasn't listening too hard." He turned away from the pasture where his cattle, mingling with the rustled ones, contentedly grazed. "That way leads into a canyon higher in the mountains."

"I know it. There're a half dozen branching canyons. Hiding out in one of them'd be a good idea. A man can get lost up there if he doesn't know the terrain."

"It's a good thing we do," Ty said.

They rode for another hour, barely talking. Then both of them drew rein at the same instant and pointed to a stand of pines. A quick exchange of looks convinced them they'd both been alerted by the same thing. Someone had ridden into the edge of the forest and waited there.

"Ready to ambush us?" Southern whispered.

Ty motioned for his friend to break off and ride in a wide

circle to come upon the trees from the west. He waited to make his approach from the south. The number of times they had gone after a road agent using a similar attack was beyond his recollection. It worked. They did it over and over.

When he was sure Southern had gotten into position, he rode directly toward the stand, making as much noise as he could. If he flushed whoever was there, they'd ride straight into Southern's leveled ten-gauge. Trying to go deeper into the forest by heading either north or east only trapped them. Southern would cover any possible escape.

Ty was ready for what greeted him, but it still surprised him. Someone opened fire rather than trying to hightail it. Lead whirred past him and caused his roan to jump about. He put his head down and galloped straight into the stream of lead seeking to kill him.

It took either a real marksman or pure luck to hit a man on a charging horse. Whoever he approached was neither. Ty saw his attacker bolt and run. When he reached the edge of the forest, he drew his six-gun and sent a few rounds after the man to speed him on his way.

The roar of Southern's Old Suzy and the dull thud that followed told Ty he had sped the outlaw on his way to hell. The Warknife marshal never missed with that barn blaster of his.

"Got one," Southern called. "Look out. There's another one farther in the woods."

Ty spotted movement an instant before someone opened up with a rifle. He grabbed his Henry and slid from the saddle. His frightened horse raced away. Ty took cover behind an old maple tree and braced the rifle on the side. This became a waiting game. But he was patient. More patient than the outlaw trying to bushwhack him.

After what must have seemed an impossible wait, the

man popped up to look around. Ty potshotted him like he was a furry marmot. The man jerked as the rifle's slug tore through him. He rose to his full height, then twisted slowly and draped himself face down over a rotting stump. He twitched a couple times and then lay still.

Ty let the ringing in his ears from the gunshots die down, then strained to hear any other sound. Southern worked his way on foot toward him from the west. But the curious silence in the woods warned him they still had company—living company—waiting for them to make a foolish mistake and show themselves.

"Let's go through their gear," Ty called. "They must have the money from the robbery." He stayed alert for any response. Luring the outlaw to make a mistake was their quickest way to end this gunfight.

"Got a gunnysack crammed with greenbacks," Southern shouted. "We're rich, Ty. We're filthy rich. There's no reason to tell anybody we found the money."

"Let's bury it here." Ty listened even harder. The normal forest sounds were still missing. Someone moved around to keep the animals and birds from stirring. His and Southern's banter about keeping the money and hiding it didn't flush their quarry. But it had to gnaw away on the robber.

"Maybe there's more. This isn't anywhere near what was taken."

"I'll see about the one I nailed." Ty gave Southern time to get into position to cover him, then advanced slowly. He had no reason to check the dead man. All he wanted was to flush anyone else hiding here. Using himself as bait was foolish, but he trusted his friend not to miss when their quarry showed himself.

There wasn't any way the robber was going to sneak off and leave behind money from the bank.

He edged around a tree and caught sight of a coarse-woven

gunnysack. It bulged, and where it had been tied shut with a double loop of twine, a single bill poked out. Seeing the money almost spelled his death. A step out from behind the tree brought him a hailstorm of bullets.

Splinters flew all around him. A spot of sticky sap splattered onto his cheek and clung with gluey ferocity. He dived forward when a lightning strike drove into his upper arm. A few quick wiggles gained him sanctuary behind a fallen log. He tapped it a couple times with his rifle barrel.

The wood was rotten all the way through. A few shots in his direction would bore through the decayed tree trunk. The log provided less cover than it did a target.

Kicking and scooting, he stretched lengthwise along the tree for maximum protection. He burrowed down and under, working his way into the soft ground. Ty did his best to ignore the rush of beetles and other swarming bugs stirred up by taking cover more in the ground than behind the log.

The ten-gauge roared twice. He heard Southern break open the breach and slam in two more shells. When the marshal fired again, Ty got his feet under him and lunged past the tree. He leveled his Henry repeater and got off round after around. He saw movement in thick bushes ahead and turned his deadly aim there.

The outlaw's luck disappeared. Ty was sure at least one round found its mark. A second slug hitting the man's torso wasn't out of the question. He vaulted a stump and stretched out on the far side. His body shot forward as straight as an arrow while his rifle came down in a precise arc. He felt metal crunch into bone. The outlaw's six-shooter fell to the ground.

"Give up or we'll kill you dead," Southern shouted.

"You've gone and made us powerful mad, but you get to choose."

Ty realized it wasn't going to be that easy. He might have disarmed the owlhoot but enough fight remained to ruin his day. Worse, the outlaw realized Southern couldn't shoot without hitting his partner.

They grappled. The outlaw grabbed the rifle barrel and tried to jerk it out of Ty's grasp. Instead of yielding, Ty drove forward. His toes dug into the soft forest loam. With his rifle in front of him, he tried to use it as a battering ram. He broke the man's grip and shoved the muzzle hard into his belly.

A screech of pure agony echoed through the forest. Ty drove forward even harder and got his arms around the man's waist. Together they tumbled to the ground, kicking and clawing, swinging and trying to land a punch. They were too entwined for a fist to have much effect. Ty realized it before his adversary.

He reached up and grabbed a handful of hair. A hard yank twisted the man's head around at a crazy angle. Even then the fight wasn't over. A powerful kick rolled Ty over onto his back. The robber came out on top and dropped down hard, his knee crushing Ty's belly.

The air blasted from his lungs, and the world spun in a crazy, blurred circle. All he knew in that instant was an existence filled with every type of pain he'd ever experienced. Sharp, dull, lingering, fleeting. Every nerve in his body told him to stop fighting.

Ty Brannigan wasn't a quitter.

Hands raised to deflect a jab aimed at his face, Ty fought to recover his senses. His lungs protested taking in air again. Pain jabbed down hard and kept him from doing anything other than defending himself however feebly.

The pummeling stopped suddenly. It took him a few seconds to realize that. He recovered and pushed himself to his feet.

"Give up," he croaked. "You're under arrest."

"I'm about ready to give up. You never quit." The man he faced sat on the ground, back against a tree. He fumbled with his six-shooter. A bullet fell from numbed fingers as he tried to reload. "But I got one bullet in here." The outlaw snapped shut the gate and held the pistol in two hands.

His aim wavered and he almost keeled over onto his side.

"Give up, and I'll see you get that gunshot patched up."

"Shot. He double-crossed me." The man's eyes glazed over, and he heaved the gun up in his attempt to plug Ty.

"You're a hair away from dyin', mister. I got you covered." Chris Southern came over, his shotgun snugged up into his shoulder. The bank robber's hand wobbled. The marshal's was rock steady.

"Can't be any worse dead, than the way I feel." The man toppled to the side. His finger curled back on the trigger and fired the single round into the ground.

"That's it for him," Ty said.

"You look like you're the one what lost the fight," Southern said.

"Where'd you get off to? I could have used help. Or were you too interested in watching me get my brains beat out?" Ty took a few shaky steps. His legs strengthened. He went to the unconscious bank robber and plucked the pistol from the man's hand. The only response was a low moan.

He was tough, this one. He hadn't died yet.

"I chased down another robber, but he got away. My time wasn't poorly spent, though." Southern reached behind a tree and lifted a bag straining its seams. "Money from the robbery. Got a second bag, too. Off his horse." He pointed his shotgun at the moaning outlaw.

"All's not completely lost. We'll have to count the money and compare it with what Hutchinson reports, but that's not twenty thousand worth," Ty said, eyeing the bags.

"If he doesn't give up the ghost, we can find out where his partners are likely to run. The money's not all lost, not yet."

"Any chance of catching the one that got away?"

"Let the posse track him. My gullet is empty, my mouth feels like a desert, and keeping my eyelids from sinkin' down is hard. In case you missed it, this has been one helluva long day."

"Back to Warknife," Ty said. He got his arms under the outlaw's armpits and heaved. If it hadn't been for the tree partially supporting his prisoner, Ty would have fallen.

With a grunt, he pulled the man completely upright.

"You walk or I'll drag you."

"Can walk. Hard, but I can walk." The man opened one eye. The other was swelling shut from a punch Ty had delivered during their fistfight. "You got my money."

"We recovered money you stole," Southern said in disgust. "My friend's too merciful. I'm for making you walk back. Or maybe draggin' you if you can't keep up."

"He has the rest of the money."

"Who's this?" Ty asked.

The man turned his battered face toward Ty and grinned. His lip was split, his nose bloodied, and he'd lost a tooth.

"I need a wild card if I don't want to spend the rest of my life in a cell."

He took another step forward and collapsed. Ty had finally achieved his knockout, even if the result was delayed long minutes.

Southern sighed. He caught up with the man and with Ty's help, lashed him belly down over his horse. It was going to be a long, slow trip back to Warknife. At least the right side had won.

CHAPTER 34

It was quite a tangle of trails. Greg Brannigan rode around in a tight circle, studying the ground for any hint where the cutthroats he had seen before had gone. His hopes of finding some spoor faded the more he hunted.

"Desperado's Den," he said softly. The words glowed in his head. Burned. He had overheard two outlaws mention it. There had to be all kinds of crooks hiding out there. When he found it, he'd have a good start on finding the man who had killed Anna's mother.

It might be coincidence that rustlers left cattle in the Circle P herd and robbed the Cutbank bank and busted men out of the Warknife jail. Anna's mother had been brutally murdered as had the man in the way station he had buried. Too many deaths, too many crimes, it had to be tied together some way. Finding the outlaw hideout was a good start to bringing a lot of bad hombres to justice.

"And one of them's murdered Anna's ma and robbed her sisters of a family." Greg realized the logic was shaky, but who'd have believed any of the other crimes?

He circled the junction again and couldn't decide. Unable to find distinct evidence, he resorted to a tried-and-true method that worked for him before. Spitting on the back of his hand and splatting down with his other thumb to see which way the gob flew was one way of choosing a direction. Such a random method failed as many times as it worked. Then an idea came to him.

A better one strained under him. Greg let his horse have its head. The gelding kept moving in a tight circle, then made a decision. The trail on the right was as good as any of the others.

After riding a half mile along the steep dirt track he tugged on the reins and dismounted. He dropped to his knees and studied the ground. Crushed grass along the trail and bright scratches on rock showed someone had ridden this way recently. Within days recently.

Greg got to his feet and walked slowly until he came to a bend in the trail. Some distance ahead, a rockslide blocked any possible passage.

He looked at the hoofprints again. Recent. There had been other tracks, fainter and partially erased by wind. One set going in this direction had been left within the past few hours.

He scratched his head. There wasn't any way a rider got past the avalanche barricade. He went to the solid wall of rock and ran his hand over the rough surface. The boulder was bigger than a house. Nobody had moved it, passed, and then dropped it back.

"The rock's been here a few days," he said. The way no mud had splashed up from rain along the base told him that. Other rocks exposed endured the rain from a week ago. This one hadn't, so it had fallen since then.

He backtracked, thinking to return to the spot he had first picked up the spoor. Before he rode ten yards he saw what he had missed in his eagerness to get on the outlaws' trail.

When he first passed this section of trail, he thought the loose gravel was part of the avalanche. He saw that it had been kicked loose as a horse scrambled up the slope. At this point, the wall wasn't as steep. Leading his horse, he clambered up. His horse followed with equal difficulty. Just when he was going to give up on all the slipping and sliding, he popped over a rim and found himself on the upper curve of the trail.

His horse flopped up a few seconds after him, snorted, and shook its head. The long mane flapped like a battle pennant.

"Victory!"

Swinging into the saddle, he continued along the trail. Evidence of recent passage excited him, but not as much as a bit of paper fluttering where it was impaled on a thorny bush. Greg swung down and snatched it. His eyes went wide. He'd seen twenty-dollar gold pieces. They were tiny little things. Once when he'd gone into Warknife with his pa, he had seen a twenty-dollar greenback. That had impressed him.

The fifty-dollar bill he held awed him. This was more than Marshal Southern earned in two months as a marshal. Almost as much. Within ten dollars.

He hurried along the trail when he spotted another bill. This time he dismounted and picked it up.

"A hundred-dollar bill!" He stared at it for a long minute. "Redeemable in gold coin," he read across the top. The crisp bill was issued by a San Francisco bank and had a picture of a sailing ship on the left side and a seated woman on the right. He couldn't make out what she held. A bundle of sticks with an axe shoved in the middle. That perplexed him.

"A hundred-dollar bill," he exclaimed again. The artwork meant less than the promise to redeem this piece of paper for one hundred in gold. Five twenty-dollar gold pieces. It was hard to imagine that much money.

He rode faster along the trail, keeping a sharp eye out for more bills. The twisting trail angled upward until the horse

began gulping in thinner air. Greg took a deep breath and
realized they had climbed several thousand feet.

"Where am I?" He looked around. This was new territory for him. He had explored the lower canyons, mostly
hunting for strays. The upper reaches of the mountains
never lost their white crowns in the summer. This late in the
year, most of the melting snow was gone. The freshets had
dried up, and streams that ran wide in the spring were puny
little trickles now.

"They need water," he said, remembering why he'd
come up here. Finding the bills had distracted him. A quick
touch on the watch pocket in his jeans convinced him the
greenbacks weren't a mirage or something that had invaded
his imagination. For a moment when he found the big bills,
he had been the Sunset Kid.

It was time to be something better. He had to be a
Brannigan now.

Two small creeks ran down into a canyon below him.
The trail had brought him out on a rim, but the canyon floor
wasn't too distant. Finding a way down was easy enough.
Along the way, he found fresh road apples and even a spot
where a horse had nibbled away at a bush. The cropped-off
sections still oozed sap.

Whoever he followed was less than a half hour ahead.
Maybe less.

He dismounted to keep a lower profile. For a moment
he felt a flash of fear. All he carried was his .410 shotgun.
If he got into a gunfight, it wasn't likely to be with a bunny
rabbit or a quail. Those were suitable victims for his shotgun. Not a human and especially not a human wielding a
six-gun.

He tried to listen for the other rider. All he heard was the
high, shrill whine of wind slipping over the canyon rim
from even higher elevations. Mingling with it came the soft

rush of the small creeks. He heard nothing more. When he inhaled deeply, he caught a hint of wood smoke.

Close!

He sniffed and turned about slowly, hunting for its source. The only place where a fire might have been built lay across the canyon, up against a sheer rock face. He thought he saw soot marks creeping upward on a flatiron.

Tracing the streams convinced him the spot he had homed in on had to be the outlaws' camp.

"Desperado's Den," he said, feeling vindicated. No one had listened to him because they probably thought this place didn't exist. Finding it showed he'd been right all along.

Never had a spot been better named. From what he could tell, there were three or four ways to get away from the camp. No posse would trap the outlaws here. To block all the ways out would take a couple dozen men.

"Try sneaking up on those cutthroats," he said softly. "One man can sneak in. One man." He puffed up a mite at that. If anyone could do it, he was it.

The idea of sentries made him cautious. He led his horse to the canyon floor, let it drink some from the nearer stream and then hiked across the open stretch to a wooded area. The piñons and spruce were sparse, but they hid Greg's advance from any guard posted high up on the side of the canyon.

He kept sniffing. The burning wood aroma mingled with boiling coffee. His heart raced. He was closer than ever to the camp. To the outlaws. To the man who had killed Anna's ma!

Greg tethered his horse and yanked out his shotgun. It wasn't likely to kill anyone, but if he shot a desperado in the face, he'd slow him down. Crouched, he made his way through the forest until he came to the edge of the camp.

He caught his breath. The gang had lit a shuck. He had seen mining camps where men simply stood up, got on their horses, and ridden away. The hideout had that look. Too much had been left behind. Pots and pans, piles of air tights, and discarded gear were all strewn about.

He sat and thought hard. If the gang had ridden out to rob the Cutbank bank, there wasn't any reason for them to return here. Steal the money, clear out of Wyoming as fast as their horses could take them. That was the smart thing to do, but his pa had told him repeatedly that crooks were seldom smart. They let greed and their own viciousness drive them to make mistakes.

A slow touch against the watch pocket in his jeans caused the bills he'd found to crinkle. Someone had returned to the camp after the robbery. Or were the bills lost some other time? If they carried this much money, why rob a bank?

"Greed," he said to himself. "Pa's right about that. They can't ever have enough money. And those bills were dropped after the bank was robbed." That was the only thing that made sense. The constant wind would have blown the bills off the trail if they'd been there very long.

But the camp was deserted.

Why would anyone carrying the loot return to such desolation?

With steps as quiet as any Cheyenne, he moved closer to the camp and began to circle it. He froze when a horse neighed. Near the farthest campfire, where soot had scarred the rock face of the canyon wall. He dropped to his belly and crawled. Everywhere around him was more proof that Desperado's Den had been abandoned. It had served its purpose.

For everyone but a solitary bandit.

"You're the one who killed Anna's ma. You've gotta be,"

he said as he advanced. There wasn't any reason why this one outlaw was the one he sought, but he knew what the Sunset Kid would do.

Capture the varmint. Make him talk. If he wasn't the killer, he'd know who was. All the outlaws hung together.

A crazy smile came to his lips.

"Hung together. They'll all hang, each and every one of them for rustling and robbery and murdering Anna's ma."

"What's that you said, kid?"

Greg turned to stone. He pulled his shotgun closer and prepared to roll over and shoot. The spread on .410 pellets wasn't great, but he heard the voice and had an idea where the owlhoot had been when he spoke from behind.

He jumped a foot when a bullet ripped past his ear and kicked up a small dust devil inches away.

"Leave the toy shotgun in the dust and stand up so I can see you better."

"Who are you? You don't have no call shooting at me like that." Greg's show of bravado hid his panic. He got his feet under him, stood, and turned slowly. Hands in the air he faced one of the outlaws. The man's Colt centered on his chest. Greg knew better than to move. Matching his reflexes against the outlaw's was suicide. Even a feint and a dive in the other direction would mean the outlaw had the problem of letting his body rot in the sun or burying it.

Greg doubted the man would do the Christian thing. He'd be left to the coyotes. Like Anna's mother.

"Who I am's no concern. You're not going to be around long enough to tell anyone who you found. Or where you found me." The man glanced around, a disgusted look turning his ugly face even uglier. "Let's say I used to be the leader of this gang."

"You're a rustler!"

The man motioned for his prisoner to step away from the

shotgun. He herded Greg toward the rock face where the fire had been built.

"You must belong to one of the ranchers around here. The Circle P? You the whelp of Ty Brannigan?"

"I'm Greg Brannigan!"

"My bad luck." The man chuckled and aimed his pistol. "No, make that *your* bad luck." The trigger finger turned white as he drew back to fire.

"Wait, if you're gonna kill me, answer a question first."

"You know who I am," the man said. "Or at least what I do. I rustle cattle."

"Did you kill her?" The question caused the outlaw to frown.

"Her? Who're you talking about? I've killed my share of men. In the past day or two more than my share. Some had it coming because they tried to double-cross me." He smiled wickedly. "The rest I double-crossed."

"Anna's mother," Greg blurted. "And Jasmine and Ruth's, too."

"I don't have any idea what you're . . ." The words trailed off. "One of the sons of a buck who tried to back-shoot me was hunting for some girls."

"Who? Who was?"

"His name's Dexter. Frank Dexter. Or it was. I shot him right about here." The rustler pressed his left index finger into the center of his chest.

"He got away," Greg said. The lie rushed out. He had no idea who Dexter was. It might be the killer he hunted down or someone entirely different. But coincidence . . .

Searching for little girls? How many cutthroats in this camp hunted for girls as well as rustling cattle and robbing banks?

"He couldn't have gotten far, not with an ounce of my lead in his gut."

"He dropped these." Greg fumbled in his watch pocket and pulled out the two greenbacks he'd found along the trail. "They were how I was tracking him."

The outlaw squinted at the sight of the hundred-dollar bill. He edged closer, keeping his six-shooter leveled. With a move like a striking snake, he snatched the bills from Greg's fingers. The instant he looked at the hundred, he shifted attention from his prisoner.

Greg sprang. He batted away the hand holding the gun. His left came around in a roundhouse blow that carried all the weight of his big body and strength of a teenager and desperation at his capture. The blow glanced off the outlaw's jaw. The impact of bone on bone might have hurt Greg more. A jolt of pain raced from his knuckles all the way up into his shoulder.

He kept moving forward. Everyone mocked him because he was so big for his age. He made that weight and muscle pay off now. Shoulder into the man's gut, he drove forward, kicking up dirt and falling forward. His arms circled the man's and pinned them to his body.

They crashed to the ground. Greg jerked about as the man fired. The bullet bypassed any real target, but the fiery hot barrel pressed between them held there by his punishing bear hug. Greg winced as the metal burned into his belly. He reared up and tried to bend his adversary double.

Somehow, the man wiggled free. He flopped around, came to his knees and fired again. Once more Greg jerked but not from lead tearing through his flesh. This bullet raked his back. He felt the dime novel rip away where he had tucked it in the back of his waistband.

"That's gotta be returned!" The idea of destroying the borrowed novel renewed his anger. He wouldn't be able to give it back to Mister Dempsey. Swinging wildly, he hit the gunman's arm again, giving him the chance to grapple once more.

They crashed to the ground. This time Greg ended up pinned under the man's weight. He felt a large, sharp rock gouging into his back—one of the rocks used to ring the fire pit. Rising to get away from the pain proved his undoing. The outlaw fell full weight on top of him. Once more that rock cracked into his spine.

Stunned, he groaned and rolled away, rubbing his back. When Greg looked up, he stared down the barrel of a very big and very deadly six-gun.

Greg expected to die but the outlaw stepped away.

"You didn't hike in. You've got a horse. Where is it?"

Greg feigned being more injured than he was. The Sunset Kid had used that trick to get out of a tight spot, too.

"My horse pulled up lame."

Greg realized this was why the outlaw had come back to a deserted camp. He hoped to find others in his gang, either with a spare horse or to steal theirs so he could escape.

"Where's your horse? Tell me!"

He shook his head. The instant he revealed where he'd tethered his horse, he was a dead man.

"I'll buy it from you. I've got two bags stuffed with more of those." He pointed to the hundred-dollar bill laying in the dust where he'd dropped it. "What's the horse worth to you if you're dead?"

"Kill me and you'll never find it."

"Five hundred dollars. No horse is worth that."

"You'll shoot me if I tell you."

The outlaw fired again. The bullet grazed Greg's cheek. He flinched away. When he touched his face, his fingers came away bloody. He'd seen worse. He'd been injured worse than this himself when a tree he and Matt had cut down snapped and kicked around. So this wasn't anything to get panicky over.

A curious calm wrapped him up like a warm wool blanket. There wasn't any chance of getting out of this alive. He accepted that now in some dim, indistinct fashion.

His only regret was not finding the man who had killed Anna's ma. That had to be Frank Dexter, who had double-crossed his partner.

His partner who was ready to gun him down.

CHAPTER 35

Every step his horse took sent a new wave of agony through him. Frank Dexter slowly inhaled. His ribs weren't broken, no thanks to the big bruiser of a rancher. More than one punch had landed on his torso. Powerful blows intended to knock him flat. Dexter had held his own against Brannigan. Next time, it'd be different. Next time he wouldn't give Brannigan a chance. A bullet in the back worked just fine for annoyances like the rancher.

He sucked in another breath and then spat. The gob wasn't tinged with bright pink. His lung hadn't been punctured, either by bullet or hammering blow. The red spot in the center of his chest reminded him with every step that Race Cooper had shot him.

He was drawing up quite a list to get even with.

"After I gunned down one of those fools for him," he muttered. He tried to remember if he'd shot Marcus or Kennard. Everything during and after the bank robbery was a blur to him. He hoped it was Kennard. He'd never liked the blow-hard, not that his partner was much better. At least Kennard mouthed off on his own. Marcus always tried to make excuses.

"What's that?" Ty Brannigan trotted up alongside and poked him. Dexter groaned. Not all of it was faked.

"What do I have to tell you and the marshal up yonder for you to let me go? It's Race Cooper you want. Not me."

"We caught you with two gunnysacks of stolen money. Or are you going to tell me you earned that? There must be five thousand dollars or more in those two bags."

"You'd never believe me if I said I found them alongside the road? I was minding my own business and came across them. Who wouldn't pick up that much money?"

"And you were riding back to Cutbank to return it," Ty said sarcastically.

"I didn't see anybody's name on the money. How was I to know it was stolen and not just lost?"

"But you're willing to give up your boss, even though you had nothing to do with any robbery?" Ty laughed harshly.

"You'll never catch Cooper without my help. Throw the little fish back into the pond. Hook the big sucker." Dexter coughed. He was glad to see now if the gob he spat carried blood. That didn't mean there weren't things busted up inside. The way he felt every time the horse took a step reminded him of lost fights.

"You're the itsy-bitsy fish, are you? If Race Cooper is such a big, bad outlaw why haven't I heard of him?"

"He's got a wanted posted on him. I'll bet my last dime on it."

"All your money's stolen," Ty pointed out.

"So I'm playing with house money? Is that so bad?"

"You're broke, in cash money and in spirit."

"Race Cooper's probably not his real name," Dexter went on, as if he hadn't heard Ty's little sermon. "Men like that rape and pillage and move on and change their names. It keeps the law hunting for the wrong man."

"You sound like someone with experience doing that."

Dexter tried to figure out what leverage worked against the big rancher. He was coming around to the sorry revelation that it wasn't possible to buy off an honest man. Even worse, the marshal carried that same incorruptible stench about him. There had to be another way to have them set him free.

"I get around. I hear things. Like everyone in Cooper's gang. I can name most of them and tell you what they all look like."

"That's not too helpful," Marshal Southern said, dropping back from the lead to listen in. "The one's that aren't worm food are going to be rounded up soon enough. There're at least two posses out hunting them down."

"Race Cooper'll get away," Dexter said with as much conviction as he could muster. "He planned this all. He got turncoats in the Army to tell him what he needed to know."

"And was he also the one who stole the Army uniforms? Like the one you've still got on?" Southern reached over and poked Dexter. He was weaker than he thought after being shot and beat up.

"You know, Chris, if he is a sergeant and deserted, Major Wallenstein would love to court-martial him and stand him in front of a firing squad."

"That's not likely to happen, Ty. I've heard tell the major's fond of a noose. He don't waste ammunition that way. That's something I can approve of."

"You two don't scare me," Dexter said. "I know facts you want to know, too. Let me go and I'll tell you everything."

"Tell us one thing we don't know," Ty said. "As a sample. That way we can tell if we want to hear more." He glanced sharply at the marshal. Dexter didn't miss the look. They were old friends who had ridden together for years. Brannigan might not wear a badge on his chest, but he acted like he did. Guessing that he had been a lawman at one time wasn't much of a stretch.

"Cooper's name. You hadn't known that 'fore I told you. Race Cooper."

"That's not much good, is it, Chris?"

"I don't recollect any such name, and I keep a stack of wanted posters from all over the territory on my desk. When I get bored, I study them, just to be sure none of them sneaks into Warknife."

"And didn't you just tell us that men like Cooper change their names more often than they do their longjohns?" Ty let his horse drift away from Dexter's, as if hinting for the outlaw to make an escape.

Dexter knew better. Even if he could escape to run, they'd fill him with lead. Escaping the Warknife jail was his best bet for freedom.

"Me and the rancher have gone over that little problem," Dexter said to Southern. "But all right. Something else." He paused as he considered the matter. "I know where Desperado's Den is."

"What's that?" Southern looked skeptical this was anything important.

"My son mentioned it. I wasn't paying much attention," Ty said.

"Matt?"

"No, Greg. He also claimed one of our horses had been stolen by outlaws from Desperado's Den."

"Yup, that was Cooper, along with Kennard and Marcus."

Brannigan and Southern rode along in silence. Something about the horse theft worked into their skulls in a way nothing else he'd said did. Dexter hardly knew what more to say, but spinning a tall tale was his ticket out of jail and on his way past the horizon, even if he rode away flat broke.

Or maybe he could find a way to steal back those bags of money. He was nothing if not clever.

"One of them's horse busted its leg and they had to shoot it. What good's a road agent without a horse to make an escape?" Dexter laughed. He saw he'd touched on something bothering both men.

"Where is it? Desperado's Den?"

"Now, Marshal, we haven't come to a deal that'll suit both of us, have we?"

"You said you'd give us a taste of what you knew. Where's Desperado's Den?" Ty watched him like a hawk. Dexter knew better than to lie. He also knew better than to give away the only high card he had left in his deck.

"I'm feeling kinda puny, what with the bullet in my chest and the beating you gave me." Dexter wobbled around in the saddle, more acting than actual weakness motivating him.

"We're almost back to town," Southern said. "I'll stay with him. Go on and fetch Doc Hickenlooper, won't you, Ty?"

"Try not to let him die before the doc and I get back," Ty said.

"Yeah, that's a good idea, Marshal," Dexter called out.

"The way the doc operates, you might want to die before he starts cutting. It's never pretty." Marshal Southern picked up the pace to reach the calaboose that much faster.

The rancher galloped off. Dexter closed his eyes and fell into the rhythm of the walking horse. It soothed him, and he drifted away until Southern poked him.

"Get down or I'll pull you out of the saddle."

Dexter blinked and saw the jailhouse. He had been here before but only to scout it for Race Cooper. Those two fools, Kennard and Marcus, had been locked up and Cooper wanted to know everything about the jail.

He almost fell to the ground. The marshal made no effort to save him from taking a nasty fall. Dexter glared at

Southern. When he got out, the lawman was on a list for him to kill. If he got back the money slung over the hindquarters of the marshal's horse, all the better. He had earned that money. The slug in his chest showed the price he'd paid.

"Cooper, too," he said, stumbling forward as the marshal untied the gunnysacks and slung them over his shoulder.

"What's that?"

"You have to pay to find out," Dexter said. The payment came in the form of an ounce of lead. He'd start writing down the names of men to kill. Otherwise, he might skip one by accident. That'd be a crying shame.

Southern shoved him into the jailhouse. The lumbering deputy, Conrad, jumped to his feet. He had been napping at the marshal's desk.

"You got one, Marshal. Good work," Conrad said.

"Lock him up. The back cell."

Dexter leaned heavily on the giant deputy and let him lock the cell door without any fuss. He watched with interest that Southern put the two bags of stolen money from Cutbank in the first cell. The empty cell between them kept Dexter from reaching out and pulling it into his.

So near and yet so far.

He collapsed onto the hard cot and leaned back against the cold stone wall. The marshal put the money in that cell to torment him. Every time he looked out toward the office, he saw the money that was his by right. He'd gone through hell to steal it.

He moaned when he touched the bullet hole in his chest. He hadn't bled much, and the slug missed his lungs. But what damage had it done? Every time he moved, it felt like liquid sloshing around inside his chest.

The sound of two men arguing caused him to look up. His vision turned a little blurry. He'd lost blood, and shock dulled his senses when he needed to be most alert. All he wanted was for Southern and the rancher to leave. It'd be the work of a few minutes to gull the big dumb deputy into letting him go free.

"You got a bullet in you? Thank your lucky stars Ty Brannigan convinced me to dig it out," the doctor said. He stood on the other side of the locked cell door, glaring at the prisoner.

"You were thinking about not operating? Don't want to show how big a butcher you are? If I die, everyone'll know you botched the operation." Dexter enjoyed poking and prodding. This way he won the silent battle whether the doctor was successful or not. If the bullet popped right out, good. Dexter lived. If he died with the sawbones digging around inside him, everyone in town would think poorly about the man's surgical skills.

"Open up, Marshal," the doctor barked. "I've got a patient to open up." He came into the cell and said, "Don't expect me to offer you a shot of whiskey to dull the pain."

"Nothing'll prevent me from being pained watching you dig around in my chest," Dexter said.

He never quite passed out as the doctor drove a steel probe into the wound, touched the bullet, then captured and drew it out with forceps. The sawbones grabbed his hand and dropped the bloody bullet into it.

"A souvenir. From what Brannigan tells me, you can keep it as a lucky charm so your hanging will be quick and merciful."

Dexter smiled weakly and closed his eyes. It was time to sleep. He wasn't aware that the doctor left but was when he heard voices in the office. Conrad's booming voice he recognized immediately. The other was high-pitched, thin, even weak.

He forced himself to sit up and saw Conrad leaving the jailhouse. A young girl stayed behind.

"You're Thomas' brat, aren't you?" he said. "Him and that whore Evangeline's."

"Uncle Frank," Anna said in a tiny voice. "You chased us."

"I owed it to you. We're family. We should be together."

"You owed it to us because you killed my mama."

Dexter sneered.

"She deserved it. Yeah, I shot her, and it was a good thing. Think about it, kid. Your pa is gone. I'm the only family you got."

"She told me about how you wanted her," Anna said. "She told me how Pa got drunk and let you have your will."

Dexter laughed. He pushed himself up even more, got to his feet and took a few weak steps to the bars. He leaned against them and reached out for the girl. She never moved an inch. His fingers raked the air a hair's breadth from her face.

"He didn't have to get drunk. He let me. *She* let me. For all I know, you're my kid."

Anna stood stock-still and said nothing.

"What's wrong? Cat got your tongue? Go fetch the keys and let your poor old uncle out before that big dumb ox of a deputy comes back."

"He'll be gone for a spell," Anna said.

"You're clever, I'll grant you that. But you need to do what I tell you because I'm your uncle. Now go get the keys and let me out!"

"I sent him on a wild-goose chase," Anna continued, as if she hadn't heard her uncle. "By the time he gives up, it'll be too late. I worry about the marshal coming back, though. Him and Mister Brannigan are in the saloon. They don't look like big drinkers."

"They're celebrating catching me," Dexter said. He

touched the bandage over the hole in his chest. "If that double-crossing Race Cooper hadn't shot me, I'd be out of the territory by now." He stopped when he realized what he said. "But that would be after I rescued you and the other two, of course. You're family. Blood comes first."

"What are their names?"

Dexter stared at her, not understanding.

"You don't even know their names."

"They're family, just like you. We need to spend more time together. Now get me out of here!"

"Jasmine and Ruth. And I'm Anna, if you don't know that, either."

"Got it. Those are their names. Now, Anna, my sweet young thing, get the key, turn it in the lock and let me go."

"You said you killed my mama. You left her for the buzzards."

"She got what she deserved. She was abandoning you."

"Why do you care?"

Dexter hesitated, then said, "I'll level with you. Your pa and me spent six months in Kansas robbing trains. Most of them never knew they'd lost a thing. We were clever and took entire freight cars loaded with food and clothing, then we sold it."

"He hid the money and never told you where," Anna said.

"He must have told you. Your ma claimed he never breathed a hint of what he'd done with close to a thousand dollars we took."

"You tortured her?"

"She wouldn't talk. It was a mercy when I put a bullet in her. Get the keys." He grabbed for the girl. This time his fingers brushed her hair. She never moved a muscle. Dexter tried again. He clamped down on her bony shoulder. "Do as I say."

"You have to let me go so I can get the keys."

Dexter began to panic. He had no choice but to release her.

Anna remained where she stood like a statue. Her expression never changed.

"Pa never told me anything about stolen money," she said.

"Get me out and we can hunt for it. You and the other two girls—what were they called?—the four of us can hunt all the places you've traveled. Thomas wasn't all that clever."

"You killed Mama," Anna said.

"I said I did. I told you I did!" Dexter shouted now. He stepped back when Anna lifted her hand from the folds of her skirt. She held a small caliber gun.

"And I killed Papa for all he'd done to her and us." She smiled just a little. The way her lips curled chilled Dexter. "That's Jasmine and Ruth and me."

She fired.

Dexter jerked. The small hunk of .32 caliber lead hit him just above the belly button. By the time the fifth bullet tore through him, he no longer cared about the pain. He was dead.

CHAPTER 36

"Well now," said Chris Southern, "there's one lucky break I caught on this." He stared into the locked cell where Frank Dexter sprawled gracelessly on the floor.

"Tell me what it is," Ty Brannigan said with a trace of bitterness. All the effort expended bringing in this cutthroat was for nothing. The gunshots and other wounds he had accumulated were in vain. Seeing Dexter stand trial had been the bright spot in finally arresting him.

The marshal picked up the key ring from the desk and jingled the keys as he walked back to the cell.

Southern smiled ruefully as he said, "All I have to do is explain this to the mayor. How much worse would it be if I had to explain to Beatriz?"

Ty looked at his friend for a moment, then laughed.

"My wife's a pistol, that's for sure. But the mayor and the folks who elected you aren't going to like it one bit that Dexter was shot like an animal in the cell."

"He was an animal," the marshal said, "but finding who did it is going to be hard unless there's a witness willing to speak his piece." He pointed to the end cell where the two bags of money had been stored. "Why he was killed is obvious. He saw whoever took the money, and they weren't inclined to leave behind anybody who could identify them."

"As if anyone would believe him," Ty said. He stared at the body and wondered if his friend was right about what had happened. If someone shot Dexter, the money was a bonus. Knowing the outlaw was locked up seemed more plausible than believing any rumor that the marshal had two bags of money in a cell. Any sensible lawman would store the money over in Diego Salazar's bank, not stash it in a spare cell.

Killing Frank Dexter had to be the primary reason someone had gotten rid of Deputy Conrad.

"Doesn't matter. A prisoner in my custody killed and a stack of money from the Cutbank robbery taken. I should have put it into the bank, but keeping it where I could watch over it seemed better."

"Getting it back to Hutchinson is real important," Ty said. He worried about the deal with the Wyoming and Colorado Railroad falling through. Losing the money he and the other ranchers had put up created a hardship. Not being able to use the spur line to move their cattle was an added problem. He'd have to hire cowhands for a drive that would put a strain on the beeves and require more feedlot time.

All of it was added expense—and he'd lost fifteen hundred dollars in the robbery.

"We'll find it, Ty. I promise. I might not be marshal much longer, but that don't mean I'm giving up running these owlhoots to ground." Southern hitched up his gun belt. "Go out with guns blazing, I say."

Ty jerked around, hand going for his Colt when Conrad came bumbling back in. He was so wide he had to turn sideways to get through the door. For a second the giant deputy stared, then he burst out, "What's happened? Marshal? Did you shoot that varmint? I coulda done it for you. I didn't like the way he mouthed off all the time."

"Where'd you go?" Southern tossed the keys back onto his desk. "You were told not to leave the office as long as the prisoner was in the cell." He cast a quick look into the cell where the two money bags had been stored.

"She said she'd watch over him whilst I helped Father Simon. He needed that stump behind the church blowed up and didn't have dynamite, so I hitched up a chain and pulled it out with a team of mules." He held out bloodied hands where the chain had cut into his flesh.

"Who're you talking about?" Ty asked.

"The padre. You know. Father Simon. He—"

"You said 'she' volunteered to watch the prisoner." Ty had a gut feeling he knew the answer. When Conrad wasn't forthcoming, he said, "Anna is a sorry little girl, isn't she?"

"I'd do anything for her. And the padre, too," Conrad said. "They're good people."

"We need to find the girl," Southern said. He chewed his lower lip. "I can't believe she shot Dexter down in cold blood, but if she didn't, she saw who did. That means she's in danger."

"Where'd she go?" Conrad scratched his head. "She said she was gonna stay here 'til I got back."

"She was either kidnapped or ran away before whoever killed Dexter got around to her."

"Why's that, Marshal?"

Southern heaved a sigh of exasperation.

"Do you see her body anywhere? She either left under her own power or was taken."

"Oh," Conrad said. "That's makes sense. What do you want me to do?"

"Get back to the church and track her down, Deputy. We've let one man get killed today. Having a little girl murdered, too, well now, that's not something else we'll allow."

Conrad gobbled like a turkey, blundered back through the door, and took off at a run.

"You built a fire under him," Ty said. "He's a tad slow, but he's determined. He won't give up until he finds Anna, one way or the other."

"Most of the men I can rely on are out in a posse. How good are you at tracking a man right here in Warknife?"

"Town tracking," said Ty, "usually comes down to asking about the varmint in one saloon after another."

"But," Southern prodded.

"If I had that much money, I'd be inclined to ride out of town and not spend any of it where you or I'd see."

"That's assuming whoever stole the money's got the sense God gave a goose."

"There's the chance they'll avoid the gin mills. We might check over at the Top Hat. Those girls are the ones most likely to take a customer this time of day. If I had a pile of cash burning a hole in my pocket but didn't want to flash it in a saloon, that's the place to go."

"As if any of the soiled doves wouldn't blab about a gent with that much money." Ty drew his Colt and spun the cylinder to be sure it carried a full load. "Whoever's got the money is on the way out of town."

"Time's a'wastin'," Southern said. "I might hang onto my job if I find Dexter's killer and recover the money 'fore everyone in town finds out."

"With Conrad asking around, that won't be long," Ty observed.

They stepped out and turned toward the livery stable when Southern's senior deputy, Glenn Beach, galloped up, waving his hat to get their attention. His horse dug in all four hooves and sent up a cloud of dust as it came a halt.

"Glad I caught you, Marshal. We found the trail." Beach panted hard from the ride. He sucked in his breath and continued, "Early's posse joined one from Cutbank led by Buckman. The trail into the mountains is obvious." He looked hard at Ty and clamped his mouth shut.

"What else, Deputy?" asked Ty. "I'll find out."

"Mister Brannigan, one of our scouts spotted your boy on the trail leading up into the hills."

"Matt?"

"Your younger son, Gregory. He was acting like he was doing the tracking just like us. When we got to the place where he was seen, we found his horse's hoofprints. And we think he picked up a couple of these along the trail." Glenn Beach fumbled around in his vest pocket and pulled out a bill.

Ty took it. He didn't understand and said so.

"We think Greg was on the trail of a robber leaking these out of a bag. Early's found a half dozen other greenbacks."

"Is the posse ready to capture whoever Greg is following?"

"We're taking it slow, but maybe not for much longer. Marshal Buckman's champing at the bit to take all his men on into the mountains and catch the bank robbers."

"Catch?" Ty said skeptically.

Beach turned grim.

"You know Buckman. He ain't seen an outlaw he wasn't inclined to gun down."

"What about the Warknife posse?" Ty started walking fast to the stables. Whatever Greg had gotten himself into was beyond his ability to escape. Tracking bank robbers willing to shoot down each other meant they'd have no hesitation in killing a nosy fifteen-year-old.

"Early's ordered them to take it slow until we know what we're up against. Our count is that four or five robbers have been killed. Nobody's been captured."

"What about the money?" asked Southern. He looked instinctively over his shoulder back into the jailhouse. Add one to the count of outlaws gunned down. And consider two bags of money back in play.

"Two bags have been recovered off robbers who fought to the bitter end. From what the banker told us, six were filled."

"We know about two more," Southern said, motioning Ty to silence. "That means these came from the remaining two." He held up the greenback.

"If we get back four of the gunnysacks, that's got to be close to the twenty thousand the ranchers put into the bank," Ty said.

"We need to get it all back, to be sure. There must have been more than just your railroad money in the safe," Southern said. To Beach he said, "Is there a way to join up with the posse without wandering all around?"

"I made it fast. We can do the same getting back." Beach looked up and made a judgment. "Before sundown, though it gets dark up in the mountains sooner than out on the plains."

"I'll get us spare horses," Ty said. We can swap off when the ones we're riding get tired."

"It's nice to have a rich friend," Southern said. "If things don't go so well here in town, do you need a ramrod on the Circle P?"

"Sorry, I'd need someone who wouldn't set around all the livelong day with his boots hiked up on my desk. The Circle P is a working man's ranch."

Marshal Southern slapped Ty on the back and said, "That's the spirit. We need taxpayers to cough up my exorbitant salary."

"Some think a dollar a day's too much," Ty said.

With more than a trace of sarcasm, Southern said, "Some days I think the same thing. One of them's today."

"Let's get in the saddle so you can earn your keep," Ty said.

* * *

"The horses are in better shape than I am," Southern said. "I'm gettin' too old for that kind of riding."

"There's Bob and the posse," Glenn Beach said. He trotted ahead and hailed the other deputy.

When his deputy was out of earshot, Southern said, "Greg'll be fine. There's nothing to show he even saw the robber."

"He's a youngster," Ty said. "Picking up big bills like he was, he won't think to lift his head and spot what troubles are ahead of him."

"Maybe so, but you might underestimate him. He's growing up fast."

"I want him to stay alive long enough to grow up, though the whipping he's gonna get for running off like he did might stunt his growth for ten years." Ty grumbled. "At least five. And then his ma will get a whack or two at him."

The two deputies rode back and waited for the marshal to notice them.

"What's the situation?" Southern asked.

"We're at the mouth of a canyon. One of the boys says there are a half dozen ways out, so we can't bottle up the mouth and expect to flush out anyone." Bob Early wiped sweat from his forehead. "One scout came back and said he's found an abandoned camp about a mile in. Leastways, he didn't see anybody pokin' around."

"How big is the camp?" Ty asked.

"There were fire pits enough for a dozen men, maybe more. If I were a betting man, I'd say this was where the gang waited before robbing the bank."

"And," added Beach, "we're not that far from your graze, Mister Brannigan. These just might be the rustlers that boosted the size of your herd."

"We took care of those rustlers," Ty said. "But there

weren't any dozen of them when we shot it out. The rest waited to rob the bank?"

"That's mighty bold of them," Southern said, "stealing cattle and robbing a bank at the same time. It certainly fits what Kennard and Marcus told us before that first robbery in Cutbank."

"One crime paid off for them." Ty looked up when a man he didn't recognize rode up.

"Deputies, we put a man on the canyon rim with field glasses. He spotted someone moving around in the camp."

"That's Marshal Buckman's right-hand man," Early said. The tone of his voice put Ty on edge. The Warknife lawman thought little of him, and probably the Cutbank marshal.

"How many?" asked Southern.

"He made out two men. One's got the other all trussed up like a Christmas goose and looks to be torturing him. I don't know what to make of that."

"Whoa, Ty, just hold your horses." Southern held his friend back. "If we charge in there, and that's Greg being held captive, the robber'll get spooked. You know what that means."

"I'll sneak in. I'll ride as close as possible, then go the rest of the way on foot. There's nobody quieter than me."

"Marshal Buckman's all fired up to lead the posse in. He's worried if we don't strike quick, they'll get away." The Cutbank deputy took a deep breath. "There's not much he won't do to get back the loot."

"Keep him in check, Chris," Ty said. "I'll handle this as quick as I can, and do it without anyone getting shot up."

"It does sound as if Buckman's plan is to go in with guns blazing," the Warknife marshal said. "You be careful. And if that is Greg, you get him out safely."

Ty grunted in reply. He hopped onto his dun and heeled the horse into the increasingly dark canyon. Twilight cast long shadows. And before he had gone half the distance, night had fallen. Guiding his horse to the narrow stream, he splashed his way deeper, hoping the sounds he made were muffled by the stream. When he saw a rope corral to the right of the stream, he kicked free and dismounted. The ropes hung empty of any stock. The piles of dung and the way the grass had been cropped told him dozens of horses has been staked out here recently.

Not a single sound of a horse slipped through the dark forest.

He drew his Henry from the saddle sheath and followed a footpath uphill toward what had to be the outlaw camp. No fire guided him. He moved on pure instinct until he reached a spot at the bottom of a long incline. At the top towered a sheer rock face. The best he could tell, soot marred the stone from the ground up fifteen feet or more. Either a large fire had burned there once or a smaller fire had been lit over weeks.

Thumb drawing back the hammer on his rifle, he walked slowly, carefully picking every step. He almost ran forward when he heard a high-pitched thin scream.

"No, no, I won't tell you. No matter what you do, I won't tell you!"

Ty ran now, stumbling over rocks and blundering through old fire pits. Caution be damned! That was his son crying out!

He reached a spot where he saw dark figures. One was stretched out on the ground. The other towered above. A raised knife blade caught a glint of the rising moon's light.

"I'll cut off your nose if you don't tell me. I've had enough."

"Go on, try to bribe me again cuz threatening me'll never work!" Greg kicked out, but his feet were lashed together.

"You should have taken the money. We'd both be happier, me on the trail and you waiting for someone to rescue you."

"Maybe you'd be happy, but I'd be all hogtied and left to

starve to death. Or maybe I'd end up as dinner for a wolf pack if I wasn't able to work myself free."

"What'll it be? Your right ear, then your left? I can save your nose for last. Better tell me what I want to know."

"Take out my tongue. I'm never telling you where my horse is!"

Ty moved closer, lifted his rifle and took careful aim. Before he drew back on the trigger, a bloodcurdling cry echoed off the canyon walls. Pistols fired and the thunder of horses' hooves approaching made him look away at the last instant.

When he swung back, his target was gone.

"Find 'em, men. Find 'em and be sure to get the money!" Paul Buckman's voice filled Ty's ears. As the Cutbank marshal galloped into view, he drew a bead. The lawman had ruined his one chance to save his son.

Somebody had to pay for it and Ty Brannigan wasn't feeling too fussy about who it would be.

CHAPTER 37

Greg Brannigan saw the silvery blade rise high. He braced himself for the inevitable pain.

"Tell me where you left your horse. I don't have time to hunt for it. Which direction did you come from? Along the stream? From which direction? Up or down?"

Greg cried out as the dull knife raked across his chest and opened a shallow cut.

"Things will get a whole lot worse for you. I've heard of how Indians make a couple dozen cuts, none very bad, but they all leak blood and you get all woozy before you die. It takes a long time. And it's supposed to be a real painful way to die."

"You've got time to torture me but not hunt for the horse?" Greg laughed weakly. Sassing the outlaw wasn't the smartest thing he could do, but it was the only weapon at his command. He lay on the ground with his hands bound behind his back and a triple turn of rope around his ankles hogtying him. He moved like a caterpillar, arching his back and inching around, but any chance at escaping his fate looked increasingly dim.

"The rest of my gang's left." Race Cooper looked around

the twilight-shrouded campsite. "I hoped to find one of them here with a spare horse."

"You can't run. Your gang's upped and abandoned you. All you can do is threaten me?"

Cooper towered over him. He lifted the knife high again. Greg sucked in his breath. He had pushed Cooper too far and was going to pay the penalty. He read death in the man's eyes.

"Nothing's gone right, nothing. I lost the rustled cattle because some of my men got greedy." He muttered under his breath but Greg caught, "and were too cowardly to take the bank."

"My horse will have wandered off by now. I don't have him ground-rein trained."

"There's no reason to let you live," Cooper said.

The way he spoke, as if to someone not visible, told Greg his life was measured in seconds now. The outlaw had come to his decision. In a way, Greg was surprised he had lasted this long as the man's prisoner. There wasn't a shred of decency in this man's being.

Greg pushed aside the pain from all the tortures inflicted on him and made what was going to be his last attempt to keep breathing.

"There's no call to kill me, either. If you set out on foot, it'll be a day or two before I can get free. Don't let me see what direction you're going. That'll give you a good head start."

"Walking?" Cooper shook his head. "And there won't be a chance you'd figure out where I went if you're dead." He lifted the knife high again. "Tell me where your horse is!"

Greg swallowed hard. This time the outlaw meant to use it with a deadly thrust into his heart.

"No, no, I won't tell you. No matter what you do, I won't tell you!"

"I'll cut off your nose if you don't tell me. I've had enough."

"Go on, try to bribe me again cuz threatening me'll never work!" Greg kicked out but his feet were lashed together.

"You should have taken the money. We'd both be happier, me on the trail and you waiting for someone to rescue you."

"Maybe you'd be happy, but I'd be all hogtied and left to starve to death. Or maybe I'd end up as dinner for a wolf pack if I wasn't able to work myself free."

"What'll it be? Your right ear, then your left? I can save your nose for last. Better tell me what I want to know."

"Take out my tongue. I'm never telling you where my horse is!"

Greg and Cooper jerked around when the soul-piercing shout echoed all around, followed by the rapid firing of six-shooters.

"They've found you," Greg gasped out. "That's the posse come to arrest you."

Greg cried out again when Cooper bent over and slashed at the ropes around his ankles. The dull knife sawed through and freed him. He tried kicking. Cooper drove the butt end of the knife into his belly.

"You quit that or I'll kill you here and now." Cooper yanked Greg to his feet and shoved him upslope.

Greg went along with the outlaw's orders. He realized that death flirted with him. The instant it benefited Cooper, he'd kill his captive. Greg had to keep being an asset.

In the distance he heard, "Find 'em, men. Find 'em and be sure to get the money!" He didn't recognize the voice. As much as he wanted that to be his pa or Marshal Southern, he was happy to hear anyone in the posse coming after him.

"You're outnumbered," he told Cooper. "If you put up a fight, they're gonna kill you right here on the spot."

"Better to go down in a gunfight than to let them drop a noose around my neck. I've seen too many men hanged to want to do a midair two-step."

He shoved Greg ahead of him. For a moment Greg thought he had a chance to escape. Cooper began digging like a badger, sending dirt and rock into the air. He yanked two bulging gunnysacks from the ground. He tied them together.

"Come here, kid." Cooper slung the bags around Greg's neck, weighing him down. "You're my pack mule. Get moving." He shoved hard and sent Greg staggering along, off balance by the bags banging into his chest and the rope tying them together cutting into the back of his neck.

Greg fought to keep his feet under him and moving. Hands tied behind his back, he kept upright by taking shorter steps. This infuriated Cooper. He slammed his hand against the back of his prisoner's head, sending Greg forward onto his knees.

"Move an inch and you're a dead man."

The cold words hung in the air for a moment before Race Cooper reacted. He threw himself into Greg. The pair of them rolled over and over.

"Give up, I told you!"

This time a bullet came along with the order. It kicked up a tiny tornado inches from Greg's head.

"Don't shoot me. Shoot him!" he called.

"Greg, stay still. Let me get him in my sights."

"Pa!" Greg kicked out and tried to get away from his captor in spite of what his father told him. This kicked up a dust cloud, obscuring everything.

"You won't get away, Cooper. Hands in the air."

"You found out my name? That must mean Dexter spilled his guts, too. Either you and that Warknife marshal are experts at torture or my men have loose tongues."

"Pa, he's—" That was all Greg got out before the cords around his neck tightened. He started to choke.

"I'll kill your kid, rancher man. I swear it. I've got nothing to lose."

"You think the marshal tortures his prisoners? You'll find out the meaning of torture if you harm one hair on my son's head. I know ways to make you last a week before you die."

"That sounds a lot like what I promised your whelp. I've got a gun put to his head. Don't make me put a bullet through his head."

"He's got the drop on me, Pa. Don't let him get away." Greg choked again when Cooper yanked on one of the gunnysacks. The cord bit harder into the boy's neck.

"If you don't get me out of this trap, you'll bury him, Brannigan. I swear it."

Greg wondered what was going on. The thunder from hooves had died down and was replaced by gunfire. He'd never been in battle, but no skirmish ever sounded fiercer. The acrid scent of gunpowder drifted uphill.

"Who're they fighting?" Cooper asked.

"Don't pay them any heed. This is between you and me, Cooper." Ty Brannigan moved from shadows into view.

"Pa, duck!" Greg felt the muzzle move from his head and knew what Cooper intended. The discharge next to his ear left him deaf.

Ty Brannigan had anticipated the move and returned fire. He shot high, hoping to hit Cooper and miss his son. For that Greg was grateful, but Cooper was a creature used to fighting such battles. The gun once more pressed hot and deadly into his temple.

"Listen good. You're dead if you try to escape." Cooper pulled Greg along to get farther from the angry sounds of Buckman's posse.

As Cooper tugged on the cord holding the gunnysacks

around Greg's neck, the boy slammed himself forward as hard as he could. The cord snapped. Both money bags tumbled to the ground. Cooper had to choose between recovering the money or going after his hostage.

He made the wrong choice.

Greg rolled over and over and past the campsite to where he had been captured. Getting his bulky body all twisted around, he slid his tied hands under his heels and brought them up in front of his body. Grasping at rocks and bushes as he slid, he stopped his downhill fall.

Not five feet away lay his shotgun. Greg wasted no time rolling over to it. He seized the gun and came to his knees. He fumbled a few seconds and aimed his shotgun in the bank robber's direction.

"Greg, are you all right?" His pa came up beside him. "Let me get those ropes off you."

Greg held out his arms. The quick movement of a sharp knife severed the ropes cleanly with a single cut. He gasped as circulation returned to his hands. His fingers felt like fat sausages. Then they began to tingle. Hanging onto his shotgun was hard but he succeeded.

"If I get a chance to shoot him, I swear, I will!"

"Calm down, son. He's not going to get away."

Ty Brannigan's words were drowned out by new gunfire from farther downhill. Then the wave moved closer.

"Marshal! Don't shoot. It's me, Ty Brannigan. Do you hear me, Buckman?"

"Hold your fire, men. It's that damned rancher." Buckman trooped closer, brandishing his six-shooter. "Who's that with you?"

"My son, you fool. You could have gotten him killed barging in the way you did."

Greg sat back on his haunches as his pa went to argue

with the Cutbank marshal about the way he and his posse had rushed in.

"What about Cooper?" he shouted. Neither his pa nor the marshal heard him. Whatever sparked the gunfight made things even worse. The level of sound echoing off the canyon walls turned everywhere above the stream into a din worse than fireworks after a crooked politician's election victory.

Greg got to his feet and rubbed circulation back into his limbs. Even after he felt more like himself, the noisy argument continued and the gunfight at lower levels. He made sure the .410 was loaded and turned back upslope.

Race Cooper had the money and nobody seemed interested in catching him. Greg was furious at being taken prisoner and used as a pawn. He stalked back to where he had been shoved to the ground.

The moon was higher in the sky, casting a silvery sheen over the land. Greg studied the ground and found boot prints leading away. He pulled the shotgun up under his arm and pressed the stock close to his body. The dozen cuts Cooper had inflicted on him all burned as if salt had been poured into the wounds. He wondered if the Sunset Kid sweat as much. He settled down and looked at the trail winding into darkness above him.

If the posse and his pa weren't going after Cooper, then he would.

The path led to a narrow footpath winding back and forth up the side of the canyon. He saw someone halfway up to the rim. Greg put his head down and began his pursuit in earnest. Race Cooper was not going to get away, not from Gregory Brannigan.

CHAPTER 38

Greg Brannigan craned his neck around, hunting the narrow foot trail above him for any sign that Race Cooper had stopped. Even plowing ahead as fast as he could, Greg worried the outlaw had enough of a head start to reach the canyon rim and then vanish into the night. On foot, Cooper couldn't make the speed as if he were on horseback, but then Greg lacked speed enough to catch a determined man, frightened for his life and liberty. Not for the first time, he cursed his clumsiness. He was like a colt, full of piss and vinegar but unable to focus it into anything useful.

His size and weight had kept him from getting killed earlier. Now it held him back. He was so broad that climbing the trail turned into an ordeal. Every time the path switched back, his body raked along the rock. Together with the torture and cuts Cooper had used on him made every step a kaleidoscope of shooting pain.

Leaning far out over the narrow trail, he hunted for any glint of moonlight off metal above. When he saw it, he pulled his shotgun to his shoulder and fired. A foot-long tongue of yellow-orange flame lanced into the night. Fifty feet away tiny bird shot pellets bounced off rock. Greg cursed. He had hoped to hit Cooper.

Failure goaded him to try even harder.

Thick legs working like pistons on a locomotive, he expended even more effort to overtake the fleeing cutthroat. As he rounded a sharp bend in the trail, he saw what he thought was a man huddled over.

"Drop your gun, Cooper!" He trained his shotgun on the middle of the darkness. Two glowing yellow-green eyes turned to him.

Greg stood his ground. Facing a cougar on the trail was about the worst that could happen. The cat padded softly toward him. A growl deep in the cougar's throat warned of an attack. He still stood his ground. If he tried to run back down the steep trail, he'd be dinner in a few seconds. Advancing on the cat challenged it.

He froze. So did the mountain lion.

They held position for long seconds. Then the standoff ended. He wondered if the sweat dropping from his forehead to the ground provoked the cougar. It came another few steps closer, let out a ferocious howl and then turned uphill. A single jump carried it away. Greg sagged in relief. Every muscle in his body trembled.

Then he looked up. Another dark figure blocked the trail. This one stood man high. Moonlight caught the worn-smooth silver of the Colt's hammer. Then it disappeared as the man reached for his iron.

Greg let out a scream of pure frustration, hoisted the butt of the shotgun to his shoulder, and fired.

The next scream came from Race Cooper.

"You put out my eye! I'm blind!"

Greg worked the action on his shotgun. It was only a .410 but inflicted pain if he hit the right spot. He fired again. Either he missed completely or Cooper endured new stinging pain better than he had the first time.

The outlaw's six-shooter flared in the dark. A heavy slug

tore past Greg's head and drove him back a few paces to a spot where the switchback in the trail protected him.

"I shoulda killed you when I had the chance. You're one more thing that didn't go right." Cooper advanced. In his right hand he carried his six-gun. His left pressed into the eye that Greg had shot out. It was as if he dared Greg to fire at him.

The small-bore shotgun belched out more bird shot. Cooper grunted, then laughed.

"You hit the money. I never thought bags of money'd work as armor. Run, little rabbit, run. Let me get you ready for the stewpot."

"Rabbits run. I'm a Brannigan. I don't run." Greg stepped out and fired again. Once more the bird shot struck Cooper without causing any significant wound.

Greg saw Cooper lift his pistol and draw a bead. Before the outlaw's trigger finger pulled back, Greg lowered his aim and fired again and again, as fast as he could pump in a new shell. After three shots, he came up empty.

But the barrage had its effect.

Race Cooper clutched his leg. When he tried to take a step it folded under him like a bad poker hand. As he fell over the brink in the narrow trail, Greg heard him moan about getting his kneecap shot off.

Greg looked over the edge. Cooper hit the trail fifteen feet below, then tumbled over the shoulder again. He cartwheeled out of sight. A meaty thunk told of him finally coming to a halt after falling almost forty feet.

Greg slung his shotgun over his shoulder. He had something else to carry. Just behind where Cooper had made his stand lay two coarsely woven sacks. Poking them produced a crinkly sound. He had recovered the two bags of greenbacks stolen from the Cutbank bank.

Slinging them over his shoulder, glad he wasn't being

strangled by them now, he made his way back down the trail into who knew what turmoil. The outlaw camp—Desperado's Den—was still lit up with gunfire. By now a hundred rounds must have been fired. And there were more to come.

"You're the south end of a northbound jackass," Ty Brannigan raged. Marshal Buckman shoved out his ample belly and tried to knock Ty back a pace. He had the weight, but Ty was taller and had planted his feet securely.

The battle of wills went on.

"You'd let him go," Buckman said. "If I hadn't led my posse in when I did, there'd be all hell to pay."

"What's going on down there?" Ty glanced toward the lower reaches of the camp. "I'd wager you a dollar to a dime that your men got spooked and are shooting at each other now."

"The outlaw gang. They're flushing them all out of hiding."

"The camp was deserted."

"What about Cooper? Are you sayin' he wasn't here?"

"He had my boy as a hostage. You're lucky Greg got away. If Cooper had harmed one hair on his head because of your attack, you'd be in a grave alongside his."

"You threatening me, Brannigan? You think you're all high and mighty because you worked as a marshal in some tough towns. There's no way you can imagine what I put up with in Cutbank. I—"

"Stuff a sock in it, Paul." Chris Southern trooped up, shoulders sagging from fatigue. "You've done nothing but put the whole herd of us in danger."

"My men'll take care of the gang. See? The shooting's dyin' down."

"They're either out of ammo," Southern said, "or they finally twigged to the fact that the only outlaw in camp was Race Cooper."

"And my son," Ty cut in.

"And Greg Brannigan," Southern finished. He slowly surveyed the deserted camp. "Where are they?"

Ty looked from his friend to Paul Buckman. He let out a low groan of disbelief at being distracted so much he forgot why they'd ridden into the mountains.

He tore past Buckman and ran up the steep slope to where his son had been held hostage.

"Greg! Where are you? Gregory Brannigan!"

The sound of a small-bore shotgun firing pulled Ty toward the base of the wall. It took him a minute to find the trail. The dirt had been scuffed up, but the rocky path wasn't much good for holding tracks. The sound of the shotgun firing again repeatedly made him step away from the base and peer upward. In the darkness he caught dim figures moving about. Then came a long, loud scream as one of them plunged over the side.

The body hit the side of the canyon wall several times and finally bounced to a halt a dozen feet from where Ty stood, not too badly banged up. He drew his six-shooter and aimed it.

"Don't reach for your iron, Cooper. You're a dead man if you do."

"Brannigan? Do I have to kill your entire family?"

"Greg? Where is he?"

Ty was faked out when Cooper turned to look up the side of the canyon face. The outlaw went for his six-gun. He got off the first shot but missed. Ty had his Colt out and firing before Race Cooper got a second shot away. In the wall of lead he sent toward the cutthroat one of them hit something vital.

Cooper grunted and sat down. His pistol slipped from dead fingers, and he slumped against the stone face. From where he stood, Ty saw the man's eyelids hadn't closed. Moonlight gleamed on sightless eyes.

He spun when a noise above him caught his attention.

"Look out below!" The warning came too late.

A heavy sack hit Ty in the shoulder, sending him reeling. He regained his balance and saw a second dark bag plunging downward. This landed several feet away.

Stretching his arm struck by the first gunnysack, he reached out and untied the cord holding it shut. Ty thrust his hands in and came out clutching a fistful of greenbacks. He stuffed it back into the bag and had just untied it to check its contents when his son came slipping and sliding down the trail.

"You got him, Pa. I saw it. You shot him!"

"And you beaned me with a bag of money."

"Sorry," Greg said contritely. He leaned out and peered around his father to stare at the dead outlaw. "I hit him in the face and pumped his leg full of shot. But you took him out."

"Come on, son. You don't need to stand around staring at a corpse. Here." Ty hefted one bag and shoved it into Greg's hands. "Carry that. And I'll carry the other one."

"Pa?"

"What?"

"Do you mind if I take both sacks? I went through hell to get them and it'd make me feel good to be the one returning them to Cutbank."

"Marshal Buckman can get them back to the bank," Ty said. "And stop swearing. You know your ma hates that."

"Yes, sir." Greg smiled and added, "Damned right she does!"

CHAPTER 39

Greg found himself pushed aside as his pa, the marshal, and about everyone else in Warknife crowded around to find out what had happened. The gathered citizens, many who had ridden with the posse, cheered when Southern held up the two bags filled with greenbacks that had been recovered.

"I got them back," Greg said to no one in particular. No one paid him any attention. He stepped back and saw nothing else happening in town. When he didn't see Anna anywhere, he drifted away from the festivities and walked to the church.

He was surprised to see Father Simon sitting on a stump at the rear of the church. Deputy Conrad had claimed to have removed that stump. Not getting it out of the ground must have affected the padre something fierce. Greg had seen men about to cry before. He had held back tears when Race Cooper tortured him, but what disturbed the priest puzzled him.

With a soft tread, he came up on him and stood until the man noticed him. It took a few seconds. Father Simon looked up and asked, "What can I do for you, Greg?"

"Everyone's over at the jailhouse. Even the mayor's making a speech. Once he gets all wound up, he's good for the rest of the afternoon. At least he's not blaming Marshal Southern for the escapes and Frank Dexter getting himself shot while in custody." Greg sighed. "It sounded like he was taking credit for bringing the Cooper gang to justice and getting back the stolen money and, well, everything good."

Father Simon nodded slowly.

"A politician's always ready to let his constituents know how good he is. A priest is the only one to hear how terrible he can be." He turned forlorn eyes to Greg. "You've heard, haven't you?"

"I've heard all of him I want to." Greg stood a little taller, and his heart skipped a beat. "What haven't I heard?"

"Anna," the priest said.

"Where is she?" Greg looked around, expecting her to pop up. "What about her sisters? Where are they?"

"Jasmine and Ruth are safe. The Gentry family—you know them?"

"Over by Bitter Creek? They lost all three of their children to the grippe last Christmas. A real shame." Greg brightened. "Are Anna and her sisters there?"

Father Simon nodded solemnly.

"That's good since the Gentrys need children to help out. They're decent people and losing all their kids like that was . . . awful." Greg grinned. "That's gonna be a big change, though. They lost three boys and now they've got three girls." His grin faded when he saw the priest didn't share his enthusiasm for Anna and her sisters finding a home in Warknife.

"I don't know how to tell you this," the cleric said. "Jasmine and Ruth went to stay with the Gentrys, but Anna . . ."

"Something's happened to her!"

The priest closed his eyes. His lips moved in a quick prayer, then he plowed ahead with the confession.

"She killed a man, Greg. She shot the outlaw who'd ridden with the gang. His name was Frank Dexter."

"Why'd she do that? He did something to her. He must have!"

"That was her uncle. And he'd killed her mother."

Greg heard the words but understanding them took a long time. He finally blurted, "He deserved it!"

The padre shook his head.

"No man deserves to be gunned down while he's caged like an animal. But she also confessed to me that she'd killed her father. He did terrible things to his family."

Greg felt as if he had stepped off a cliff. He started to speak but words clogged his throat. Then he coughed and felt the block go away. Unexplained details all came crashing together and fit together in a way he hardly wanted to believe.

"I might have buried him. Anna's father." He explained to the priest. "I never knew. She never said a word, but then I didn't want to upset her bragging on how I found the body and all."

"She took the money Dexter had with him after the bank robbery."

Greg tried to sort out what he felt about that. Hearing that a girl he had sought to impress was a killer confused him. Anna hadn't seemed the type to kill the way she had confessed. Even if she had good reasons, shooting down a man locked up in a cell wasn't what decent folks did. Killing was bad, but he had an awful feeling about what Anna had done with the money taken from the Cutbank robbery.

"No, Greg, no. She did the right thing. She gave it all to me. For the church she said, but knowing where it came from, keeping it was out of the question."

"Where is it?"

"In the bank. The Warknife bank. Your grandfather's taken custody of it. When things settle down, the marshal can transfer it back to Cutbank however seems best."

"Or when it's sent to the railroad they can stop here and add it to the rest." Greg felt adrift. "We've got four gunny-sacks of the six taken. It might be all the railroad needs in those four money bags."

"It'd be better if Marshal Southern and your pa and the other ranchers around town delivered it."

"Where's Anna? I want to talk to her. We can figure this out."

"She's gone, Greg. She left. I think she kept a few dollars, but she didn't tell anyone where she headed."

"Jasmine. She must have told Jasmine. Or Ruth."

"They claim she just left in the middle of the night. I believe them. It's Anna's only way to protect them."

"Protect them," Greg said dully. That made sense. Anna had killed to protect them, to avenge their mother's death. If the two girls had no idea where their oldest sister went, they'd never be able to betray her, even accidentally.

If she had told him, he'd keep her secret. He had endured Race Cooper's torture when all that mattered was revealing where he'd tethered his horse. For something this important, Greg would die before telling anyone where she had gone.

"Greg," the priest said, putting his hand on the boy's shoulder. "She just lit a shuck. She didn't have anywhere in particular in mind. She's just running."

"That's no way to live," he said.

"I hope she'll find peace, but with two mortal sins weighing down her soul . . ." Father Simon shook his head.

"Even with a few dollars to live on, how can she . . . ?"

"She never said but there might be some legacy from her father she can claim. From some dealing with her uncle back in Kansas having to do with food and boxcars. She wasn't too specific."

"Her pa left her money?" Greg's mouth turned dry. She willingly killed him. How had her father and uncle made that money? "You said this was back in Kansas? Where her family lived?"

Father Simon gripped Greg's shoulder so hard he winced. The priest inadvertently opened some of the shallow cuts Race Cooper had inflicted.

"Let her go, Greg. She needs to face her own demons and find her own angels."

Greg turned away and stared into the distance. Asking around, he was sure he could find which direction Anna had gone. Or could he? She'd sneaked out in the middle of the night like some kind of thief. Kansas? Where? She'd never told him but her sisters had to know. If he asked . . .

"What would the Sunset Kid do?"

"What did you say, Greg?"

"Nothing, Father. Nothing."

"Will I see you and the rest of the Brannigan clan this Sunday?"

"It's been a while since we all made it into town," he said. He thought it over for a minute. "Ma would like that but it might be Father Ralph's turn to see us all."

"In Cutbank," the priest said, nodding. "Dividing your piety isn't ideal, but I applaud your family keeping traditions. He was the priest who conducted their wedding mass, wasn't he?"

Cheers from the crowd drew Greg again. The mayor must be close to finishing. That had to be why everyone applauded. He let the padre hug him before letting him go.

* * *

"Your dedication to what's right is admirable, son," Ty Brannigan said. "But your friend did some terrible things."

"I know, but she had reasons."

"Self-defense is one thing. Revenge is another." Ty pursed his lips, then asked, "Do you have any idea where she'd go?"

"I reckon I don't know her at all. Not once did I think she'd kill her own pa, much less her uncle. Her family was hunting for a safe place to live. It wasn't Warknife."

"Her sisters will be in good hands at the Gentrys." Ty knew the couple and how devastated they had been losing all their children within three weeks around Christmas. "Don't try to make either of the girls tell you if Anna comes back to see them."

"I know. Better to wash my hands entirely. Walk away. Forget her."

"No, not that. Don't forget her, Greg. Learn from knowing her."

"I never thought she'd kill anyone!" he blurted.

"Come on. Let's go to the barbershop. We can both use a bath. You first. You stink to high heaven."

"Me? That's you, Pa. You're the one that smells like a pig wallow."

Joking, they went to Merlin Dempsey's barbershop. Greg hurried through his bath so his pa could linger. Ty Brannigan moaned and stretched and complained about his aching joints. While the bathwater was changed, Greg pulled out the battered copy of the epic adventures of the Sunset Kid and handed it to Mister Dempsey.

"You sure read that one to pieces, son," the barber said, hardly glancing at the dime novel.

"That's all right, Merlin. Put it on the bill," Ty called from the back room. "He deserves something for all he's been through."

"I enjoyed it a whole bunch, sir. I'm sorry it kinda fell apart."

"They're meant to be read and thrown away," Merlin Dempsey said. "Wait a minute." The barber opened a drawer and pulled out another dime novel. Solemnly, he handed it to Greg.

"I'll take real good care of this one, Mister Dempsey. I promise."

"Keep it. Your pa says you deserve a reward for everything you've done. And I'll put it on the Brannigan bill!"

Greg looked up in surprise.

Dempsey winked and said, "Word gets around. The Sunset Kid doesn't hold a candle to you."

Greg looked at the dime novel. His pa saw his pleasure and winked at him. Then Ty Brannigan sank down under the sudsy water and let out a small sigh of pleasure.

CHAPTER 40

"Finished saddle soaping all the tack, Greg?" Ty Brannigan poked his head into the barn. "Good work. Now get on over and gather the eggs. Your ma's fixing something special for dinner and needs them."

"Done here, sir," Greg said. It had been a week since the bank robbery and the shootout in Desperado's Den and all the rest. In spite of himself and resolving never to forget Anna, he found her less in his thoughts as more and more chores were piled on him.

"Your ma wants you to go over the ranch accounts before supper, too. She says there's a discrepancy."

"I tracked down a fifty-dollar mistake." Greg had been given the added authority over ranch finances. It hadn't been what he expected when his pa told him he was getting greater responsibilities. Greg had thought that meant the family would treat him like a grown-up. Instead it meant keeping all his old chores with added ones.

With his ma watching him like a hawk, he had the feeling any mistakes would be laid on his shoulders. The Circle P spent a pile more money than he had ever believed. Now keeping track of it and not wasting a penny was his responsibility.

"That's good. Investing that fifteen hundred dollars with the Wyoming and Colorado about drained our account."

"When does the railroad begin laying track up to Cutbank?"

"Any day now. They have to get close enough for all the ranches to move the cattle to the main line by the end of next month. It's already getting chilly out."

"Snow'll be here soon," Greg said.

"But it's not going to be a cold winter. Your ma said the caterpillars aren't anywhere near as woolly as last year. That's a good sign. And Matt saw a bear up in the north graze. It hardly had any fat on it. Another sign the winter's going to be mild."

Greg filed away those signs about the weather. It mattered a lot whether the ranch had to prepare for a vicious winter or one with only a bit of snow. Since that fifteen hundred dollars had been spent, there wasn't much in the ranch account to buy extra forage for the horses until the herd was moved, sold, and money from that flowed back. The notion amused Greg. Cash flow. Like money was a river that dried up at times and at others flooded everything.

"If it looks like we need extra grain, go on over to the bank and get the ranch a loan. I've signed the papers letting you do some borrowing. Your grandpa will be happy to see you. He complained that we hide out here to avoid him."

"A Brannigan never hides from anything," Greg said.

"Except you and your chores. Get to them. And don't worry about the rooster. He's going to join us for dinner. Now get moving. Make hay while the sun shines."

Greg sighed. More work, more responsibility. He had to figure out how much grain the horses needed if they were snowed in for weeks on end and then it was his responsibility to put the Circle P in debt because of it.

"Pa, can Caroline tend the chickens and get the eggs?"

"What are you going to do?"

"I'm trying to figure out how to divert the stream into a new stock pond. That'll let us water a couple hundred head more next summer."

"How in the world are you going to do that? The pasture's way above the stream. You'd have to pump water up fifty feet or more."

"I've got an idea or two," Greg said. He reached behind his back and touched the dime novel tucked into his waistband.

"Be back for supper. You know how your ma gets if you're late. And it's her special chicken and dumplings, if you hadn't guessed."

"I won't miss that, sir."

Greg gathered the odds and ends he needed, lashed them together in a bundle and then loaded them on his horse. All the way to the pasture he thought and schemed and tried to keep from getting too anxious.

After dropping all the parts and tools to the ground near the stream, he let his horse run free. Greg pulled out the dime novel Mister Dempsey had given him and found the spot with the dog-eared page where he had stopped reading the night before. For close to an hour he read, frowning at times and grinning at others. When he completed a section, he put the book away and went to his pile of wood and gears.

He had spent a fair amount of time putting some of the equipment together. Now it was time to see if he was clever enough to duplicate what he read into a working paddle-wheel. Another hour's work finished his model. He yanked out a dowel rod used as a brake and the crude pump began work, using the speed of the stream to spin the wheel that lifted water up into a small pond he had dug near the running water.

Greg stood back and watched his tiny lake form all by

itself. He had built this model after getting inspiration from the dime novel.

He took out the Frank Reade dime novel *Steam Man of the Plains,* about steam power and machines and how to improve everything. If he figured out how to use details in the book to supply water for the herd in a new spot next year, what else might he do?

Gregory Brannigan had a lot of planning to do if he wanted to change the Circle P for the better before getting back to his chores.

**TURN THE PAGE
FOR AN EXCITING PREVIEW!**

**JOHNSTONE COUNTRY.
WITH A DETOUR THROUGH HELL.**

**Legendary gunfighter Perley Gates
always fights on the side of the angels.
But in the East Texas county of Angelina,
the war is half over—and the devils are winning . . .**

In spite of his holy-sounding name, Perley Gates is not his brother's keeper. Even so, he can't refuse a simple request by his elder brother Rubin. Rubin is starting his own cattle ranch, and he wants Perley to deliver the contract for it—through a lawless stretch of land called Angelina County. Perley can't blame his brother for wanting a piece of the American Dream. But for the famed gunslinger, it means a nightmare journey through hell itself . . .

The trouble starts when Perley and his men meet some damsels in distress—a lovely group of saloon girls with a broken wagon wheel. Being a Good Samaritan, Perley feels honor-bound to help them. But when the travelers cross paths with an ornery gang of vicious outlaws, things turn deadly—and fast. It only gets worse from there. Angelina County is infested with a special breed of vermin known as the Tarpley family. And this corrupt clan has a gunslinger of their own— who'd love nothing more than to take down a living legend like Perley Gates . . .

National Bestselling Authors
William W. Johnstone and J.A. Johnstone

THE LONESOME GUN
A Perley Gates Western

On sale now wherever Pinnacle Books are sold.

Live Free. Read Hard.
www.williamjohnstone.net

Visit us at www.kensingtonbooks.com

CHAPTER 1

"Becky, another hungry customer just walked in," Lucy Tate said. "I'm getting some more coffee for my tables. Can you wait on him? He looks like trouble." She looked at Beulah Walsh and winked, so Beulah knew she was up to some mischief.

"I was just fixing to wash up some more cups," Becky said. "We're about to run out of clean ones. Can he wait a minute?"

"I don't know," Lucy answered. "He looks like he's the impatient kind. He might make a big scene if somebody doesn't wait on him pretty quick."

"I don't want to make a customer mad," Beulah said as she aimed a mischievous grin in Lucy's direction. "Maybe I can go get him seated."

"Oh, my goodness, no," Becky said. "I'll go take care of him." She was sure there was no reason why Lucy couldn't have taken care of a new customer, instead of causing Beulah to do it. Beulah was busy enough as cook and owner. She dried her hands on a dishtowel and hurried out into the hotel dining room. Lucy and Beulah hurried right after her as far as the door, where they stopped to watch Becky's reaction.

"Perley!" Becky exclaimed joyfully and ran to meet him.

Surprised by her exuberance, he staggered a couple of steps when she locked her arms around his neck. "I thought you were never coming home," she said. "You didn't say you were gonna be gone so long."

"I didn't think I would be," Perley said. "We were just supposed to deliver a small herd of horses to a ranch near Texarkana, but we ran into some things we hadn't counted on. And that held us up pretty much. I got back as quick as I could. Sonny Rice went with Possum and me, and he ain't back yet." She started to ask why, but he said, "I'll tell you all about it, if you'll get me something to eat."

"Sit down, Sweetie," she said, "and I'll go get you started." He looked around quickly to see if anyone had heard what she called him, but it was too late. He saw Lucy and Beulah grinning at him from the kitchen door. Becky led him to a table right outside the kitchen door and sat him down while she went to get his coffee. "I was just washing up some cups when you came in. I must have known I needed a nice clean cup for someone special."

He was both delighted and embarrassed over the attention she gave him. And he wanted to tell her he'd prefer that she didn't do it in public, but he was afraid he might hurt her feelings if he did. Unfortunately, Lucy and Beulah were not the only witnesses to Becky's show of affection for the man she had been not so secretly in love with for a couple of years. Finding it especially entertaining, two drifters on their way to Indian Territory across the Red River spoke up when Becky came back with Perley's coffee.

"Hey, darlin'," Rafer Samson called out, "bring that coffeepot out here. Sweetie ain't the only one that wants coffee. You'd share some of that coffee, wouldn't you, Sweetie?"

"Dang, Rafer," his partner joined in. "You'd best watch what you're sayin'. Ol' Sweetie might not like you callin' him that. He might send that waitress over here to take care of you."

That was as far as they got before Lucy stepped in to put a stop to it. "Listen, fellows, why don't you give it a rest? Don't you like the way I've been taking care of you? We've got a fresh pot of coffee brewing on the stove right now. I'll make sure you get the first cups poured out of it, all right?"

"I swear," Rafer said. "Does he always let you women do the talkin' for him?"

"Listen, you two boneheads," Lucy warned, "I'm trying to save you from going too far with what you might think is fun. Don't force Perley Gates into something that you don't wanna be any part of."

"Ha!" Rafer barked. "Who'd you say? Pearly somethin'?"

"It doesn't matter," Lucy said, realizing she shouldn't have spoken Perley's name. "You two look old enough to know how to behave. Don't start any trouble. Just eat your dinner, and I'll see that you get fresh coffee as soon as it's ready."

But Rafer was sure he had touched a sensitive spot the women in the dining room held for the mild-looking young man. "What did she call him, Deke? Pearly somethin'?"

"Sounded like she said Pearly Gates," Deke answered. "I swear it did."

"Pearly Gates!" Rafer blurted loud enough for everyone in the dining room to hear. "His mama named him Pearly Gates!"

Lucy made one more try. "All right, you've had your fun. He's got an unusual name. How about dropping it now, outta respect for the rest of the folks eating their dinner in here?"

"To hell with the rest of the folks in here," he responded, seeming to take offense. "I'll say what I damn-well please.

It ain't up to you, no how. If he don't like it, he knows where I'm settin'."

Lucy could see she was getting nowhere. "You keep it up, and you're liable to find out a secret that only the folks in Paris, Texas, know. And you ain't gonna like it."

"Thanks for the warnin', darlin'. I surely don't want to learn his secret. Now go get us some more coffee." As soon as she walked away, he called out, "Hey, tater, is your name Pearly Gates?"

Knowing he could ignore the two no longer, Perley answered. "That's right," he said. "I was named after my grandpa. Perley was his name. It sounds like the Pearly Gates up in Heaven, but it ain't spelt the same."

"Well, you gotta be some kinda sweet little girlie-boy to walk around with a name like that," Rafer declared. "Ain't that right, Deke?"

"That's right, Rafer," Deke responded like a puppet. "A real man wouldn't have a name like that."

"I know you fellows are just havin' a little fun with my name, but I'd appreciate it if you'd stop now. I don't mind it all that much, but I think it upsets my fiancée."

Perley's request caused both his antagonists to pause for a moment. "It upsets his what?" Deke asked.

"I don't know," Rafer answered, "his fi-ant-cee, whatever that is. Maybe it's a fancy French word for his behind. We upset his behind." He turned to look at the few other customers in the dining room, none of whom would meet his eye. "We upset his fancy behind."

"I'm sorry, Becky," Perley said. "I sure didn't mean to cause all this trouble. Tell Beulah I'll leave, and they oughta calm down after I'm gone."

Beulah was standing just inside the kitchen door, about ready to put an end to the disturbance, and she heard what Perley said. "You'll do no such thing," she told him. "Lucy shouldn't have told 'em your name. You sit right there and let Becky get your dinner." She walked out of the kitchen then and went to the table by the front door where the customers deposited their firearms while they ate. She picked up the two gun belts that Rafer and Deke had left there, took them outside, and dropped them on the steps. When she came back inside, she went directly to their table and informed them. "I'm gonna have to ask you to leave now, since your mamas didn't teach you how to behave in public. I put your firearms outside the door. There won't be any charge for what you ate if you get up and go right now."

"The hell you say," Rafer replied. "We'll leave when we're good and ready."

"I can't have you upsettin' my other customers," Beulah said. "So do us all the courtesy of leaving peacefully, and like I said, I won't charge you nothin' for what you ate."

"You threw our guns out the door?" Deke responded in disbelief. He thought about what she said for only a brief moment, then grabbed his fork and started shoveling huge forkfuls of food in his mouth as fast as he could. He washed it all down with the remainder of his coffee, wiped his mouth with his sleeve, and belched loudly. "Let's go, Rafer."

"I ain't goin' nowhere till I'm ready, and I ain't ready right now," Rafer said, and remained seated at the table. "If you're through, go out there and get our guns offa them steps."

"Lucy," Beulah said, "Step in the hotel lobby and tell David we need the sheriff."

"Why, you ol' witch!" Rafer spat. "I oughta give you somethin' to call the sheriff about!" He stood up and pushed his chair back, knocking it over in the process.

That was as far as Perley could permit it to go. He got up and walked over to face Rafer. "You heard the lady," he said. "This is her place of business, and she don't want you and your friend in here. So why don't you two just go on out like she said, and there won't be any need to call the sheriff up here."

Rafer looked at him in total disbelief. Then a sly smile spread slowly across his face. "Why don't you go outside with me?"

"What for?" Perley asked, even though he knew full well the reason for the invitation.

"Oh, I don't know. Just to see what happens, I reckon." Finding a game that amused him now, he continued. "Do you wear a gun, Perley?"

"I've got a gun on the table with the others," Perley answered. "I don't wear it in here."

"Are you fast with that gun?" When Perley reacted as if he didn't understand, Rafer said, "When you draw it outta your holster, can you draw it real fast?" Because of Perley's general air of innocence, Rafer assumed he was slow of wit as well.

"Yes," Perley answered honestly, "but I would only do so in an emergency."

"That's good," Rafer said, "because this is an emergency. You wanna know what the emergency is? When I step outside and strap my gun on, if you ain't outside with me, I'm gonna come back inside and shoot this place to pieces. That's the emergency. You see, I don't cotton to nobody tellin' me to get outta here."

"All right," Perley said. "I understand why you're upset. I'll come outside with you, and we'll talk about this like reasonable men should."

"Two minutes!" Rafer blurted. "Then if you ain't outside, I'm comin' in after you." He walked out the door with Deke right behind him.

Becky rushed to Perley's side as he went to the table to

get his gun belt. "Perley, don't go out there. You're not going to let that monster draw you into a gunfight, are you?"

"I really hope not," Perley told her. "I think maybe I can talk some sense into him and his friend. But I had to get him out of here. He was gettin' too abusive. Don't worry, I'll be all right. He oughta be easier to talk to when he doesn't have an audience."

He strapped his Colt .44 on and walked outside to find Rafer and Deke waiting. Seeing the expressions of gleeful anticipation on both faces, Perley could not help a feeling of uncertainty. If he had looked behind him, he would have seen everyone in the dining room gathered at the two windows on that side of the building, that is, everyone except Becky and Beulah. All of the spectators were confident of the unassuming young man's gift of speed with a handgun. As far as Perley was concerned, his lightning-fast reactions were just that, a gift. For he never practiced with a weapon, and he honestly had no idea why his brain and body just reacted with no conscious direction from himself. Because of that, he was of the opinion that it could just as easily leave him with no warning. And that was one reason why he always tried to avoid pistol duels whenever possible. He took a deep breath and hoped for the best.

"I gotta admit, I had my doubts if you had the guts to walk out that door," Rafer said when Perley came toward them. Aside to Deke, he said, "If this sucker beats me, shoot him." Deke nodded.

"Why do you wanna shoot me?" Perley asked him. "You've never seen me before today. I've done you no wrong. It doesn't make any sense for you and me to try to kill each other."

"The hell you ain't done me no wrong," Rafer responded. "You walked up to my table and told me to get outta there. I don't take that from any man."

"If you're honest with yourself, you have to admit that you started all the trouble when you started makin' fun of my name. I was willin' to call that just some innocent fun, and I still am. So, we could just forget this whole idea to shoot each other and get on with the things that matter. And that's just to get along with strangers on a courteous basis. I'm willing to forget the whole trouble if you are. Whaddaya say? It's not worth shootin' somebody over."

"I swear, the more I hear comin' outta your mouth, the more I feel like I gotta puke. I think I'll shoot you just like I'd shoot a dog that's gone crazy. One thing I can't stand is a man too yellow to stand up for himself. I'm gonna count to three, and you'd better be ready to draw your weapon when I say three 'cause I'm gonna cut you down."

"This doesn't make any sense at all," Perley said. "I don't have any reason to kill you."

"One!" Rafer counted.

"Don't do this," Perley pleaded and turned to walk away.

"Two!" Rafer counted.

"I'm warnin' you, don't say three."

"Three!" Rafer exclaimed defiantly, his six-gun already halfway out when he said it, and he staggered backward from the impact of the bullet in his chest. Deke, shocked by Perley's instant response, was a second slow in reacting and dropped his weapon when Perley's second shot caught him in his right shoulder. He stood, helplessly waiting for Perley's fatal shot, and almost sinking to his knees when Perley released the hammer and returned his pistol to his holster.

"There wasn't any sense to that," Perley said. "Your friend is dead because of that foolishness, and you better go see Bill Simmons about your shoulder. He's the barber, but he also does some doctorin'. We ain't got a doctor in town yet. You'd best just stand there for a minute, though, 'cause

I see the sheriff runnin' this way." Deke remained where he was, his eyes still glazed with the shock of seeing Rafer cut down so swiftly. Perley walked over and picked up Deke's gun, broke the cylinder open and extracted all the cartridges. Then he dropped it into Deke's holster.

"Perley," Paul McQueen called out as he approached. "What's the trouble? Who's that?" He asked, pointing to the body on the ground, before giving Perley time to answer his first question.

"I think I heard his friend call him Rafer," Perley said. "Is that right?" He asked Deke.

Deke nodded, then said, "Rafer Samson."

"Rafer Samson," McQueen repeated. "I'll see if I've got any paper on him, but I expect you could save me the trouble," he said to Deke. "What's your name?"

"Deke Johnson," he replied. "You ain't got no paper on me. Me and Rafer was just passin' through on the way to the Red."

"I don't expect I do," McQueen said, "at least by that name, anyway. You were just passin' through, and figured you might as well cause a little trouble while you were at it, right?" He knew without having to ask that Perley didn't cause the trouble. "How bad's that shoulder?"

Deke nodded toward Perley. "He put a bullet in it."

"You musta gone to a helluva lot of trouble to get him to do that," the sheriff remarked. "Perley, you wanna file any charges on him?" Perley said that he did not. "All right," McQueen continued. "I won't lock you up, and we can go see Bill Simmons about that shoulder. Bill's a barber, but he also does some doctorin', and he's our undertaker, too. He's doctored a lotta gunshots, so he'll fix you up so you can ride. Then I want you out of town. Is that understood?"

"Yessir," Deke replied humbly.

"Perley, you gonna be in town a little while?" McQueen

asked. When Perley said that he was, McQueen told him he'd like to hear the whole story of the incident. "I'll tell Bill to send Bill, Jr. to pick up Mr. Samson." He looked around him as several spectators from down the street started coming to gawk at the body. "You mind stayin' here a while to watch that body till Bill, Jr. gets here with his cart?"

"Reckon not," Perley said.

Bill, Jr. responded pretty quickly, so it was only a few minutes before Perley saw him come out of the alley beside the barbershop, pushing his hand cart. Perley helped him lift Rafer's body up on the cart. "Sheriff said he called you out," Bill, Jr. said. "They don't never learn, do they?" Perley wasn't sure how to answer that, so he didn't.

CHAPTER 2

When he turned back toward the dining room again, he saw the folks inside still crowded up at the two small windows on that wall, and he thought maybe he'd just skip his dinner. But then he saw Becky standing in the open door, waiting for him to return. He truly hated for her to have seen the shooting. The incident she just witnessed was the kind of thing that happened to him quite frequently. There was no reason for it that he could explain. It was just something that had been attached to him at birth. The same as his natural reaction with a handgun, he supposed. He often wondered if when The Lord branded him with the cowpie stigma, He thought it only fair to also grant him with lightning-fast reactions. He had his brother, John, to thank for the saying, "If there wasn't but one cowpie in the whole state of Texas, Perley would accidentally step in it."

Becky broke into his fit of melancholy then when she became impatient and stepped outside the door. "Perley, come on in here and eat your dinner. It's almost time to clean up the kitchen." He reluctantly responded to her call.

Inside, he kept his eyes focused on the space between Becky's shoulder blades, avoiding the open stares of the customers as he followed her to the table by the kitchen door. "Sit down," Becky said, "and I'll fix you a plate." She picked up his coffee cup. "I'll dump this and get you some fresh."

When he finally looked up from the table, it was to catch Edgar Welch's gaze focused upon him. The postmaster nodded and calmly said, "Attaboy, Perley." His remark caused a polite round of applause from most of the other tables. Instead of feeling heroic, Perley was mortified. He had just killed a man. It was certainly not his first, but it was something he was most definitely not proud of.

Becky returned from the kitchen with a heaping plate of food. She was followed by Beulah, who came to thank him for taking the trouble outside her dining room. "There ain't no tellin' how many of my customers mighta got shot, if you hadn't gone out there with him. He was gonna come back in here if you hadn't. There certainly ain't gonna be no charge for your dinner. Becky, take good care of him."

"I will," Becky said and sat down at the table with him. She watched him eat for a few minutes after Beulah went back into the kitchen before she asked a question. "Before all that trouble started, when you first came in, you said you came by to tell me something. Do you remember what it was?"

"Yeah," he answered. "I came to tell you I've gotta take a little trip for a few days."

"Perley," she fussed, "you just got back from Texarkana. Where do you have to go now?"

"Rubin wants me to take a contract he signed down to a ranch somewhere south of Sulphur Springs. It's for fifty head of Hereford cattle. Him and John have been talkin' about cross-breedin' 'em with our Texas longhorns to see if they can breed a better meat cow."

"Why can't one of them go?" Becky asked.

"John and Rubin both work pretty hard to run the cattle operation for the Triple-G. I never cared much for workin' on the ranch, and there wasn't anything tyin' me down here, till I found you. So, I have always been the one to do things like takin' this contract, and takin' those horses to Texarkana." He saw the look of disappointment in her face, so he was quick to say that there would surely be a change in his part of running the Triple-G after they were married. Judging by her expression, he wasn't sure she believed him. Their discussion was interrupted at that point when Paul McQueen walked in the dining room. He came straight to their table.

"Mind if I sit down?" Paul asked.

"Not at all," Becky answered him. "I've got to get up from here and help Lucy and Beulah. Can I get you a cup of coffee?" She knew he had been in earlier to eat dinner.

"Yes, ma'am, I could use a cup of coffee," he said. When she left to fetch it, he said, "Bill's workin' on that fellow to get your bullet outta his shoulder. I asked him how it all happened, but I swear, he seemed to be confused about how it did happen. I asked him why he pulled his weapon, if it was just you and his partner in a shootout. He said he wasn't sure why he pulled it. Said maybe he thought you might shoot him and damned if you didn't. I don't think he really knows what happened, but I can pretty much guess. Anyway, I don't think you have to worry about him. I told him I wanted him outta town as soon as Bill's finished with him, and I think he's anxious to go. Bill, Jr. was already back with the body before I left there."

"If you're wonderin' about that business at all, you've got plenty of eye-witnesses," Perley suggested. "Everybody you see sittin' in here now was at those two windows up front. So they can tell you better than I can. I'm a little bit like the one I shot. It happened so fast, I ain't sure I remember what happened."

"Don't get me wrong, Perley, I don't doubt you handled

it any other way than you are about everything, fair and square. I just wanted the whole picture, in case the mayor asks me."

McQueen didn't have to wait long before he received the first eye-witness report. It came when Edgar Welch finished his dinner. Before leaving, he walked over to the table. "That was one helluva bit of shootin' you done today, Perley. Sheriff, you shoulda seen it." He then took them through the whole encounter. "Perley wasn't even facing that devil when he drew on him, and he still beat him."

"Maybe it ain't such a good idea to tell too many people about it, Edgar," McQueen said. "You might not be doin' Perley or the town any favors if we talk about how fast he is with that six-gun of his. We might have the kind of men showin' up in town that we don't wanna attract, like them two today."

"I see what you mean," Edgar said. "And I agree with you. We might have more drifters like those two showing up in town. Point well taken. Well, I'll be gettin' back to the post office."

The sheriff left soon after the postmaster, leaving Perley to finish up his dinner with a brief word here and there from Becky as she helped Lucy and Beulah clean up the dining room. He promised her that he would stay in town the entire day and eat supper there that night before going back to the Triple-G. She gave him a key to her room on the first floor of the hotel, right behind the kitchen, so he could wait for her to finish her chores. She would have a couple of hours before it was time to prepare the dining room for supper. He was concerned about Buck, so he took the bay gelding to the stable so he could take his saddle off and turn him loose in Walt Carver's corral.

He suspected that Possum was going to give him a goodly portion of grief for slipping out that morning without telling him where he was going. He was halfway serious when he wondered what he was going to do with Possum after he and Becky were married.

It was after two o'clock when Becky showed up at her room. They embraced briefly before she stepped away, apologizing for her sweaty condition, the result of just having cleaned up the kitchen. She seemed strangely distant, he thought, not like her usual lighthearted cheerfulness. "Maybe I ought to go on back to the ranch now," he suggested, "and let you get a little bit of rest before you have to go back to the dining room."

"I guess I'm just a little more tired than I thought," she said. "But I don't want to rush you off. I know you stayed in town because of me." She didn't want to tell him that the incident that took place right outside the dining room made a tremendous impact upon her. She had sought the council of Beulah Walsh, the closest person to a mother she had. Her own mother had passed seven years ago, leaving her father a widower living alone in Tyler. While they had worked cleaning up the kitchen, Beulah, and Lucy, too, had tried to help her understand the man she had fallen in love with.

"The thing that happened in the dining room today is not that unusual in Perley's life," Beulah had told her. "His skill with a firearm is a curse that he has to live with," she said. "To Perley's credit, he tries to avoid it, but it always finds him sooner or later. And like you saw today, even his name is a curse and an open invitation to a troublemaker. So you have to be prepared for that day when Perley's not the fastest gun."

"I know how you feel, honey," Lucy had suggested. "But why don't you wait to see if he's gonna be working full time at the ranch before you marry him? The way it is now, him and Possum are gone who knows where most of the time.

You said he's leaving tomorrow to go somewhere for a few days, and that ain't good for a marriage. You don't wanna spend your life wondering if your children's daddy is coming home or not."

Those words were still ringing in her mind now as she tried to sort out her true feelings, and she could see the confusion in Perley's eyes as they searched hers. This was the first time since she had met Perley that she wondered if she was about to make the wrong decision. In spite of her love for the man, she reluctantly decided that Lucy's advice might be best. "Perley," she finally managed to say, "you're leaving tomorrow to take that contract for the cows. Why don't we wait till you get back to talk about any plans we want to make? I must confess, that business today really got to me. And working in the kitchen afterward just seemed to drain all the energy I had. I hope you understand. I love you."

He didn't understand at all, but he said that he did. She seemed to be a Becky he had never met before. "That's a good idea," he said. "I'm gonna go now, so you can rest up before you have to go back to work tonight. We'll talk about everything when I get back. I love you, too." She stepped up to him and gave him another brief embrace, a fraction longer than the one she had greeted him with. He reached in his pocket and pulled out her door key. "Here," he said, "I don't reckon I'll be needin' this."

She stood in the door and watched him walk down the hallway to the back door. "Perley," she called after him, "be careful." He acknowledged with a wave of his hand.

"That last kiss felt more like a goodbye kiss," he told Buck as he followed the trail back to the Triple-G Ranch. "It sure didn't seem like Becky a-tall. I feel like I just got fired." Walt Carver was sure surprised when he showed up at the stable to get Buck. Perley gave him no reason for returning so soon, other than the simple fact that he changed his mind. Without pushing Buck, he arrived at the ranch in plenty of time to get supper at the cook shack, which was where he generally ate his meals. His eldest brother, Rubin, and his family lived in the original ranch headquarters. His other brother, John, had built a house for him and his family. Perley was welcome to eat at either house, but he found it more to his liking to eat with the cowhands at the cook shack. He always felt that he was imposing, even though he knew he was a favorite with his nephews and nieces. Since he had time, he decided to stop by the house and pick up the contract and the money for the Herefords from Rubin.

"Howdy, Perley," Link Drew greeted him when he rode up to the barn. Young Link had grown like a weed since Perley brought him home with him, after the brutal death of Link's mother and father in the little store they operated. Link was nine when he came to the Triple-G. Looking at him today, Perley couldn't remember if he'd had one or two birthdays since he had arrived. "You want me to take care of Buck for you?" Link asked.

"I think Buck would appreciate it," Perley replied. "If you'll do that, I'll run up and get something at the house, and I'll see you at supper." He climbed down out of the saddle and handed Link the reins. He hesitated half a minute to watch the boy lead the big bay gelding away before turning to walk up to the house. "Knock, knock," he called out as he walked in the kitchen door. In reality, the house was as much his home as it was Rubin's, but being practical, he didn't want to surprise anybody.

"Oh, hello, Perley," Lou Ann, Rubin's wife, greeted him. "If you're lookin' for Rubin, he's in the study."

"Thank you, ma'am," Perley said and headed for the hallway door.

"You stayin' for supper?" Lou Ann asked. "You're welcome, you know."

"No, thank you just the same, Lou Ann. I'm just gonna pick up a paper and some money from Rubin, and I'll be outta your way." Just as Lou Ann said, he found Rubin at his desk in the study. "You got that contract and the money for those cattle?" Perley asked as he walked in.

"Thought you weren't comin' back till after supper," Rubin said as he opened a drawer and pulled out a big envelope. "What happened? Becky kick you out?" He joked. "When are you gonna bring her down here to officially meet the family?"

"I don't know," Perley answered. "Might be a while. There ain't no hurry."

"Well, you might be wise to take your time and be sure it's what you really want. You stayin' for supper?"

"Nope," Perley answered. "I just came to get this." He picked up the thick envelope and tested its weight. "You got a thousand dollars in here?"

"Plus a contract that Weber has to sign, sayin' he got the money," Rubin answered. "He wouldn't deal with anything but cash. Take Possum with you. That's a lot of money you're carrying."

Perley couldn't help chuckling when he thought of the remote possibility of getting away without Possum. "I'll tell him you said to take him. That way, he'll feel like he has a right to complain if something doesn't suit him. We'll leave right after breakfast in the mornin'." He turned and headed for the door.

"You take care of yourself, Perley," Rubin called after him.

"I will," Perley replied and went out the front door in

time to hear Ollie Dinkler banging on his iron triangle to announce supper was ready.

"Beans is ready, Perley," Ollie said when Perley walked on past him.

"Right," Perley replied. "I'll be right back, soon as I put this in the barn. He folded the thick envelope Rubin gave him, took it in the barn, and stuck it in his saddlebag. When he returned to the cook shack, he found Possum waiting for him.

"I thought you said you was gonna eat supper in town with Becky," Possum said. "What's wrong? And I know somethin' is, so tell me what happened."

"What makes you think somethin's wrong?" Perley asked. "She just had a hard-workin' day, and I thought she could use a little rest. Besides, we gotta get an early start in the mornin', and I didn't wanna get back too late tonight."

"You stickin' with that story?" Possum asked.

"I reckon," Perley answered. "Let's eat while there's still some beans in the pot."

Possum followed him inside where Ollie was serving. "You think you can find that Weber Ranch?" He asked Perley.

"I expect so," Perley answered. "I wouldn't think it would be too hard." He paused to let that simmer a little while in Possum's brain until he saw him working up his argument for the wisdom of accompanying him. "Oh, and Rubin said it might be a good idea to take you along." Possum sighed as he exhaled his argument.

"That brother of yours knows what's what," Possum said.

They carried their plates and a cup of coffee to the table and sat down across from Fred Farmer, who at forty-four was the oldest of the cowhands. Were it not for the fact that Perley's brother, John, filled the role as foreman, Fred would most likely have been the best candidate. "Did

I hear Possum say you and him are ridin' down below Sulphur Springs in the mornin'?" Fred asked.

"That's a fact," Perley said. "So, it might be a little hard to keep things runnin' smooth without Possum and me," he joked.

"That's true," Fred came back. "'Course, you two are gone somewhere half the time, anyway, so we're kinda used to it. Besides, we picked up another man today."

"Is that right?" Perley asked. Fred nodded toward the door and Perley turned to look. "Well, I'll be . . ." he uttered when he saw Sonny Rice walk through the door. He looked at Possum. "Did you know?"

"Yeah, I was fixin' to tell you Sonny came back. I just ain't had a chance to," Possum said.

Sonny filled a plate and brought it and a cup of coffee to join them. Fred slid down the bench to make a place for the young man. "Howdy, Perley," Sonny greeted him.

"Sonny," Perley returned. "I swear, I never expected to see you again. Are you back for good, or just a visit?" The last time he saw Sonny was when they were on their way back from Texarkana. Sonny left him and Possum to escort pretty young Penny Denson and her brother to their farm on the Sulphur River.

"I'm back for good," Sonny answered. "You know there ain't no way I could ever be a farmer."

"The way the sparks were flyin' between you and that young girl, I thought love conquers all, even walkin' behind a plow," Perley commented. "She was hangin' on you like a new pair of curtains on the window."

"I reckon I thought so, too," Sonny confessed. "And things was lookin' pretty good there till the feller she's engaged to marry came to supper the next night after we got back. She introduced me as her brother, Art's new friend. I started back to the Triple-G the next day. End of story."

"Sonny, you're better off in the long run," Fred told him. "You'da missed all this good companionship you get at the Triple-G."

"The mistake you made was goin' back to that farm with her and her brother," Possum remarked. "If you was so danged struck by her, you shoulda just picked her up and run off with her."

"Now, there's some good advice," Perley declared sarcastically. "What would you do with a wife right now, anyway. You're better off without the responsibility."

"I reckon that could apply to everybody settin' here," Possum said.

The remark was not lost on Perley. He knew it was aimed at him, and Possum wasn't buying the story he told him about coming back early to give Becky some rest.

Visit our website at
KensingtonBooks.com
to sign up for our newsletters, read
more from your favorite authors, see
books by series, view reading group
guides, and more!

BOOK **CLUB**
BETWEEN THE **CHAPTERS**

Become a Part of Our
Between the Chapters Book Club
Community and Join the Conversation

Betweenthechapters.net